ISABEL WOLFF

The Very Picture of You

HARPER

Harper
An imprint of HarperCollins*Publishers*
77–85 Fulham Palace Road,
Hammersmith, London W6 8JB

www.harpercollins.co.uk

A Paperback Original 2011
1

Set in Sabon by Palimpsest Book Production Limited,
Falkirk, Stirlingshire

Printed and bound in Great Britain by
Clays Ltd, St Ives plc

THE VERY PICTURE OF YOU

Isabel Wolff was born in Warwickshire and read English at Cambridge. She is the author of eight other bestselling novels, which are published in 28 languages. She lives in London with her family.

For more information on Isabel Wolff, visit her website: www.isabelwolff.com

Praise for Isabel Wolff:

'She'll make you laugh out loud and tug your heart-strings.'   *Hello!*

'Feel-good, gritty and full of surprises.'
                                          Cosmopolitan

'A touching, compulsive read. Love it!'   *Heat*

'Charming, funny and unpredictable.'   *Company*

'You won't be able to put this romantic comedy down!'   *Closer*

'Pure feel-good escapism. Perfect.'   Sophie Kinsella

'Far more depth and sensitivity than you might anticipate . . . an absolute delight. Warm and wittily perceptive about human foibles.'
                                          Kirkus UK Reviews

'An engaging read and an intriguing page-turner.'
                                          Sainsbury's Magazine

'It's effervescent and heart-warming and somehow the pages just turn themselves.'   *Big Issue*

By the same author

For my parents in-law, Eva and John

Are we to paint what is on the face, what's inside the face, or what's behind it?

Pablo Picasso

PROLOGUE

'Ella . . .? *El*-la?' My mother's voice floats up the stairs as I sit hunched over my sketchpad, my hand moving rapidly across the cartridge paper. 'Where *are* you?' Gripping the pencil I make the nose a little more defined then shade in the eyebrows. 'Could you *answer* me?' Now for the hair. Fringe? Swept back? I can't remember. 'Gabri-*el*-la?' And I know I can't ask. 'Are you in your room, darling?' As I hear my mother's light, ascending tread I stroke a soft fringe across the forehead, smudge it to add thickness, then swiftly darken the jaw. As I appraise the drawing I tell myself that it's a good like-ness. At least I *think* it is. How can I know? His face is now so indistinct that perhaps I only ever saw it in a dream. I close my eyes, and it *isn't* a dream. I can see him. It's a bright day and I'm walking along and I can feel the warmth rising from the pavement and the sun on my face, and his big, dry-feeling hand enclosing mine.

1

I can hear the slap of my sandals and the click-clack of my mother's heels and I can see her white skirt with its sprigs of red flowers.

He's smiling down at me. 'Ready, Ella?' As his fingers tighten around mine I feel a rush of happiness. 'Here we go. One, two, *three* . . .' My tummy turns over as I'm lifted. 'Wheeeeeee . . . !' they both sing as I sail through the air. 'One, two, three – and *up* she goes! Wheeeeeeeeee . . . !' I hear them laugh as I land.

'More!' I stamp. 'More! *More!*'

'Okay. Let's do a *big* one.' He grips my hand again. 'Ready, sweetie?'

'I rea-dee!'

'Right then. One, two, three and . . . *u-u-u-u-u-p*!'

My head goes back and the blue dome of the sky swings above me, like a bell. But as I fall back to earth, I feel his fingers slip away and when I turn and look for him, he's gone . . .

'*There* you are,' Mum is saying from my bedroom doorway. As I glance up at her I quickly slide my hand over the sketch. 'Would you go and play with Chloë? She's in the Wendy house.'

'I'm . . . doing something.'

'Please, Ella.'

'I'm too *old* for the Wendy house – I'm eleven.'

'I know darling, but it would help me if you could entertain your little sister for a while, and she loves you to play with her . . .' As my mother tucks a strand of white-blonde hair behind one ear I think how pale and fragile-looking she is, like porcelain. 'And I'd rather you were outside on such a warm day.' I will her to go back downstairs; instead, to my alarm, she is walking towards

2

me, her eyes on the pad. I quickly flip the page over to a fresh sheet. 'So you're drawing?' My mother's voice is, as usual, soft and low. 'Can I see?' She holds out her hand.

'No . . . not now.' I wish I'd torn out the sketch before she came in.

'You *never* show me your pictures. Let me have a look, Ella.' She reaches for the pad.

'It's . . . private, Mum – *don't* . . .'

But she is already turning over the spiral-bound sheets. 'What a *lovely* foxglove,' she murmurs. 'And these ivy leaves are perfect – so glossy; and that's an *excellent* one of the church. The stained glass must have been tricky but you've done it brilliantly.' My mother shakes her head in wonderment then gives me a smile; but as she turns to the next page her face clouds.

Through the open window I can hear a plane, its distant roar like the tearing of paper.

'It's a study,' I explain. 'For a portrait.' My pulse is racing.

'Well . . .' Mum nods. 'It's . . . very good.' Her hand trembles as she closes the book. 'I had no idea that you could draw so well.' She puts it back on the table. 'You really . . . capture things,' she adds quietly. A muscle at the corner of her mouth flexes but then she smiles again. 'So . . .' She claps her hands. '*I'll* play with Chloë if you're busy, then we'll all watch the royal wedding. I've put the TV on so that we don't miss the start. You could draw Fergie's dress.'

I shrug. 'Maybe . . .'

'We'll have a sandwich lunch while we watch. Is cheese and ham okay?' I nod. 'Actually, *could* make coronation

3

chicken – that would be *very* suitable, wouldn't it!' she adds with sudden gaiety. 'I'll call you when it starts.' She walks towards the door.

I take a deep breath. 'So have I captured *him*?' My mother seems not to have heard me. 'Does it look like him?' I try again. She stiffens visibly. The sound of the plane has dissolved now into silence. 'Does my drawing look like my *dad*?'

I hear her inhale, then her slim shoulders sag and I suddenly see how expressive a person's back can be. 'Yes, it does,' she answers softly.

'Oh. Well . . .' I say as she turns to face me. 'That's good. Especially as I don't really remember him any more. And I don't even have a photo of him, do I?' I can hear sparrows squabbling in the flower beds. '*Are* there any photos, Mum?'

'No,' she says evenly.

'But . . .' My heart is racing. 'Why *not*?'

'Because . . . there just . . . aren't. I'm sorry, Ella. I know it's not easy. But . . .' She shrugs, as if she's as frustrated by it as I am. 'I'm afraid that's just . . . how it *is*.' She pauses for a moment, as if to satisfy herself that the conversation has ended. 'Now, would you like tomato in your sandwich?'

'But you must have *some* photos of him?'

'Ella . . .' My mother's voice remains low, but then she rarely raises it. 'I've already told you – I don't. I'm sorry, darling. Now I really *do* have to—'

'What about when you got married?' I imagine a white leather album with my parents smiling in every photo, my father darkly handsome in grey, my mother's veil floating around her china-doll face.

4

She blinks, slowly. 'I *did* have some photos, yes – but I don't have them any more.'

'But there must be others. I only need *one*.' I pick up my heart-shaped rubber and flex it between my thumb and forefinger. 'I'd like to put his photo on the sideboard. There's that empty silver frame I could use.'

Her large blue eyes widen. 'But . . . that simply wouldn't *do*.'

'Oh. Then I'd buy a frame of my own: I've got some pocket money. Or I could make one, or you could give me one for my birthday.'

'It's not the *frame*, Ella.' My mother seems helpless suddenly. 'I meant that I wouldn't *want* to have his photo on the sideboard – or anywhere else, for that matter.'

My heart is thudding. 'Why *not*?'

'Because . . .' She throws up her hands. 'He's not part of our *lives*, Ella, as you very well know – and he hasn't been for a long time, so it would be confusing, especially for Chloë – he wasn't *her* father; and it wouldn't be very nice for Roy. And Roy's been so good to you,' she hurries on. '*He's* been a father to you, hasn't he – a wonderful father.'

'Yes – but he isn't my *real* one.' My face has gone hot. 'I've *got* a "real" father, Mum, and his name is John I don't know where he is, or why I don't see him and I don't know why you never ever *talk* about him.' Her lips have become a thin line, but I'm not going to stop. 'I haven't seen him since I was . . . I don't even know that. Was I three?'

My mother folds her slim arms and her gold bangle gently clinks against her watch. 'You were almost five,' she answers softly. 'But you know, Ella, I'd say that the

5

person who *does* the fathering *is* the father, and Roy does everything that any father *could* do, whereas . . . John . . . well . . .' She lets the sentence drift.

'But I'd still like a photo of him. I could keep it here, in my room, so that no one else would have to see it – it would just be for me. Good,' I add quickly. 'So that's settled then.'

'Ella . . . I've already told you, I don't *have* any photos of him.'

'Why . . . *not*?'

She heaves a painful sigh. 'They got . . . lost . . .' She glances out of the window. '. . . when we moved down here.' She returns her gaze to me. 'Not everything came with us.'

I stare at her. 'But those photos *should* have come. It's mean,' I add angrily. 'It's *mean* that you didn't keep just one of them for me!' I am on my feet now, one hand on my chair to steady myself against the clamour in my ribcage. 'And why don't you *talk* about him? You never, *ever* talk about him!'

My mother's pale cheeks are suddenly pink – as if I'd brushed a swirl of rose madder on to each one. 'It's . . . too . . . *difficult*, Ella.'

'*Why*?' I try to swallow, but there's a knife in my throat. 'All you ever say is that he's out of our lives and that it's better that way, so I don't know what *happened* . . .' Tears of frustration sting my eyes. 'Or why he left us . . .' My mother's features have blurred. 'Or if I'll ever *see* him again.' A tear spills on to my cheek. 'So that's why – *that's* why I—' In a flash I'm on the floor, reaching under the bed, and dragging out my box. It has *Ravel* printed on it and Mum's best boots came in

6

it. I get to my feet and place it on the bed. My mother looks at it, then, with an anxious glance at me she sits down next to it and lifts off the lid . . .

The first drawing is a recent one, in pen and ink with white pastel on his nose, hair and cheekbones. I was pleased with it because I'd only just learned how to highlight properly. Then she takes out three pencil sketches of him that I'd done in the spring, in which, with careful cross-hatching, I'd managed to get depth and expressiveness into the eyes. Beneath that are ten or twelve older drawings in which the proportions are all wrong – his mouth too small or his brow too wide or the curve of the ear set too high. Then come five sketches in which there is no hint of any contouring, his face as flat and round as a plate. Mum lifts out several felt-tip images of my dad standing with her and me in front of a red-brick house with a flight of black steps up to the dark green front door. Then come some bright poster-colour paintings in each of which he's driving a big blue car. Now Mum lifts out a collage of him with pipe cleaners for limbs, mauve felt for his shirt and trousers and tufts of brown woollen hair that are crusted with glue. In the final few pictures Dad is barely more than a stick man. On these I have written, underneath, *dad* but on one of them the first 'd' is the wrong way round so that it says *bad*.

'So many,' my mother murmurs. She returns the pictures to the box, then she reaches for my hand and I sit down next to her. I hear her swallow. 'I should have told you,' she says quietly. 'But I didn't know how . . .'

'But . . . why didn't you? Tell me what?'

'Because . . . it was . . . so awful.' Her chin dimples

7

with distress. 'I was hoping to be able to leave it until you were older . . . but today . . . you've forced the issue.' She presses her fingertips to her lips, blinks a few times then exhales with a sad, soughing sound. 'All right,' she whispers. Her hands drop to her lap and she takes a deep breath; and now, as the 'Wedding March' thunders out to us from Westminster Abbey she talks to me, at last, about my father. And, as she tells me what he did, I feel my world suddenly lurch, as though something big and heavy has just shunted into it . . .

We stay there for a while and I ask her some questions, which she answers. Then I ask her the same questions all over again. Then we go downstairs and I fetch Chloë in from the garden and we all sit in front of the TV and exclaim over Sarah Ferguson's billowing silk dress with its seventeen-foot, bee-embroidered train. And the next day I take my box down to the kitchen and lift out the pictures. Then I thrust them all deep into the bin.

ONE

'Sorry about this,' the radio reporter, Clare, said to me early this evening as she fiddled with her small audio recorder. She tucked a hank of Titian red hair behind one ear. 'I just need to check that the machine's recorded everything . . . there seems to be a gremlin . . .'

'Don't worry . . .' I stole an anxious glance at the clock. I'd need to leave soon.

'I really appreciate your time.' Clare lifted out the tiny batteries with perfectly manicured fingers. I glanced at my stained ones. 'But with radio you need to record quite a lot.'

'Of course.' How old was she? I'd been unsure to start with, as she was very made up. Thirty-five I now decided – my age. 'I'm glad to be included,' I added as she slotted the batteries back in and snapped the machine shut.

'Well, I'd already heard of you, and then I read that piece about you in *The Times* last month . . .' I felt my stomach clench. 'And I thought you'd be perfect for my programme – if I can just get this damn thing to *work* . . .' Even through the foundation I could see Clare's cheeks flush as she stabbed at the buttons. *And when did you first realise that you were going to be a painter?* 'Phew . . .' She clapped her hand to her chest. 'It's still there.' *I knew I wanted to be a painter from eight or nine* . . . She smiled. 'I was worried that I'd erased it.' *I simply drew and painted all the time* . . . Now, as she pressed 'fast forward', my voice became a Minnie Mouse squeak then slowed again to normal. *Painting's always been, in a way, my* . . . *solace.* 'Great,' she said as I scratched a blob of dried Prussian blue off my paint-stiffened apron. 'We can carry on.' She glanced at her watch. 'Can you spare another twenty minutes?'

My heart sank. She'd already been here for an hour and a half – most of which had been spent in idle chatter or in sorting out her tape recorder. But being in a Radio 4 documentary might lead to another commission, so I quelled my frustration. 'That's fine.'

She picked up her microphone then glanced around the studio. 'This must be a nice place to work.'

'It is . . . That's why I bought the house, because of this big attic. Plus the light's perfect – it faces north-east.'

'And you have a glorious view!' Clare laughed. Through the two large dormer windows loomed the massive rust-coloured rotunda of Fulham's Imperial Gas Works. 'Actually, I like industrial architecture,' she added quickly, as if worried that she might have offended me.

'So do I – I think gas containers have a kind of grandeur; and on the other side I've got the old Lots Road Power Station. So, no, it's not exactly green and pleasant, but I like the area and there are lots of artists and designers around here, so I feel at home.'

'It's a bit of a no-man's land, though,' Clare observed. 'You have to trail all the way down the King's Road to get here.'

'True . . . but Fulham Broadway's not far. In any case, I usually cycle everywhere.'

'That's brave of you. Anyway . . .' She riffled through the sheaf of notes on the low glass table. 'Where were we?' I slid the pot of hyacinths aside to give her more room. 'We started with your background,' she said. 'The Saturdays you spent as a teenager in the National Gallery copying old masters, the foundation course you did at the Slade; we talked about the painters you most admire – Rembrandt, Velázquez and Lucian Freud . . . I *adore* Lucian Freud.' She gave a little shiver of appreciation. 'So lovely and . . . *fleshy*.'

'Very fleshy,' I agreed.

'Then we got to your big break with the BP Portrait Award four years ago—'

'I didn't win it,' I interrupted. 'I was a runner-up. But they used my painting on the poster for the competition, which led to several new commissions, which meant that I could give up teaching and start painting full time. So yes, that was a big step forward.'

'And now the Duchess of Cornwall has put you right on the map!'

'I . . . guess she has. I was thrilled when the National Portrait Gallery asked me to paint her.'

'And that's brought you some nice exposure.' I flinched. 'So have you had many famous sitters?'

I shook my head. 'Most are "ordinary" people who

11

simply like the idea of having themselves, or someone they love, painted; the rest are either in public life in one way or another, or have had a distinguished career which the portrait is intended to commemorate.'

'So we're talking about the great and the good then.'

I shrugged. 'You could call them that – professors and politicians, captains of industry, singers, conductors . . . a few actors.'

Clare nodded at a small unframed painting hanging by the door. 'I love that one of David Walliams – the way his face looms out of the darkness.'

'That's not the finished portrait,' I explained. 'He has that, of course. This is just the model I did to make sure that the close-up composition was going to work.'

'It reminds me of Caravaggio,' she mused. I wished she'd get *on* with it. 'He looks a bit like Young Bacchus . . .'

'I'm sorry, Clare,' I interjected. 'But can we . . .?' I nodded at the tape recorder.

'Oh – I keep chatting, don't I! Let's crack on.' She lifted her headphones on to her coppery bob then held the microphone towards me. 'So . . .' She started the machine. 'Why do you paint portraits, Ella, rather than, say, landscapes?'

'Well . . . landscape painting's very solitary,' I replied. 'It's just you and the view. But with portraits you're with another human being and that's what's always fascinated me.' Clare nodded and smiled for me to expand. 'I feel excited when I look at a person for the very first time. When they sit in front of me I drink in everything I can about them. I study the colour and shape of their eyes, the line of their nose, the shade and texture of the skin, the outline of the mouth. I'm also registering how they *are*, physically.'

'You mean their body language?'

'Yes. I'm looking at the way they tilt their head, and the way they smile; whether they look me in the eye, or keep glancing away; I'm looking at the way they fold their arms or cross their legs, or if they don't sit on the chair properly but perch forward on it or slouch down into it – because all that will tell me what I need to know about that person to be able to paint them truthfully.'

'But—' a motorbike was roaring down the street. Clare waited for the noise to fade. 'What does "truthfully" mean – that the portrait looks like the person?'

'It ought to look like them.' I rubbed a smear of chrome green off the palm of my hand. 'But a good portrait should also reveal aspects of the sitter's character. It should capture both an outer and an *inner* likeness.'

'You mean body and soul?'

'Yes . . . It should show the person, body and soul.'

Clare glanced at her notes again. 'Do you work from photographs?'

'No. I need to have the living person in front of me. I want to be able to look at them from every angle and to see the relationship between each part of their face. Above all, I need to see the way the light bounces off their features, because that's what will give me the form and the proportions. Painting is all about seeing the light. So I work only from life, and I ask for six two-hour sittings.'

Clare's green eyes widened. 'That's a big commitment – for you both.'

'It is. But then a portrait is a significant undertaking, in which the painter and sitter are working together – there's a complicity.'

She held the microphone a little closer. 'And do your sitters open up to you?' I didn't reply. 'I mean, there you are, on your own with them, for hours at a time. Do they confide in you?'

'Well . . .' I didn't like to say that my sitters confide the most extraordinary things. 'They do sometimes talk about their marriages or their relationships,' I answered carefully. 'They'll even tell me about their tragedies, and their regrets. But I regard what happens during the sittings as not just confidential, but almost sacrosanct.'

'It's a bit like a confessional then?' Clare suggested teasingly.

'In a way it *is*. A portrait sitting is a very special space. It has an . . . intimacy: painting another human being *is* an act of intimacy.'

'So . . . have you ever fallen in love with any of your sitters?'

I smiled. 'Well, I did once fall in love with a dachshund that someone wanted in the picture, but I've never fallen for a human sitter, no.' I didn't add that as most of my male subjects were married they were, in any case, off-limits. I thought of the mess that Chloë had got herself into . . .

'Is there any kind of person you particularly enjoy painting?' Clare asked.

I was silent for a moment while I considered the question. 'I suppose I'm drawn to people who are a little bit dark – who haven't had happy-ever-after sort of lives. I like painting people who I feel are . . . complex.'

14

'Why do you think that is?'

'I . . . find it more interesting – to see that fight going on in the face between the conflicting parts of someone's personality.' I glanced at the clock. It was half past six. I *had* to go. 'But . . . do you have enough material now?'

Clare nodded. 'Yes, plenty.' She lifted off her headphones, then smoothed down her hair. 'But could I have a quick look at your work?'

'Sure.' I suppressed a sigh. 'I'll get my portfolio.'

As I fetched the heavy black folder from the other side of the studio, Clare walked over to my big studio easel and studied the canvas standing on it. 'Who's this?'

'That's my mother.' I heaved the portfolio on to the table then came and stood next to her. 'She popped by this morning so I did a bit more. It's for her sixtieth birthday later this year.'

'She's beautiful.'

I looked at my mother's round blue eyes with their large, exposed lids beneath perfectly arching eyebrows, at her sculpted cheekbones and her aquiline nose, and at her left hand resting elegantly against her breastbone. Her skin was lined, but time had otherwise been kind. 'It's almost finished.'

Clare cocked her head to one side. 'She has . . . poise.'

'She was a ballet dancer.'

'Ah.' She nodded thoughtfully. 'I remember now, it said so in that article about you.' She looked at me. 'And was she successful?'

'Yes – she was with the English National Ballet, then with the Northern Ballet Theatre in Manchester – this was in the seventies. That's her, actually, on the wall, over there . . .'

15

Clare followed my gaze to a framed poster of a ballerina in a full-length white tutu and bridal veil. 'Giselle,' Clare murmured. 'How lovely . . . It's such a touching story, isn't it – innocence betrayed . . .'

'It was my mother's favourite role – that was in '79. Sadly, she had to retire just a few months later.'

'Why?' Clare asked. 'Because of having children?'

'No – I was nearly five by then. It was because she was injured.'

'In rehearsal?'

I shook my head. 'At home. She fell, breaking her ankle.'

Clare's brow pleated in sympathy. 'How terrible.' She looked at the portrait again, as if seeking signs of that disappointment in my mother's face.

'It was hard . . .' I had a sudden memory of my mother sitting at the kitchen table in our old flat, her head in her hands. She used to stay like that for a long time.

'What did she do then?' I heard Clare ask.

'She decided that we'd move to London; once she'd recovered enough she began a new career as a ballet mistress.' Clare looked at me enquiringly. 'It's something that older or injured dancers often do. They work with a company, refreshing the choreography or rehearsing particular roles: my mother did this with the Festival Ballet for some years, then with Ballet Rambert.'

'Does she still do that?'

'No – she's more or less retired. She teaches one day a week at the English National Ballet school, otherwise she mostly does charity work; in fact she's organised a big gala auction tonight for Save the Children, which is why I'm pushed for time as I have to be there but in here—'

16

I went over to the table and opened the folder – 'are the photos of all my portraits. There are about fifty.'

'So it's your Facebook,' Clare said with a smile. She sat on the sofa again and began to browse the images. '*Fisherman* . . .' she murmured. 'That one's on your website, isn't it? *Ursula Sleeping* . . . *Emma, Polly's Face* . . .' Clare gave me a puzzled look. 'Why did you call this one *Polly's Face* – given that it's a portrait?'

'Oh, because Polly's my best friend – we've known each other since we were six; she's a hand and foot model and was jokingly complaining that no one ever showed any interest in her face, so I said I'd paint it.'

'Ah . . .'

I pointed to the next image. 'That's Baroness Hale – the first woman Law Lord; this is Sir Philip Watts, a former Chairman of Shell.'

Clare turned the page again. 'And there's the Duchess of Cornwall. She looks rather humorous.'

'She is, and that's the quality I most wanted people to see.'

'And did the Prince like it?'

I gave a shrug. 'He seemed to. He said nice things about it when he came to the unveiling at the National Portrait Gallery last month.'

Clare turned to the next photo. 'And who's this girl with the cropped hair?'

'That's my sister, Chloë. She works for an ethical PR agency called PRoud, so they handle anything to do with fair trade, green technology, organic food and farming – that kind of thing.'

Clare nodded thoughtfully. 'She's very like your mother.'

'She is – she has her fair complexion and ballerina

physique.' Whereas I am dark and sturdy, I reflected balefully – more Paula Rego than Degas.

Clare peered at the painting. 'But she looks so . . . *sad* – distressed, almost.'

I hesitated. 'She was breaking up with someone – it was a difficult time; but she's fine now,' I went on firmly. Even if her new boyfriend's vile, I didn't add.

My phone was ringing. I answered it.

'Where *are* you?' Mum demanded softly. 'It's ten to seven – nearly everyone's here.'

'Oh, sorry, but I'm not quite finished.' I glanced at Clare, who was still flicking through the portfolio.

'You said you'd come *early*.'

'I know – I'll be there in twenty minutes, promise.' I hung up. I looked at Clare. 'I'm afraid I have to go now . . .' I went to my work table and dipped some dirty brushes in the jar of turps.

'Of course . . .' she said, without looking up. 'That's the singer Cecilia Bartoli.' She turned to the final image. 'And who's this friendly looking man with the bow tie?'

I pulled the brushes through a sheet of newspaper to squeeze out the paint. 'That's my father.'

'Your father?'

'Yes.' I did my best to ignore the surprise in her voice. 'Roy Graham. He's an orthopaedic surgeon – semi-retired.' I went to the sink, aware of Clare's curious gaze on my back.

'But in *The Times*—'

'He plays a lot of golf . . .' I rubbed washing-up liquid into the bristles. 'At the Royal Mid-Surrey – it's not far from where they live, in Richmond.'

'In *The Times* it said that—'

'He also plays bridge.' I turned on the tap. 'I've never played, but people say it's fun once you get into it.' I rinsed and dried the brushes, then laid them on my work table, ready for the next day. 'Right . . .' I looked at Clare, willing her to leave.

She put the tape recorder and notes into her bag then stood up. 'I hope you don't mind my asking you this,' she said. 'But as it was in the newspaper, I assume you talk about it.'

My fingers trembled as I screwed the top back on a tube of titanium white. 'Talk about what?'

'Well . . . the article said that you were adopted when you were eight . . .' Heat spilled into my face. 'And that your name was changed—'

'I don't know where they got that.' I untied my apron. 'Now I really *must*—'

'It said that your real father left when you were five.'

By now my heart was battering against my ribcage. 'My real father is Roy Graham,' I said quietly. 'And that's all there is to it.' I hung my apron on its hook. 'But thank you for coming.' I opened the studio door. 'If you could let yourself out . . .'

Clare gave me a puzzled smile. 'Of course.'

As soon as she'd gone, I furiously rubbed at my paint-stained fingers with a turps-soaked rag then quickly washed my face and tidied my hair. I put on some black trousers and my green velvet coat and was about to go and unlock my bike when I remembered that the front light was broken. I groaned. I'd have to get the bus, or a cab – whichever turned up first. At least Chelsea Old Town Hall wasn't far.

I ran up to the King's Road and got to the stop just as a number 11 was pulling up, its windows blocks of yellow in the gathering dusk.

As we trundled over the bridge I reflected bitterly on Clare's intrusiveness, yet she'd only repeated what she'd read in *The Times*. I felt a burst of renewed fury that something so intensely private was now online . . .

'Would you *please* take that paragraph out,' I'd asked the reporter, Hamish Watt, when I'd tracked him down an hour or so after I'd first seen the article. As I'd gripped the phone my knuckles were white. 'I was horrified when I saw it – please *remove* it.'

'No,' he'd replied. 'It's part of the story.'

'But you didn't *ask* me about it,' I'd protested. 'When you interviewed me at the National Portrait Gallery last week you talked only about my work.'

'Yes – but I already had some background about you – that your mother had been a dancer, for example. I also happened to know a bit about your family circumstances.'

'*How?*'

There was a momentary hesitation. 'I'm a journalist,' he answered, as though that were sufficient explanation.

'Please cut that bit out,' I'd implored him again.

'I can't,' he'd insisted. 'And you were perfectly happy to be interviewed, weren't you?'

'Yes,' I agreed weakly. 'But if I'd known what you were going to write I'd have refused. You said that the article would be about my painting, but a good third of it was very personal and I'm uncomfortable about that.'

'Well, I'm sorry you're unhappy,' he'd said unctuously.

20

'But as publicity is undoubtedly helpful to artists, I suggest you learn to take the rough with the smooth.' With that, he'd hung up . . .

It would be on the Internet for ever, I now thought dismally – for anyone to see. Anyone at all . . . The thought of it made me feel sick. I'd simply have to find a way to deal with it, I reflected as we passed the World's End pub.

My father is Roy Graham.

My father is Roy Graham and he's a wonderful father.

I've got a father, thank you. His name is Roy Graham . . .

To distract myself I thought about work. I was starting a new portrait in the morning. Then on Thursday Mike Johns, MP, was coming for his fourth sitting – there'd been quite a gap since the last one as he said he'd been too busy; and yesterday I'd had that enquiry about painting a Mrs Carr – her daughter, Sophia, had contacted me through my website. Then there'd be the new commission from tonight – not that it was going to make me any money, I reflected regretfully as we passed Heal's. I stood up and pressed the bell.

I got off the bus, crossed the road and followed a knot of smartly dressed people up the steps of the town hall. I walked down the black-and-white tiled corridor, showed my invitation, then pushed on the doors of the main hall, next to which was a large sign: *Save The Children – Gala Auction.*

The ornate blue-and-ochre room was already full, the stertorous chatter almost drowning out the string trio that was valiantly playing away on one side of the stage.

Aproned waiters circulated with trays of canapés and drinks. The air was almost viscous with scent.

I picked up a programme and skim-read the introduction. *Five million children at risk in Malawi . . . hunger in Kenya . . . continuing crisis in Zimbabwe . . . in desperate need of help . . .* Then came the list of lots – twenty of which were in the Silent Auction, while the ten 'star' lots were to be auctioned live. These included a week in a Venetian palazzo, a luxury break at the Ritz, tickets for the first night of *Swan Lake* at Covent Garden with Carlos Acosta, a shopping trip to Harvey Nichols with Gok Wan, a dinner party for eight cooked by Gordon Ramsay and an evening dress designed by Maria Grachvogel. There was an electric guitar signed by Paul McCartney and a Chelsea FC shirt signed by the current squad. The final lot was *A portrait commission by Gabriella Graham, kindly donated by the artist.* As I looked at the crowd I wondered who I'd end up painting.

Suddenly I spotted Roy, waving. He walked towards me. 'Ella-Bella!' He placed a paternal kiss on my cheek.

Damn Clare, I thought. *Here* was my father.

'Hello, Roy.' I nodded at his daffodil-dotted bow tie. 'Nice neckwear. Haven't seen that one before, have I?'

'It's new – thought I'd christen it tonight in honour of the spring. Now, *you* need some fizz . . .' He glanced around for a waiter.

'I'd love some. It's been a long day.'

Roy got me a glass of champagne and handed it to me with an appraising glance. 'So, how's our Number One Girl?'

I smiled at the familiar, affectionate appellation. 'I'm fine, thanks. Sorry I'm late.'

'Your mum was getting *slightly* twitchy, but then this is a big event. Ah, here she comes . . .'

My mother was gliding through the crowd towards us, her slender frame swathed in amethyst chiffon, her ash-blonde hair swept into a perfect French pleat.

She held out her arms to me. '*El*-la.' Her tone suggested a reproach rather than a greeting. 'I'd almost given *up* on you, darling.' As she kissed me I inhaled the familiar scent of her Fracas. 'Now, I need you to be on hand to talk to people about the portrait commission. We've put the easel over there, look, in the presentation area, and I've made you a label so that people will know who you are.' She opened her mauve satin clutch, took out a laminated name badge and had already pinned it to my lapel before I could protest about the mark it might leave on the velvet. 'I'm hoping the portrait will fetch a high price. We're aiming to raise seventy-five thousand pounds tonight.'

'Well, fingers crossed.' I adjusted the badge. 'But you've got some great items.'

'And *all* donated,' she said wonderingly. 'We haven't had to buy anything. Everyone's been *so* generous.'

'Only because you're so persuasive,' said Roy. 'I often think you could persuade the rain not to fall, Sue, I really do.'

Mum gave him an indulgent smile. 'I'm just focused and well organised. I know how I want things to *be*.'

'You're formidable,' Roy said amiably, 'in both the English *and* the French meaning of that word.' He raised his glass. 'Here's to you, Sue – and to a successful event.'

I sipped my champagne then nodded at the empty podium. 'So who's wielding the gavel?'

Mum adjusted her pashmina. 'Tim Spiers. He's ex-Christie's and brilliant at cajoling people into parting with their cash – having said which, I've instructed the waiters to keep topping up the glasses.'

Roy laughed. 'That's right – get the punters pissed.'

'No – just in a good *mood*,' Mum corrected him. 'Then they're much more, well, biddable,' she concluded wryly. 'But if things are a bit slow . . .' she lowered her voice '. . . then I'd like *us* to do a little strategic bidding.'

My heart sank. 'I'd rather not.'

Mum gave me one of her 'disappointed' looks. 'It's just to get things going – you wouldn't have to *buy* anything, Ella.'

'But . . . if no one outbids me, I *might*. These are expensive lots, Mum, and I've a huge mortgage – it's too risky.'

'You're donating a portrait,' said Roy. 'That's more than enough.' Too right, I thought crossly. '*I'll* do some bidding, Sue,' he added. 'Up to a limit, though.'

Mum laid her palm on his cheek – a typical gesture. '*Thank you*. I'm sure Chloë will bid too.'

I glanced around the crowd. 'Where *is* Chloë?'

'She's on her way,' Roy replied. 'With Nate.'

A groan escaped me.

Mum shook her head. 'I don't know *why* you have to be like that, Ella. Nate's delightful.'

'Really?' I sipped my champagne again. 'Can't say I'd noticed.'

'You hardly know him,' she retorted quietly.

'That's true. I've only met him once.' But that one time had been more than enough. It had been at a drinks party that Chloë had given last November . . .

'Any special reason for having it?' I'd asked her over the phone after I'd opened the elegant invitation.

'It's because I haven't had a party for so long – I've neglected my friends. It's also because I'm feeling a lot more cheerful at the moment, be*cause* . . .' She drew in her breath. 'Ella . . . I've met someone.'

Relief flooded through me. 'That's *great*. So . . . what's he like?'

'He's thirty-six,' she'd replied. 'Tall with very short black hair, and lovely green eyes.'

To my surprise I had to suppress a pang of envy. 'He sounds gorgeous.'

'He is – and he's *not* married.'

'Well . . . that's good.'

'Oh, and he's from New York. He's been in London about a year.'

'And what does this paragon do?'

'He's in private equity.'

'So he can stand you dinner then.'

'Yes – but I like to pay for things too.'

'So are you . . . an item?'

'*Sort* of – we've been on five dates. But he said he's looking forward to the party, so that's a good sign. I know you're going to *love* him,' she added happily.

So, a fortnight later, I'd cycled over to Putney, through a veil of fog. And I was locking up my bike outside Chloë's flat at the end of Askill Drive when I heard a taxi pull up just around the corner in Keswick Road. As the door clicked open I could hear the passenger talking on his mobile. Although he spoke softly his voice somehow carried through the mist and darkness.

'I'm *sorry*, but I can't,' I heard him say. He was American. Realising that this could be Chloë's new man I found myself tuning in to his conversation. 'I really *can't*,' he reiterated as the cab door slammed shut. 'Because I've just gotten to Putney for a drinks party, that's why . . .' So it *was* him. 'No . . . I don't *want* to go.' I felt my insides twist. 'But I'm here now, honey, and so . . . just some girl,' he added as the cab drove away. 'No, no . . . she's nothing special,' he added quietly. By now my face was aflame. 'I *can't* get out of it,' he protested. 'Because I promised, that's why – and she's been going on and *on* about it.' My hands shook as I unclipped my front light. 'Okay, honey – I'll come over later. Yes . . . that *is* a promise. No . . . I'll let myself in . . . You too, honey . . .'

I stood there, filled with dismay, expecting the wretch to come round the corner and walk up Chloë's path; and I was just wondering what to do when I realised that he was going in the opposite direction, his footsteps snapping across the pavement then becoming fainter and fainter . . .

So it *wasn't* him. I exhaled with relief. I went up to Chloë's front door and rang the bell.

'Ella!' she exclaimed as she opened it. She looked lovely in a black crêpe shift that used to be Mum's, with a short necklace of over-sized pearls. 'I'm glad you're the first,' she said quickly, 'I've just poured the champagne, but if you could give me a hand with the eats that would be . . .' I was aware of steps behind me as Chloë's gaze strayed over my shoulder. Her face lit up like a firework. 'Nate!'

I turned to see a tall, well-dressed man coming up the path.

'Hi, Chloë.' As I recognised his voice my heart sank. 'I just went completely the wrong way – I was halfway down Keswick Road before I realised. I shoulda used my sat-nav,' he added with a laugh.

'Well, it *is* foggy,' she responded gaily. I stepped past her into the house so that she wouldn't see my face. 'It's *so* nice that you're here, Nate,' I heard her say.

'Oh, I've been looking forward to it.' As I glanced at him I tried not to show my contempt.

Chloë drew him inside; then, still holding his hand, she grabbed *mine* so that the three of us were suddenly linked, awkwardly, as we stood there in the hallway. 'Ella,' she said happily, 'this is Nate.' She turned to him. 'Nate, this is my sister, Ella.'

He was just as Chloë had described. He had very short dark hair that receded slightly above a high forehead, and eyes that were a pure mossy green. He had a sensuous mouth with a tiny indentation at each corner, and a long, straight nose that had a slender bridge, as though someone had pinched it.

'Great to meet you, Ella.' He was clearly unaware that I'd overheard his conversation. I gave him a cold smile and saw him register the slight. 'Erm . . .' He nodded at my head. 'That's a nice helmet you've got there.'

'Oh.' I'd been too distracted to remove it. I unclipped it while Chloë relieved Nate of his coat.

She folded it over her arm. 'I'll just put this on my bed.' She put her hand on the banister. 'But have a glass of champagne, Nate – the kitchen's through there. Ella will show you.'

'No – I . . . need to come up too.' Turning my back on Nate, I followed Chloë upstairs.

27

We crossed the landing and went into Chloë's bedroom. She half-closed the door then put her finger to her lips. 'So what do you *think*?' She laid Nate's charcoal cashmere coat on her bed then turned to me eagerly. 'Isn't he attractive?'

I took off my cycling jacket. 'He is.'

'And he's really . . . *decent*. I think I've landed on my feet.'

I fought the urge to tell Chloë that she'd almost certainly landed flat on her face.

I put my jacket and helmet down, then went over to the large gilded wall mirror. I opened my bag. 'So how did you meet him?' My hand shook as I pulled a comb through my fog-dampened hair.

Chloë came and stood next to me. 'Playing tennis.' As she checked her own appearance I was momentarily distracted by the physical difference between us – Chloë with the alabaster paleness of my mother, next to me, with my olive skin, brown hair and dark eyes. 'Do you remember telling me that I should try and go out more – maybe play tennis?' I nodded. 'Well, I took your advice, and booked some lessons at the Harbour Club.' Chloë licked her ring finger then ran it over her left eyebrow. 'Nate was on the next court; and I had to retrieve my ball from behind his baseline a few times . . .'

I put the comb back in my bag. 'Really?'

'So of course I said sorry. Then I saw him in the café afterwards and I apologised again . . .'

I snapped my bag shut.

'Then we had a coffee – and that's how it started. So I have *you* to thank,' she added happily. My heart sank. 'It's still early days – but he's keen.'

I looked at her. 'How do you know?'

'Well . . . because he calls me a lot and because . . .' She gave me a puzzled smile. 'Why do you ask?'

It was on the tip of my tongue to tell Chloë that Nate was in fact a disingenuous, two-timing creep. But then, reflected behind us on the wall I saw my portrait of her, her face so thin, and almost rigid with distress; her blue eyes blazing with pain and regret.

'Why do you ask?' she repeated.

As I looked at Chloë's happy, hopeful expression I knew I couldn't tell her. 'No reason.' I exhaled. 'I was just . . . wondering.'

'*Ella*?' Chloë was peering at me. 'Are you okay?'

'I'm . . . fine.' I went to the corner basin and washed my hands. 'Actually, a van jumped the lights by the bridge and nearly knocked me off. I'm still feeling shaken,' I lied as I dried them.

'I *knew* something was up. I *wish* you didn't cycle – and in fog like this it's crazy. You've *got* to be careful.'

I laid my hand on Chloë's arm. 'So have you.'

'What do you mean?' She gave a little laugh. 'I don't cycle.'

I shook my head. 'I mean be careful . . .' I tapped the left side of my chest. '*Here.*'

'Oh.' She heaved a sigh. 'I see. Don't worry, Ella. I'm not about to make another . . . well, mistake, if that's what you're thinking. Nate's free of complications, thank God.' My stomach lurched. 'But he'll be wondering what we're doing.' She opened the door. 'Let's go and talk to him.'

This was the last thing I wanted to do, not least because I didn't think I'd be able to hide my hostility;

29

and I was just wondering how I could get out of it when the bell rang, so I said I'd do door duty, then I offered to heat up the canapés and by the time with a tray of drinks, been round Chloë's flat was heaving, and I'd managed to avoid Nate. As I left, pleading an early start, I glanced at him as he chatted to someone in the sitting room and hoped that his romance with Chloë wouldn't last. Having overheard what I had done, it didn't seem likely.

So my heart sank when Chloë phoned me three days later to say that Nate was taking her to Paris for the weekend in early December. Then just before Christmas they gave a dinner party at his flat; Chloë wanted me to be there, but I said I was busy. In January they invited me to the theatre with them but I made some excuse. Then last month Mum asked us all to Sunday lunch, but I told Chloë I'd be away.

'What a shame,' she'd said. 'That's three times you've been unable to meet up with us, Ella. Nate will think you don't like him,' she added with a good-natured laugh.

'Oh, that's not true,' I lied . . .

'Well, *I* like Nate,' I heard Mum say above the pre-auction chatter 'Nate's attractive and charming.' Her voice dropped to a near whisper. 'And we should all just be thankful that he makes Chloë so happy after . . .' Her mouth pursed.

'Max,' said Roy helpfully.

I nodded. 'Max *was* a bit of a mistake.'

'Max was a dis*aster*,' Mum hissed. 'I told Chloë,' she went on quietly. 'I told her that it would *never* work out, and I was *right*. These situations bring nothing but heartbreak,' she added with sudden bitterness, and I knew that she was thinking of her own heartbreak three decades ago.

'Anyway, Chloë's *fine* now,' said Roy evenly. 'So let's change the subject, shall we? We're at a party.'

'Of course,' Mum murmured, collecting herself. 'And I must circulate. Roy, would you go and see how the Silent Auction's going? Ella, you need to go and stand next to the easel, but do make the portrait commission sound *enticing,* won't you? I want to get the highest possible price for every item.'

'Sure,' I responded wearily. I hated having to do a hard sell – even for a good cause. I made my way through the crowd.

The easel was standing between two long tables on which the information about all the star lots was displayed. The Maria Grachvogel gown was draped on to a silver mannequin next to a life-size cut-out of Gordon Ramsay. On a green baize-covered screen were pinned large photos of the Venetian palazzo and the Ritz and next to these was a Royal Opera House poster for *Swan Lake*, flanked by two pendant pairs of pink ballet shoes. The guitar was mounted on a stand, and next to it the Chelsea FC shirt with its graffiti of famous signatures.

As I stood beside the portrait a dark-haired woman in a turquoise dress approached me. She glanced at my name badge. 'So you're the artist.' I nodded. The woman gazed at the painting. 'And who's she?'

'My friend Polly. She's lent it to us tonight as an example of my work.'

'I've always wanted to have my portrait done,' the woman said. 'But when I was young and pretty I didn't

31

have the money and now that I *do* have the money I feel it's too late.'

'You're still pretty,' I told her. 'And it's never too late – I paint people who are in their seventies and eighties.' I sipped my champagne. 'So are you thinking of bidding for it?'

She sucked on her lower lip. 'I'm not sure. How long does the process take?' I explained. 'Two hours is a long time to be sitting still.' She frowned.

'We have a break for coffee and a leg stretch. It's not too arduous.'

'Do you flatter people?' she asked anxiously. 'I hope you do, because look –' She pinched the wedge of flesh beneath her chin, holding it daintily, like a tidbit. 'Would you be able to do something about this?'

'My portraits are truthful,' I answered carefully. 'But at the same time I want my sitters to be happy; so I'd paint you from the most flattering angle – and I'd do some sketches first to make sure you liked the composition.'

'Well . . .' She cocked her head to one side as she appraised Polly's portrait again. 'I'm going to have a think about it – but thanks.'

As she walked away, another woman in her mid-forties came up to me. She gave me an earnest smile. 'I'm definitely going to bid for this. I *love* your style – realistic but with an *edge*.'

'Thank you.' I allowed myself to bask in the compliment for a moment. 'And who would you want me to paint? Would it be you?'

'No,' she replied. 'It would be my father. You see, we never had his portrait painted.'

'Uh-huh.'

'And now we regret it.' My spirits sank as I realised what was coming. 'He died last year,' the woman went on. 'But we've got lots of photos, so you could do it from those.'

I shook my head. 'I'm afraid I don't do posthumous portraits.'

'Oh.' The woman looked affronted. 'Why not?'

'Because, to me, a portrait is all about capturing the essence and spirit of a living person.'

'Oh,' she said again, crestfallen. 'I see.' She hesitated. 'Would you perhaps make an exception?'

'I'm afraid I wouldn't. I'm sorry,' I added impotently.

'Well . . .' She shrugged. 'Then I guess that's that.'

As the woman walked away I saw my mother go up the flight of steps at the side of the stage. She waited for the string trio to finish the Mozart sonata they were playing, then she went up to the podium and tapped the mike. The hubbub subsided as she smiled at the crowd then in her soft, low voice, thanked everyone for coming and exhorted us to be generous. As she reminded us all that our bids would save children's lives, the irritation that I'd been feeling towards her was replaced by a sudden rush of pride. Next she expressed her gratitude to the donors and to her fellow committee members before introducing Tim Spiers, who took her place as she gracefully exited stage left.

He leaned an arm on the podium, peering at us benignly over his half-moon glasses. 'We have some *wonderful* lots on offer tonight – and remember there's no buyer's premium to pay, which makes everything *very* affordable. So, without further ado, let's start with the week at the *fabulous* Palazzo Barbarigo in Venice . . .'

An appreciative murmur arose as a photo of the palazzo was projected on to the two huge screens that had been placed on either side of the stage. 'The palazzo overlooks the Grand Canal,' Spiers explained as the slideshow image changed to an interior. 'It's one of Venice's most splendid palazzos and has a stunning *piano nobile*, as you can see . . . It sleeps eight, is fully staffed, and in high season a week's stay there costs ten thousand pounds. I'm now going to open the bidding at an *incredibly* low *three* thousand.' He affected astonishment. 'For a mere *three* thousand pounds, ladies and gentlemen, *you* could spend a week at one of Venice's most glorious private palaces – the experience of a lifetime. So do I hear three thousand . . . ?' His eyes raked the room. 'Three thousand pounds – anyone? Ah, *thank* you, sir. And three thousand five hundred . . . and four thousand . . . thank you – at the back there . . . five thousand . . .'

As the bidding proceeded a girl in her early twenties approached me and looked at the portrait of Polly. 'She's very pretty,' she whispered.

I gazed at Polly's heart-shaped face, framed by a helmet of rose-gold hair. 'She is.'

'Do I hear six thousand?' we heard.

'What if you have to paint someone who's plain?' the girl asked. 'Or ugly, even? Is that difficult?'

'It's actually easier than painting someone who's conventionally attractive,' I answered softly, 'because the features are more clearly defined.'

'Seven thousand now – do I hear seven *thousand* pounds? Come *on*, everyone!'

The girl sipped her champagne. 'And what happens if you don't *like* the person you're painting – could you still paint them then?'

'Yes,' I whispered. 'Though I don't suppose I'd enjoy the sittings very much.' Suddenly I noticed the doors swing open and there was Chloë, in her vintage red trench coat, and behind her, Nate. 'Luckily I've never had a sitter I disliked.'

'Going once,' we heard the auctioneer say. 'At eight thousand pounds. Going twice . . .' His eyes swept across us, then, with a flick of his wrist he tapped the podium. '*Sold* to the lady in the black dress there.' I glanced over at Mum. She looked reasonably happy with the result. 'On to lot two now,' said Spiers. 'An evening gown by Maria Grachvogel, who designs dresses for some of the world's most glamorous women – Cate Blanchett, for example, and Angelina Jolie. Whoever wins this lot will receive a personal consultation and fitting with Maria Grachvogel herself. So I'm going to start the bidding at a *very* modest five hundred pounds. *Thank* you, madam – the lady in pale blue there – and seven hundred and fifty?' He scrutinised us all. 'Seven hundred and fifty pounds is still a snip – thank you, sir. So do I hear one thousand now?' He pointed to a woman in lime green who'd raised her hand. 'It's with you, madam. At one thousand two hundred and fifty? Yes – and one thousand five hundred . . . thank you. Will anyone give me two thousand?'

I glanced to my right. Chloë was making her way around the room, leading Nate by the hand.

I know you're going to love *him, Ella . . .*

She'd been wrong about that. I loathed the man. I watched her as she spotted Roy and waved.

'Is that two thousand pounds there?' The auctioneer was pointing at Chloë. 'The young woman at the back in the scarlet raincoat?'

Chloë froze; then with a stricken expression she shook her head, mouthed *sorry* at Spiers, then looked at Nate with horrified amusement.

'So *still* at one thousand five hundred then – but *do* I hear two thousand? There was a pause then I saw my mother raise her hand. 'Thank you, Sue,' the auctioneer said. 'The bid's with our organiser, Sue Graham, now at two *thousand* pounds.' Mum's face was taut with tension. 'Will anyone give me two thousand two hundred? *Thank* you – the lady in the pink dress.' Mum's features relaxed as she was outbid. 'So at two thousand two hundred pounds . . . going once . . . twice *and* . . .' The gavel landed with a 'crack'. '*Sold* to the lady in pink here – well done, everyone,' he added jovially. 'On we go to lot three.'

As the bidding for the weekend at the Ritz got underway I saw Chloë greet Mum and Roy. Mum smiled warmly at Nate, then as Chloë leaned closer to say something to her, Mum clapped her hands in delight then turned and whispered in Roy's ear. I wondered what they were talking about.

'So for three thousand pounds now . . .' Tim Spiers was saying. 'A weekend at the Ritz in one of their deluxe suites – what a *treat*. Thank you, sir – it's with the man with the yellow tie there. Going once . . . twice . . . *and* . . .' He rapped the podium. 'Sold! You have got yourself a bargain,' Spiers said to the man amiably. 'If you'd like to go the registration desk to arrange payment, thank you. Now to the dinner party for eight, cooked by Gordon Ramsay himself – *well* worth all the shouting and swearing. Let's start with a very modest eight hundred pounds – to include wine, incidentally . . .'

The sound of the auction faded as I silently observed Chloë and Nate. Chloë seemed to do most of the talking while Nate just nodded now and again, absorbing her conversation, rather than responding to it. I saw him look at his phone and wondered if the woman he'd promised to meet that night was still in his life.

'Now for the portrait,' I heard the auctioneer say, and as my picture of Polly was projected on to the screens he indicated me with a sweep of his hand. 'Ladies and gentlemen, Gabriella Graham is an outstanding young artist.' I felt a warmth suffuse my face. 'You've probably seen media coverage of the lovely painting she did of the Duchess of Cornwall which was commissioned by the National Portrait Gallery for its permanent collection. Now you too have the chance to be immortalised by Ella. So I'm going to open the bidding at all *pitifully* low – two thousand pounds. Do I hear two thousand?' Spiers looked at us over his spectacles. 'No? Well, let me tell you that Ella's portraits usually command between six and twelve thousand pounds, depending on the size and composition. So who'll give me a trifling *two* thousand? Thank you, madam!' He beamed at the woman in the turquoise dress who'd spoken to me earlier. 'And two thousand five hundred?' I heard Spiers say. 'Just two and a half thousand – anyone?' He smiled indulgently. 'Come *on*, folks. Let's see some bidding now! *Thank* you, Sue.' My mother's hand had gone up. 'So it's with Sue Graham now at two thousand five hundred pounds . . . and three thousand – the lady in turquoise again. Who'll offer me *four* thousand?' I was startled. That was a big jump. 'Four thousand pounds?' There was silence. '*No* takers?' he said with mock incredulity. I felt a pang of disappointment tinged with embarrassment that no one thought it worth that much. Suddenly Spiers' face lit up. '*Thank* you, young lady!' He grinned. 'I hope you *mean* it this time!'

I followed his gaze and to my surprise saw that this remark had been directed at Chloë, who was nodding enthusiastically. So she was bidding in order to help Mum. 'Do I hear four thousand five hundred now?' Spiers demanded. 'Yes, madam.' The woman in turquoise had come back in. 'And who will give me five thousand pounds for the chance to be painted by Ella Graham? You'll be getting not just a portrait but an heirloom. *Thank* you! And it's the young woman in the red raincoat again.' I stared at Chloë – why was she still bidding? 'It's with you at five thousand pounds now.' I held my breath. 'And five thousand five hundred? Yes? Now it's back with the lady in turquoise.' Chloë was off the hook – thank God. 'So at five thousand five hundred pounds – to the lady in the turquoise dress there – going once . . . twice . . . and . . . SIX thousand!' Spiers shouted. He beamed at Chloë then held out his right hand to her. 'The bid's back with the lady in the red coat, at six *thousand* pounds now! Any advance on six K?' This was *crazy*. Chloë couldn't spare six thousand – she probably didn't *have* six thousand. Now I felt furious with Mum for asking her to bid. 'So at six thousand pounds – still with the young woman in red,' Spiers continued. 'Going once . . . twice . . .' He looked enquiringly at the woman in the turquoise dress, but to my dismay she shook her head. The gavel landed with a 'crack', like a gun firing. '*Sold!*'

I expected Chloë to look appalled; instead she looked thrilled. She made her way through the crowd towards me, leaving Nate with Mum and Roy.

'So what do you think?' She was smiling triumphantly.

'What do I think? I think it's *insane*. Why didn't you stop when you had the chance?'

'I didn't *want* to,' she protested. 'I decided I was going to get it – and I did!'

I stared at her. 'Chloë – how much champagne have you had?'

She laughed. 'I had some at lunchtime, but I'm not drunk. Why do you assume I am?'

'Because you've just paid six thousand pounds for something you could have had for *free*. What on earth were you *doing*?'

'Well . . . today I was made a director of PRoud – with a thirty per cent pay rise.' So *that* was what Mum had been looking so thrilled about. 'And I've just had a tax rebate – plus I want to support the charity.'

'That's very generous of you,' I told her. 'But it was at five and a half grand, which was already a good price, plus I've *done* a portrait of you, remember?'

'Of course I do – don't be silly, Ella – but the point *is*—'

I suddenly twigged. 'You want me to do it again.' I thought of how distressed Chloë had been at the time. She'd broken up with Max shortly after I'd started painting it. I'd urged her to wait, but she'd refused. She'd insisted that she *wanted* me to paint her in that state, so that she would never forget how much she'd felt for him. 'You know, Chloë,' I said, 'it probably *would* be good to do another portrait of you now that—'

'Ella,' she interrupted. 'That's *not* why I bid. Because it isn't me you're going to paint.'

'No?'

'It's Nate.'

My heart sank. And now here he was. I gave him a thin smile. 'Erm . . . apparently it's you I'm to paint, Nate.'

He looked at Chloë in confusion.

'Yes, you,' she confirmed happily.

'Oh . . . Well . . .' He was clearly as dismayed as I was. 'I don't know whether I *want* Ella to paint me. In fact I *don't* want her to – I mean, I don't want *anyone* to paint me.' He shook his head. 'Sorry, Chloë, it's *not* my kinda thing, so I'm going to have to say thanks – it's *very* sweet – but *no* thanks.'

Chloë gave him a teasing smile. 'I'm sorry, but you're not allowed to refuse, because the portrait's to be a present from me to you – a very special one.'

'His birthday present?' I asked her.

'No.' Chloë smiled delightedly. 'His *wedding* present.' She slipped her arm through Nate's. 'We're engaged!'

TWO

'I will be keeping the sittings to a *minimum*,' I said to Polly grimly the following morning as we sat in her bedroom overlooking Parsons Green. I'd taken her portrait, carefully bubble-wrapped, back to her flat. 'I am *not* relishing the prospect of spending twelve hours with that creep in order to paint his face – or rather his *two* faces. I'll paint him as Janus,' I added darkly.

Polly's nail file paused in mid-stroke. 'So I take it you still don't like him?'

I shuddered with distaste. 'I thoroughly *dis*like him – and I don't trust him.' I went and sat on the window seat. 'I told you how he behaved before her party.'

'Hmm.' Polly scrutinised the tip of her left index finger then began filing it again, the rasp of the emery board masking the drone of morning traffic.

'He was very disparaging about Chloë – plus it was obvious that he was already in a relationship with the woman he was on the phone to. So for those two *very* good reasons I have taken against him.'

Polly shifted on the bed. 'Fair enough, although – let's assume he *was* in a relationship with this other woman . . .'

'He was.'

'But at that stage he hadn't known Chloë long – so he was hedging his bets.' She shrugged. 'Lots of men do that.'

'Well . . . okay. Not that it's any excuse.'

'Or it *could* be that he was only *pretending* that he wasn't keen on Chloë in order to protect the other woman's feelings.' Polly blew on her fingertips. 'I'd hardly condemn him for that.'

'But if he'd wanted to protect the other woman's feelings then he shouldn't have told her about Chloë's party at *all*. He should have lied.'

Polly looked at me. 'Now you're saying you don't trust him because he didn't lie?'

'Yes. *No* . . . but . . . what if that other woman's still on the scene?'

She began to file her thumbnail. 'As he and Chloë are engaged, I doubt it.'

'But it's not that long ago, so she could be – and he's clearly duplicitous. I don't want Chloë having her heart broken again. It was bad enough last time.'

Polly reached for the tub of hand cream on her bedside table. 'Ella – how old is Chloë now?'

'She's . . . nearly twenty-nine.'

'Exactly – *oh* . . .' She grimaced as she tried to twist off the lid. 'Open this for me, would you?' She leaned forward and handed me the pot. 'I daren't snag a nail – I'm working tomorrow.'

'What's the job?' I asked as I unscrewed it.

'A day's shoot for a feature film. My hands are going to double for Keira Knightley's – I have to put them up to her face, like this.' Polly held her palms to her cheeks. 'I'll be kneeling behind her and won't be able to see, so I hope I don't stick my fingers up her nose. I did that to Liz Hurley once. It was embarrassing.'

'I can imagine.' I handed Polly the opened tub.

She scooped out a blob of cream and dabbed it on her knuckles. 'Chloë's got to make her *own* mistakes.'

'Of course: the trouble is she makes such *bad* ones – like getting involved with a married man. The first thing she ever knew about Max was that he was someone else's husband.'

'Remind me how she met him?'

'Chloë and I had gone into Waterstone's on the King's Road; we saw that Sylvia Shaw was signing copies of her new book and, as Chloë had liked her first two, we decided to stay. While Chloë was queuing to have her copy signed, she started chatting to this man – I could see she really liked him – who said that he was Sylvia Shaw's husband. So that's how it started – *right* under his wife's nose!'

'And his wife never found out?'

'No. Chloë said that she was too absorbed in her writing to notice. But Chloë was crazy about him. Do you remember the state she got herself in when it finally ended?' Polly nodded grimly. 'She went down to seven stone. And what she did to her hair?'

'It was a bit . . . severe.'

'It was *savage*. She looked as though she'd been in some . . . war.'

Polly stroked cream on to her other hand. 'That was

a year and a half ago,' she pointed out calmly. 'Chloë's on an even keel again now.'

'I hope so – but she's always been fragile. She's not like Mum, who has this core of *steel*.'

'That's ballerinas for you,' Polly said simply. 'They have to learn to dance through the agony, don't they, whether they've got a broken toenail or a broken heart. *Damn . . .*' She peered at her left hand then reached for the magnifying glass on the bedside table and examined it through that. 'I've got a *freckle*.' How did *that* happen?' she wailed. 'I use factor 50 on my hands all year round – my rear end gets more UV than they do. Where's my Fade Out?'

Polly went over to her dressing table and rummaged amongst all the hand creams, nail polishes and jars of cotton-wool puffs. 'I can't afford to have *any* blemishes,' she muttered. She lifted up a framed photo of her daughter, and my god-daughter, Lola. '*Here* it is . . .' She sat down on the bed again then held out the pot for me to open. 'I know you've always looked out for Chloë.'

I loosened the lid and passed the pot back to her. 'Well, she's a lot younger than me, so yes . . . I have.'

'That's nice; but now you should just . . . let go.' Polly looked at me. 'As I've known you since we were six, I feel I can say that.' She began to massage the skin lightener on to the offending brown mark. 'Chloë's got over Max enough now to be able to marry Nate – just be happy for her.'

'I'd be *thrilled* if Nate was someone I liked.' I groaned. 'And *why* does she have to give him a portrait? If she wants to spend that much, then why can't she give him something normal, like a gold watch or . . . diamond cufflinks or something?'

Polly squinted at her hand. 'Why don't you paint them together?'

'I suggested that, but Chloë wants a picture of Nate on his own. She's going to give it to him the day before the wedding.'

'Which will be when?'

'July third – which is also her birthday.'

'Well, she's always wanted to be married before she was thirty.'

'Yes – so perhaps *that* explains the quick engagement – as though anyone could care less what age a woman is when she gets married or whether she gets married at all: I mean, I'm thirty-five and still single, but I really don't . . .' I let the sentence drift.

'I'm thirty-five,' said Polly, 'and I'm divorced.' She tucked a hank of red-gold hair behind one ear. 'But it doesn't bother me. Lola has a good relationship with Ben and that's the key thing. He's being tricky about maintenance though,' she added wearily. 'Lola's school fees are fifteen grand now with all the extras, so thank God my digits give me an income.'

I considered Polly's hands with their long, slim fingers and gleaming nail beds. 'They *are* lovely. Your thumbs are *fantastic*.'

'Oh, thanks. But it isn't just about looks – my hands can *act*. They can be sad or happy.' She wiggled her fingers. 'They can be *angry* . . .' She clenched her fists. 'Or playful.' She 'walked' her fingers through the air. 'They can be inquisitive . . .' She turned up her palms. '. . . Or pleading.' She clasped them in supplication. 'The whole gamut, really.'

'There should be an Oscar category for it.'

45

'There should. Anyway . . .' She examined them again. 'They're done. Now it's time for my tootsies.'

'Have they got a part in the film too?'

'No. But they've got a Birkenstock ad next week, so I need to get them tip-top.'

Polly kicked off her oversized sheepskin slippers and examined her slender size six feet with their perfectly straight toes, shell-pink nails, elegantly high arches and smooth, rosy heels. Satisfied that there were no imperfections to attend to, she put them in the waiting foot spa and switched it on.

'Ooh, that's nice,' she crooned as the water bubbled around them. 'So what does your mum think about Chloë's engagement?'

'She's elated. But then, she couldn't stand Max.'

'Well, he was married, so you could hardly expect her to have been crazy about him.'

'True – though it went deeper than that. Mum only met Max once, but she seemed to loathe him – as though it was personal. I'm sure that was because . . . well, you know the background.'

Polly nodded. 'I still remember when you told me. We were eleven.'

The window was misted with condensation. I rubbed a patch clear and sighed. 'I hadn't known it myself until then.'

'That was a long time for your mother to keep it from you,' Polly observed quietly.

I shrugged. 'I don't really hold it against her – she'd been terribly hurt. Having made a new life, I suppose she didn't want to remember the awful way in which her old one had ended.'

Your father was involved with someone else, Ella. I knew about it and it made me desperately unhappy – not least because I loved him so much. But one day I saw him with this . . . other woman; I came across them together: it was a terrible shock. I begged him not to leave us, but he abandoned us and went far, far away . . .

'Do you think about him?' I heard Polly say.

'Hm?'

She turned off the foot spa. 'Do you think about him much? Your father.'

'No.' I registered the surprise in her eyes. 'Why would I when I haven't seen him since I was five and can barely remember him?'

One, two three . . . up in the air she goes.

'You must have *some* memories.'

Ready, sweetie? Don't let go now!

I shook my head. 'I used to, but they've gone.'

Through the smudged window pane I watched the children playing on the green below.

Again, Daddy! Again! Again!

Polly reached for the towel on the end of the bed and patted her feet with it. 'And where in Australia did he go?'

'I don't know – I only know that it was Western Australia. But whether it was Perth or Fremantle or Rockingham or Broome, or Geraldton or Esperance or Bunbury or Kalgoorlie I've *no* idea and I'm not interested.'

Polly was looking at me again. 'And he made *no* attempt to stay in touch?'

I felt my lips tighten. 'It was as though we'd never existed.'

'But . . . what if he wanted to find you?'

47

I heaved a sigh. 'That would be hard—'

'Oh, it probably *would* be,' Polly interjected. 'But you know, Ella, I've always thought that you should at least *try* to—'

I shook my head. 'It would be hard for him to *do* – given that he doesn't even know my surname.'

'Oh.' She looked deflated. 'I see. Sorry – I thought you meant . . .' She swung her legs off the bed. 'I remember when your name was changed. I remember Miss Drake telling us all at register one morning that you were Ella *Graham* now. It was a bit confusing.'

'Yes. But it was so that Chloë and I would be the same – and Roy had adopted me by then, so I can understand why they did it.'

I had a sudden memory of Mum cutting the old name tapes out of my school uniform and sewing in new ones, pulling up the thread with a vehement tug.

You're not Ella Sharp any more . . .

Now I remembered Ginny Parks, who sat behind me, endlessly asking me *why* my name had been changed and where my *real* father was. When I tearfully told Mum this she said that Ginny was a nosy little girl and that I didn't have to answer her questions.

You're Ella Graham now, darling.

But—

And that's all there is to it . . .

'What if he got in touch?' Polly tried again. 'What would you do?'

I looked at her. 'I'd do . . . nothing. I wouldn't even respond.'

Polly narrowed her eyes. 'Not even out of . . . curiosity?'

I shrugged. 'I'm *not* curious about him. I *was* – until Mum told me what he'd done; after that I stopped thinking about him. I have no idea whether he's even *alive*. He'd be sixty-six now, so perhaps he isn't alive any more, perhaps he's . . . *not* . . .' A shiver convulsed me. I looked out of the window again, scrutinising the people below as though I somehow imagined I might spot him amongst them.

'I think it's sad,' I heard Polly say.

'I suppose it is. But if your father had behaved like mine, you'd probably feel the same.'

'I don't know *how* I'd feel,' she said quietly.

'Plus I wouldn't want to upset Mum.'

'*Would* it still upset her – after so long?'

'I know it would, because she *never* mentions him – he broke her heart. But I'm sure that's why she had it in for Max, because his affair reminded her of my father's betrayal. She and Chloë had huge rows about it – I told you.'

Polly nodded. 'I guess your mum just wanted to protect Chloë from getting hurt.'

'She did. She kept telling her that Max would never leave his wife – and she was right; so Chloë finally took Mum's advice and ended it.' I shrugged. 'And now she's with Nate. I hope *he's* not going to cause her any grief, but I've got the awful feeling he is.'

Polly put her slippers on again then stood up. 'So when did they decide to tie the knot?'

'Yesterday, over lunch. They went to Quaglino's to celebrate her promotion and came out engaged. They told Mum and Roy at the auction. Mum's so thrilled, she's offered to plan it all for them.'

'She hasn't got long then. Only – what? Three and a half months?'

'True, but she has a tremendous talent for arranging things – it's probably all the choreography she's done.' I glanced at my watch. 'Yikes! I must go.' I shot to my feet. 'I've got to get to Barnes for a sitting.'

'Anyone of note?' Polly asked as we went on to the landing.

'Not really – she's a French woman married to a Brit. Her husband's commissioned me to paint her for her fortieth. He sounds quite a bit older – but he kept telling me how beautiful she is: I could hardly get him off the phone.'

Polly heaved a sigh of deep longing. 'I'd love to have someone appreciate *me* like that.'

'Any progress in that area?' I asked as we went downstairs.

'I liked the photographer at the Toilet Duck shoot last week. He took my card – not that he's phoned,' she added balefully as I opened the cupboard and got out my parka. 'What about you?'

I thrust my arms into the sleeves. 'Zilch – apart from a bit of flirting at the framer's.' I looked at the bare patch of wall where Polly's portrait usually goes. 'Shall I hang you up again before I go?'

She nodded. 'Please – I daren't do *anything* practical until the shoot's over; the tiniest scratch and I'll lose the job; there's two grand at stake and I'm short of cash.'

I pulled the bubble wrap off the painting. 'Me, too.'

Polly leaned against the wall. 'But you seem to be busy.'

I lifted the portrait on to its hook. 'Not busy enough

– and my mortgage is *huge*.' I straightened the bottom of the frame. 'Perhaps I could offer to paint the chairman of the Halifax in return for a year off the payments.'

'Maybe one of Camilla Parker Bowles's friends will commission you.'

I picked up my bag. 'That would be great. I've just joined the Royal Society of Portrait Painters, so I'm on *their* website – and I've got a Facebook page now . . .'

'That's good. Then there's that piece in *The Times*. I *know* you didn't like it,' Polly added hastily, 'but it's great publicity and it's online. So . . .' She opened the door. 'Who knows *what* might come out of it?'

I felt my gut flutter. 'Who knows . . . ?'

There was a sharp wind blowing as I walked home so I pulled up my hood and shoved my hands into my pockets. As I cut across Eel Brook Common, with its bright stripe of daffodils, my mother phoned.

'*El*-la?' She sounded elated. 'I've just had the final figures from last night. We raised *eighty* thousand pounds – five thousand more than our target, and a record for the Richmond branch of the charity.'

'That's wonderful, Mum – congratulations.'

'So I just wanted to thank you again for the portrait.' I resisted the urge to say that had I known who the sitter was to be I wouldn't have offered it. 'But *how* funny that you're going to paint Nate.'

'Yes . . . extremely amusing.'

'It'll give you an opportunity to get to *know* him before the wedding. I've just booked the church, by the way.'

'Mum . . . they've been engaged less than twenty-four hours.'

'I know – but July third's *not* that far off! So I phoned the vicar at St Matthew's first thing and by some *miracle* the two p.m. slot for that day had become free – apparently the groom had got cold feet.'

'Oh dear.'

There was a bewildered silence. 'No, not "oh dear", Ella – "oh *great*"! I didn't think we'd find *any* churches in the area free at such short notice, let alone our own one.'

'And where's the reception going to be?'

'At home. We'll come out of the church then stroll down the lane to the house through a cloud of moon daisies.'

'There aren't any moon daisies in the lane, Mum.'

'No – but there will be, because I'm going to plant some. Now we'll need a large marquee,' she went on. 'Eighty feet by thirty feet, minimum: the garden's *just* big enough – I paced it out this morning; I think we should have the "traditional" style, not the "frame" – it's *so* much more attractive – and I'll probably use the caterers from last night, although I'll get a couple of other quotes . . .'

'You've got the bit between your teeth then.'

'I *have* – but most weddings take at least a year to plan: I've got less than four months to organise Chloë's!'

'Doesn't she want to do any of it herself?'

'No – she's going to be very busy at work now that she's been promoted, and it means that she can enjoy the run-up to her big day without all the stress. She'll make the major decisions, of course, but I'll have done all the legwork.'

'Can *I* do anything?'

'No – thanks, darling. Although . . . actually there is

one thing. Chloë's thinking about having a vintage wedding dress. Could you give her a hand on that front? I don't even know who sells them.'

'Sure. Steinberg & Tolkien's gone now, hasn't it, but there's Circa, or Dolly Diamond, and I think there's a good one down in Blackheath – or hang on, what *about* . . .?'

'Yes?'

'Well . . .' I bit my lip. 'What about *yours*?'

'But . . . Roy and I got married in a register office, Ella. I wore that pale-blue silk trouser suit.'

'I know – but what about when you got married . . . before?' During the silence that followed I tried to imagine what my mother wore when she married my father in the early 1970s. A sweet, pin-tucked dress perhaps, Laura Ashley style, with a white velvet choker – or maybe something flowingly Bohemian by Ossie Clark. 'It would probably fit Chloë,' I went on. 'But . . . maybe you didn't keep it,' I added weakly as the silence continued. Why *would* she have done, I now reflected, when she hadn't even kept the wedding photos? I had a sudden vision of the dress billowing out of a dustbin. 'Sorry,' I said, as she still didn't respond. 'Obviously not a good idea – forget I suggested it.'

'I have to go,' Mum said smoothly. 'There's a beep in my ear – I think it's Top Tents. We'll speak again soon, darling.'

As she ended the call, I marvelled at my mother's ability to blank things that she didn't want to talk about. I'd steer a conversation away from a no-go area, but my mother simply pretends that the conversation isn't happening.

When I got home, I booked my minicab to Barnes then quickly packed up my paints, palette and my portable box easel. I took three new canvases out of the rack, unhooked my apron and put everything ready by the front door.

While I waited for the car I went to my computer and checked my e-mails. There was one from Mike Johns, MP, confirming his sitting for nine o clock on Thursday morning – his first for two months. I was looking forward to seeing him as he's always great fun. There was some financial spam, which I deleted, and a weekly update on the number of visits to my official Facebook page. The last message was from Mrs Carr's daughter, confirming that the first sitting with her mother would be on Monday, at Mrs Carr's flat in Notting Hill.

Hearing a beep from outside I lifted the slats of the Venetian blind and saw a red Volvo from Fulham Cars pulling up. I gathered my things and went out.

'I've driven you before, haven't I?' the driver asked as he put my things in the boot.

'That's right. I use your firm quite a bit.'

'Can't you drive then?'

'I can. But I don't have a car.'

As we drove up Waterford Road we passed the Wedding Shop. Seeing the china and cut glass in its windows I wondered how many guests Chloë and Nate would have. I speculated about where they'd go on honeymoon; but that only made me think about the woman that Nate had called 'honey'. Now I tried to guess where he and Chloë would live. It suddenly struck me that they might move to New York, a prospect that only made me feel more depressed.

'Shame,' I heard the driver say as we idled at the lights at Fulham Broadway.

'I'm sorry?'

'It's a shame.' He nodded to our right.

'Oh. Yes,' I said feelingly.

The railings at the junction were festooned with flowers. There were perhaps twenty bouquets tied to them, their cellophane icy in the sunlight. Some were fresh but most looked limp and lifeless, their leaves tinged with brown, their ribbons drifting in the breeze.

'Poor kid,' he murmured.

Tied to the top part of the railings was a large, laminated photo of a very pretty woman, a little younger than me, with short, blonde hair and a radiant smile. *Grace,* it said beneath.

'The flowers keep coming,' I observed softly.

The driver nodded. 'There're always new ones.' Today there was also a big teddy bear on a bike; it was wearing blue cycling shorts, a silver helmet and a sensible hi-vis sash.

Two months on, the large yellow sign was still there. *Witness Appeal. Fatal accident, 20 Jan., 06.15. Can you help?*

'So they still don't know what happened?' I murmured.

'No,' replied the driver. 'It happened very early – in the dark. One of our drivers said he saw a black BMW drive off, fast, but he never got the number and the CCTV wasn't working properly – typical.' He shook his head again. 'It's a shame.' The lights changed and we drove away.

The rest of the journey passed quietly, apart from the stilted commands of the sat-nav as it coaxed us over Hammersmith Bridge towards Barnes.

Mrs Burke lived halfway down Castlenau, in one of the imposing Victorian houses that line the road. The cab swung through the lion-topped gateposts then the driver got out and opened the boot.

He handed me the easel. 'You paint *me* one day?'

I smiled. 'Maybe I will.'

I rang the bell and the door was opened by a woman in her late fifties who said she was the housekeeper.

'Mrs Burke will be down shortly,' she said, as I stepped inside. The hall was large and square, with a marble-tiled floor and large architectural prints in black and gold frames. On the sideboard was a big stone jug with branches of early cherry blossom.

The housekeeper asked me to wait in the study, to our right. It had floor-to-ceiling bookshelves, an antique Chesterfield that gleamed like a conker, and a big mahogany desk on which were ranged several family photos in silver frames. I looked at these. There were two of Mrs Burke on her own, a few of the couple's son from babyhood to teens, and three of her with a man I assumed to be her husband. He was patrician-looking, with a proud, proprietorial expression, and, as I'd imagined, he was at least a decade older than his wife. She had large grey eyes, a long, perfectly straight nose and a curtain of dark hair that fell in waves from a high forehead. She *was* beautiful. I began to make imaginary marks on the canvas to define her cheeks and jawline.

The appointment had been for eleven, but by twenty past I was still waiting. I went into the hall to try and find out what was happening. Hearing a creak on the stairs I looked up to see Mrs Burke coming down. She was slim and petite, and wore a pink silk shirtwaister that was cinched in by a very wide, black patent-leather belt. I felt a flash of annoyance that she didn't seem to be in any hurry.

'I'm sorry to keep you waiting,' she said flatly as she reached the bottom step. 'I was on the phone. So . . .' She gave me a restrained smile. 'You're here to paint me.'

'Yes,' I said, taken aback by her clear lack of enthusiasm. 'Your husband said it's to celebrate your birthday.'

'It is.' She heaved an anxious sigh. 'If hitting the big "Four O" is a cause for "celebration".'

'Well, forty's still young.'

'Is it?' she said flatly. 'I only know that it's when life is supposed to *begin*. So . . .' She drew her breath through her teeth. 'We'd better get on with it then.' You'd have thought she was steeling herself for root-canal treatment.

'Mrs Burke—'

'Please.' She held up a hand. 'Celine.'

'Celine, we can't start until you've chosen the size of canvas. I've brought along three . . .' I nodded at them, propped against the skirting board. 'If you know where the portrait's going to hang, that'll help you decide.'

She stared at them. 'I haven't the faintest idea.' She turned to me. 'My husband's sprung this on me – I would *never* have thought of having myself painted.'

'Well . . . a portrait's a nice thing to have. And it'll be treasured for generations. Think of the *Mona Lisa*,' I added cheerfully.

Celine gave a Gallic shrug then pointed to the smallest canvas. 'That one is more than big enough.'

I picked it up. 'Now we need to choose the background – somewhere where you'll feel relaxed and comfortable.'

She blew out her cheeks. 'In the drawing room then, I suppose. This way . . .'

I followed her across the hall into a large yellow-papered room with a cream carpet and French windows that led on to a long walled garden, at the end of which a huge red camellia was in extravagant flower.

I glanced around the room. 'This will be fine. The colour's very appealing, and the light's lovely.'

On our left was an antique Knole sofa in a dark-green damask. The sides were very high, almost straight, and were secured to the back with thickly twisted gold cord, like a hawser. Celine sat on the left-hand side of it then smoothed her dress over her knees. 'I shall sit here . . .'

I studied her for a moment. 'I'm sorry, but that won't look right.'

Her face clouded. 'You said I should feel comfortable – this *is*.'

'But the high sides make you look . . . boxed in.'

'Oh.' She turned to look at them. 'I see. Yes . . . I am, as you say, boxed in. That is perfectly true.' She stood up then looked around. 'So where *should* I sit?' she added petulantly.

'Perhaps here . . .?' To the left of the fireplace was a mahogany chair with ornately carved arms and a red velvet seat. Celine sat in it while I moved back a few feet to appraise the composition. 'If you could just turn this way,' I asked her. 'And lift your head a little? Now look at me . . .'

She shook her head. 'Who would have thought that sitting could be such hard work?'

'Well, it's a joint effort in which we're both aiming to get the best possible portrait of you.' Celine shrugged as though this was a matter of sublime indifference to her. I held up my hands, framing her head and shoulders between my thumbs and forefingers. 'It's going to be great,' I said happily. 'Now we just have to decide what you're going to wear.'

Her face fell. 'I'm going to wear *this*—' She indicated her outfit.

'It's lovely,' I said as I considered it. 'But it won't work.'

'Why not?'

'Because the belt's so big and shiny that it will dominate the picture. If you could wear something a little plainer . . .'

'Are you saying I have to change?'

'Well . . . it would be better if you did, yes.' She exhaled irritably. 'Could I help you to choose? That's what I usually do when I paint people in their homes.'

'I see,' she snapped. 'So you control the whole show.'

I bit my lip. 'I don't mean to be controlling,' I replied quietly. 'But the choice of outfit is very important because it affects the composition so much – I did explain that to your husband.'

'Oh.' Celine was rubbing her fingertips together, impatiently, as if sifting flour. 'He forgot to tell me – he's away this week.' She stood up. 'All right,' she said grudgingly. 'You'd better come.'

I followed her across the room and up the stairs into the master bedroom, the far wall of which was taken up by an enormous fitted wardrobe. Celine slid open the middle section then stood there, staring at the garments. 'I don't know *what* to wear.'

'Could *I* look?'

She nodded. As I began to pull out a few things her mobile phone rang. She looked at the screen, answered in French, then left the room, talking rapidly in a confidential manner. It was more than ten minutes until she returned.

Struggling to hide my irritation, I showed her a pale-green linen suit. 'This would look wonderful.'

Celine chewed on her lower lip. 'I no longer wear that.'

'*Would* you – just for the portrait?'

She shook her head. 'No. I don't like myself in it.'

'O-kay, then . . . what about this?' I showed her an oyster satin dress by Christian Dior.

Celine pursed her mouth. 'It's not a good fit.' Now she began pulling things out herself: 'Not that,' she muttered. 'No . . . not that either . . . this is horrible . . . that's much too small . . . this is *so* uncomfortable . . .' Why did she keep all these things if she didn't even like them? She turned to me. '*Can't* I wear what I'm wearing?'

I began to count to ten in my head. 'The belt will wreck the composition,' I reiterated quietly. 'It will draw all the attention away from your face. And it's not really flattering,' I added, then instantly regretted it.

Celine's face had darkened. 'Are you saying I look fat?'

'No, no,' I replied as she studied her reflection in the cheval mirror. 'You're very slim. And you're really attractive,' I added impotently. 'Your husband said so and he was right.'

I'd hoped this last remark might mollify her, but to my surprise her expression hardened. 'I adore this belt.

It's Prada,' she added, as though I could have cared less whether she'd got it in Primark.

By now I was struggling to maintain my composure. 'It won't look . . . good,' I tried again. 'It'll just be a big block of black.'

'Well . . .' Celine folded her arms. 'I'm going to wear it and that's all there is to it.'

I was about to pretend that I needed the loo so that I could take five minutes to calm myself down – or quite possibly cry – when Celine's mobile phone rang again. She left the room and had another long, intense-sounding conversation which drifted across the landing in snatches.

'*Oui, chéri . . . je veux te voir aussi . . . bientôt, chéri.*'

By now I'd decided to admit defeat and was just working out how best to minimise the monstrous belt when Celine returned. To my surprise her mood seemed to have lightened. Now she took out a simple linen shift in powder blue, then held it against her.

'What about this?'

I could have wept with relief. 'That will look *great*.'

The next morning, as I waited for Mike Johns to arrive for his sitting I looked at Celine's portrait – so far no more than a few preliminary marks in yellow ochre. She was the trickiest sitter I'd ever had – obstructive, unreasonable, and entirely lacking in enthusiasm.

Her attitude struck me as bizarre. Most people give themselves up to the sittings, recognising that to be painted is a rather special thing. But for Celine it was clearly something to be endured, not enjoyed. I wondered why this should be.

I once had to paint a successful businessman whose

company had commissioned the portrait for their board-room. During the sittings he kept glancing at his watch, as though to let me know that he was an extremely busy and important man whose time was very precious. But when I at last started to paint Celine she told me that she didn't work, and that now that her son was at boarding school she led a 'leisured' sort of life. So her negativity can't have been because she didn't have time.

Thank God for Mike Johns, I thought. A big bear of a man, he was always genial, cooperative and expressive – the perfect sitter. As I took out his canvas I was pleased to see that even in the painting's semi-finished state, his amiability and warmth shone through.

Mike's portrait had been commissioned by his constituency association to mark his fifteenth anniversary as their MP: he'd been elected very young, at twenty-six. He'd said he wanted to get the painting done well before the run-up to the general election began in earnest: so we'd had two sittings before Christmas, then the third early in the New Year. We'd scheduled another for 22 January but Mike had suddenly cancelled it the night before. In a strangely incoherent e-mail he'd put that he'd be in touch again 'in due course', but to my surprise I hadn't heard from him in the intervening two months, which had surprised me, not least because he lives nearby, just on the other side of Fulham Broadway. Then last week he'd messaged me to ask if we could continue. I was glad, partly because it would mean I'd get the other half of my fee, but also because I liked Mike and enjoyed chatting to him.

We'd arranged for him to come early so that the sitting

wouldn't eat into his working day. At five past eight the bell rang and I ran downstairs.

As I opened the door I had to stifle a gasp. In the nine weeks since I'd last seen him, Mike must have lost nearly three stone.

'You're looking trim,' I said as he stepped inside. 'Been pounding the treadmill?' I added, although I already knew, from his noticeably subdued air, that his weight loss must be due to some kind of stress.

'I *have* shed a few pounds,' he replied vaguely. 'A good thing too,' he added with a stab at his usual bonhomie, but his strained demeanour gave him away. He was friendly, but there was a sadness about him now – an air of tragedy almost, I realised as I registered the dead look in his eyes. 'Sorry about the early start,' he said as we went up to the studio.

'I don't mind at all,' I replied. 'We can do all the remaining sessions at this time, if you like.'

Mike nodded then took off his jacket and put it on the sofa. He sat in the oak armchair that I use for sittings. 'Back in the hot seat then,' he said with forced joviality.

The morning light was sharp so I lowered the blinds on the Velux windows to soften it. As I put Mike's canvas on the easel I realised that I was going to have to adjust the portrait. His torso was much slimmer, his face and neck thinner, the collar of his shirt visibly gaping. His hands looked less fleshy as he clasped them in his lap. He fiddled with his wedding ring, which was clearly loose.

I scraped a pebble of dried paint off the palette then squeezed some new colour out of the tubes, enjoying, as I always did, the oily scent of the linseed.

'I forgot to wear the blue jumper,' Mike said. 'I'm sorry – it slipped my mind.'

'Don't worry.' I mixed the colour with a palette knife, then selected a fine brush. 'I'll be working on your face today, but if you could wear it next time, that would be great.'

Now I looked at Mike, and began to paint; I looked at him again, then painted a little more. And so it went on, just looking and painting, looking and painting.

Mike usually chatted away, but today he was virtually silent. He directed his gaze towards me but avoided eye contact. His mouth and jaw were tight. Aware that I must have noticed the change in him, he suddenly confided that he was 'a bit strung out' with all the extra work he was doing in preparation for the general election.

I wondered if he was worried that he might lose his seat, but then remembered reading somewhere that he had a huge majority. I shaded a slight hollow into his left cheek. 'Have you been away?' I wondered whether that was why he'd been unable to sit for me lately.

He nodded. 'I went to Bonn last month on a cross-party trip.'

I cleaned the brush in the pot of turps. 'What was that for?'

'We were looking at their tram system. I'm on a transport committee.'

I dipped the brush in the cobalt to make the flesh tone around his jaw a bit greyer. 'Then please will you do what you can to help cyclists – it's not easy on two wheels in this city.'

Mike nodded, then glanced away. Then I asked him

64

about his wife, a successful publisher in her late thirties.

He shifted on the chair. 'Sarah's fine. She's incredibly busy though – as usual.'

I thinned the paint with a little turps. 'I saw a photo of her in the business pages the other day – I can't remember what the story was, but she looked terribly glamorous.'

'She's just bought Delphi Press – to add to her empire,' Mike added with a slightly bitter smile. Now I remembered him confiding that his wife's career was all-consuming. I wondered again at the change in him; maybe she'd decided that she didn't want children, and he did: or maybe they couldn't have them and it was getting to him. Maybe, God forbid, he was ill.

Suddenly he heaved a sigh so deep, it was almost a groan.

I lowered my brush. 'Mike,' I said quietly. 'Are you okay? I hope you don't mind my asking, but you seem a bit—'

'I'm . . . fine,' he said brusquely. He cleared his throat. 'As I say, I'm just a bit stressed . . . with polling day looming . . . and it's particularly tense this time round.'

'Of course. Would you like to have a coffee break now – if you're tired?' He shook his head. 'Well . . . shall we just listen to the radio then?' He nodded gratefully. So I found my paint-spattered tranny and switched it on.

Ra-di-o Two . . . It's ten to nine. And if you've just joined us, you're listening to me, Ken Bruce, taking you through the morning . . . Eric Clapton's on tour – he'll be playing the O2 next week, then he'll be in Birmingham and Leeds . . .

The doorbell rang. As I ran down I heard a gentle guitar introduction, then Clapton's voice.

> *Would you know my name*
> *If I saw you in heaven*
> *Will it be the same*
> *If I saw you in heaven . . .*

I opened the door. It was a courier with the new bank card I'd been expecting. As I signed for it, Clapton's sad ballad drifted down the stairs.

> *Would you hold my hand*
> *If I saw you in heaven*

I went back up to the studio. 'Sorry about that.' I went to my desk and put the letter in a drawer.

> *I must be strong, and carry on*
> *Because I know I don't belong*
> *Here in heaven . . .*

I returned to the easel, picked up my brush, then looked at Mike . . .

> *. . . don't belong*
> *Here in heaven.*

He was crying.

I turned the radio off. 'Let's stop,' I murmured after a moment. 'You're . . . upset.'

'No. No.' He cleared his throat, struggling to compose

himself. 'I'm fine – and the picture needs to be finished.' He swallowed. 'I'd like to continue.'

'Are you sure?'

He nodded, then raised his head to resume the pose, and we continued in silence for another fifteen minutes or so, at the end of which Mike stood up. I wondered whether he'd come and look at the painting, as he usually does; but he just picked up his jacket and went out of the studio.

I followed him downstairs. 'So just two more sittings now.' I opened the front door. 'And is the same time next week okay for you?'

'That'll be fine,' he said absently. 'See you then, Ella.'

'Yes. See you then, Mike. I look forward to it.'

I watched him walk to his car. As I stood there, Mike lifted his hand, gave me a bleak smile, then got into his black BMW and drove slowly away.

THREE

'Ella?' said Chloë over the phone a few days later. 'I need to ask you something.'

'If it's that you want me to be a bridesmaid, the answer's no.'

'Oh . . .' She sounded disappointed. 'Why not?'

'Because I'm nearly seven years older and two stone heavier than you are – that's why. I don't fancy being a troll to your fairy.'

'How about maid of honour then?'

'No. See answer above.'

'Actually, that wasn't what I was going to ask you – Nate has a five-year-old niece who's going to do the honours.'

'That sounds perfect. So what did you want to ask?' My insides were churning, because I knew.

'I'd just like to set up the first sitting with Nate. I was half expecting you to get in touch about it,' she reproached me.

'Sorry, I've been working flat out,' I lied.

'Can we fix up some times now?'

'Sure,' I said breezily.

I rummaged on the table for my diary and found it under this month's *Modern Painters*. I scribbled in Chloë's suggested date.

'So where are you going to paint him? His flat's near to yours, if you want to paint him there.'

'No – he'll have to come to me.' Disliking Nate, I preferred him to be on my ground.

'That's eleven a.m. next Friday then,' said Chloë. 'It's Good Friday.'

'So it is. I'll get some hot cross buns in for the break.'

As I tossed the diary back on the table I remembered the girl at the auction asking me if I could paint someone I didn't like. I was about to find out.

'Nate will be a good sitter,' I heard Chloë say.

'I hope so.' I sighed. 'I've had some tricky ones lately.'

'Really?'

I wasn't going to tell her about Mike – I felt a growing concern for him and wondered what had happened to make him so unhappy.

'So how are your sitters being tricky?' Chloë persisted. I described Celine's behaviour. 'How odd,' said Chloë. 'It's as though she's trying to sabotage the portrait.'

'Exactly. And when we finally got to start, she took two *more* calls then went to the front door and spoke to her builder for fifteen minutes. The woman's a nightmare.'

'Well, Nate will be very good. He's not that keen on it all either, as you know. But at least he'll behave well during the sittings.'

'In that case, we should be able to get away with five

69

rather than the usual six.' The thought cheered me. 'Or even four.'

'Please don't cut corners,' I heard Chloë say. 'I've paid a lot for this portrait, Ella. I want it to be . . . wonderful.'

'Of . . . course you do.' I felt a wave of shame. 'Don't worry, I'll do a good job, in at least six sittings – *more* if they're needed,' I added recklessly.

'And please make it truthful, not just attractive. I want the portrait to *reveal* something about Nate.'

'It will do,' I assured her, then wondered *what* – that he was cynical and untrustworthy, probably. Convinced that my negativity about him would show, I now regretted the commission even more and wished I could get out of it. I fiddled with a paintbrush. 'I saw the engagement announcement in *The Times*, by the way.' Seeing it in black and white had depressed me . . .

Mr Nathan Roberto Rossi to Miss Chloë Susan Graham.

Chloë snorted. 'Mum also put it in the *Telegraph*, the *Independent and* the *Guardian*! I told her it was over the top, but she said she "didn't want anyone to miss it".' I immediately suspected that what Mum really intended was for *Max* not to miss it.

'She is *amazing*, though,' Chloë went on. 'She's already booked the church, the photographer, the video man, the caterers, the florist *and* the marquee – or Raj tent, rather. She's now decided on a Moghul pavilion – she says it's the most elegant way to dine under canvas.'

'Is it going to be a sit-down affair then?'

'Yes. I told Mum that finger food would be fine, but she insists we do it "properly" with a traditional, wait-ered wedding breakfast – poor Dad. He keeps joking that it's a good job he's an orthopaedic surgeon as he knows where to get more arms and legs.'

I smiled. 'And Mum said you wanted a vintage wedding dress.'

'If I can find one that's perfect for me, yes.'

While Chloë chatted about her preferred style I went to my computer and, with the phone still clamped to my ear, found three specialist websites. I clicked on the first, the Vintage Wedding-Dress Store.

'There's a wonderful fifties dress here,' I said to her. 'Guipure lace top with a billowy silk skirt – it's called "Gina".' I told Chloë the name of the site so that she could find it. 'There's also a thirties one called "Greta" – see it? That column of ivory satin – but it's got a very low back.'

'Oh yes . . . It's lovely, but I'm not sure I'd want to show that much flesh.'

'That sixties one would suit you – "Jackie": it's a twelve though, so you'd have to take it right in, which might ruin it.'

'I can't see it. Hang on a mo' . . .'

While I waited for Chloë to find it, I clicked on my e-mails. There were three new ones including a request for my bank account details, an advert for 'bedding bargains' from 'Dreamz' and some offers from Top Table. I deleted them all.

'*Here's* a gorgeous dress,' Chloë said. 'It's called "Giselle".'

I navigated back to the site. The dress was ballerina style with dense layers of silk tulle below a fitted satin bodice that spangled with sequins. 'It *is* gorgeous. You'll look just like Mum in her dancing days.'

'It's perfect,' Chloë breathed. 'And I know it would suit me – *but* . . .' She was making little clicking noises.

'It might be inauspicious to wear a wedding dress called "Giselle" – don't you think?'

'Oh . . . because she has such bad luck in the husband department, you mean?'

'Exactly – Albrecht's such a cad, two-timing the poor girl like that. I hope Nate isn't going to do that to *me*,' she snorted. 'Otherwise I might have to kill myself, like Giselle does.'

'Don't be silly,' I said faintly. 'After all, he's asked you to marry him.'

'That's . . . true. Anyway, if you see any really great dresses, let me know.'

'Sure. But I'd better go, Chloë – I've got a sitting.'

'And I've got some press packs to check – but I'll tell Nate that he's got a date with you on Friday.'

A date with Nate, I thought dismally as I hung up.

I ordered the cab then began to get my things together for the sitting with Mrs Carr. Her daughter had already specified the size of canvas, so I took out the one that I'd primed, checked that it was properly stretched, then put my canvas bag and easel by the front door. I was just reaching for my coat when the phone rang.

I picked it up. 'Ella? This is Alison from the Royal Society of Portrait Painters. Do you remember we spoke before Christmas – when you were first elected?'

'Of course I do. Hi.'

'Well, I've just had an enquiry about you.'

'Really?' My spirits lifted at the possibility of another commission. 'Who's it from?' Through the window I could see the cab pulling up.

'It's slightly unusual in that it's for a posthumous portrait.'

My euphoria evaporated. 'I'm afraid I don't do them. I find the idea too sad.'

'Oh, I didn't realise that you felt like that – I'll make a note. Some of our members do do them, but we'll put on your page that you don't. Not that these requests arise all that often, but it's good to know the position. Anyway, I'm sure there'll be other enquiries about you before long.'

'Fingers crossed . . .'

'So I'll be in touch again sometime.'

'Great. Erm . . . Alison, do you mind if I ask you . . .?'

'Yes?'

'Just out of curiosity – who was it from? This enquiry?'

'It was from the family of a girl who was knocked off her bike and killed.' I felt goose bumps stipple my arms. 'It happened two months ago,' Alison went on. 'At Fulham Broadway. In fact, there's been a bit about it in the press because the police still don't know what caused the accident – or who, rather.'

I thought of the black BMW speeding away. 'I live near there,' I said quietly. 'I've seen where it happened . . .'

'There'll be a memorial service in early September, at the school where she taught – she was a primary teacher. Her parents have decided to commission a portrait of her for it.'

'Grace. Her name was Grace.'

'That's right. It's terribly sad. Anyway, her family realise that any painting's going to take time, so her uncle called me to discuss it. He said that they'd been looking at our artists and had particularly liked your work – plus the fact that you're a similar age to Grace.'

'I see . . .'

73

'In fact, they're very keen for you to do it.'

'Ah.'

'But I'll tell him that you can't, shall I?'

'No . . . I mean, yes. Tell him . . . that . . .'

'That you paint only from life?' Alison suggested.

'Yes . . . But please say I'm sorry. And give them my condolences.'

'I will.'

From outside I heard the impatient beeping of the cab's horn so I said goodbye, locked up, then went out to the car. It was the red Volvo again; the driver put my easel and canvas in the boot while I climbed into the back.

He sat behind the wheel then looked at me in the mirror. 'Where to this time?'

I gave him the address and we set off.

'So who are you painting today?' he asked me as we drove through Earl's Court.

'An elderly lady.'

'Lots of wrinkles then,' he laughed.

'Yes – and lots of character. I like painting old people. I love looking at paintings of old people too.' I thought of Rembrandt's tender and dignified portraits of the elderly.

'You're going to paint me, one day – don't forget now!'

'Don't worry – I won't forget,' I said. He had an interesting, craggy sort of face.

Mrs Carr's flat was in a mansion block in a narrow street close to Notting Hill Gate. I paid the driver, got out of the cab, then he handed me my equipment. To my left was an antique shop, and to the right a primary school. I could hear children's voices and laughter and the sound of a ball being kicked about. I pressed the bell for flat 9 and after a moment heard Mrs Carr's daughter, Sophia, over the intercom.

'Hi, Ella.' The door buzzed open and I pushed on it. 'Take the lift to the third floor.'

The interior of the Edwardian building was cold, its walls still clad in the original Art Nouveau tiles in a fluid pattern of green and maroon. I stepped into the antiquated lift and rattled up to the third floor where it stopped with a sonorous 'clunk'. As I pulled back the grille I could see Sophia waiting for me at the very end of the semi-lit corridor. Mid-fifties, she was dressed youthfully in jeans and a brown suede jacket, her fair hair scraped into a ponytail.

'It's nice to see you again, Ella.' As I walked towards her she looked at the equipment. 'But that's a lot to lug about.' She stepped forward. 'Let me help you.'

'Oh – thanks. It's not heavy,' I added as she took the easel. 'Just a bit awkward.'

'Thanks for coming to us,' she said as I followed her inside. She shut the door. 'It makes it so much easier for my mother.'

'That's fine.' I didn't add that I like painting people in their own homes: it gives me important insights into who they are – their taste, how much comfort they prefer and how tidy they like these things; I can tell, from the number of family photos, how sentimental they are and, if there are invitations to be seen, how social. All this gives me a head start on my subjects before painting even begins.

'Mum's in the sitting room,' Sophia said. 'I'll introduce you, then leave you to it while I do a bit of shopping for her.'

I followed her down the hallway.

75

The sitting room was large with two green wing-back chairs, a lemon-yellow chaise longue and a cream-coloured sofa. A large green-and-yellow Persian rug covered most of the darkly varnished parquet-tiled floor.

Mrs Carr was standing by the far window. She was tall and very slim, but slightly stooped, and she leaned on a stick. Her hair was tinted a pale caramel colour and was set in soft layered waves. In profile her nose was Roman, and her eyes, when she turned to look at me, were a remarkable dark blue, almost navy.

Sophia put the easel down. '*Mummy?*' She'd raised her voice. 'This is *Ella*.'

'Hello, Mrs Carr.' I extended a hand.

She took it in her left one. Her fingers felt as cool and smooth as vellum. As she smiled, her face creased into dozens of little lines and folds. 'How nice to meet you.'

Sophia took my parka. 'Can I get you a cup of coffee, Ella?'

'Oh, no thanks.'

'What about *you*, Mummy? Do you want some *coffee*?'

Mrs Carr shook her head, then went over to the sofa and sat down, leaning her stick against the arm.

Sophia waved to her. 'I'll be back around four – *four*, Mummy! *Ok-ay*?'

'That's fine, darling. No need to shout . . .' As we heard Sophia's retreating steps Mrs Carr looked at me, then shrugged. 'She thinks I'm deaf,' she said wonderingly. The front door slammed, creating a slight reverberation.

I took a closer look at the room. One wall was lined with books; the others bore an assortment of prints and paintings that hung, in attractive chaos, from the picture rail. I opened my bag. 'Have you lived here long, Mrs Carr?'

She held up her hand. 'Please call me Iris – we'll be spending quite a lot of time together, after all.'

'I will then – thanks.'

'But to answer your question – fifteen years. I moved here after my husband died. We'd lived not far away, in Holland Street. The house was too big and too sad for me on my own; but I wanted to stay in this area as I have many friends here.'

I opened up the easel. 'And do you have any other children?'

Iris nodded. 'My younger one, Mary, lives in Sussex. Sophia's just down the road in Brook Green; but they're both very good to me. This portrait was their idea – rather a nice one, I think.'

'And have you ever been painted before?'

Iris hesitated. 'Yes. A long time ago . . .' She half-closed her eyes as if revisiting the memory. 'But . . . the girls suddenly said that they wanted a picture of me. I did wonder whether I *wanted* to be painted at this age – but I have to accept the fact that my face is now an *old* face.'

'It's also a beautiful one.'

She smiled. 'You're being kind.'

'Not really – it's true.' I felt that Iris and I were going to get on well. 'So . . . I'll just get everything ready.' I got out the paints and my palette. I tied on my apron and spread a dustsheet around the easel. 'And did you have a career, Iris?'

She exhaled. 'Ralph was in the Foreign Office, so *that*

was my career, being a diplomatic wife – dutifully flying the flag in various parts of the globe.'

'Sounds exciting – so where did you live?'

'In Yugoslavia, Egypt and Iran – this was before the revolution – and in India and Chile. Our last posting was in Paris, which was lovely.' As Iris talked I studied her face, seeing how it moved, and where the light fell upon her features.

I got out my pad and a stump of charcoal. 'It sounds like a wonderful life.'

'It was – in most ways.'

I sat in the wing-backed chair nearest Iris, looked at her, and began to make rapid marks: 'I'm just doing a preliminary sketch.' The charcoal squeaked across the paper. 'And do you come from a diplomatic background yourself?'

'No. My stepfather was in the City. So are you going to paint me sitting here?'

'Yes.' I lowered the sketchpad. 'If you're happy there.'

'I'm perfectly happy. And is the light satisfactory?'

'It's lovely.' I glanced at the window, through which I could see the dome of the Coronet Cinema and behind it a patch of pale sky. 'There's a lot of high cloud today, which is good because it eliminates strong shadows.' I carried on drawing, then turned the pad round to show Iris what I'd done. 'I'm going to paint you like this, in a three-quarters position.'

She peered at it. 'Will my hands be in the picture?'

'Yes.'

'In that case I'll wear one or two rings.'

'Please do – I love painting jewellery.' I wiped a smudge of charcoal off my thumb.

'And what about my clothes?' Iris asked. 'Sophia told me that you like to have some say in what your sitters wear.'

'I do – if they don't object.' I thought of Celine.

'I don't object in the slightest.'

'You're very easy to work with,' I said gratefully.

Iris looked puzzled. 'Why shouldn't I be? You're going to deliver me up to *posterity* – the least I can do is to cooperate. My daughters say that your portraits are so vibrant that one almost expects the people in them to climb out of the frames.'

'Thank you – what a lovely compliment.'

'But *I've* not yet seen one myself.'

'Ah.' I should have brought some photos of them with me. 'Do you have a computer, Iris?' She shook her head. 'Then I'll show you some images of them on my mobile phone – it's got a good screen.'

I got out my phone, went to 'Gallery' then touched one of the thumbnail images and handed the phone to Iris.

She brought it close to her eyes then nodded appreciatively. 'That's Simon Rattle.'

I nodded. 'The Berlin Philharmonic commissioned it last year – I went there for a week and painted him every day in between rehearsals. He was a good, patient sitter.'

'I'll try to be the same.'

I took the phone from Iris, touched another image, then handed it back to her. 'This is P. D. James.'

'So it is . . . I see what my daughters mean – there's such a *vitality* to your work.'

As Mrs Carr gave me back my phone I noticed that I had new e-mails. I touched the inbox and saw a flyer from the V&A and a message from Chloë. At that moment a new e-mail arrived – one that had been forwarded automatically from my website. I felt a tingle of excitement because it was likely to be an enquiry; I could see a bit of the first line, *Dear Ella, My* . . . but resisted the temptation to open it as I didn't want to risk annoying Iris – I was here to paint her, not to read my messages. I put the phone in my bag.

'So now we'll decide what I'm to wear,' said Iris. 'Please come.'

Reaching for her stick, she pushed herself to her feet and I followed her down the corridor into her bedroom. It was large and light, with pale-blue chintz curtains and a blue candlewick bedspread. Against one wall was a big Art Deco wardrobe in a walnut veneer. As Iris opened its doors, a faint scent of lily-of-the-valley drifted out.

'Can I help you get things out?' I asked her.

'No . . . I can manage. Thank you.' Iris leaned her stick against the wall, then, with slightly shaky hands took out a pink, lightly patterned dress and a blue tweed suit. She laid them on the bed. 'What about these?'

I looked at the garments, then at Iris. 'Either would look good. But . . . the suit, I think.'

Iris smiled. 'I hoped you'd say that. Ralph bought it for me in Simpson's on a home leave one time – he couldn't really afford it, but he saw how much I liked it and wanted me to have it.'

'It's perfect. So what jewellery will you wear?'

'A lapis lazuli necklace that I had made when I was in India and my engagement ring.'

Iris went to her dressing table and lifted the lid of an ornately carved sandalwood box. As she did so I glanced round the room. There was a gilded mirror on one wall, flanked by a pair of small alpine paintings. Over the bed was a silk wall hanging of a crested crane. A blue Persian glass vase stood in the window, casting a cobalt shadow on to the sill.

'Would you kindly get my stick?' I heard Iris say. 'It's leaning against the wall there, by the wardrobe.'

As I did so I noticed a painting hanging next to her bed. It was of two little girls playing in a park. They were about five and three and were throwing a red ball to each other while a small dog darted at their feet in a blur of brown fur. On a bench close by, a woman in a white apron sat knitting.

I stared at it. 'What a lovely picture.'

Iris turned. 'Yes . . . that painting is very special. In fact, it's priceless,' she added quietly.

I tried to disguise my curiosity. 'It's certainly very fine.' I handed Iris her stick then looked at the painting again. 'So is it an . . . heirloom?'

She hesitated. 'I bought it in an antique shop in 1960, for ten shillings and sixpence.'

I turned to her. 'So you just . . . liked it.'

Iris was still gazing at it. 'Oh it was much more than "liked" . . .' She paused. 'I was drawn to it – *guided* to it, I sometimes think.'

I waited for her to elaborate, but she didn't say any more. 'Well,' I said after a moment, 'it's easy to understand why you fell in love with it. It's beautifully composed and has so much – I was going to say charm – but what I really mean is *feeling*.'

Iris nodded. 'There's a lot of feeling there. Yes.'

'The woman on the bench must be the girls' nanny.'

'That's right.'

'She seems absorbed in her knitting, but she's actually looking at the artist, covertly, which gives it a kind of edge. It looks as though it's from the early 1930s. I wonder where it was painted . . .'

'In St James's Park, near the lake.'

I studied the silvery-grey water shining in the background. 'Well, it's lovely. It must lift your spirits, just looking at it.'

'On the contrary,' Iris murmured. 'It makes me feel sad.' She lowered herself on to the bed. 'But now I'll change, so if you could give me a few moments . . .'

'Of course.'

I went back to the sitting room. As I tied on my apron I wondered why the painting would have that effect on Iris. Of course we all see different things in works of art; yet the scene was, objectively, a happy one, so why should it make her sad?

While I was preparing my palette, my phone rang. I quickly answered.

'He's *called* me,' Polly declared excitedly.

'Who has?'

'Jason – from the Toilet Duck shoot; he's *just* called and asked me to have lunch with him on Saturday.'

'Great,' I whispered. 'But I can't chat, Pol – I'm in a sitting.'

'Ooh, sorry – I'll leave you to it.'

As I pressed the 'end call' button I looked at the envelope icon; I was tempted to open the e-mail from my website, but then I heard Iris's footsteps.

'So . . .' She was standing in the doorway. The suit fitted her perfectly and brought out the intense blue of her eyes; she'd applied some powder and a touch of pink lipstick.

'You look beautiful, Iris.' I put my phone back in my bag.

She smiled. 'Thank you. So now we can start.'

Iris sat on the sofa, smoothed down her skirt then turned towards me. As I looked at her, I felt the frisson I always feel when I begin a new portrait. We were silent for a while, the brush scraping softly across the canvas as I began to block in the main shapes with an ochre wash.

After a couple of minutes Iris shifted her position.

'Are you comfortable?' I asked her, concerned.

'I *am* – though I confess I feel a little self-conscious.'

'That's normal,' I assured her. 'A portrait sitting's quite a strange experience – for both parties – because there's this sudden relationship. I mean, we've only just met, but here I am, openly gawping at you: it's a pretty unnatural first encounter.'

Iris smiled. 'I'm sure I'll soon get used to your . . . scrutiny. But wouldn't you rather be painting someone young?'

'No. I prefer painting older people. It's much more interesting. I love seeing a whole life etched on to a face, with all that experience, and insight.'

'And regret?' Iris suggested quietly.

'Yes . . . that's usually there too. It would be strange if it wasn't.'

'So . . . do your sitters ever get upset?'

My brush stopped. 'They do – especially the older ones, because as they sit there they're looking back on their lives. Sometimes people cry.' I thought of Mike and

83

wondered again what could have happened to make him so unhappy.

'Well, I promise *not* to cry,' Iris said.

I shrugged. 'It doesn't matter if you do. I'm going to paint *you*, Iris, in all your humanity, as you *are* – or as I see you, at least.'

'You have to be perceptive then, to do what you do.'

'That's true.' I exhaled. 'And I couldn't even *try* to do this if I didn't believe that I was. Portrait painters need to be able to detect things about the sitter – to try to work out who that person *is*.'

We continued in silence for a few moments.

'And do you ever paint yourself?'

My brush stopped in mid-stroke. 'No.'

Surprise flickered across Iris's features. 'I thought portrait artists usually did do self-portraits.'

You're Ella Graham now . . .

'Well . . . I don't – at least not for years now.'

And that's all there is to it . . .

'But . . . I'd love to hear more about your time abroad, Iris. You must have met some remarkable people.'

'I did,' she said warmly. 'Well, they weren't just people, they were *personalities*. Let me see . . . Whose names can I drop?' She narrowed her eyes. 'We met Tito,' she began. 'And Indira Gandhi – I have a photo of Sophia, aged five, sitting on her lap. I also met Nasser – the year before Suez; I danced with him at an embassy ball. In Chile we met Salvador Allende: Ralph and I liked him enormously and were outraged at what the Americans did to help overthrow him, though we could never say so openly. Discretion is a frustrating, if necessary, aspect of diplomatic life.'

84

'What was your favourite posting?'

Iris smiled. 'Iran. We were there in the mid-1970s – it was paradisally beautiful and I have wonderful memories of our time there.'

'But presumably your daughters went to boarding school?'

She nodded. 'In Dorset. They weren't able to join us for every holiday, so that was hard. Their guardian was very good, but we hated being separated from our two girls.'

There was another silence, broken only by the dull rumble of traffic in Kensington Church Street.

'Iris . . . I hope you don't mind my asking you – but the painting in your bedroom . . .'

She shifted slightly. 'Yes?'

'You said it made you feel sad. I can't help wondering why – as it's such a happy scene.'

Iris didn't at first reply, and for a few moments I wondered whether she *wasn't*, in fact, slightly deaf; and I was considering whether to ask her again when she exhaled, painfully. 'That picture makes me feel sad because there is a sad story attached to it – one I learned a few years after I'd bought it.' She heaved another deep sigh. 'Perhaps I'll tell you . . .'

I felt crass suddenly. 'You don't have to, Iris – I didn't mean to pry: I was just surprised by your remark, that's all.'

'That's perfectly understandable. It *is*, on the surface, a happy scene. Two little girls playing in a park . . .' She paused, then looked at me intently. 'I *will* tell you the story, Ella – because you're an artist and I believe you'll understand.' Understand what, I wondered. What

85

could the sad story behind the painting be? It now occurred to me, with an anxious pang, that the girls might not have survived the war – or perhaps something awful had happened to the nanny. Now I wasn't sure that I *wanted* to hear the story, but Iris was beginning.

'I bought the painting in May 1960,' she said. 'We were in Yugoslavia then – our first posting; but I'd come home with Sophia, who was then three, to have my second child, Mary. There were good hospitals in Belgrade, but I decided to have the baby in London so that my mother could help me. Also, she was widowed by then and I wanted to take the opportunity to spend some time with her; so I went to stay with her for three months.'

I studied Iris, and drew in the curve of her right cheek.

'My mother's house was in Bayswater. She'd spent most of her married life in Mayfair but, as I say, my stepfather lost everything after the war.' I wondered about Iris's own father. 'The week before the baby was due I took Sophia out in her pushchair. We had an ice cream in Whiteleys then walked slowly up Westbourne Grove: and I was just passing a small antique shop when I glanced in the window and saw that painting. I remember stopping dead and staring at it: I was completely taken with it – as you have been today. Sophia turned round and squawked at me to go on, so I did. But I couldn't get the picture out of my mind. So, a few minutes later I turned back and pushed on the door.

'The man who owned the shop told me that the painting had come in the week before. It had been brought in with some other things by a woman who'd found it in her late brother's attic – she'd been clearing his house. She wasn't sure who it was by, as it was unsigned, but on the back of the canvas was the year it was painted, 1934. I couldn't really afford it, but I bought it, and as I carried it back I remember feeling what I can only describe as a kind of *relief*.

'I showed it to my mother and she looked at it closely, but said nothing. I felt hurt by her lack of enthusiasm, but assumed that it was because she felt I'd been extravagant. I volunteered that it *was* a lot of money, but added that I'd fallen in love with it and simply "had to have it". Then I hung it in my room.

'The following week Mary was born, and I stayed with my mother for another two months. She was very helpful, but seemed sad, despite the birth of the new baby; I assumed it was because she knew I'd soon be going back to Yugoslavia with her grandchildren and that it would be a long time before she saw us again.'

'Did you have any siblings?'

'Yes – an older sister, Agnes, who lived in Kent. Anyway, before I went back to Belgrade I put the painting in storage, along with all the other things that Ralph and I had stored.'

'Could you lift your head a little, Iris? I'm just marking out your brow.' I squinted at her. 'That's better. So . . . what happened then?'

Iris folded her hands in her lap. 'In 1963 we returned to London for a two-year stint before our next foreign posting. We were glad to be back, the only sadness being that my mother had died a few months before. I think she knew that she might not see me again, because her later letters to me had been full of sorrow – she said that she hadn't been a good mother in some critical ways; she said she had so much to regret. I simply thought that the distance between us had made her feel vulnerable; so I wrote back saying that she'd been a very loving and caring mother, which, in most ways, she had been . . .'

Iris brushed a speck off her skirt. 'Anyway . . . Ralph and I had returned to our house in Clapham – it had been let while we were away. I remember the day our things came out of storage and Sophia and Mary, who were then six and three, delightedly helping us unpack the crates. For them it was a bit like Christmas. Eventually we came to the china and glass, then to the few pictures we possessed and there, wrapped in some old pages of the *Daily Express*, was my painting. I was *so* glad to see it again . . .'

Iris paused for a moment then continued.

'This was the first time Ralph had seen it, although I'd talked to him about it. As he looked at it he said that it was clearly very good and added that he'd ask our neighbour, Hugh, who worked at Sotheby's, to take a look at it. So a few days later Hugh came round, and he said that the reason it was unsigned was because it was probably a model for a larger painting. He was almost sure that it was by Guy Lennox, who had been a successful portraitist in the twenties and thirties. Ralph asked Hugh about its possible value and I remember feeling alarmed because I knew that I could never part with it – especially as I was now mother to two little girls myself. And this made me feel that *that* was what had first drawn me to the picture; when I was pregnant I was *sure* that I was going to have another daughter

– and I did. Anyway, I was very relieved to hear Hugh say that the picture wouldn't be worth a huge amount, because Lennox was simply a good figurative artist, painting portraits to commission. And I was about to put the girls to bed when he added that his uncle had known Lennox well; he remembered him saying that Lennox had had a sad life.

'Really?'

'Hugh said that he could find out more about him, if I was interested – which I was. So he showed his uncle the painting on a visit to him in Hampshire not long afterwards. When Hugh brought the painting back a month later, he confirmed that it *was* by Guy Lennox, whose life story he now knew. He told us that he was born in 1900, had fought in the First World War, but had been badly gassed at Passchendaele and was sent back. While recuperating, he'd taught himself to paint, and after the war he went to the Camberwell School of Art – which is where he met Hugh's uncle. He then decided to specialise in portraits and so in 1922 he went to study portraiture at the Heatherly School of Fine Art in Chelsea. I'm sure you know it.'

'Yes – very well; I used to teach at Heatherly's.'

'While he was there, Guy fell desperately in love with one of the models – a beautiful girl named Edith Roche. His parents tried to discourage the relationship but in 1924 Guy and Edith were married at the Chelsea Town Hall. In 1927 they had a baby girl, followed fifteen months later by another. By this time Guy was becoming successful, fashionable even. He was much in demand, painting anyone who was "anyone" – literary and political figures, and members of the aristocracy. He became a Royal Academician, and was able to buy a house in Glebe Place with its own studio. His life seemed gilded – until the day he was commissioned to paint a man called Peter Loden . . .' Iris fell silent.

'So . . . who was Peter Loden?' I asked after a few moments.

Iris blinked, as if surfacing from some dream. 'He was an oil trader,' she replied. 'He was very rich – he'd laid the first pipeline to Romania. He had a huge house just off Park Lane; it was like something out of the *Forsyte Saga*,' she added absently.

'How old was he?'

'Thirty-eight – still a bachelor – and quite a ladies' man. In May 1929 he won a Conservative seat in the general election and, to celebrate, he asked Guy Lennox to paint his portrait. He liked the painting so much that he decided to hold an official unveiling for it. So in the September of that year he held a lavish party, to which he invited *tout le monde*. He also invited Lennox – and his wife: and when Peter Loden met Edith . . .'

'Ah . . .'

'He was absolutely infatuated with her beauty: she was flattered to have the attentions of such a rich and powerful man. Soon everyone knew that Edith Lennox was involved with Peter Loden; worse, Guy had to carry on working, knowing that the society figures he painted were gossiping about his wife.'

'How horrible for him.'

Iris nodded. 'It must have been agonising. And it was to have a devastating effect on his life, because within three months Edith had petitioned Guy for divorce. And you'd think that she and Loden had done him enough harm,' Iris added wearily. 'But then it all became truly heartbreaking for that poor man because—'

Iris looked up. The front door was being opened, there was a grunt as it banged shut, then footsteps and there was Sophia, clutching four bulging green carrier bags, her face pink with exertion.

'I'm pooped!' She smiled at us benignly. 'I carried this lot back from Ken High Street. Still, the exercise is good for me.' She nodded at the easel. 'So how are you two getting along?'

'Oh . . . fine,' Iris replied. She glanced at her watch. 'But you're early, Sophia. It's a quarter to four.'

'I know, but I'd got everything you needed – except the Parma ham: there was *no Parma ham*, Mum – so I thought I'd head back. But don't let me disturb you. I'll put all this away.' She disappeared and now we heard cupboards being opened and banged shut.

Iris gave me a rueful smile. 'Well . . . I think this is a good moment for us to stop.'

I nodded reluctantly then clipped the canvas into the canvas carrier. 'So I'll see you next time, Iris.' I collapsed the legs of the easel.

'It will have to be after Easter,' Iris said. 'I'm staying with my other daughter, Mary, for a week.' I got my diary out of my bag.

As we were making a date, Sophia came back. 'Will you need me to be here again?' she asked. 'I can be, if you want.'

'That's kind, darling,' Iris replied. 'But now that Ella and I know each other, we can just carry on from where we've left off.'

I nodded. Sophia handed me my coat and I put it on. 'I've enjoyed the sitting, Iris.'

'I have too,' she replied. '*Very* much. So until next time . . .'

I smiled my goodbye then picked everything up.

Sophia held the door open for me. 'Can I give you a hand?' she asked good-naturedly.

'I'll be fine, thanks.' I hitched my canvas bag a little higher on to my shoulder. 'Bye, Sophia . . .'

'Bye, Ella.' The door shut behind me.

I clanked down in the lift then went out on to Kensington Church Street and hailed a cab. As I sat in the back, my mind was full of Guy Lennox and the beautiful Edith and Peter Loden, and the two little girls, the nanny and the dog: they felt almost as real to me as if I'd known them myself. Soon we were passing Glebe Place and I craned my neck to look down it, wondering which house Lennox had lived in.

Suddenly the driver's intercom came on. 'Did you say Umbria Place, miss?'

'Yes – it's next to the Gasworks.'

'I know it – we'll be there in three minutes, if the traffic keeps moving.'

I rummaged in my bag for my purse. Seeing my phone, I now remembered the unread e-mail from my website. So I went to the inbox and opened it, and as I began to read it the story of Guy Lennox evaporated. A jolt ran down my spine.

Dear Ella, My name is John Sharp . . .

FOUR

On the morning of Good Friday I prepared for my first sitting with Nate. I got out the canvas, which I'd primed with a cream emulsion base a few days before. I cleaned the brushes and laid them neatly on my work table. I put the oak chair in place and, behind it, the folding screen that I sometimes use as a background. I mixed some burnt sienna with turps to make the thin wash. Then, still with half an hour before Nate was due, I got out my mother's portrait: I simply wanted to look at it and to think about the e-mail which I'd now read so many times that it was seared on my mind.

Dear Ella, My name is John Sharp, and I am your father.

I shook my head. 'I've got a father, thanks.'

I hope you'll forgive me for contacting you . . .

'Shouldn't that be for *not* contacting me?' I said angrily.

It must be a bit of a shock.

'It certainly is!'

. . . but I came across an interview with you on The Times *website.*

I exhaled, sharply. 'Just what I'd dreaded.' I silently cursed the journalist, Hamish Watt.

There was a link to it from the Western Australian, *and when I saw your face I knew at once who you were.*

'No,' I murmured. 'You have *no* idea who I am.'

I recognised in your strong, dark features my own, and your story fitted with the life we shared so many years ago.

'So many,' I echoed bitterly.

And though I have no right to say that I feel proud of you, I do . . .

'Well, it isn't mutual . . .'

Ella, I'm going to be in London the last week of May.

Adrenalin scorched through my veins. I went to my desk, picked up my phone and opened the message.

I would so much like to meet you . . .

'Oh God . . .'

I've always wanted to try and explain –

'Explain *what?*' I demanded. 'That you deserted your wife and child? I don't *need* that explaining – I can remember it.'

Now I looked at my painting of Mum and saw her sitting at the kitchen table in our old flat, crying softly, while I sat next to her, helpless with anxiety and fright. I remembered drawing pictures of my father to cheer her up. And I remembered thinking that if I drew him well – so that it really *looked* like him – then perhaps, by some magic, he'd come back.

Ella, I've always felt very guilty about what happened.

'About what you *did*, you mean.'

I'd like to try and make amends . . .

I went to 'Options' then to 'Delete message?'.

. . . if it's not too late to do so.

I hesitated for a few moments, then pressed 'Yes'. My father's words vanished.

With a shaking hand I put my phone away.

Drrrrrrrrnnnnnnnng.

Nate had arrived – exactly on time. I breathed deeply to steady my nerves then walked slowly downstairs and opened the door.

Chloë stood beside him.

'I know I said I *wouldn't* come . . . But I'm meeting Mum at Peter Jones – we're going to look at wedding invitations – so I thought I'd just pop in on my way.' She stepped inside, then peered at me. 'Are you all right, Ella? You look a bit . . . tense.'

'No,' I said, my insides churning. 'I'm fine.'

Chloë turned to Nate. 'Come *in*, darling!' With palpable reluctance, he did. He was wearing jeans and a green cashmere jumper that had a collar, with dark-brown brogues. As I looked at him a current of antagonism flashed between us.

I wrested my features into a pleasant expression. 'Hello, Nate.'

He gave me a wary smile. 'Hi.'

'The studio's on the top floor,' Chloë explained as she climbed the stairs. 'Ella lives under the shop – don't you, Ella?'

'That's right,' I said, as Nate followed her up. We passed the bathroom, then the spare room, then my room, through the open door of which the wrought-iron bedstead was visible – I quickly pulled the door to. Then we went up the last flight and into the studio.

Nate looked around him in surprise.

'You wouldn't think there'd be this much space up here, would you?' Chloë said to him.

'No,' he answered.

'I mean, the house doesn't look much from outside – sorry, Ella.' Chloë gave me an embarrassed smile.

I shrugged. 'It's true. But it's got a steeply pitched roof, which makes for this big, high attic.'

Now Chloë went over to the chair, put her hand on the back of it then smiled at Nate. 'All you have to do is sit here looking handsome – not hard in your case,' she added with a laugh.

Nate rolled his eyes. 'For how long?'

I unhooked my apron. 'Two hours.'

He grimaced.

'It'll *fly* by,' Chloë assured him. 'You can just chat.'

'Or not,' I said as I put on the apron. 'It's up to you. You can be quiet, if you want – or I can put the radio on; if you want to bring an iPod, that's fine.' That would be my preferred option, I decided – then I wouldn't have to talk to him.

'You *should* chat,' Chloë said. She looked from me to Nate. 'I mean, you hardly know each other – you've only met, what – three times?'

'Twice,' Nate and I said simultaneously. We glanced awkwardly at each other then looked away.

Chloë crossed the room and picked up my portfolio. She staggered back with it. 'Have a look at Ella's portraits, darling.' She set it down on the table with a thump, and Nate sat on the sofa and began to look through the images while Chloë sat next to him, occasionally explaining who the sitters were. 'That's Simon Rattle, that's P. D. James, that's Roy, of course . . .' Nate turned to the final page. 'And that's me!'

'I know.' He smiled indulgently. 'I've seen the original often enough.' I pushed away the unwelcome image of him in Chloë's bedroom. 'I still can't understand why you'd want to have yourself painted in this state though.'

Chloë shrugged. 'That was in the middle of the boyfriend trouble I mentioned – all water under the bridge now,' she added airily. I suddenly wondered how much she'd told Nate about Max. 'But as Ella had started the picture we thought we'd just . . . carry on. Isn't that right, Ella?'

I looked at her. 'Erm . . . yes.' Chloë could hardly tell Nate the truth – that the portrait was for her a record of the deep attachment she'd had for his predecessor. 'Anyway . . .' She threw her arms around him. 'Thank God I met *you*!'

As she planted a kiss on Nate's cheek I saw his gaze stray to the portrait of Mum. I'd leaned it against the wall. 'That's really good,' he said quietly.

Chloë turned to look at it. 'It is – it's really come on: you can see Mum's inner strength now, Ella, and her self-discipline and her . . . what's the word I'm looking for?'

Pain, I thought. The wound that she'd sheltered for so long was visible in her eyes, and in the slightly hard set of her mouth – it was visible even in her pose. On the surface it was the pose of a ballerina taking a curtain call, her left hand spread elegantly across her chest. But it was also a defensive gesture – she was shielding her heart.

I knew now that I was right not to have told her about my father's e-mail. It would have been cruel to stir up such painful emotions, and quite unnecessary, given that I wasn't going to meet him.

'*Resolve*,' Chloë concluded. She pointed to the *Giselle* poster. 'That's Mum too. That was two years before I was born,' she explained to Nate, 'but Ella saw her in it, didn't you?'

'I did.' I remembered sitting in the front row, mesmerised by my mother's arabesques and her graceful *jetés*; she was so light that at times she seemed to be poised in mid-air, her slender limbs extending into infinity. Now I suddenly recalled my father sitting next to me, gazing at her, his profile bathed in the light from the stage: and when Mum grabbed Albrecht's sword then fell down dead he held my hand and whispered that she was 'just pretending'. And when we went backstage afterwards Mum was still in her long tutu and veil, and she threw her arms round my father and stood up on her *pointes* and kissed him, and They were both laughing and I was laughing too because my parents were happy and loved each other. But within a few weeks my father had gone . . .

'I wish *I'd* seen Mum dance,' I heard Chloë say. 'But her career was over by the time I was born.'

Nate looked at her. 'You said she was injured.'

Chloë nodded. 'She had a fall and broke her ankle – I'm not sure where it happened. Do you know, Ella?'

'No – I did once ask her, but she didn't want to talk about it.' I knew only that it had happened more or less when my father left. So within a short space of time both her marriage and her career had ended abruptly, and in great pain.

'That's how Mum met my dad,' Chloë said to Nate. 'He was the surgeon who did the second operation a few months after her accident. He managed to make it a lot better than it had been, but he had to tell her that the injury had been career ending.'

'How heartbreaking for her,' Nate said, his eyes still on the portrait.

'It was,' Chloë agreed. 'Though at least she got *him* out of it – he was completely smitten with her, wasn't he, Ella?' I nodded. 'Mum often says that he was her silver lining.'

I thought of my father's desertion. 'He was her golden lining,' I said feelingly.

Chloë smiled. '*Ah* . . .' She glanced at her watch. 'But I'd better go – she's a stickler for punctuality.' She blew Nate a kiss. 'I'll see you later, darling.'

He gave her an anxious smile. 'Ciao.'

'Chloë,' I said as she turned to go, 'will you want to see the portrait while I'm working on it?'

She made a clicking noise with her tongue while she considered the question. 'No,' she said. 'I think I'd rather see it when it's finished, to have that wonderful sense of . . . revelation.' She gave us a cheery wave and was gone.

We heard her light, descending tread, then the sound of the front door being opened and then slammed shut. The house fell silent . . .

I put the portrait of Mum back in the rack then lifted Nate's blank, primed canvas on to the easel.

'So . . .' My pulse was racing. 'Let's start . . .'

I nodded at the chair and Nate went and sat in it, gingerly, as though he feared it might be booby-trapped. He crossed his legs then folded his arms.

'Erm . . . if you could sit in a slightly more relaxed way, Nate.'

'Oh.' He uncrossed his legs. 'Like that?'

'Yes . . . and if you could maybe put your hands on your knees.' They were large and sinewy, I noticed, with strong, straight fingers. 'Now lift your head . . . and look this way . . .' I heard him exhale as if already exasperated. 'That's great . . . in *fact* . . .' I felt a sudden frisson as I decided on the composition. 'I'm going to paint you looking straight out of the canvas. It's not something I do very often, but your features are strong enough, and I think it'll look powerful.' Nate nodded uncertainly. 'So you'll need to look right *at* me.' As Nate's gaze fell on me I felt a shiver of awkwardness, but this was quickly dispelled by my growing excitement at the possibilities of the portrait. Okay, the man wasn't that nice, but at least he had a great face. 'That's good . . .' I murmured. 'Now I'm just going to stare at you, if that's okay . . .'

Nate nodded apprehensively, but I decided to ignore his discomfiture and simply focus on the task in hand. So I took in the shape of his head, the square of light that fell on his brow and the almost bluish shine to his hair; I registered the planes of his cheeks and the different textures and shades of his skin. There were two short lines above his nose, like a number eleven, and a small round scar, like a watermark, on the right side of his brow. His eyes, I realised, weren't so much a mossy green as dark sage, with flecks of gold. Then I stared at him from either side, examining the angle of his jaw, the swell of his mouth, and the long, slender triangle of his nose.

Then I went back to the canvas, dipped my brush in the wash and, still looking at him, made my first mark.

100

I worked in silence, aware only of the shapes that flowed from the tip of my brush, and the sound of Nate's gentle, steady breathing. I gazed at the lower part of his face. The runnel between lip and nose was very clearly defined. I was seized by the bewildering urge to place my fingertip in it.

As I dipped the brush in the wash again I heard a deep sigh.

I looked at Nate. 'Are you okay?'

He shifted on the chair. 'Well . . .'

'Do you need a cushion?'

'No. I'm . . . fine.' I turned back to the canvas and carried on painting for a minute or two, then the chair creaked again and he exhaled wearily. 'Are you sure you can't do this from a photograph?'

'I *could* – but it wouldn't make for a good portrait.'

'Why not?'

I ignored the edge in his tone. 'Because a photo is only a snapshot of a single moment. But a portrait represents an accumulation of moments – *all* the moments of the sitter's life. So although it might *look* like you, it wouldn't show who you *are*, which is what I'll be trying to do.'

'I see,' he said grimly.

I worked for four or five minutes; then I heard another pained sigh and the chair creaked again.

I lowered my brush. 'You do seem a bit . . . uncomfortable, Nate.'

'I . . . *am*.'

'Then do let me get you a cushion.'

'No. Thanks. My discomfort isn't physical.' His meaning lay between us, like a grenade.

101

'Sitting for a portrait isn't easy,' I said, nervously. 'It's an . . . odd situation; there's often a . . . tension.'

'There is,' Nate agreed. 'Especially if the sitter feels that the artist doesn't like him.'

My brush stopped in mid-stroke. 'I don't know what you mean.'

'I think you do,' he countered. 'Because you haven't exactly been . . . *simpatico*.' He shrugged. 'Maybe you think I'm not good enough for your sister.'

'No, that's not . . .' I faltered. 'I mean . . . Chloë's obviously happy with you, which is all that matters.' My hand was shaking, making it hard to hold the brush.

'In fact, you've been pretty hostile, right from the start.'

I wiped a little splash of blue off the corner of the canvas. 'You know, Nate, I really don't think this conversation is very helpful – especially as we have to spend another eleven and a half hours in each other's company.'

'It's *because* we have to spend another eleven and a half hours in each other's company that I think it *is* helpful,' Nate shot back. 'Because you say you're going to show who I *am* in this portrait.'

'Yes,' I said weakly.

'Well, I'm not happy about that – given your obvious negativity toward me. I see the portrait as a potential attack.'

I silently cursed Chloë for landing me with a commission that wasn't just awkward – it was becoming downright embarrassing.

Nate shifted on the chair again. 'You've clearly got a big problem with me. I don't know why . . .'

I glared at him. 'Don't you?'

'No. I don't.'

'Really?'

He gave me a challenging stare. 'So you *do* have a problem with me. Would you mind telling me what it is?' I dipped the brush in the wash again then turned back to the canvas. 'If you're going to paint me, then I need to know,' I heard him say. 'And if you don't tell me, then I might just walk out and give Chloë the money for the wasted commission.'

I could hear the tick of the clock. 'All right,' I said quietly. 'I *will* tell you – as you've pushed me to it.' A part of me was glad to be able to get it off my chest. So I told him about the night of the party. 'You didn't see me, because I was on the other side of Chloë's fence, locking my bike. But I heard you talking to someone – another woman – about Chloë. I didn't *like* what I heard – and yes, it's affected how I feel about you. *There*,' I concluded. 'Now you know.'

Nate was staring at me. 'You listened to my private conversation?'

'No – because it *wasn't* private, given that you were having it on a mobile phone in the street. I couldn't help hearing it, and I wish I hadn't, because it was pretty upsetting.'

Puzzlement furrowed Nate's brow. 'So . . . *what* did you hear?'

I heaved a sigh. 'You said that you didn't want to go to Chloë's party – but that you felt you couldn't get out of it because she'd been going on and on about it – as though she'd pestered you.'

'Well . . .' Nate turned up his palms. 'She *did*. She

103

must have phoned me ten times a day about it. It got to be pretty annoying.'

I ignored this. '*Then* I heard you making arrangements to go and see this woman, who you kept calling "honey", later that night. That didn't exactly endear you to me either.'

'Ah . . .' He put his head on one side.

'But what really got up my nose was the fact that you were *discussing* Chloë with this other woman – and in disparaging terms!' My face was suddenly burning with retrospective indignation. 'You reassured her that Chloë was "nothing special".'

Nate was nodding slowly. 'I *remember* this conversation now – and I *did* say that, yes.'

The man was brazen! 'So I heard *all* that,' I said, 'then, lo and behold, a few minutes later I see you greet Chloë warmly and tell her how much you've been looking forward to her party. At which point I decided that you were a cynical, disingenuous, hypocritical, *two*-faced, two-*timing* . . .'

'Creep?' said Nate helpfully.

'*Yes*. And to be frank, I hoped that Chloë wouldn't be seeing too much more of you, but now she's engaged to you and she's paid a lot of money for me to paint you, which for *her* sake is what I intend to *do*.' My heart was pounding. 'And having answered your question, I suggest we now get *on* with the sitting – if only to minimise the time that we have to spend together!'

I picked up my brush and began stabbing at the canvas with it.

I could hear Nate sucking on his lower lip. 'So you heard me talking to "honey"?'

'Yes.' I picked a bristle off the canvas. 'I did. And I *don't* like men who date two women at a time – especially if one of the women is my sister!'

'I see. You didn't *tell* Chloë any of this, did you?'

'No. Don't *worry*,' I said. 'Your secret is safe. I *was* tempted to tell her, but couldn't bring myself to rain on her parade – so I didn't.'

'Well, that's a shame,' he said, with irritating calm. 'Because if you *had* done then you would have found out from Chloë that the woman I called "honey" is my first cousin.'

I looked at him. 'Then you appear to have an unhealthily close relationship with her.'

'Her name is Honeysuckle, but everyone calls her "Honey" or "Hon".'

My mouth had suddenly dried to the texture of felt. 'But . . . you had keys to her place. You said that you were going to let yourself in, so it sounded as if she was your—'

'I *do* have keys,' he interrupted. 'Not to her "place", but to her office – *our* office – because Honey's also my boss. She's CEO of the firm I work for, Blake Investments, which was set up twenty years ago by her father, Ted Blake, who's married to my mom's younger sister, Alessandra.'

I tried to swallow. 'I see . . .'

'And the reason *why* I was going to go and see Honey was because when I was on the way to Putney she'd called me on my cell to ask me to go back to the office – a problem had blown up with an acquisition that we were handling. I didn't want to disappoint Chloë, so I told Honey I was going to a party but promised I'd come back afterwards. I said I'd let myself in because the security guy leaves at eight – and that's what I did. I returned to the office at nine, and Honey and I worked until two in the morning and got it all sorted.' He looked at me. 'Happy now?'

My cheeks were burning. '*No* – because you were *rude* about Chloë. You'd made out that it was a chore to have to go to her party.'

'That's true – because, although Honey's great, she can be very inquisitive, so I was talking it down.'

'Okay.' His smug tone infuriated me. 'But you didn't have to tell her that Chloë was "nothing special" did you?'

'Well . . . the minute she thinks I *am* seeing "someone special" – as she invariably puts it – I never hear the *end* of it. Worse, she tells her mom, who then tells *mine*. The next thing I know, *all* my sisters are phoning me, demanding information.'

'So . . . how many sisters . . . have you got?'

'Five – all older.'

'Oh.' Now I vaguely remembered Chloë saying that Nate came from a big family.

'Plus, I'd only known Chloë for a couple of months, so I wasn't *ready* to talk about it to Honey.'

'Well . . . this all sounds perfectly plausible, but—'

'It isn't just plausible, Ella,' he interrupted firmly. 'It's *true*.' Nate emitted an amused snort, then folded his arms. 'So, on the basis of that one overheard conversation you decided that I was seeing another woman while dating Chloë, who I spoke about *to* this other woman in disrespectful, if not downright contemptuous, terms. That's it, in a nutshell, isn't it?'

'Yes. But that's how it *sounded*,' I countered helplessly.

Nate sucked on his lower lip again. 'The way it may have sounded was quite different from the way it *was*.'

'Well . . . I'm . . . very glad to know that. And I'm . . . sorry . . .' I faltered, 'if I *have* been, yes, a bit cool with you.'

'Cool?' Nate was shaking his head. 'You were arctic, Ella.'

'Okay, but that . . . coldness, was based on what I *now* understand to be a *mis*understanding.' My face was aflame. 'But I am perfectly happy to accept that you are *not* . . .'

'. . . a cynical, disingenuous, hypocritical, two-faced, two-timing creep?' Nate suggested pleasantly.

'Exactly.'

'Well I'm glad we've established *that*.'

'Me too,' I said sheepishly. I picked up my brush. 'So *now* will you let me paint you?'

Nate unfolded his arms then smiled at me. 'Yes.'

'So you got the wrong end of the stick?' Polly said on the Tuesday after Easter. We were having coffee in her small garden. As the sun was out, she was wearing one of her many pairs of white cotton gloves.

'I got *completely* the wrong end.' I cringed at the memory. 'I feel awful.'

'Don't – it's easy to see why you thought what you did.' Polly nodded at the cafetière. 'Would you mind?'

'Oh, sure.' I pushed the plunger down to spare Polly's hands, then poured her a cup.

'Thanks.' She reached for the milk. 'So what did you think of Nate after that?'

'Erm . . . Nice. Very. Yes.'

Polly smiled. 'That's great. After all, he's going to be your brother-in-law so it must be a relief to find that you like him after all.' I tried to stifle the feeling that I'd been happier when I *dis*liked him. 'So – is he attractive?'

'He *is*.' I filled my cup. 'Definitely. I can't . . . deny it.'

Polly gave me a puzzled look. 'Why would you want to?'

'Erm . . . No reason. He's, as I say . . . very attractive.'

'Lucky Chloë,' Polly sighed.

'Yes . . .'

'So what's his background?'

'Italian – his parents were from Florence but emigrated to New York in the early fifties.'

Polly sipped her coffee. 'Why would anyone want to leave *Florence*?'

'That's what I asked him – it was because jobs were hard to come by, post-war. He said he was a surprise baby – his mother was forty-five when she had him; she's eighty-one now and a bit frail. His father died ten years ago and he's got five older sisters – Maria, Livia, Valentina, Federica *and* . . . oh yes, Simonetta.'

'I see,' said Polly slowly. 'So why hasn't *he* got an Italian name?'

'Because he was named after the taxi driver who delivered him. He arrived three weeks early and his father, who worked for Steinway, was in Philadelphia at the time taking a new concert grand to the Academy of Music there – not that he was a delivery man or anything; he was a master tuner, and a wonderful pianist himself, apparently. He used to give *very* good recitals at a local church.'

108

Polly was looking at me. 'Really?'

'Oh yes.' I stirred my coffee. 'Anyway, he was in Philadelphia,' I went on, 'and so Nate's mother, realising that the baby was starting, phoned for an ambulance but it didn't come. So she got in a cab but didn't make it as far as the hospital. Nate was born *in* the taxi with the help of the driver, whose name was Nathan. So Mrs Rossi promised that she'd name her son after him. He came to Nate's baptism and gave him a pair of silver cufflinks that Nate still wears. Isn't that nice?'

Polly smiled. 'Well . . . it sounds like you had a really good chat.'

I laid the spoon in the saucer. 'I was just trying to be extra friendly to make up for not having been terribly *simpatico* before.'

Polly gave me a quizzical look. '*Simpatico?*'

'Yes. What's the problem?'

'Nothing. It's just that you don't usually use that word.'

'Don't I?' I batted away a fly. 'Anyway, Nate's sisters have all long since had kids and they've been piling the pressure on him to get married – especially as his mother's getting on. He said they've been driving him crazy about it.'

'What a pain.'

'That's why he moved to London – to get away from them.'

'Poor chap. So they must be thrilled about Chloë then.'

'I guess they must be . . .'

'Has she met them?'

'Yes – she and Nate went to New York for the weekend about a month ago.'

'And are his family all coming over for the wedding?'

'I . . . don't know.'

'You could ask Chloë.'

'Yes . . . I could.'

The idea of discussing Nate with Chloë made me flinch. I decided that this was only natural, because I regard the sittings as such private affairs.

'So when are you seeing him next?'

'On Saturday morning. I'll get some croissants in for the break – we didn't have a break last time because we were talking so much and forgot; or maybe I'll get biscotti.' I put my cup down. 'What do you think?'

'What do I think about what?'

'Should I get croissants or biscotti? Biscotti,' I said, before she could answer. 'Or perhaps Florentines, in honour of his origins – as long as he's not allergic to nuts,' I added anxiously.

'Ella?' Polly put down her cup.

'What?'

'Erm . . . you seem to have really enjoyed the sitting with Nate.'

I felt my skin prickle. 'I *did* . . . because I was just . . . happy that we'd cleared the air. It *was* a relief – as you say. So . . .' I clapped my hands. 'How was your date?'

'Well . . .' She sighed, wearily. 'It *started* promisingly. I dropped Lola off at Ben's, then I went to Islington to meet Jason. We had lunch at Frederick's, during which we both talked about our work – he didn't know that I do feet as well as hands, and I told him about the Step by Step Pedicure Guide I'm doing for *Woman's Own*. He seemed quite interested in that, and at the end of lunch he asked me if I'd like to go back to his place for coffee. I was feeling pretty mellow so I said yes, and as we strolled through Camden Passage he took my hand—'

'He didn't squeeze it, did he?'

'No, no – I told him to be careful. Anyway, I felt really happy and hopeful, so we went to his flat, which is in a converted warehouse at the top of Peter Street, but *then*—' She grimaced.

'His wife came back?'

'No – he's single. It was *weirder* than that. We went into his studio and he pulled me on to the sofa and I thought he was going to kiss me, which I wouldn't have minded. Instead, he asked me to take off my shoes. So I *did*. He gazed at my feet and said how beautiful they were, and he lifted them on to his lap and began to stroke them, which was nice, in a way, but *then* . . .'

'Oh God – he tried to suck your toes.'

She pulled a face. 'Not *quite*. He left the room and when he came back he was holding this pair of red patent-leather shoes with *eight*-inch heels, three-inch platforms with metal spikes round the sides, and black leather thonging right up to mid-high.'

'So what did he want you to do – stand on him in them while he screamed for mercy?'

'No.' Polly shuddered. 'He just asked me to put them on, very slowly, and then lace them up, very *slowly* . . .'

'Uh huh.'

'While he filmed me.'

'Oh.'

Polly's eyes were like tea-plates. 'That's *all* he wanted – to film me putting on those horrendous shoes!'

'So . . . *did* you?'

'And risk getting bunions and fallen arches? No way! My feet are paying the school fees. He *begged* me to do it, but I refused.'

'You'd have ended up on YouTube if you had.'

'Exactly. Or he could have sold the footage – ha ha – to some fetishist site. Anyway, I put my Hush Puppies back on and left.'

'So . . . a bit disappointing then.'

'It was. All I'd wanted was a cup of Nescafé and a cuddle.' Polly rolled her eyes. 'I get this *all* the time. The minute I tell a man I'm a foot model he goes all pervy on me. Anyway . . . so much for Mr Toilet Duck.'

'There'll be others, Pol.'

'That's what worries me.'

'No – your prince will come, bearing a nice comfy . . . glass slipper.'

'I'd rather he came bearing a nice comfy Ugg! Anyway, Cinderella's slippers weren't glass – that's a common misconception.'

'Is it?'

'In the earliest French versions of the legend she wore *"pantoufles de vair"* – v, a, i, r, – which were slippers of squirrel fur; by the time Charles Perrault was reading those early versions, that word was no longer in use; so it's believed that he assumed *"vair"* to be a mis-translation of *"verre"* – v, e, double r, e – and therefore made Cinderella's slippers in *his* version, glass.'

'I see. You're a mine of information on the foot front, Polly.'

She shrugged. 'You pick these things up if you're in the toe business.' She looked at me. 'So . . . any other news?'

'No.' I replied. 'Actually . . . *yes*.' I told her about my father's e-mail.

Polly's hand flew to her chest. 'Your father contacted you?' Her eyes were round with amazement. 'Because of that piece in *The Times*?'

'Yes – which is *exactly* what I was worried about. *That's* why I tried to get that journalist to change it.'

'I assumed it was because you thought it was too personal.'

'I *did* think that; but my main worry was that if my father happened to see it he might get in touch – and now he *has*.' I let out a sigh. 'I still don't know *how* Hamish Watt knew what he did. I never talk about it to anyone, nor does Chloë; and I know you wouldn't discuss it.'

'Not in a million years.'

'But that wretched article is the reason for my father's e-mail.'

'Perhaps he was already looking for you.'

'He said that the *Western Australian* had a profile of the Duchess of Cornwall in which it mentioned my portrait of her and put a link to the interview with me in *The Times*. That's all that prompted his message – a chance sighting of me online. But I've deleted it.'

'*Ella* . . .' Polly's face was a mask of dismay.

My heart sank. '*Don't* look at me like that, Pol. I've had no contact with the man for more than three decades and I don't want it now – I've told you that.'

'I feel sorry for him.'

I put down my cup. 'Why do you have to be on his side?'

'I'm not,' she protested quietly. 'I'm on yours, but I just feel . . . well, you *know* what I feel, Ella.'

I shrugged. 'He said he'd like to "make amends", but what he really wants is to make himself feel better about what he did. Why should I help him do that?'

'Because . . . you may deeply regret it in the future if you don't.'

'I'll take that risk.'

'And *maybe* . . .' Polly looked at me apprehensively. 'Maybe there's another side to the story: maybe, somehow, it's not as bad as you think.'

'No.' I felt a rush of indignation. 'It was just an awful betrayal. My mother adored him – he was the love of her life. She said she did everything she could to make him happy, and I believe her. But in September 1979 he deserted us, and we never heard of him again – until now.'

'Okay. What he did was heartless. But he's going to be in *London* – perhaps even close by.' I had an image of my father walking towards me. Would I recognise him? I didn't even have a photograph of him. I remembered that his hair was dark, like mine – it would be grey now, perhaps even white. He might not *have* much hair. He might be thinner than he was when I knew him, or heavier. His face might be very lined.

'Wouldn't it be good to *meet* him,' Polly was saying, 'if only once? Just to talk to him, and find a bit of . . . closure.'

'I don't need "closure", thank you – I'm *fine*.'

'But there must be things you'd like to ask him.'

'Oh, there *are*. I'd like to ask him why his marriage vows meant so little to him and how he could abandon my mother when she loved him so much. I'd like to ask him how he could bring himself to leave his only child, and why he didn't, at the very least, try and explain it to me, or even say goodbye.'

'So you didn't know that he was . . . going?'

'No.' I searched my memory. 'He just stopped being . . . *around*. I kept asking my mother where he was, and she simply wouldn't answer – but then she must have been in turmoil, not least because she'd just had her fall. Eventually my grandmother told me that I was going to have to be brave, because my father had gone away and wouldn't be returning. I was convinced she was wrong. So I sat in the window of our flat on Moss Side and looked out for him. I sat there for weeks, but he didn't come. And I began to connect his leaving with my mother's accident, and I came to believe that my father must have left because Mum couldn't dance any more . . .'

'You told me you didn't remember much about your father, but you obviously do,' Polly observed quietly.

I nodded. 'And I've been remembering more and more since he got in touch . . .'

One two three, up in the air . . . Why *was* that such a clear memory? I wondered now. How could I remember it at all, given how young I would have been? And why did my mother's white-and-red skirt stand out in my mind?

Polly laid her hand on my arm. 'I *wish* you'd see him, Ella.'

'No.' I pursed my lips. 'He's left it too late. He should have contacted me years ago.'

'He didn't know where you *were*.'

'True – but he could have traced Mum. He could have

made enquiries through English National Ballet or at the Northern Ballet Theatre. He could have put out all sorts of leads. Okay, he wouldn't have known that she was no longer Sue Young – that was her maiden name and the name she danced under. But if he'd been determined enough, he could have found her, and if he *had* done, he'd have found me.'

'Well . . . maybe he *did* contact her.'

'He didn't. There's been nothing from him all these years. Then, one day, he comes across me online and with two clicks of the mouse he's in touch. It's been too *easy* for him, Polly – so it doesn't *mean* much.'

'I can understand why you feel like that, but perhaps he felt he *couldn't* contact your mother after what he'd done.'

'That *is* possible. Maybe he felt too ashamed – he *should* have done; especially as he left her with no money.'

Polly's eyes widened. 'Surely she got something after they divorced?'

'I don't think she did.'

'Then she must have had a useless solicitor.'

'Maybe, but wives didn't get such a good deal then – the law's changed.'

'And was he well off?'

'I've no idea. He was an architect – whether successful or not, I don't know.'

'So how long were your parents married?'

I shrugged. 'Five or six years?'

'Surely he had to pay maintenance?'

'I haven't a clue. I do remember Mum swearing that she'd never take a penny from him after what he'd done; she was very bitter, and still is. So I'm not about to open a can of worms by telling her that he's been in touch with me, let alone that he's coming to London.'

'Couldn't you see him, but not say anything to her?'

I hesitated. 'I have wondered about that . . . but it's too big a thing to conceal, and telling her might be incredibly disruptive – it could spoil Chloë's wedding.'

'And will you mention it to Chloë?'

'No – I can't take the chance, in case she tells Mum. Not that Chloë ever thinks about my father,' I added. 'As far as she's concerned, my father's Roy: and that's another thing – I want to protect *his* feelings.'

'But he'd be happy for you.'

'No – he'd be upset.'

'I think he'd understand. He'd support you,' Polly went on. 'I know he would. He loves you, Ella . . .'

Polly was pushing this too far. I stood up. 'I'd better go, Pol. I've got stuff to do . . . canvases to prime – that kind of thing.'

'Okay,' she said wearily as we went into the hall. 'But there's a bit of time until your father comes . . .' She looked at me earnestly. 'I hope you'll change your mind, Ella. I hope you'll see him.'

I shook my head. 'Well I won't.'

In any case I *couldn't* change my mind, I reflected as I went over to Barnes the next morning: I'd double deleted my father's message. I had no record of him. He'd gone. As the cab swung into Celine's drive I decided to forget that he'd ever been in touch.

I paid the driver, rang the bell and the housekeeper let me in and once again asked me to wait in the study; I told her that I'd prefer to set everything up to save time.

So she showed me into the drawing room and put down some dustsheets while I unfolded the easel and put the chair into position; then I mixed the yellow ochre wash, put the canvas out and waited. I glanced at the mantelpiece, on which, amongst the bits of antique silver, were a number of formal-looking invitations. On the glass coffee table was a copy of *Hello!* so I flicked through it. Amongst the ads I saw Clive Owen's face being stroked by Polly's hands; I'd know her fingers anywhere. As I turned to the next page I was surprised to find myself staring at a photo of Max. He had a champagne glass in his hand and was standing next to his wife, *best-selling crime writer Sylvia Shaw at the launch of her latest novel,* Dead Right. Max looked smarter than I remembered him – his face clean shaven, his collar-length fair hair now short; but the photo did nothing for Sylvia, whose angular features seemed to jostle together, like a late Picasso. She'd be interesting to paint, I reflected.

'I'm sorry, I'm a bit late,' I heard Celine say. I glanced up. She was *very* late, but at least she was wearing the blue dress. 'I see you're all ready,' she added pleasantly.

I resisted the temptation to tell her that I'd been ready for twenty minutes. I put the magazine back on the table then went over to the easel.

Celine sat in the chair, placed her bag at her feet then turned towards me. 'I was sitting like this, wasn't I?'

'You were. But if you could just sit a little further back . . . you're rather on the edge of your seat there: that's great.' As I picked up my brush we heard the 'ker-plink' of a text alert.

'Sorry,' Celine muttered as she leaned down and reached into her bag. She fished out the phone, read the message and then, to my astonishment, began to text back. 'I *just* have to reply . . .' she murmured as she thumbed away. 'Almost done . . . *et . . . voilà!*' She put the phone back then resumed the pose.

I began to work. 'I'm still doing the under-painting,' I explained. 'I'll start to build up the detail next week, using thicker and thicker paint each time – we call that "thin to fat" – until – oh . . .'

We heard the synthesised jingle of Celine's ring tone. She was rummaging in her bag.

'Celine—' I protested. But she'd taken the call.

'*Oui?*' She stood up. '*Oui, chéri, je t'entends . . .*' she said softly, furtively almost. '*Bien sûr, chéri . . .*' As she left the room I flung silent curses at her. I wished I could glue her rear end to the seat.

Ten minutes later she returned. She dropped her mobile back in her bag then sat down. 'Okay.' She placed her hands in her lap. '*Now* we can start.'

'Great,' I said brightly. I loaded the brush again, looked at Celine, and began to delineate the left side of her face. I'd been working for three or four minutes when we heard the doorbell ring.

Celine stood up. 'I'd better get that.'

'Surely your housekeeper—'

'She's at the top of the house – I don't want to derange her.'

'Celine—' I protested, but she was already halfway across the room. 'You're "deranging" *me*,' I mouthed at her back. I heard her heels click across the hall then the front door was opened. There now followed a long and animated conversation, in English, about . . . I strained to listen – the church?

119

When Celine at last returned she blew out her lips in a dumb show of exasperation. 'I'm sorry about that, but the Jehovah's Witnesses are *very* persistent.'

I felt my jaw go slack. 'You were talking to the Jehovah's Witnesses?'

'I was.'

'For ten minutes?'

'Yes. I wanted to make it *quite* clear that they were wasting their time. I told them that they *mustn't* come here again. I don't think they *will*,' she added with voluptuous satisfaction. 'So . . .' She sat down. 'Shall we carry on?' I didn't reply. 'I'd like to continue the sitting,' Celine added with an air of dignified patience, as though I had kept *her* waiting.

I lowered my brush. 'I *can't*.'

Celine stared at me. 'Why not?'

'Because "sitting" is the one thing you won't *do*. You keep *getting up*, Celine; you keep taking phone calls and making phone calls, and sending texts and going to the front door – this happened last time, too. So I'm not going to continue until two things have happened – firstly that you've turned off your phone . . .'

Celine's eyes widened. 'I *have* to have it on. It could be important.'

'The sittings are important.'

'The caller could take offence.'

'*I* could take offence. In fact, I *am* taking offence. Second thing, would you please *stay* in that chair. You're only allowed to leave it if the house is on fire.'

Celine looked at me as though I'd slapped her. '*Don't* tell me what I can and can't do in my own home!'

I began to count to ten in my head. 'Celine, if you

don't give me your attention, then I'm not going to be able to paint you.' She shrugged as though she couldn't care less. 'And I *want* to paint you – not least because your husband's already paid me quite a lot of money to do so.'

'I didn't *ask* him to!' Celine's face had flushed. 'I didn't *want* to be painted. I *don't* want to be!'

'Well . . .' She'd trumped me. 'That's pretty obvious. But . . . could you tell me why *not*?'

Celine sighed. 'Oh . . . I don't know . . . I just . . . feel . . .'

I put down my brush. 'Are you worried that the portrait won't flatter you?' She didn't answer. 'You're very attractive, Celine, and that's how you're going to look, because I'll simply be painting what I see – a beautiful woman.'

'Of forty.' She looked stricken. 'I'm going to be *forty*.' For a moment I thought she was going to cry.

'Forty's not *old*.' Was *this* what it was all about? Some neurosis about her age? 'You don't even *look* forty. You look younger than I do.'

Celine peered at me. 'How old *are* you?'

'Thirty-five.'

'And are you married?'

'No.'

'You have kids?' I shook my head. Celine looked at me sadly. 'So you've never married or had children?'

I tried not to bridle at her air of sympathy. 'I haven't – but I'm perfectly happy – there are many ways to live.' Celine nodded slowly, her expression mournful almost. 'But look, Celine, can we please talk about you. It would help if I knew *why* you don't want to be painted.'

She exhaled. 'I don't . . . *know*. It's hard to explain . . . I just . . . can't . . . I don't . . .' She gave a defeated shrug. Whatever the reason, she wasn't going to say.

'Being painted *isn't* easy,' I offered. 'For the painter, the sitting's an absorbing, intense experience, but for the sitter it can be frustrating because they basically have to sit there staring at the same piece of wall. Is that why you seem so . . . *restless*?'

She blinked slowly. 'Yes. I find it a strain,' she said. 'Just sitting here . . . that's the reason. Exactly.'

'Well, you'll find it a lot easier if we chat. But we can only do that if you ignore the front door, and if you turn off your phone.'

She took her mobile out of her bag. 'I *won't* turn it off . . .' She began pressing the buttons again and my heart sank. 'But I *will* put it on "answer" and "silent".' I closed my eyes in relief. 'And I promise *not* to get up – unless I see flames.'

'*Thank* you.'

Celine placed the phone in her lap then resumed the pose. Desperate to establish some kind of rapport, I began chatting to her. I asked her which part of France she came from, and she told me that the family home was in Fontainebleu near Paris. Then I asked her what her husband did.

'He's Chairman of Sunrise Insurance. That's how we met. I wanted to work in London for a year or two – I'd studied English at university – so I got a job in the department that Victor was then running. We married when I was twenty-three; I had Philippe not long afterwards . . . and . . .' She shrugged. 'Here I still am.'

'You said Philippe's at boarding school. Does he enjoy it?'

'He loves it,' she said flatly. 'He was very keen to go, so he left his day school and went to Stowe to do his A levels.'

'So he's what – sixteen?'

'Yes – and already *very* independent. He hardly comes home.' Celine looked at me balefully. 'Life passes *so* fast. Yesterday I was pushing him down to Barnes pond in his buggy to feed the ducks. Today he's a teenager with an iPod and a laptop; tomorrow he'll have a job and a flat; the day after that he'll have his own children and then . . . But you've never been married.'

I suppressed an irritated sigh. 'That's right.'

'But you have someone.'

'No.' I squeezed a little manganese violet on to the palette. 'My last relationship ended more than a year ago.'

'Who was he?'

'A sculptor called David. He was quite a bit older than me.'

'By how much?'

'Eleven years.'

Celine looked at me intently. 'So *you* ended it?'

'Yes – though not because of that – it was because . . .'

'Because *what*?' It was as though my answer somehow mattered to her.

I didn't want to discuss my private life, nor did I wish to alienate Celine now that she was being cooperative. 'I'd been with him for two years,' I explained. 'We got on well, but it just felt too, I don't know – comfortable – too . . .'

'*Safe*?'

I looked at Celine. 'Yes. He was very nice – but I wanted to feel . . . *more*; I may never find that, but at least I have hope.'

Celine nodded thoughtfully. 'But there's someone you like now.'

I began to outline her bottom lip. 'No. There isn't.'

'There *is*,' she insisted. 'There's someone you're very attracted to – I can see it in your face.' I felt my skin prickle. 'I can sense it – I'm very intuitive.'

'I'm sure you are.' I wiped the brush. 'But you're mistaken.'

The rest of the sitting passed uneventfully. Celine's mobile buzzed a couple of times, but she just glanced at the screen. The doorbell rang again, but she let her housekeeper answer. She seemed to have resigned herself to the portrait at last.

At five past one we finished. Celine stood up and came to see what I'd done.

'As I say, these are just the basic shapes,' I explained. 'But as I say, from next time I'll start to define your features. So . . .' I clipped the portrait into the canvas carrier. 'Same time next week?'

'That'll be fine – and do you need a taxi now?'

'I've booked one for one-fifteen.'

It arrived on the dot. I put my easel and the spare canvases in the boot, and placed the portrait on the seat beside me. Then we set off. As we drove over Hammersmith Bridge, the river glinted like sheet metal in the sunlight.

There's someone you like.

Celine was wrong. I wondered what colours I'd use to paint Nate's eyes . . .

I can see it in your face.
Cerulean blue with raw sienna . . .
I can sense it.
With a touch of yellow cadmium light.

The journey seemed to pass quickly – I looked at my e-mails as we sped along. There was one from Mum asking me whether, as I'd painted Cecilia Bartoli, I might approach her to sing at Chloë's wedding. I texted a one-word reply. *No!!!* There was an e-mail from Clare, the radio journalist, with the date and time that her documentary was to be broadcast. As I scribbled it into my diary I became aware that the cab hadn't moved for a while.

'*What* the eff?' the driver said. I looked up. He was gripping the wheel, staring ahead. 'Look at this!' We were close to Fulham Broadway, where the traffic on our side of the road was at a standstill.

'Is there a football match on?' I asked him.

'No. There's a dead bus – up there, look: it's blocking both lanes.'

We crawled towards the lights and, amid a cacophony of blaring horns, watched them go red, then green, then red again.

I got my purse out of my bag. 'I'll walk home from here. It's not far.'

The driver turned his head. 'Will you manage with all your stuff?'

'Yes, thanks.' I passed him the fare. 'It's not that heavy, just a bit awkward.'

'Well, mind yourself as you get out.'

I quickly retrieved my easel and the canvases from the boot. Then I walked the two hundred yards or so to the pedestrian crossing. The yellow sign was still there, and there were more bouquets, one of them still with its price tag. As I pressed the button on the 'wait' box I looked at the photo of Grace. It was the first time I'd seen it close up. Her face was alight with a kind of surprised happiness, as though she'd just been told some wonderful news. And now, beneath the photo, I saw a laminated note:

Dedicated to the Life of Grace Clarke

Beautiful, sparkling, funny, warm, happy, loyal, brave, strong, cyclist, determined, thoughtful, cool, snappy dresser, teacher, fizzing, unique, kind, reliable, Nutella, big heart, sensitive, friendly, Lake District, bright, energy, gardener, sympathetic, Three Peaks, Gracie, patient, children, green, Tic-Tacs, adventurer, open, mint tea, inspiring, sunny, caring, hugs, joyous, salsa, surfer, snowboarder, colleague, cousin, niece, aunt, sister, daughter, grand-daughter, Miss Clarke, best friend in the world, our darling, loved by all.

At the periphery of my vision I had been aware of the green man appearing, then disappearing, then appearing again with his jaunty emerald stride. Now I looked up, and saw that the red man was showing but it didn't matter because the cars weren't moving. So I crossed the road, lost in thought.

I walked home, unlocked the front door, went to my desk, opened my address book, found the number I wanted and dialled. It rang three times then picked up.

'Royal Society of Portrait Painters – Alison speaking.'

'Alison, it's Ella Graham here.'

'Hi, Ella. What can I do for you?'

'Well . . . you remember the commission that you phoned me about before Easter? The one for the portrait of the cyclist . . . Grace?'

'Of course I remember. I did tell the family that you didn't feel it was something you could do.'

'I *did* feel like that. But could you please tell them that I've changed my mind?'

FIVE

On Saturday morning I decided to give the studio a quick clean before Nate arrived. At half past nine the phone rang. I instantly knew that it must be him, phoning to cancel.

I picked up the handset. 'Hello?'

'Ella?'

'Oh, *hi*, Pol. I'm so glad it's you.' I clamped the phone to my shoulder and began vigorously wiping the table.

'You sound out of breath. What are you doing?'

'I'm getting ready for Nate's second coming.'

'His what?'

'His second *sitting*, I mean. Nate's coming for his second sitting, so I'm just . . . tidying up.'

'I see . . . and what did you decide about the refreshments – biscotti or Florentines?'

'Hobnobs, actually.' I walloped the sofa cushions to get out the dust. 'I wonder if he likes them?'

'Ella, he's American – he probably doesn't know what a Hobnob *is*.'

'That's true.' I put *John Singer Sargent: Late Portraits* back on the bookshelf. 'In that case I might be better off with chocolate digestives – or I've got some Penguins. Perhaps I should have made cupcakes.' I glanced at the clock. 'I *could* make some now – there's just time.'

There was an odd silence. 'Ella?' said Polly.

I chucked an empty paint tube into the bin. 'Yes?'

'Ella . . .?'

I scooped some old sketches off the floor. 'What?'

'Erm . . . you don't . . .?'

'*What?*' I repeated.

'Nothing.' I heard Polly exhale. 'It's okay.'

'Then in that case I'm going to go – I'm busy, Pol.'

'*Wait!* I phoned you for a reason. Do you remember Ginny Parks from primary school?'

'I do.' I began tidying my work table, putting the brushes into the pots. 'In fact I was thinking about her just the other day. She was very annoying, with short brown hair, and pink glasses.'

'Well, she's very attractive now with long, blonde hair and contact lenses.'

'So . . . is that why you've phoned? To tell me that Ginny Parks's looks have improved since we were six?'

'No. I'm phoning because yesterday she befriended me on Facebook and I've just read her profile: it says that she's a solicitor . . .'

'Jolly good . . .' I suddenly noticed that the windows were dirty. I went to the sink and rinsed a sponge.

'. . . for a City law firm.'

'Marvellous . . .'

'Specialising in commercial litigation . . .'

'*Super.*' I began to clean the glass.

129

'And that she's "in a relationship" with Hamish Watt.'

My hand stopped in mid-wipe. 'That jerk who interviewed me?'

'That's the one.'

'So *that's* how he knew what he did.' Through the window I could see a plane tracking across the blue vault, leaving a bright, snowy contrail. 'Ginny was always asking me about my father. I used to hate it. And now . . . this is strange, Polly, but I've just realised that in a funny roundabout sort of way . . . she's *reunited* me with him.' I felt goose bumps rise up on my arms.

'Reunited?' Polly echoed. 'So does that mean that you've decided to—'

'No, no – it *doesn't*.' I heard a frustrated sigh. 'Sorry, Polly, but can we please *close* the subject? There's nothing more to say. My father, after three decades of neglect, has decided to get in touch. *I've* decided not to respond. The *End*.'

There was silence for a moment. 'Sorry, Ella . . . I didn't mean to be interfering.'

'It's okay, Pol. I know you mean well – but now I'm going to draw a line under it. But thanks for telling me about Ginny.' I glanced at the clock again. 'I've only got an hour until Nate gets here, so I'm going to say *ciao*.'

'"Ciao"?' I heard her say as I hung up.

I finished tidying up, got the coffee things ready, then showered and dressed, did my hair, put on a little make-up and, with a few minutes to spare, went online to look at the news. Then, just out of curiosity, I Googled 'John Sharp, Architect, Western Australia'. Nothing came up, except a link to the Australian Architect's Association, which I clicked on, but his name wasn't there. Then, in an online architectural magazine I found a reference to a John Sharp who, in 1986, had designed a primary school in Busselton. I guessed that it was him, but as I could find no other references to anything he'd built, I presumed that he hadn't practised in Australia for very long. And I was about to do a further search to find out what he *had* gone on to do when I remembered that I wasn't interested and stopped.

Instead I went to my Facebook page. In the last week I'd acquired two more fans, one of them a boy that I'd taught at Heatherly's. He'd left a friendly message on the Wall, so I replied in kind, and all this set me thinking about Heatherley's, then about Guy Lennox, who'd also studied there, nearly a century ago; I thought about how Lennox had fallen for someone that he'd painted. I imagined him standing at his easel, gazing at Edith, falling more and more hopelessly in love with each stroke of his brush.

Drnnnnggggggg.

I started at the sound of the bell, then quickly checked my appearance in the wall mirror and ran downstairs.

I opened the door and there was Nate, smiling at me self-consciously, as though he was still amused by the idea that we had declared a truce. 'Hi, Ella.'

'Hi,' I said happily.

As Nate came in, he kissed me on the cheek – a gesture of peace, I assumed. He smelt deliciously of vetiver and lime.

'So . . . how did you get here?'

'I walked – it's only ten minutes. We're almost neighbours,' he added as he took off his jacket.

'Let me take that. Oh, good – you remembered to wear the green jumper.'

131

'Does that get me a gold star?'

'It does. It's a pain when my sitters forget to put on what they're being painted in.'

Nate followed me upstairs. 'So . . . how's your week been?'

'Oh . . . not bad.' I pulled the bedroom door to. 'Though it's felt a bit long for some reason. Anyway . . .' We were in the light and space of the studio. 'Here we are again.' I tied on my apron then nodded at the chair. 'Get posing!'

Nate laughed then sat down. 'I'll try.'

I pulled my hair through a yellow scrunchie then picked up my palette. As Nate lifted his head and gazed at me, I felt a sudden voltage: I told myself that this was just an artistic frisson because I was excited about the portrait.

I stood behind the easel. 'Here's looking at you then.'

I began to study Nate's face, the landscape of which was already so familiar that I could have painted him from memory. I looked at his nose, then his eyes – his lashes were very dark and his right lid was a little more exposed than his left; I studied his forehead and wondered how he'd got that small round scar. His hair was cut close to his head and grew down in front of his ears in a shape that tapered to a point, like the outline of India.

Nate was smiling. 'I don't think I've ever been looked at quite so closely by *anyone* – not even my mom.'

I held up a pencil and squinted at him as I measured the distance between his lower lip and his chin. 'Well, . . . that's my job. Basically, I stare at people for a living.'

'That must feel pretty weird.'

'It does.' I put the pencil down and picked up a brush.

'It makes me feel a bit predatory – like a stalker almost – especially when my sitters tell me that I've "captured" them.' I began to mix the wash.

'Well . . . I hope you'll capture me.'

Nate had said it matter-of-factly, but I felt my face flush. 'I'll try to,' I faltered. 'I mean . . . I just want my sitters to be happy.'

'And are they?'

'Usually. If they're not, they're too nice to say.'

'Do you ever stay in touch with them?'

'Yes – a few have become friends.'

'So you've painted them into your life.'

I smiled at the idea, then reflected that Nate was already in my life. He's going to be my brother-in-law, I reminded myself. He's marrying Chloë. My sister is going to be his *wife*. 'So . . . how's the wedding shaping up?' I asked brightly.

'Well . . . the answer is *fast*.' Nate drew the breath through his teeth. 'Your mom's efficiency is awesome, if not . . . downright terrifying.'

I dipped my brush in the turps, aware that he hadn't exactly paid my mother a compliment. 'Well, to be fair to her, three and a half months isn't long.'

Nate blinked. 'Not long at all.'

'But then a short engagement's romantic,' I pointed out. 'And it's nice that you're getting married on Chloë's birthday.'

'That was your mom's idea too.'

'Really?' I smiled to myself at her manipulation.

Nate nodded. 'Chloë and I had only gotten engaged a few hours before. We'd vaguely mentioned October, but then your mom suddenly said why didn't we get married on Chloë's birthday as it fell on a Saturday: Chloë looked so thrilled I felt I couldn't say no – not that I *wanted* to say no,' he added hastily. 'I was just . . . taken aback.'

'It'll make it easier to remember your wedding anniversary.'

'That's true. And, as your mom pointed out, it's the Fourth of July weekend, so that will make it easier for people coming from the States as the Monday's a holiday, so . . .' He held up his hands in a gesture of surrender. 'July third's . . . *great*.'

'And will your sisters be there?' I imagined them, in a gang, outside the church, with fistfuls of rice.

Nate nodded. 'There's no *way* they'd miss it: they'll all be standing there, telling me what to do.'

'It's going to be a big wedding then.'

'It looks like it. The guest list seems to be . . . *huge*, but . . .' He shook his head.

'But what?'

'The idea of making such private vows in front of so many people . . .'

'Oh . . . you'll be fine: all you have to do is stand there and say "I do".

Then I decided that I didn't want to talk about the wedding any more, so I steered the conversation to Florence and New York – we talked about the Uffizi gallery and the Frick; I asked Nate about his childhood, and he told me some more about growing up in Brooklyn with his sisters, about how he'd got the scar on his brow, and about the dog that he'd had when he was a boy. Then we discussed films and plays we'd both seen, books we'd read, and suddenly Nate was getting to his feet.

134

'Do you need to stretch your legs?' I asked him.

'No . . .'

'Let's have a break anyway.' I put down my brush. 'It must be at least an hour since we started.'

Puzzlement furrowed Nate's brow, then he nodded at the clock on the wall behind me. 'Ella. It's been two and a half.'

'It can't be.' I looked. It was. 'I had *no* idea . . .'

'Well, we were talking a lot – like last time.'

'Even so . . .' I turned back to him. '*How* can it be five to one?'

Nate smiled. 'Maybe we hit a time warp, or got sucked down a wormhole?'

'That's the only credible explanation.' I put my palette on the worktable. My hand ached from holding it for so long. 'Why didn't you *say* something? You must have been desperate for a break.'

'No – I was . . . happy.'

'But you haven't even had a cup of coffee – let alone a Hobnob.'

'A what?'

'They're biscuits. Fancy one now?'

Nate shook his head. 'Thanks, but I'm meeting Chloë for lunch.'

I felt a piercing sensation, as though someone had plunged a skewer into my chest. I smiled. 'Please give her my love. Tell her I'll call her soon. So . . .' I untied my apron and hung it up. 'Is next Saturday okay?'

'That'll be fine.'

Nate came over to look at the canvas. He was standing so close to me that I could almost feel the warmth of his body. 'It's still in the early stages,' I said as we looked at the broad lines and massed areas of flat colour. 'But I've got down the basic structure of your face, and from next week you'll see yourself begin to . . .'

'Emerge?'

'Yes. Each time you'll recognise a little more of yourself until we get, well . . . the whole picture of you. Or as I see you.'

'I wonder what you'll make of me.'

I shrugged. 'I don't know – I'm still working you out. But you're a good sitter.'

'That's because I'm enjoying it.'

I glanced at him. 'That's . . . great.'

He shifted his weight then turned back to the unfinished painting. 'It's funny to think that I was dreading these sessions. Now, well . . . I'm looking forward to them.'

I felt a bewildering burst of euphoria. 'Me too.'

We went downstairs and I unhooked Nate's jacket, then opened the door. I turned to him. 'So I'll see you next week then. Ten-thirty again?'

He nodded. 'I'll be here.'

I waited for him to leave, but for some reason he was still standing there, just looking at me intently. My heart did a swallow dive.

'Ella?' Nate murmured after a few moments.

'Hm?' Suddenly his eyes didn't look as green as they had done. They looked quite dark.

'Ella?' he repeated gently.

'Yes?'

'Could I have my coat?'

'*Oh.*' I was still holding it – hugging it almost. 'Sorry . . .' I laughed. 'Here you go.'

Nate slipped the jacket on then leaned forward and

136

kissed me on the cheek. '*Ciao*, Ella.' He walked out of the house, then turned, smiling. 'See you.'

'See you,' I echoed.

I closed the door then leaned against it, listening to his fading footsteps.

There's someone you like . . .

'Yes,' I murmured.

You're very attracted to him.

'I am.'

I can see it in your face.

'But he's engaged to my sister.'

My euphoria gave way to dismay.

I wasn't falling for Nate, I reasoned as I lay in bed the following morning. It was just a crush – a silly, no, in the circumstances, *insane* – infatuation. If I simply ignored it, it would soon pass. Once, when my mother was having yet another go at Chloë about Max, she'd told her that she *shouldn't* have fallen in love with him. Chloë had retorted that she hadn't chosen to fall in love with him. 'You *could* have chosen not to!' Mum had flung back.

I decided that Mum had been right. I would now make the deliberate and rational choice *not* to fall in love with my sister's husband-to-be. For the remaining sittings Nate and I would have a pleasant but purely professional relationship, after which we'd default to the friendly rapport expected of us as in-laws.

'Good.' I swung my legs out of bed. 'Got that sorted.'

I quickly showered and dressed. As I picked up my mobile I saw that another message had come in overnight from my father. With a sinking heart, I opened it.

Dear Ella, I hope you received my message of a fortnight ago.

'I did.'

I realise that you may not wish to respond.

'I don't.'

But this is to let you know the dates that I'm going to be in London in case you do decide that you'd like to meet up. I'll be there for four days from 23 May.

I felt my pulse quicken.

It would mean so much to me if I could see you.

A wave of anger ran through me. 'It would have meant so much to *me* if I could have seen *you* anytime in the last thirty years!'

*In the meantime here's my mobile phone number –
and a photo.
Sincerely,
Your father*

'My *ex*-father,' I muttered. At least he hadn't signed off as 'Daddy' or 'Dad'.

I read the message six or seven times. Then, with a shaking hand, I opened the attachment.

I felt a sudden 'thud' in my ribcage as I saw myself,

aged about four, standing hand in hand on a beach somewhere with a man I knew instantly was my father. I was wearing a blue-and-white striped dress and was squinting into the late afternoon sun, my short brown hair whipped by the breeze. My father, barefoot, in knee-length shorts and a casual shirt, was dark-haired and powerfully built with broad shoulders – a big, handsome man. In the hand that wasn't holding mine, he held a red spade while, behind us, on a yellow towel were a picnic basket and a white sunhat. I had no idea where we were, but knew that the photo had been taken by my mother because in the foreground I could see her shadow stretching towards us across the pale sand.

I realised with a shock that this was the only photograph of my father that I'd ever seen. I consoled myself with the thought that he'd loved me enough to keep it; but sending it to me now was just an act of manipulation. I scrolled down to 'options'. *Delete message?*

I hesitated: then on his left hand I spotted his wedding ring gleaming in the sunshine. I exhaled, closed my eyes, then touched *Yes* . . .

I thought I'd feel relieved; instead I felt upset – so much so that I then tried to retrieve the photo but couldn't. With a rising sense of panic I ran up to the studio and yanked open the bottom drawer of my desk. From the back of it I pulled out a large white envelope, the edges of which were yellowed with age. I lifted the flap and slid out the drawing of my father – the one that I'd never been able to throw away. It was very much like him, I now saw. I must have been pleased with it because I'd signed it. And I was just trying to work out how old I would have been when I'd sketched it – nine

139

or ten – when I heard a car pulling up. I looked out of the window and saw Mike parking his BMW. I quickly put the drawing back in its envelope, returned it to my desk then ran down and opened the door.

'Hi, Mike.' I was glad to have the distraction of the sitting.

'Morning, Ella.' He locked his car then came in.

'Would you like a cup of coffee?'

'No. Thanks. I'm fine.'

As he took off his jacket I grimaced. 'You forgot to wear the blue jumper.'

He groaned. 'Sorry – but I've got *so* much on my mind.'

'Of course, but the next sitting will be the last one, so I'll text you the day before to remind you about it, okay?'

'Sure . . .'

We went up to the studio and I got Mike's canvas out of the rack and put it on the easel. As I mixed the colours we chatted about the election, the date of which had at last been announced. 'That must be a relief.'

'It is,' he answered wearily. He sat in the chair. 'But it's going to be tough.'

I squeezed a little Prussian blue on to the palette. 'But you have a big majority, haven't you?'

'I do, but I can't take anything for granted.'

Now Mike talked about the opinion polls and about how hard he found the door-to-door canvassing, having to persuade and cajole. 'I feel like a Jehovah's Witness,' he said ruefully. 'Only less welcome.'

'I don't know.' I thought of Celine. 'Some people are quite pleased to have the Jehovah's Witnesses turn up.'

'Maybe . . . and who else are you painting at the moment?'

'A beautiful French woman – but it's been a battle as she doesn't *want* to be painted.' I imagined Celine and I locked in combat over the canvas.

Mike looked puzzled. 'Why doesn't she?'

'She says she finds sitting frustrating, which in some ways it *is*, but . . .' I shrugged, not wanting to add that I believed that there was more to it than that. 'Then I'm painting a very elegant Englishwoman who's in her eighties.' I thought about how much I was looking forward to seeing Iris again, but it wouldn't be for at least another week as Sophia had phoned me to say that her mother had a bad cold. 'I'm also painting my sister's fiancé.' I felt my face flush. 'And I'm still working on the portrait of my mum.' I nodded at her canvas, leaning against the wall. 'It's almost finished now.'

Mike turned to it. 'She's beautiful.' He cocked his head to one side. 'Her expression's interesting.'

'What do you see?' I asked, out of curiosity.

'She looks . . . guarded.'

'She does look a bit guarded, that's true.' I dipped the brush in the turps.

'I mean secretive,' he mused. 'As though she's hiding something.'

'Oh. . . .' I looked at the painting again. 'Well . . . I don't see that.' Now I regretted having asked Mike for his opinion – what did *he* know? 'I don't do proper sittings with her,' I explained. 'She usually pops in for half an hour after she's been teaching at the English National Ballet School. She's going to be there tomorrow, so we'll do a bit more.'

141

'So you're busy,' Mike remarked.

'Yes, pleasantly so.' I studied the tip of his nose, then added a highlight to its painted counterpart. 'And I've just been commissioned to do a posthumous portrait.'

'Really? They must be . . . strange.'

I picked up a smaller brush. 'I'm about to find out. I've never done one before – I've always avoided them because they're rather sad and probably quite tricky, technically. In fact, when I was first approached I said no.'

'What made you change your mind?'

'Because I read a tribute to the person who'd died – her friends had each contributed one word that they felt encapsulated this girl. It . . . touched me and for some reason I don't seem able to stop thinking about her.'

I felt the tension in the room tighten. 'So who . . . was she?'

As I told Mike he closed his eyes for a moment, as though he'd just been given bad news.

'There's been quite a bit about her death in the press,' I said. 'You must have seen it.'

The chair creaked as Mike turned away. 'Yes . . .'

'It's so hard for her family, not least because they still don't know how it happened – or why she was cycling through Fulham Broadway at that time of day, given that she didn't live or work anywhere near there.'

Now I thought of my meeting with Grace's uncle. A quiet man in his late fifties, he'd come to the studio the day before and had talked to me about Grace for a couple of hours. He told me that she'd lived in Chiswick and had taught at a primary school in Bedford Park. He'd brought with him four photo albums – two that had been hers and two that belonged to her parents.

I'd looked at pictures of Grace on the swings aged three, smiling gappily at five, riding her new bike at six, on a brown pony at eight, starting secondary school at eleven, atop Mount Snowdon at fourteen, arm in arm with friends in her graduation robes, and on a sunny day last September on the steps of her school, surrounded by the children she'd taught.

'It was a hit-and-run,' I said to Mike.

The corners of his mouth clenched. 'They don't know that. The driver might have had no idea what had happened.'

'Surely he would have realised what he'd done.'

'Why do you say "he"?' Mike snapped.

'Well . . .' Mike's tone had taken me aback.

'How do you *know* it was a "he"?'

'I . . . *don't*.' I conceded. My heart was thudding.

'Whoever it was . . .' Mike's sudden anger had vanished and now he just looked distressed, '. . . they might very well *not* have known.' He was blinking rapidly, as though trying to work something out. 'Especially as it happened in the dark.'

I exhaled. 'That's true. The wing mirror might have just clipped her, and helmets don't always offer enough protection in a bad fall.' Mike nodded, dismally. 'But they're trying to enhance the CCTV: apparently the images were very grainy and they don't have the registration number, but there are things that they can do . . . to . . . anyway.' I dipped the brush in the white spirit. 'That's my latest commission – Grace.'

A mournful look came into Mike's eyes as silence fell.

I had no idea what to make of Mike's intensity. He was clearly already on edge, but he also seemed . . . defensive.

As I continued painting him, a shiver ran through me. Perhaps he *did* know what had happened to Grace. After all, he often drove through Fulham Broadway, and he had a black BMW. I'd thought about that, but had dismissed it as coincidence; but perhaps it had been *his* car that had struck her, and he'd had no idea at the time, only realising afterwards from the media coverage . . .

That would explain his turmoil. He'd be horrified at what he'd done, and he'd be dreading what the enhanced CCTV tape might reveal. He'd be in terror, too, at the thought of the newspaper headlines, given that he was an MP – and on a transport committee – a protector of cyclists. He'd be vilified for failing to stop. He might face criminal charges. This would destroy his career; if not his life . . .

As my mind raced through this scenario I remembered that Mike had abruptly cancelled his sittings at the end of January, a couple of days after Grace had died. The e-mail he'd sent me saying that he'd 'suddenly got very busy' had been so incoherent that when I'd read it I'd thought that he must have been drunk. Now he was a shadow of the big, happy, self-confident man whom I'd started to paint less than four months ago. And he'd cried at a sad song on the radio. He was clearly under huge emotional strain. Perhaps that was why he'd seen what he had in my mother's face – because of what he himself was desperately trying to conceal.

He exhaled, painfully. 'So . . . have you started the painting?'

'Erm, no, not yet.' I felt awkward now, discussing the commission with Mike, but he seemed to want to know about it. 'First I need to get some feeling for who Grace was. I have photos of her.' Mike flinched. 'But I want the portrait to be more than just a likeness: I want it to capture Grace's spirit. But as I never met her, that isn't going to be easy.'

'No,' Mike agreed quietly. 'It's going to be hard.'

'I can only stay for half an hour,' Mum announced when she arrived that afternoon. 'I've *so* much to do. It's unending,' she added, with a curious blend of satisfaction and annoyance. She slipped off her coat and handed it to me. 'The invitations have gone off to be printed,' she said as I hung it up. 'I've decided to enclose RSVP cards; people can be shockingly casual, even about weddings. Will you help me write them?' she added as we went upstairs.

'Sure. I'll come over with my calligraphy pen.' I pushed on the studio door. 'So how many people are you inviting?'

'Two hundred and ten.'

'Good God!'

'Well, there are people who've invited us to *their* children's weddings, and of course Nate has a very large family.' I imagined his sisters, lined up like Russian dolls. 'Chloë has a lot of friends,' Mum went on, 'plus she wants to invite some of her colleagues, so it's not hard to get up to that kind of figure.' She went over to the wall mirror and checked her appearance. 'Luckily, we *can* accommodate that number as the garden's so big.' She opened her bag and took out her gold compact. 'But it's nice to make a bit of a statement.'

'Is it?' I asked as she reapplied her lipstick.

'Yes.' She snapped the compact shut. 'It is.' She put

145

it back in her bag then glanced around the studio. 'It's looking nice up here, Ella – less of a jumble.'

'I've tidied up.' I unhooked my apron and put it on. 'Oh, well done,' I added as Mum took off her cardigan. 'You remembered to wear the silk shirt.'

'I'm amazed that I did as I've *so* much to think about.' She shook her head as if to stop it spinning, then she sat down, lifted her chin, and laid her left hand on her chest.

My mother was still every inch the prima ballerina. She didn't just 'sit' in a chair – she folded herself into it, ensuring that there was a graceful 'line' to her body, that her limbs were positioned harmoniously and that her head was at an elegant angle to her neck.

'I'm *very* upset with the organist,' she confided.

I adjusted the blind. 'Why's that?'

'He's trying to insist that we have Purcell's "Trumpet Tune", but I've heard it at *so* many weddings.'

I returned to the easel. 'It's joyful though.'

Mum inclined her head. 'That's true. And Chloë's wedding is going to be *very* joyful.'

I felt the skewer turn in my heart. 'It is.' For everyone except me, I reflected, then felt ashamed at the thought.

'But I'm putting my foot down about the Widor Toccata.'

I picked up my palette. 'That *is* over-used. Could you look this way?'

Mum turned her pale-blue gaze on me. 'But I've found a *wonderful* soprano. She's in the chorus at Covent Garden and her *voice* . . .' Mum closed her eyes in an attitude of ecstasy, then slowly opened them. 'We'll all be in floods. In fact, I *may* staple a tissue into each Order of Service.'

'Good idea. I'm sure *I'll* need one,' I added balefully. I dipped my brush in the light skin tone that I'd prepared. 'So what's this diva going to sing?'

'"Ave Maria" after the first reading – the Bach-Gounod, not the Schubert – then "Panis Angelicus" during the signing of the register: I *adore* both.'

'Does Chloë?'

Mum shrugged. 'She seems to be happy with *all* my ideas. She's being surprisingly easy-going about everything.'

'That's lucky.'

'It *is* – especially as I have so little time; I couldn't cope with any arguments, and you know how stubborn she can be.' Mum tucked a stray wisp of hair behind her ear. 'But she still hasn't chosen her dress. I thought *you* were helping her on that front, darling.'

'I *am*,' I said, trying not to bridle at the suggestion that I'd been dragging my heels. 'I'm going to a vintage wedding-dress shop with her next week. She's going to try on a few that we've seen on their website.'

Mum was making 'tutting' noises. 'I *wish* she'd have something contemporary – I really don't want to see her in yellowed lace.'

'You won't, Mum.' I began to work on her left hand. 'These gowns are beautifully restored – and they're expensive: you'd better warn Roy that the one she most likes the look of costs two thousand pounds.'

Mum's eyes were round. 'She could get an Amanda Wakeley for that.'

'Something old – that's what she wants.'

'Well, *I* shall be wearing something *new*.'

Now Mum told me about the outfit she'd ordered from

Caroline Charles, the Philip Treacy 'fascinator' that would adorn her head, the menus that she was keen on but had yet to confirm with Chloë and Nate, the ice sculpture that she was considering and whether I thought a peacock might be preferable to a swan. She talked about the hardwood flooring she'd ordered for the wedding tent and about the work Roy was doing in the garden to get it looking 'tip-top'. Then she discussed the flowers.

'The church will already have flowers from the eleven o'clock service,' she said as I painted a cream highlight on to the gold of her wedding ring. As I did this I wondered what Mum had done with her first wedding ring. Perhaps she'd flushed it away, or flung it into the sea. More likely, she'd kept it in a box inside another box inside a bag at the back of a drawer.

'That's good,' I said. 'Then you won't have to buy any.'

'It *isn't* good at all,' Mum protested. 'They might be hideous, and I *don't* want to find that we're stuck with carnations and chrysanthemums. So I've asked the florist to strip them all out, and we'll have tuberoses, pink peonies and green viburnam for the larger arrangements, with posies of sweet peas at the end of each pew. I *love* sweet peas . . .' Mum shivered with happiness, like a small child anticipating Christmas.

I found her excitement touching. It was as though it was *she* who was . . .

I dipped my brush in the zinc yellow. 'Can I ask you something, Mum?'

'Yes.'

'I've never asked you this before – or probably not since I was very young, but . . . what with Chloë getting married, I've been wondering . . .'

'Wondering what?' she asked serenely.

'Did *you* have a big wedding? The first time, I mean.' I suddenly imagined my mother standing at the altar with the entire *corps de ballet* fanned out behind her.

'No,' she said. 'I didn't.'

'So . . . it was just . . . a small one, was it? But in church, presumably.'

Mum blinked. 'No.'

'Didn't you want to get married in church?'

'*I* did,' she replied. 'But, well . . . your father didn't *believe*. But you know, it was such a *long* time ago and I really don't want to . . .'

I raised my hands in surrender. 'Okay.'

So Mum had got married in a register office both times. That would go a long way to explaining why she wanted to make such a 'statement' with Chloë's wedding – she was turning it into the big, glamorous meringue-and-marquee number that she'd never had.

I dipped the brush in the pot of turps. 'There's one other thing I wanted to ask you.'

Mum suppressed an annoyed sigh. 'What's that?'

'Did we go to the seaside somewhere – when I was about four?'

She inclined her head, like a bird suddenly aware of a predator. 'Why do you ask?'

'Because . . . I recently had a memory of being on a beach somewhere. In a blue-and-white striped dress.'

I held my breath as Mum considered the question. For a moment I thought she wasn't going to answer. 'We had a holiday in Wales,' she replied slowly. 'The summer before you were five. We went to Anglesey

149

for three days. You *did* have a blue-and-white striped dress – I'm amazed that you remember it.'

'So . . . that holiday must have been with my father. Is that right?' I added.

'Yes,' she answered reluctantly. '*Now,* I'd just like to—'

'Three days for a holiday isn't long,' I interrupted, before she could change the subject.

'Well . . .' I heard Mum swallow. 'We didn't *have* long holidays.'

'Oh. Why not?'

'Be*cause* . . . we couldn't.' She brushed a bit of fluff off her skirt. 'I was dancing principal roles, and so taking a fortnight, or even a week off, simply wasn't *possible.*'

'I see . . .'

'So we just took a few short breaks – where we could.' I nodded, blankly. 'Are you all *right*, Ella? You seem rather . . . intense.'

I stared at her.

My father's sent me two e-mails and a photo. He'll be in London in a few weeks' time. He wants to see me, but I know that that would cause big problems for you, so I've been ignoring him, but it's making me feel confused and unhappy – plus I've fallen for Nate, which is also making me feel confused and unhappy – so, all in all, I'm feeling, yes, rather intense.

'I'm fine,' I said.

Mum smiled. '*Good.* Now I've got to find a jazz band – there's one that plays down by the river on Thursday evenings, so Roy and I are going to go and hear them this week. I've also been wondering about having an entertainer – a caricaturist might be amusing. What do you think, darling?'

150

'That would be fun.'

'I wish *you'd* find someone.'

'I don't know any caricaturists.'

'I mean a *man*.' Mum sighed, extravagantly. 'I've always thought it a shame you didn't settle down with David.'

I picked up the tube of cadmium green. 'I didn't want to.' I unscrewed the cap.

'Why not?'

I squeezed a little on to the palette. 'Because he was very nice, but it was terribly . . . cosy. I felt too young to be in the comfort zone for the rest of my life.'

Mum shifted on her chair. 'The comfort zone is preferable to many other, more hazardous zones, Ella. I hope you won't come to regret that decision.'

'I know I won't – because a few weeks ago I bumped into David at the Chelsea Arts Club; he was with someone new, and I didn't mind. But if you've *loved* someone it must be hard to see them with anyone else.'

'Very hard . . .' Mum agreed quietly.

I knew that she must be thinking of my father, because she'd seen *him* with someone else – the woman for whom he would eventually leave her. She'd once told me that she'd 'come across them', which suggested that this encounter had happened outside. Would *I* have been with her? I wondered. Suddenly I felt sure that I *was*, because I had a vision of my father's startled face, and I saw that white skirt with its bold red flowers . . .

'Isn't there *some* nice man that you like?' Mum was asking me now.

'Er . . . no. There's no one . . .'

My mother touched her cheek, then put her hand back on her chest. 'Now what about *Nate?*'

151

It was as though I'd plunged down a manhole. 'What do you mean?'

'I mean, what about Nate's portrait? Sorry, darling, I've changed the subject – my mind's all over the place. How's his painting going? Do tell me.'

I exhaled with relief, as though I'd committed a crime and had narrowly escaped detection. 'It's going . . . fine.' My heart rate slowed. 'We've had two sittings.' So only four more, I reflected with a pang. How odd to think that I'd hoped to keep them to a minimum: now I wished I could have dozens more.

'So when will it be ready?'

'I'll aim to finish it by mid-June so that it has time to dry. Then Chloë will collect it the day before the wedding. I hope she'll like it.'

'I'm sure she'll love it. I know you'll bring out Nate's intelligence and charm – and his *kindness:* he's a compassionate sort of man.' Mum shook her head in bewilderment. 'I still can't understand *how* you could have disliked him, Ella.'

The conversation was making me so tense that I accidentally smudged the line of Mum's hand. 'I just . . . did.'

'But you like him now?'

I know you're going to love *him!*

'I do.' So Chloë *had* been right.

'And you're coming to the engagement party, aren't you? It's next Saturday.'

I began to correct my mistake. 'Chloë told me about it, but I'm not sure . . .'

'Well, you'll have to let them know, because it's a sit-down dinner just for close friends and family – they're

152

not having a big party because the wedding's so soon: Nate's having it at his flat.'

'I see . . .' I wished I didn't have to go. It would be painful seeing him with Chloë. I wondered how I could get out of it . . .

Mum lifted her chin. 'By the way, I presume you chat to Nate during the sittings.'

'Ye-es.'

'Well, please don't let on, should the subject arise, that Chloë's last boyfriend was married.'

'I wouldn't dream of it. I don't discuss Chloë with Nate.'

'Good. Because I've told her that it's better if he doesn't know.'

'Why?' I looked at her. 'It's got zero to do with him.'

'Yes, but men can be . . . *funny* about things: it doesn't do to tell them everything.' I wondered what sort of things Mum hadn't told Roy. 'After all, they haven't known each other that long,' she went on. 'So I've advised her to say nothing about it until they've been married at least a year – or better still, not to tell him at all.'

I picked a stray bristle off the canvas. 'You know, Mum, I think it's for Chloë to decide what she does and doesn't tell her own fiancé.'

'Well, I don't think that her association with Max is something that she should shout about.'

I shrugged. 'Nate would have to be a prig to care one way or another, and I don't think he is.'

'Anyway, that's how *I* feel and Chloë agrees.' The chair creaked as Mum shifted her position. 'But thank *God* she met Nate. I still can't bear to think how unhappy she was before – thanks to Max's awful treatment of her.'

I squeeze a little Naples yellow on to the palette. 'Max

153

wasn't "awful" to Chloë, Mum. She said he treated her well. She was only unhappy because she couldn't *be* with him.'

Mum laughed. 'Of course she couldn't – the man was married!' Mum was always so censorious about adultery, I reflected. But then she knew only too well the damage it does. 'In any case, he *didn't* treat her well – he stayed with his wife.'

'Oh . . .' I was about to challenge my mother's somewhat skewed analysis of the situation, but she was hurrying on.

'*Why* he stayed with her, I really don't know. It's not as though they had children, so I assume it was because she earned a lot with those books of hers.'

'I've *no* idea. Maybe he loved her – maybe he loved them *both*. Maybe he was just . . . *confused*.'

'Confused?' Mum gave me a glacial stare. 'Allowing men to be "confused" gives them an excuse to just . . . string other women along, offering them *nothing*.'

'Then those "other women" should keep away.' A muscle at the corner of Mum's mouth twitched – she'd always loathed the idea that her daughter had been an 'other woman'. I pulled the brush through a rag. 'But Chloë really fell for Max.'

Mum sniffed. 'Goodness knows *why*. He's not attractive – and he can't earn much, working for a charity.'

'He doesn't just work for a charity, Mum – he runs Well-Spring, the international clean-water charity, and he isn't *un*attractive – just a bit unkempt.'

'All right – what he does is worthwhile,' Mum conceded. 'But that doesn't alter the fact that he should have left Chloë alone.'

'She should have left *him* alone – I was appalled when she told me that she'd become involved with him. But she believed him when he told her that his marriage was unhappy.'

Mum smiled unctuously. '*So* much so that we now see him proudly posing with his wife in *Hello!*'

Mum had a point there. 'So you saw that.'

'I did – and it made me feel sick. But it also made me realise that I was *right* to give Chloë the guidance that I gave her.' Mum's lips had become a thin line. 'Because once she started talking about having his baby, then I knew that things *couldn't* continue. Do you remember that, Ella?'

'Yes.' I reached for the paint rag again. '*Not* a great idea.'

'So I decided that it was time that Max's wife knew what was going on. I mean – there she was, writing detective fiction while failing to detect that her own husband had been having a year-long affair!'

I looked at Mum, aghast. 'You weren't really going to tell Max's wife – were you?'

'I *was* . . .' She exhaled through her nose. 'But Roy dissuaded me.'

I lowered my palette. 'Thank God! Chloë was a grown woman. You have to let her make her own mistakes; it would have been *dreadful* to have talked to Sylvia.'

'I *know*,' Mum said tetchily. 'But I was sorely tempted, because I could see that Chloë was on the verge of wrecking her *life*. I told her that time was marching on, and that it was quite clear that Max was never going to leave Sylvia. Chloë had convinced herself that if she got pregnant he would. So it was up to me to tell her that she was deluded and that it would be . . .'

155

'Wrong?' I suggested.

The flanges of Mum's nostrils flared. 'Too big a risk. I was determined to *protect* her,' she added quietly. 'Just as I'd have protected you; not that *you* would have been stupid enough to fall for a man who wasn't available.'

'Hm . . .'

'So I told Chloë, yet again, just what the realities of life *are* for a mistress.' Mum's voice, normally so soft and low, had begun to rise. 'I told her that she'd be forever waiting for him to call, and that she wouldn't be able to do anything with him openly and honestly. I said that her relationship with Max was *low*. She insisted that they were in love. I told her that, in that case, Max had to prove that he loved her – by committing to her, which he *wasn't*. Chloë finally recognised the bitter truth of that and ended it – at *last*.' Mum inhaled through her nose as though calming herself after some trauma.

'Mum,' I said gently. 'Why are you getting so worked up? It's all in the past now.'

She blinked, as if waking from some dark dream. 'Yes,' she murmured. 'It *is*.' She gave a little laugh. 'Why am I even *talking* about it? Chloë's *not* with Max, she's with Nate; they're getting married and we're all just thrilled.' She gave a little shudder of happiness. 'Aren't we, Ella?'

'Yes. Yes, of course we are . . .'

SIX

'Thanks for coming with me,' Chloë said the following Thursday at 6.30. We were standing outside the Vintage Wedding-Dress Store in Covent Garden's Neal Street. She pressed the old-fashioned brass bell. 'It's good that they do evening appointments – I don't feel I can take *any* time off during the day.'

'So your nose is to the grindstone?'

'It is – as are my cheeks, mouth and chin. I'm surprised I've still got a *face,*' she added with a laugh. Then the door was buzzed open and she pushed on it.

'But you're enjoying the work?' I asked her.

'Yes – and it's great to have the responsibility. Oh. Hi.' Chloë was smiling at the proprietor, who was walking towards us. 'Are you Annie?'

'I am – you must be Chloë.' Annie, was about my age, slim, with short, dark hair. She was wearing a nineteen fifties circle skirt, with a pattern of strawberries, with a yellow cashmere jumper and white pumps.

'This is my sister, Ella,' Chloë explained. 'She's going to give me a second opinion on everything.'

'Great.' Annie smiled. 'Come on in.'

We followed her to the back of the shop. The walls were painted a restful pale green and were hung with framed sketches of wedding gowns by Balenciaga, Norman Hartnell and Dior. On the display stands were antique veils, vintage headdresses and exquisitely embroidered satin slippers. Beneath our feet the cream velvet carpet was voluptuously thick – a comforting surface for stressed-out brides.

The changing room was very big, with two carved mahogany chairs with blue velvet seats like thrones. Hanging from the antique brass pegs were several wedding gowns, just visible inside their muslin bags, like cabbage whites about to emerge from their chrysalises.

'I've brought out the ones we discussed on the phone,' Annie told us. 'So that's "Gina" here.' She began to unzip the bag. 'I've also put out "Greta", the slipper silk gown from the 1930s, and the sixties one that you liked – "Jackie".' She nodded at it. 'It's by Lanvin – hence the price. There are also three others I thought you might try, including one designed by Marc Bohan before he went to work for Dior. Do you wear much vintage?' she asked Chloë.

'Quite a bit,' Chloë answered. 'But I'd always thought that if I ever got married I'd wear a vintage dress, in order to have something . . . original.'

'Well, these are unique,' Annie said.

'Where do you get them?' Chloë asked.

'I buy them at auction,' Annie replied. 'I get quite a few in New York – like this one.' She gently pulled the

'Gina' out of its bag. 'It's by Will Steinman, which was a big name in America in the forties and fifties. And, of course, people bring dresses in to show me. I also have a friend who owns a vintage dress shop in Blackheath – Village Vintage.'

'I've heard of it,' said Chloë.

'This friend – in fact, I used to work for her – doesn't sell wedding gowns herself, so if she comes across a particularly lovely one she kindly sends it my way.' Annie put her hand in her pocket and produced a pair of white cotton gloves of the sort Polly often wears. 'So . . .' She pulled them on. 'Let's make a start.'

'Should *I* wear gloves?' Chloë asked.

'No – but could I ask if you're wearing much make-up?'

'Almost none,' Chloë replied, 'but I'll be very careful.' She turned to me. 'Will you come in with me, Ella?'

'Sure.'

I sat in one of the chairs and Annie drew the calico curtain across, then left us. Chloë quickly got undressed. It was a long time since I'd seen her in just her bra and pants.

'You've lost weight again, Chloë.' She'd put it back on over the past year, but now you could see the jut of her hips.

She glanced anxiously at her reflection. 'It must be the stress of the job – and of getting married, of course, and, well . . . everything really.' She put her clothes on the other chair.

'I wish I could give you some of my pounds.' I smiled ruefully.

'You're not fat, Ella – just strong.'

'I know – it's hard to believe that Mum ever gave birth to me!' I had the sturdiness and broad shoulders of my father, I'd realised since seeing that photograph. I saw myself standing beside him on that beach in Anglesey, my hand in his. I wondered if he'd known then, as he'd smiled for my mother's camera, that he'd soon be leaving us. He probably did. Another good reason for not keeping the photo, I decided.

'I'm ready, Annie,' Chloë called.

Annie parted the curtain and came in. She took the 'Gina' dress off its hanger, and held it up, the silk swishing softly. Chloë stepped into it, gingerly, as though getting into hot water.

Annie lifted the dress on to Chloë's shoulders, did up a few of the loop fastenings then gently pulled it in at the back so that Chloë could see the fitted effect in the mirror.

Chloë appraised her reflection. 'It's gorgeous,' she murmured. 'But I'm too thin for it.' Her hand went to her chest. 'I don't have enough up here – and a dress like this needs to be . . . filled.' She glanced at me. 'It would suit *you*, Ella.'

'I'm not the one getting married,' I said – a bit too sharply, I realised, as I saw Chloë blink at my tone. 'You . . . could always stuff it with those chicken-fillet things.'

She shook her head. 'That would make me feel fake; and your wedding day is surely one day in your life when you want to feel that you're being true to yourself.'

'I agree,' said Annie. 'You *are* a bit slender for it.' She undid the fastenings. 'Let's try the "Greta".'

Chloë put the 'Greta' on. It looked much better than

the 'Gina' had done, and the drape and gleam of the satin was lovely. Chloë didn't mind the low back, but the dress had clearly been made for someone tall, because even when she put on a pair of heels, the fabric pooled at her feet.

Now she tried on another fifties dress, 'Grace'. It didn't suit her, but it made me think of Grace Clarke, whose portrait I had now begun. The photos that her uncle had lent me were good, but it was still going to be hard to create the illusion of three dimensions out of these two-dimensional images. I decided to ask her uncle if there was any recent video footage of Grace that I might see.

Now Chloë was putting on the 'Jackie', which was made of thick shantung silk which gave it a structured, architectural look. It was a beautiful dress, but, as we had suspected, it was far too big.

Next she tried on another sixties dress with a pleated skirt, then the Marc Bohan gown, which was a simple ivory tunic with a silvery lace overlay, like a cobweb; she then put on an eighties duchesse silk dress with lace-trimmed, elbow-length sleeves. As Chloë looked at herself she grimaced.

Annie agreed. 'It's not really you. It's very like Sarah Ferguson's wedding dress. That was way back in 1986, so I don't suppose you remember it.'

'I don't,' Chloë replied as she took the dress off.

'You did see the wedding,' I told her. 'You'd just turned five. I remember it very well.' I'd never forgotten it, because of what my mother had told me that day.

'Are you sure you won't try on the "Giselle"?' Annie asked as she hung the dress up.

'I'm quite sure,' Chloë replied. 'I wouldn't want my dress to have *any* negative associations, and Giselle has a hard time of it on the wedding front.'

Annie zipped up the bag. 'Why? What happens to her?'

'She's an innocent girl,' Chloë began, 'who falls in love with this handsome huntsman, Loys, who's been madly flirting with her. When Giselle finds out that Loys is really Duke Albrecht, and that he's engaged to Princess Bathilde, she goes insane with grief and grabs Albrecht's sword and stabs herself—'

'No,' I interrupted. 'She collapses because of her already frail health, *before* she can stab herself.'

'Okay,' Chloë conceded. 'Anyway, heartbroken, she dies and then becomes a Wili – a ghost of a jilted bride – which is the only time she gets to wear a wedding dress, poor girl.' I thought of Mum, in that poster, in her long tutu and veil. 'Do you ever get to know the history of these dresses?' Chloë asked Annie.

'Sometimes,' she replied. 'In fact, I know the story behind *this* one . . .' Out of the last bag she took a nineteen fifties gown with a ruffled silk tulle skirt and a heart-shaped satin bodice. The small bustle was topped with dainty blue flowers.

Chloë's face lit up. 'It's *lovely*.'

Annie took the dress off its hanger. 'I bought it from my next-door neighbour. When I told her that I was setting up my own vintage wedding-dress shop, she offered it to me. She'd kept it beautifully, but the red roses on the bustle had faded, so I replaced them with these forget-me-nots.'

'Something blue,' said Chloë happily as Annie held it

162

out to her. She stepped into it and Annie pulled up the zip. Chloë looked at herself in the mirror and her eyes widened with pleasure. 'It's . . . beautiful.'

As I looked at Chloë's reflection I imagined Nate waiting at the altar, then turning and seeing her walking towards him in this glorious gown. I saw his face light up with delighted pride.

'Are you okay, Ella?' I heard Chloë ask. 'You look a bit sad.'

'Oh, I'm . . . just tired. But it's a *lovely* dress.'

'It is,' Annie murmured. 'And it's a terrific fit.'

Chloë turned to Annie. 'So what's the story behind it?'

'The story *is* . . . that it was never worn.'

'Really?' said Chloë. 'Why not?' she added anxiously.

'My neighbour, Pam, told me that she'd got engaged in 1958 to a boy called Jack whom she adored. She was twenty-three and still living at home, in a village near Sevenoaks. She saw the dress in Dickins & Jones – it cost forty guineas, which was a lot back then, but her parents wanted her to have her dream wedding so they bought it. Pam told me that she couldn't wait for Jack to see her walk up the aisle in it. But a week before her big day Jack came to the house and told her that he couldn't go through with it.'

Chloë looked stricken, then she examined her reflection again, as if suddenly seeing the dress in a different light.

'Pam's parents tried to persuade Jack to change his mind, but he said he was sorry – he didn't want to get married. He said he had too many doubts. Her parents then realised that they had no choice but to cancel everything and let the guests know. So there was no wedding – and their relationship was over, because Pam told him that she never wanted to see him again. Everything was ruined. She was distraught.'

'*Poor* girl.' Chloë's face was a mask of sympathy. 'But . . . I don't think I'd *want* the dress now, knowing this.' I wondered what on earth had induced Annie to tell such a negative story. Didn't she *want* to sell it?

She held up her hand. 'Wait, there's more. Three years later . . .'

'She met someone else?' Chloë anticipated. 'I hope she *did*.'

'Pam had moved to London by then, partly to get away from the memory of what had happened; and she was walking to work down Regent Street one morning when she looked up, and in the crowd she spotted Jack, coming towards her. Her heart started to pound. She told me that she'd decided to walk straight past him, as though she'd never known him.' That's what Mum would have done, I thought. 'But some inner voice told her *not* to do that; so instead she called his name, and he stopped, clearly shocked. So there they both were, in the middle of the pavement with all these people weaving around them; and Pam asked him how he was, and he said fine, and he asked her how she was, and she said fine. And she was about to smile goodbye and walk on, when he asked her if she'd have time to have a cup of coffee with him. Pam hesitated, but then agreed. Then he rang her at work the next day and asked her if she'd have dinner with him one evening, and to cut a long story short . . .'

'They got back together,' Chloë murmured.

Annie nodded. 'They were married a few weeks later, in a register office, with just two friends as witnesses.

Pam wore a suit, but she'd kept her wedding dress because she'd been unable to part with it. So . . . that's why it was never worn. She didn't get her dream wedding, but she did have her happy ending – in fact, she said that she was happier with Jack because she believed she'd lost him.'

'Was it hard for her to forgive him?' Chloë asked.

'She said it *wasn't,* because she still loved him – she'd never stopped.'

'But why didn't he get in touch with her in the interim?'

'He'd desperately wanted to, but didn't feel that he could – remember, she'd told him that she never wanted to see him again. But they were married for forty-five years and had two sons. So it *was* a happy story . . .'

'In the end,' said Chloë quietly. As she gazed at her reflection, she frowned slightly, as though she was struggling with something.

'Nate wouldn't do that to you,' I said. 'If that's what you're thinking.'

'I can put the dress on hold,' said Annie. 'If you're not sure.'

Chloë looked at herself, steadily, then the doubt in her face vanished. 'No, I *am* sure. I'm going to buy it right now.'

I'd hoped that helping Chloë choose the dress in which she was to marry Nate might have a calming effect on my feelings. It didn't. Over the next few weeks they only intensified. In addition I became prey to a kind of schizophrenia in which I looked forward to seeing Nate but at the same time dreaded it. I had to gaze at him professionally, when I longed to do so personally. I had to stroke his face on to the canvas as if it were just a technical exercise when it had already become a labour of love. I'd think of Guy Lennox, and imagine his frustration at having to look at Edith from behind his easel when he'd probably wanted nothing more than just to stride up to her and take her face in his hands.

In between sittings my mind would default to Nate, like a screensaver. I'd open my eyes in the morning and there he'd be, just as he was when I closed them at night. I would wake with a feeling of euphoria, then, as reality returned I'd feel sad and confused. I didn't even know whether it was Nate's own face I saw or the image of it that I was painting – they seemed to morph into one. I'd work on his portrait as a way of feeling close to him. I was in a state of exhilarated despair.

So as I waited for Nate to arrive for his fourth sitting, I decided to be reserved with him, in order to re-establish a distance between us. But although my mind was happy with this strategy, my body rebelled. With five minutes before he arrived, my pulse began to race. It was as though all my nerve endings were attached to twitching wires. The ring of the bell induced an adrenalin charge that was like an electric shock. As I opened the door to him my heart was pounding so hard that I thought he'd see it beating. He smiled, and a sudden heat suffused my face.

I'd never felt a physical longing like this for any man. As Nate followed me up the stairs, past my bedroom, the door of which was ajar, allowing a glimpse of bed, I imagined taking his hand and pulling him inside and putting my hand on the back of his head and drawing his mouth to mine and unbuttoning his shirt and—

What was I *thinking?* The man was marrying my *sister!* I felt a wave of guilt and shame.

As we went into the studio, I wished that Chloë had *never* asked me to paint him. Then I could have gone on believing that Nate was a duplicitous creep rather than the decent and desirable man I now knew him to be.

I remembered my resolve to be remote. So I asked him how the project he was working on in Finland was going and what he thought of the coalition. I told him that I was looking forward to the engagement party that night, which was a lie because I was dreading it and had been obsessing about how I could get out of it. I'd say I had a migraine: Chloë knew that I got them sometimes . . .

'Ella . . .' Nate was looking puzzled. 'Are you okay?'

'Sure. Why shouldn't I be?'

'No reason – you seem a bit . . . subdued.'

'Oh.'

'Are you sure you're all right?'

'No . . . I mean, yes. I *am* – though I might be getting a migraine.'

'Do you need an aspirin? Or a glass of water?'

'No, I'm *fine* . . . really . . . thanks . . .' I dipped the brush in the flesh tone. 'I'm . . . perfectly . . . okay, I'm . . .'

To *hell* with being reserved, I thought. Why shouldn't I chat to Nate, and just enjoy being with him? I'd done nothing wrong, and I wasn't *going* to do anything wrong. Was I?

So we started talking about Nate's schooldays, and about mine, about his dog, Chopsy, and about the opera singer, Raymond, who'd lived in the apartment below

167

them and who used to get them free tickets for the Met. Then Nate talked about his first girlfriend, Suzanne, whom he'd dated at Yale.

'Suze and I were together for two years – I was crazy about her.' I felt a stab of jealousy. 'After we graduated, I wanted us to get an apartment together in New York, but she'd just gotten a news traineeship with NBC and said she didn't want a full-on relationship. She said she needed to feel free as she'd be spending a lot of time on assignment, with periods abroad, and so . . .' Nate drew his finger across his throat.

'She ended it?'

He nodded. 'Broke my heart.'

Another shard pierced me. 'And . . . after Suze?'

He shrugged. 'I had a few relationships, none of them special. I tended to date women who I knew I could never feel serious about.'

'Why? Out of fear of committing yourself to anyone?'

He thought about it for a moment. 'No. It was because I still hoped that it would work out with Suze. Whenever she was back in New York we'd see each other; we'd often e-mail and phone; we both kept fanning the embers when we should have doused them. We'd often joke that we'd get it together one day. But then a couple of years ago Suze phoned me to tell me that she was getting married to this guy she'd met three months before, and that she was very happy – and so . . .' He gave a philosophical shrug. '*Finita la comedia*. Honey had been badgering me to come and work with her in London, so it seemed a good time to accept.'

'I see. So it wasn't so much because your mum and sisters were hassling you to settle down?'

'Well, they *were*. They'd been telling me for ages to forget Suze and just try and find someone I could *live* with, without expecting a great love or anything. And I'd just come round to their way of thinking when I met Chloë.'

'At the Harbour Club?'

'Yes.' Nate grinned. 'She annoyed the hell out of me to start with, because she kept rushing on to my court to retrieve her balls, but then I realised what was going on and I thought it was quite funny; then we got chatting in the bar—' He gave a bemused shrug. 'Which is how we come to be where we are today. But Chloë's really . . . sweet.'

'Oh, she *is*. She's lovely – and there's got to be some material in that for your wedding speech. You can joke about her putting the ball in your court, or wanting to play doubles.' Or making all the running, I thought wryly. Chloë wasn't exactly shy when she set her sights on a man. She'd met Max right in front of his wife.

'She'd obviously had a bad time with her last boyfriend,' I heard Nate say. 'Not that she talks about it, but it's there, in your portrait of her. You can see it.'

'He . . . just wouldn't commit to her,' I said truthfully. 'The usual story,' I added casually. 'But she's so happy to have met you.'

'She does seem happy, yes.' There was a silence. 'Anyway . . . now you know all about my past.'

'I'm disappointed that it isn't more lurid.'

'Sorry.' He shrugged. 'But c'mon, Ella – it's your turn now – what about your past?'

'Oh. Do I have to?'

'Sure you do. You can't just get all this information out of me, without revealing anything about yourself.'

'Fair enough. Okay . . .' I cleared my throat. 'Let's see . . .' I talked about Patrick, who I'd dated at the Slade and about the two or three brief relationships I'd had in my twenties, and then I told Nate about David.

'Two years is a long time,' Nate remarked. 'So what was wrong with the guy?'

'Nothing. He was nice – and very talented. But . . . I don't know. We liked each other, but we weren't in love . . .'

'I see.'

'I tend to date men that I'm not really in love with.'

'Why? To make it easier when it ends?'

'Maybe.' I knew the real reason, though I didn't want to discuss it with Nate. And suddenly I didn't want to talk about relationships any more because I didn't want to hear him tell me how adorable he found Chloë or how happy he was with her, so I steered the conversation back to the safer topic of his family, then, as I re-drew the line of his left shoulder – I'd got the angle all wrong – Nate told me how much he liked Roy.

'Roy's a lovely man,' I agreed proudly. 'He'll be a *great* father-in-law,' I added, to remind myself again of Nate's impending marriage.

Nate was looking at me quizzically. 'So you've always called him "Roy"?'

'Yes; because I was five and a half when I met him; so I could never bring myself to call him "Dad" if that's what you mean.' Nate nodded. 'Plus I knew that my own dad was out there somewhere . . . not that I had any idea where.' I suddenly wanted Nate to know my story. 'Maybe Chloë's mentioned it.'

'She said very little – only that you haven't seen your father since you were five.'

'That's right. He'd run off to Australia with his girl-friend – not that I knew that until I was eleven.'

'So, where did you think he was – before that?'

I shrugged. 'I had no idea. My mother would say only that he'd left us and that it was best not to think about him. But I was convinced that he was somewhere nearby. I kept imagining that I'd see him drive up in his big blue car, like he used to do when we lived in our flat.'

I had a memory of how my mother used to stand by the sitting-room window, looking down the street. Then I'd hear her call out, 'Daddy's here!' and I'd run to her and we'd see him pulling up . . .

I heard the chair creak as Nate shifted. 'You must have missed him so much.'

'I did – and of course I *did* think about him – all the time. Whenever I saw a car like his, I'd look to see if he was driving it. I'd search for his face in crowds and in the windows of passing buses and trains. I remember once, when I was ten, following this man around the supermarket because he looked like my father. But if I ever asked my mother where he was, she'd give me the same answer – that he'd gone, and wasn't coming back. I remember panicking, thinking that he must be dead. Mum assured me that he was alive, but that as we couldn't see him any more it was best to put him out of our minds. Every time I asked her *why* we couldn't see him, she'd make me feel that it was too painful for her to discuss – so I learned not to ask.'

Nate shifted on the chair. 'Did *she* know where he was?'

'Yes . . .'

'Then why didn't she just . . . *tell* you?'

I rubbed a drip of paint off the corner of the canvas. 'She said that it had been to protect me from unnecessary hurt: she said it would have felt like another rejection to know that he'd gone so far away – and she was right, because when she *did* eventually tell me, I was very shocked and upset, because then I understood not only that he *wasn't* coming back, but that he'd never intended to.'

'So . . . who was his girlfriend?'

'I don't know – I only know that she was Australian and that her name was Frances. In fact, I didn't even know that until I was in my teens; my mother had only ever referred to her as "the other woman". But Frances must have had an amazing hold over my father for him not just to give up his wife and child for her, but to let her take him so far away from them.'

'Did Roy know that he was in Australia?'

I shook my head. 'Mum had concealed it from him too, because she was worried that, if he knew, then he'd tell me. She'd drawn a veil over her first marriage because of the awful way it ended. She'd been aware that there was this other woman: she once told me that she'd found a hotel bill in his jacket pocket, and another time a love letter that Frances had written him. But when my mother actually saw them together it was a terrible shock: she said it was "traumatic" . . .'

'Even though she'd known about the affair?'

'Yes. It would have made it horribly *real*. Then, not

long after that, Mum had her fall. She said that she was so upset and distracted that she missed her footing, so she seemed to blame my father for that too. In her darker moments she'd say that he hadn't just betrayed her, he'd "destroyed" her.'

'Poor woman . . .'

'But she was very lucky, because a few months later she met Roy, who fell in love with her, and she saw that with him she had the chance for a new start. That's why she wanted Roy to adopt me – in order to erase my father. So when I was eight I became Ella Graham.'

'That must have felt . . . weird.'

'It . . . altered my whole sense of who I *was*; it took me years to get used to it.' Now, as I squeezed some zinc white on to the palette, I wondered how the adoption had worked. Did the natural father have to agree to it – especially where he'd been married to the child's mother? And was there any formal hand-over of paternal responsibility? I decided to ask Roy about this some time.

I began to outline Nate's right arm. 'But Roy's been the most wonderful father to me. Though it wasn't easy to start with . . . I remember my mother telling me that she was having a baby with him – I was very upset. She then dropped several more bombshells because she said that she and Roy would be getting married and that we'd be moving to London where we'd all live together in a place called Richmond. She said that Roy would work in a hospital nearby and that I'd go to a nice new school, even though I liked the school I was already at.'

'So much change in your life,' Nate murmured sympathetically.

I nodded. 'I told my mum I didn't *want* her to marry Roy and I didn't want there to be a new baby.' I dipped the brush in the cobalt blue. 'I said that we *couldn't* leave our flat in case Dad came back and didn't know where we were. On the day of the move I had to be prised out of it, screaming, and would only agree to go once I'd been allowed to leave a note for him to say where we'd gone – not that it would have been particularly legible, as my writing couldn't have been up to much at that age . . .'

'Poor little kid,' Nate said.

'So I hated Roy because I saw him as the cause of all this change. I used to clamp myself to my mother to keep him away from her; if he spoke to me I wouldn't reply; I used to hide his shoes in the garden. I hated seeing his pictures and his books and told my mother that she should burn them on a big fire. But Roy was always wonderful to me. He told me that he understood why I felt cross: he said that *he'd* feel cross if he were me. But he added that perhaps I wouldn't feel so cross once I met the baby.'

Now, as I mixed the colour for Nate's hair, I remembered being in the garden of the house we'd first lived in, in Richmond. Roy sat next to me on the bench and told me that the baby would be coming soon – in the next day or two. I started to cry. And he told me that there was no need to be upset because the point was that someone was coming into the world who was going to love me. He said that that was all I needed to know . . .

I looked up from the painting. 'And Roy was right. Because when I saw Chloë for the first time my anger just . . . vanished. Roy would put her in my arms and I'd just gaze at her, and talk to her for hours, telling her all the things that I was going to show her when she was older. I almost fought with my mother to push the pram. In the mornings they'd find me asleep on the floor by her cot. And from then on I didn't mind Roy being in my life, because I understood that without him I wouldn't have had Chloë. But of course I still hoped . . .' My brush stopped. 'I'd never stopped hoping . . .' I could hear the tick of the clock.

'To see your father again?' Nate asked quietly.

I nodded. 'But this was very hard to imagine, because I was already forgetting what he looked like.'

'Didn't you have any photos of him?'

'No. My mother said that she'd lost them. So I drew and painted him, obsessively, to try and remind myself.' I thought of the faded drawing of him in my desk. 'And I believed that if I did a really *good* picture of him – so that it was the *very* picture of him – then that would somehow make him come back.'

'Which is why you became a portrait painter,' said Nate softly.

I nodded. 'It probably is. Because I was searching for this one *face;* hoping to see him again. I kept *on* hoping . . . even after I knew the truth.' I felt my throat constrict. 'I'd tell myself that I didn't want to see him.' The image on the canvas had blurred. 'But of course I did want to, I *did* . . .' My hands sprang to my face.

I heard the chair creak, then footsteps, then I felt Nate's arms around my shoulders. A tear seeped into the corner of my mouth with a salty tang.

I was aware of the softness of Nate's jumper, of the

175

gentle pressure of his arms, and of his breath, warm against my ear.

I closed my eyes for a moment, then pulled away, awkwardly. As I did so I saw that there was a red stain on Nate's chest. 'I've got paint on you,' I croaked. 'From my brush. I'll fix it.' I went to my work table and tipped some white spirit on to a tissue; then I walked back over to Nate and without even thinking about it, slid my left hand under his jumper then gently rubbed at the wool with my right. 'There . . .' I murmured. 'It's gone.'

I knew that if I looked at Nate I would want to kiss him; so I turned away; but he put out his hands, caught my face, and stroked away my tears with his thumbs.

'I'm fine,' I whispered. 'I'm fine now. Thanks . . .' I went to the sink and started cleaning the brush, in order to disguise my turmoil.

'Now I know why you seemed so subdued,' I heard Nate say. 'Your father must have been on your mind.'

'He has been.' I turned off the tap. 'Very much so.' I didn't tell Nate why, or that he himself had also been on my mind.

'Maybe you'll hear from him one day . . .'

I exhaled. 'Maybe . . .'

'What would you do if he *did* ever get in touch? Would you want to talk to him – see him?'

'See him?' I looked at Nate. 'I . . . really don't know.'

So much for being reserved, I thought grimly as I got ready for the party a few hours later. I'd bared my soul to Nate – impulsively telling him things that I'd never even told Polly – and had ended up being held in his

176

arms. Now I was going to have to go and make polite small talk with him at his engagement party.

The invitation was for eight o'clock, but I was so anxious about it that I was running late. I couldn't decide what to wear and changed my outfit three times; then I made up my mind not to go, then I decided that I *would* go but ended up walking because my front tyre was flat, then the bus didn't come and I didn't have enough money for a cab because I'd forgotten to go to the cashpoint. So by the time I turned into Redcliffe Square it was a quarter past nine and I was feeling flustered and unhappy.

Nate's flat was on the south side of the square in a big porticoed house with a huge magnolia in front that was shedding its last waxy white petals. I rang the bell and an aproned caterer opened the door, took my coat then offered me a glass of champagne from the tray on the hall table. I gratefully took one and had two large, nerve-steadying sips. I was bracing myself to enter the room on my left where the party was clearly in full swing, when Chloë came out into the hallway. I felt a stab of envy, then loathed myself for it.

Chloë gave me a radiant smile. 'There you are, Ella!'

'I'm so late,' I mumbled. 'Sorry.'

'Never mind – you're here now: come and join the party.'

'Can I just take a moment? I'm a bit . . . stressed.' I could hardly tell Chloë why. I had another sip of champagne and began to feel its sedative effects. I managed to smile. 'You look lovely.' Chloë was wearing a turquoise silk shift that skimmed her slight frame. She seemed so young, but now it struck me that she was just the age that Mum was when my father left – except that Mum had a five-year-old child. I thought again how unusual it was for an ambitious young dancer to jeopardise her career by having a baby. Perhaps Mum's pregnancy was accidental and that was the real reason why she and my father had had a register office wedding. What she'd said about his lack of religious belief had somehow rung false.

'Thanks,' Chloë said.

As she tucked a strand of hair behind her ear I saw something sparkle and the skewer twisted again. 'Oh, show me your ring!'

She held out her hand. A large marquise diamond winked and flashed. 'Now I *really* feel engaged,' she said, widening her eyes with mock anxiety. 'We chose it a month ago, but it needed to be made smaller so I collected it this morning while you were painting Nate. He's enjoying the sittings,' she added as I followed her into the living room. Anxiously I wondered whether Nate discussed them with her. 'Not that he tells me *what* you two talk about.' I exhaled with relief. 'But he came back reeking of turps – I teased him that he must have been doing some painting himself . . .'

There were perhaps twenty people in the room, which was long and wide with a deep bay window. On the white marble mantelpiece were a number of engagement cards and on the wall above it hung a large, semi-abstract seascape in boiling blues and greens. On the other side of the room was a pale-gold damask sofa on which I instantly imagined Chloë and Nate curled up together.

At the garden end of the room I saw Nate, in jeans and a white shirt, chatting to his guests. Seeing me, he extricated himself and walked towards me. It was like one of the dreams I have of him, in which his face slowly emerges out of a crowd of strangers and I have this sense of happiness and relief. Now though, knowing how powerfully I was drawn to him, I felt only pain and dismay.

'Ella,' he said warmly.

I recalled the gentle pressure of his arms around my shoulders, the feel of his hands on my face.

'Hi, Nate – sorry I'm late. What a great flat!' I turned to Chloë. 'So is this where you'll live after the wedding?'

'That's the idea. Nate rents it, so when the lease is up we'll buy a place of our own. In fact, I like the streets where you are, Ella.'

My heart plunged at the prospect of having Chloë and Nate living nearby – seeing them walking along hand in hand, or unloading their shopping from the car, or pushing a buggy . . .

'That would be great,' I said. 'Though bear in mind it can be tricky living near the football stadium.'

'True,' Chloë agreed. 'How often do Chelsea play at home?'

'Every other Saturday, but also during the week: the roads get *so* congested – and it's dreadfully noisy.' I suddenly wished that she and Nate would go and live in New York – a scenario I'd dreaded when they'd first got engaged.

'Well, we'll see,' she said. 'There's no rush – is there, Nate?'

'No. No . . . rush at all.'

Suddenly Chloë's 'old phone' ringtone drilled through the noise and chatter. She took her mobile out of her

179

pocket and peered at the screen. She frowned. 'I'm sorry . . . I'll just . . .' She went out into the hall, leaving Nate and me to chat.

So we talked about property prices in this part of London and about when interest rates might start to rise. Without the intimacy of the studio we were politely going through the conversational motions. This is how it'll have to be, I reflected, once the portrait's done.

Then one of the caterers came to speak to Nate; as I glanced around, I saw that Chloë had returned and was talking to an old school friend of hers, Jane. So I squeezed past them to talk to Mum and Roy, who were standing near the window. I caught snatches of party babble on the way.

– *Wedding's not long now.*

– *So did he get down on bended knee?*

– *Capri's* a lovely *honeymoon destination.*

– *Actually,* I *asked* him!

Mum was deep in conversation with another friend of Chloë's, Trish, and her husband Don. Seeing me, Mum extended an elegant arm and drew me to her while she continued to wax lyrical about Nate.

'He's *so* attractive,' Trish agreed. 'Obviously very steady . . . yes . . . perfect for Chloë – well, he'd be perfect for *any* woman, really – but not as perfect as *you*,' she added to Don with a laugh. Then Trish began telling my mother about the jazz band she and Don had hired for their wedding, and about the awful problems they'd had seating his divorced parents. As she and Mum began discussing the pros and cons of a formal receiving line, I broke away to talk to Roy.

He smiled at me. 'So how's our Ella-Bella?'

'Fine, thanks.' I took another sip of champagne. 'A bit wedding-weary though.'

Roy sighed. 'I know what you mean . . . but . . .' He fiddled with his bow tie. 'I do hope you're pleased for Chloë, Ella.'

I looked at him, shocked. 'Of course I am. Why do you ask?'

A red stain had spread up Roy's neck. Did he *know*? I wondered. Had he seen it in my face like Celine had done? Did I have *I ♥ Nate!* stamped on my brow?

'Why are you asking?' I repeated nervously.

'Well . . .' Roy shifted his weight. 'To be honest, I thought you might not be entirely happy about her getting married.'

'Why wouldn't I be?' My pulse began to race.

Roy ran a finger round his collar. He knew. He and Mum both knew. 'Because it must be *hard* for you,' he said, 'seeing your mother and me *fussing* over your sister like this, not to mention spending such *vast* amounts on her, so I just hope . . .'

'Oh, I *see* . . .' I emitted a burst of relieved laughter. 'You think I'm *envious* of Chloë – because she's getting married.'

'Well . . . I didn't really think that, but I want you to know that we'll push the boat out *just* as far for you. I've been saving for both you girls for years now.'

I smiled. '*Thank you*, Roy.' He really was the nicest man. I laid my hand on his arm. 'But as I doubt it'll ever be needed for me, I hope you'll spend it on you and Mum.'

He sipped his champagne. 'You don't know what the future holds, Ella. Anyway, it's good to know that you're happy for your sister.'

'Of course I am.' I just wished that she were marrying anyone but Nate.

Now everyone was moving towards the wide wooden staircase that curved down to the basement.

'I think dinner is served,' said Roy. 'Very nice of Nate to do this.'

'It is. But I'd like to wash my hands first – I'll see you down there.'

I went out into the hall and a caterer told me that the bathroom was just at the top of the stairs. I walked up. As I pushed on the door I saw a big, claw-footed Victorian tub on the rim of which were Chloë's shampoo and conditioner and some jewel-coloured glass tea-light holders. I tortured myself with visions of her and Nate having a candle-lit soak. Beside the basin, among Nate's shaving things, were Chloë's Cath Kidston wash-bag, a pink toothbrush and a big tub of Elizabeth Arden body cream.

I *should* have pleaded a migraine, I reflected miserably as I turned on the tap. I lifted my eyes to the mirror then looked away, unable to face myself. 'I'm *not* in love,' I whispered as I splashed water on my burning cheeks. 'It *is* just a . . . crush – a silly, and completely inappropriate, crush.' I felt ashamed to acknowledge it, even to myself; I certainly didn't want anyone *else* to know about it. I resolved to keep my feelings concealed.

As I came out of the bathroom I saw that the door of the room next to it was ajar. Through the gap I could see Nate's green jumper lying on a chair, one arm dangling over the side, as though exhausted. Without thinking, I pushed on the door then stood there looking at the big sleigh bed, masochistically imagining Chloë and Nate spooned together in it, or lying face to face, their limbs plaited like rope.

On the chest of drawers I could see some photos in silver frames. I wanted to look at them – to know *more* about Nate, so, feeling like a trespasser, I went in.

There was a photo of a young couple – Nate's parents, presumably – leaning against a stone wall, with Florence's *Duomo* rising above the buildings behind them. There was a close-up of a young woman on her wedding day – I guessed that it must be Maria, Nate's youngest sister, as he'd told me that she was the sister to whom he's always been close. There was a photo of Nate as a boy of eight or nine, sitting on a sofa, cradling his dog like a baby. In a glass frame was a snap of Chloë and Nate at some black-tie dinner, her arm stretched around the back of his chair. I felt another stab of jealousy. The force of it took me aback.

I went out, pulled the door shut behind me, then ran downstairs.

The kitchen was very large with a big conservatory dining room, the glass of which was strung with little lights that twinkled in the gathering dusk. Everyone was finding their places at the trestle table that hugged the sides of the room.

I found my name – written in Chloë's large, round hand – and was joined by a forty-ish woman with shoulder-length blonde hair and a slash of cyclamen lipstick.

'Hi,' she said, smiling warmly. 'I'm Nate's cousin, Honeysuckle.'

I returned her smile. 'That's a great name.'

'Well my father adored Fats Waller so I'm "Honeysuckle Rose", but everyone calls me Honey or Hon.'

I remembered my misunderstanding about 'Honey' on the night of Chloë's party. I'd been furious at the idea that Nate might be two-timing Chloë: now some dark part of me *wanted* him to two-time her – with *me!*

'This is my husband, Doug.' Honey indicated the sandy-haired man who was standing on my left.

I shook his outstretched hand. 'I'm Ella – Chloë's sister.'

'I've *heard* about you,' Doug said. 'You're painting Nate, aren't you?'

'That's right.'

'Is he behaving himself in the sittings?' Honey asked as we all sat down.

'Of course he is.' I saw Honey register my indignant tone. I felt my face flush. 'I just mean . . . he keeps *very* still and he's . . . nice.'

'Oh, Nate's a darling,' Honey said as Doug poured us all some white wine. 'We grew up together in New York, then my folks moved to London when I was twelve – hence my nearly English accent, but Nate and I always got on well, and now we work together.'

'He's told me a lot about you,' I said. 'Nice things,' I added hastily. Then I remembered that Nate had said that Honey could be inquisitive. I'd have to be on my guard.

She smiled. 'So . . . how long do the sittings take?' I explained. 'And how well did you know him at the start?'

'I didn't know him – I'd met him twice. But then, I don't usually know my sitters before I paint them.'

Honey shook her head. 'How weird – spending so

184

much time closeted with a stranger.' She laughed. 'It must be like being on a blind date!'

I nodded. 'In some ways it is.' Except that in Nate's case there'd been no possibility of the encounter ever developing into anything more. I felt a burst of anger with Chloë: in asking me to paint Nate she had, albeit unwittingly, put before me a feast that I could never touch. I felt like Tantalus, neck-deep in water that he could never drink, grasping at fruit that was always just out of reach.

I stole a glance at Nate, sitting on the other side of the conservatory, next to Chloë. I tried to work out what had happened between us this morning; then I told myself that there was nothing *to* work out. Seeing me become upset, he'd instinctively comforted me. That was *all* there was to it. And yet . . .

Now Nate's friend James came and sat next to me with his wife Kay: I already knew that James worked in London, for Citibank, had been at high school with Nate, and was to be his best man. James and Honey clearly knew each other, so as they struck up a conversation I chatted to Kay, who told me that she was doing a part-time art history degree.

The caterers brought in our starters but I was too stressed to eat. As I picked at my smoked trout, I wondered how soon I'd be able to leave. My dinner companions were very pleasant, but it was an effort to make small talk with them in my present mood: thankfully they seemed interested in portraiture, so at least I didn't have to scrape the mental barrel for things to say.

'Is there anyone you *wouldn't* want to paint?' Kay asked me.

I lowered my fork. 'I find young children difficult, because their expressions are so fleeting. And I *don't* like painting women who've had plastic surgery – it's difficult to deal with because it never looks . . . right. Last year I painted this fifty-something woman who'd clearly had her eyelids lifted; it just looked as though two stun grenades had gone off in her sockets. But I'm currently painting a woman of eighty-three who's had nothing done and is still very beautiful.' I hoped that I'd soon be able to start painting Iris again, not least because I longed to hear what had happened to Guy Lennox – his tragic story had got under my skin.

Now Kay began talking about self-portraits – about Rembrandt's, Francis Bacon's and Lucian Freud's. 'And there's a self-portrait by Dürer that I adore,' she added. 'It's *so* sexy.'

'You mean the Christ-like one?' I said. 'With the long, curling hair?'

'Yes – *that* one – he's *gorgeous*.' She giggled. 'I had a massive crush on him when I was a teenager because of that picture!'

I smiled in recognition. 'Me too. It was as though he was *real* – not a two-dimensional image of himself that he'd painted five centuries before.'

'So will Nate look as "real" as that?' Honey asked. 'With women swooning over him hundreds of years hence?'

I smiled. 'I'd like to think so. But I'm certainly ambitious for his portrait.'

'Ambitious?' Honey echoed. 'In what way?'

'In that a competent portrait just catches a likeness, and a good portrait reveals aspects of the sitter's

186

character. But a *great* portrait will show something about the sitter that they didn't even know themselves. That's what I hope to achieve with Nate's.'

Doug raised his glass to me. 'Then here's to a great portrait of Nate. He'll have to have an official unveiling for it.'

'Terrific idea,' Honey said. 'We'll all come and see it – but I know it'll be gorgeous, because he is.' At that she caught Nate's eye and blew him a kiss.

Nate smiled back at Honey, then, as she turned to say something to Doug, Nate let his gaze rest, just for a few moments, on me. I flashed him a brief smile then looked away, my face aflame. He's just checking that I'm okay, I told myself firmly.

'Don't forget that little scar on his head.' I looked at Honey. 'One of his sisters dropped him when he was a baby,' she added. 'I think it was Valentina.'

'No.' I lowered my glass. 'It was Maria.'

Surprise flickered across Honey's features. 'How do you know?'

'Because Nate told me that Maria dropped him when he was four months old. She was six and had lifted him out of his cot because she wanted to cuddle him. They rushed him to hospital and Maria was so upset that they had to buy her a big doll to make her stop crying. He said that she still can't bear to talk about it.'

Honey nodded, slowly. 'I'd . . . forgotten.'

As our plates were taken away, Honey reminisced about Nate's father, Roberto. 'Uncle Rob knew so many famous pianists,' she said to Kay. 'He worked with Ashkenazy, Horowitz, Martha Argerich and Alfred Brendel; and he was a terrific pianist himself – he used to give recitals in a local church, Saint Thomas Aquinas.'

'It was St Vincent de Paul,' I corrected her without thinking.

Honey looked at me in surprise. 'Was it?'

'Yes. At least . . . that's what Nate told me.'

'Then . . . that must be right. You obviously take in what he says.'

'I . . . always take in what my sitters say; in order to paint them I have to get to know them. Don't I?' I added, then wished that I hadn't.

Nate had stood up and was chinking his glass. I assumed that he was about to make a speech, but he simply asked if some of us would pick up our wine glasses and swap places for dessert and coffee. Doug moved round, as did Kay and a few moments later Mum came over and sat in Kay's chair. As I introduced her to everyone I realised that, like me, she'd had too much to drink.

'So how are the wedding plans going?' James asked her pleasantly.

'*Fine*,' she answered with a smile. 'We're sending the 'vitations out next week. That's going to be quite a job as we've got a *huge* cast list.'

'I . . . think you mean guest list,' Honey suggested.

Mum looked puzzled. 'Isn't that what I said?'

'Will there be any Italian elements?' Honey asked her.

'Yes. The soprano's going to sing some Rossini and I'm thinking of releasing a pair of doves outside the church, to add a bit of *drama*.'

'Not that one wants *too* much drama at a wedding,' Kay cautioned.

Mum heaved a tipsy sigh. 'That's true. It's a pity we're not Catholic, like Nate, otherwise he and Chloë could have had a Nuptial Mass – they're rather beautiful; but we'll *definitely* have those little bags of sugared almonds and I *do* want Chloë and Nate to smash a glass.'

I had another sip of wine. 'What's that about?'

'During the reception, the bride and groom smash a glass,' Honey explained. 'The number of fragments denotes the number of years that they'll be happily married – like in a Jewish wedding.'

'That's right,' said Mum, as Chloë now joined us. 'Hello, darling.' Chloë sat down next to her. 'We're talking about the wedding, and I was *just* saying that I want you and Nate to smash a glass. I've *also* been wondering about confessi.'

'Confessi?' Chloë smiled. 'What have you got to confess, Mum? Come on – out with it!'

'Confe*tti*,' Mum corrected herself with a laugh. 'I'm trying to make up my mind between delphinium petals and hydrangea – *not* an easy decision.'

Honey, clearly bored with the minutiae of the wedding preparations, was reminiscing about Nate. 'He had this dog, Chopsy,' she said to James. 'He was one *ugly* little mutt, but Nate adored him.'

'He wasn't ugly,' I protested. 'He looked very sweet. And he wasn't a mutt – he was a pedigree Border terrier.'

'Really?' said Honey. 'Actually . . . you're *right*. I'd completely forgotten.' She gave a bewildered laugh. 'But how would *you* know what Nate's dog looked like?'

My heart stopped. I could hardly admit that I'd snooped in Nate's bedroom. 'Nate described him to me,' I replied truthfully. 'I have a vivid image of him.'

189

Honey nodded. 'Ah.'

Now as our coffee arrived Nate came and sat in the chair next to Honey's. I hardly dared look at him in case my face betrayed my emotions. I pressed my knees against the underside of the table to stop them trembling. And I thought how weird it was, that in the studio I could stare at him uninhibitedly – brazenly, even – but here I hardly dared throw him a glance.

Honey laid her hand on Nate's arm. I envied her the easy familiarity with which she was able to do this. 'I was just telling everyone about Chopsy,' she told him.

Nate grinned. 'He was a *great* little dog.'

'Why was he called Chopsy?' Chloë asked him. 'Was it because he liked chops?'

'No, it was short for Chopin,' I explained. 'Nate's dad got him from a rescue centre. He'd come in half starved, with cigarette burns on his legs – Chopsy, that is – not Nate's dad. He lived to fourteen, though he might have been as much as sixteen, as they weren't sure how old he was when they first got him.'

'Oh,' said Chloë. 'I didn't know that.'

I was suddenly aware of Honey's gaze, shrewd and knowing. 'Well . . .' I stood up. 'I'd better get back.' I blew Mum a kiss then turned to Nate. 'Thanks, Nate,' I said pleasantly. 'It's been *lovely*.' He pushed back his chair, as if to show me out, but Chloë was already on her feet.

'I'll come up with you, Ella.'

'Okay . . .' I lifted my hand to everyone. 'I'll see you all at the wedding.'

Mum smiled. 'Not long now.'

I followed Chloë up the stairs. 'What a great evening,'

I said as we went into the hall. 'I really enjoyed myself,' I lied.

She handed me my coat and I put it on then picked up my bag. 'Ella . . .?' As I saw Chloë's tortured expression my heart plunged. She knew. How could she *not* know when I'd jabbered on about Nate and his father and his dog like that? So much for concealing my feelings – I'd drunk too much and had displayed them for all to see. 'Ella . . .?' Chloë said again.

'Yes?'

'I'm feeling rather . . . anxious and upset, actually.'

'Why?'

'I . . . think you *know* . . .'

'Know what?' I said innocently. *That I've fallen in love with your fiancé? Yes. I have. I didn't mean to. I'm sorry.* I braced myself for Chloë's censure.

'Well . . .' She pursed her mouth. 'That . . . getting married is . . . *scary.*'

'Oh.' Relief flooded through me. 'It *is* . . . I mean, it must be – but . . .' I fought down my emotions. 'At least you've made a good choice. Nate's . . . very . . . nice.'

Chloë closed her eyes then opened them again. 'I'm *so* glad you said that – he *is.* And he's decent and hardworking – he's intelligent, *and* kind. And he's steady,' she added earnestly. 'That's important, isn't it? He's also very generous – and loyal. And he's attractive – did I say that?' I shook my head. 'Well, he *is* attractive, very, and I know I'm just so . . . *lucky.*' Chloë's mouth quivered, then a tear splashed on to her cheek. 'Sorry, Ella . . . I'm a bit . . . overwrought.'

I fumbled in my pocket and found some tissues. 'That's

very understandable . . .' I pulled a few out and Chloë pressed them to her eyes. 'It's the emotion of it all.'

She nodded, then regained her composure. 'So . . .' She looked at me, her eyes red-rimmed. 'How will you get home? Do you want me to call you a cab? I can wait with you until it arrives,' she added, brightening suddenly. 'We could sit here and chat.'

'It's okay, Chloë, I'm going to walk – I need the air. And you ought to get back to your guests.'

'You're right,' she sighed. 'So . . .' She flashed me a regretful smile. 'I'll see you soon, Ella.'

'Yes – and . . . don't worry, sweetie.' I kissed her on the cheek.

As I went down the steps, Chloë's words rang in my ears. She loved Nate so much that just the thought of it made her cry. She would soon marry him, and I would just have to be happy for her and try to view him in a different way.

When I got home I went up to the studio. Then I got out Nate's canvas, put it on the easel, picked up my palette and began to work on it. As I did so I tried to understand why I was so drawn to him. Was it because I'd hated him to start with and found the realisation that I liked him exhilarating somehow? Was I competing with Chloë? If so I'd never competed with her before; I'd only felt protective towards her – I was six years older than her after all: nor had I felt even a flicker of interest in any of her previous boyfriends. I was drawn to Nate, I realised, for the simple reason that I found him so attractive and decent and so easy to be *with*. We had an almost effortless rapport.

I worked on his portrait for the best part of two hours;

then, satisfied with what I'd done, I cleaned the brushes and went to my computer to check my e-mails before going to bed.

There was a new enquiry from a Mr and Mrs Berger about painting them to mark their silver wedding anniversary. That was good news. There was also a message from Sophia, to say that her mother was over her cold, asking if we could arrange the next sitting. I was glad. It would be good to see Iris again. I typed my reply and as I pressed 'send' another message arrived. It was from my father.

Dear Ella,
I've still had no word from you, but I continue to
hope that you'll find it in your heart to see me,
even if it's only for a few minutes. So this is to let
you know where I'll be staying – at the Kensington
Close Hotel, in Wright's Lane. I'll be in touch again
nearer the time, but for now I send you my
sincerest wishes, and my love.
Your father,
John

I stared at his message. *Hope . . . heart . . . love*. It was far too late for him to be using words like that.

I scrolled down to 'options'. *Delete message?* I high-lighted *Yes*.

Then, without knowing why, I changed my mind and pressed *No*.

SEVEN

'Wasn't the party fun?' Mum said the following Saturday morning. We were sitting at the kitchen table in Richmond, having a cup of coffee before starting the invitations. She was in her dancewear, having already done the hour of Pilates with which she starts each day. 'I think I drank a little more than was wise,' she added. 'I didn't say anything *silly*, did I?'

'No – you just had a bit of trouble with the word confetti.'

'Oh yes.' Mum rolled her eyes. 'But it was a lovely evening – I liked Nate's friends.' She moved the well-thumbed copies of *Brides* magazine, *You & Your Wedding* and *Perfect Wedding* to the end of the table. 'You know he's in Finland at the moment?'

'I do – otherwise I'd be painting him right now.' I wished I *were*, I reflected ruefully. I longed to see him again.

Through the French windows I could see Roy, at the very end of the garden, by Chloë's old wooden Wendy house, toiling away in the long flowerbed that skirted the lawn.

'I hope Nate won't have to do too much travelling,' I heard Mum say.

I looked at the horse chestnut waving its white candles. 'I think it goes with the job.' I sipped my coffee. 'What he does is to look at companies with a view to buying them – so at the moment he's putting together a leveraged bid for a liquid chemicals transport business in Helsinki. Its primary operations are in Scandinavia, but they're expanding into Estonia, Latvia and Lithuania. He's also looking at a shipping company in Sweden.'

Mum's brow furrowed. 'You seem to know a lot about it, darling.'

'Well . . . Nate talks about his work during the sittings.'

She opened her glasses case. 'It's sweet the way you pay so much attention to the people you paint – it must really put them at their ease.' She took out the spectacles, looping the mauve cord over her head. 'And have you had a busy week?'

'No – the election threw everything into disarray. I couldn't paint my MP, Mike Johns, for obvious reasons. Another sitter, Celine, had to go to France to see a friend – she said it was very important – so she cancelled our sitting. Other than that, I've been working on the posthumous portrait I'm doing. Did I tell you about it?'

'You did.' My mother shook her head. 'That poor girl. And how's her picture going?'

'Not well.' I heaved a frustrated sigh. 'It's just . . . flat. What I need is some close-up video footage of her, but there isn't any.' I refilled my coffee cup. 'Then I had

195

another sitting with a lovely woman called Iris who's in her eighties.' I'd hoped that Iris would continue the story about Guy Lennox, but an electrician had been there, doing some re-wiring, so we'd only made small talk. I looked at the garden again. 'What's Roy doing?'

'He's planting lots of delphiniums, foxgloves and holly-hocks – they should flower just in time for July third. Then he's going to do some weeding – with last week's rain the beds are like Papua New Guinea.'

'I'll help him with that,' I volunteered. 'It's too much for him on his own. Or maybe Chloë could give him a hand – she's coming over today, isn't she?'

'No – she phoned first thing to say that she can't.'

'Why not?'

'She said she needs to go into the office.'

'I see. But however busy she is, she should help you and Roy – I mean, this is all for *her*,' I added crossly.

'*I'll* help Roy later,' Mum said soothingly. She lifted her glasses on to her nose. 'But you and I *must* get on with the invitations.'

'Okay.' I put my cup in the sink. 'We'll start.'

I went over to the large green box standing on the end of the kitchen table, lifted the lid and pulled out the first invitation. The card was so thick that it could almost stand up unaided.

'Isn't the font lovely?' Mum said.

I looked at the flowing curlicues and extravagant swashes. 'It's . . . a bit fancy for my tastes.'

'Well, *I* love it. It took me ages to choose it.'

'Didn't Chloë want to choose it?'

'No. She's left *all* the arrangements to me – except for the dress, which I've now seen, and I must say it's

196

gorgeous.' Mum took her glasses off. 'Chloë told me that she'd been a bit unsure about it, given its history, but I said that there was no way Nate would try and get out of *their* wedding.'

'I'm sure he wouldn't.' I felt a stab of guilt for then wishing that he *would*.

Mum put some printed sheets in front of me. 'Here's *your* copy of the guest list. I want you to do A to M while I do N to Z. The addresses are all in *here . . .*' She thumped her Filofax on to the table.

I opened my backpack, got out my calligraphic pen and practised on a piece of scrap paper. *Nate, Nate, Nate, Nate.* I saw Mum peering at it, so then I wrote *Chloë, Chloë, Chloë, Chloë* then *Nate & Chloë.* 'It's fine,' I said.

'Good.' Mum unscrewed the top of her fountain pen then took an invitation out of the box, put her glasses on again, then began to write. I could hear the nib scratch across the card.

I inscribed an invitation to Mum's friend Janet Allen and her husband Keith; then I looked up their address, wrote it on the envelope and carefully blotted it. 'There's the first one done.' I slid it into the envelope.

Mum peered at it over her spectacles. '*Very* nice: don't seal them, will you – we'll be adding the accommodation list and RSVP cards afterwards. Right . . .' She turned back to her card. 'Here's *my* first one.' She inserted the invitation into the envelope then put it next to mine. I picked it up.

When I'd done my calligraphy course we'd studied graphology. I'd been sceptical at first, but studying my mother's writing had convinced me that there must be something to it, as all her personality traits seemed to be there. Her hand was forward sloping, indicating ambition and drive; the words were evenly spaced and of a uniform height, denoting organisational ability and self-control; the 'i's were beautifully dotted, indicating a meticulous character. Now I noticed that the tops of her letters were perfectly closed. This, I now recalled, pointed to a secretive nature.

'What are you doing?' Mum asked.

I put the envelope down. 'Just admiring your writing.'

'Thanks – it's not as elegant as yours, of course, but it'll do. Now, shall we listen to the radio while we work?'

'Yes – in *fact* . . .' I looked at the clock. 'I'm *on* the radio – in five minutes time. I'd completely forgotten.' I told Mum about the BBC documentary that I'd been interviewed for.

She went to the dresser and switched on the kitchen radio and we heard the tail end of *Travelling Light*.

'Now *Artists of the Portrait*,' said the announcer, 'in which our reporter, Clare Bridges, examines the fine art of painting people . . .'

We heard Clare talking about why it is that human beings have always sought to portray themselves, from the earliest scratchings at Lascaux to Marc Quinn's iconic bust, *Self*, carved out of eight pints of his own frozen blood. There were contributions from Jonathan Yeo and June Mendoza, and a rare clip of Lucian Freud. Then I heard my voice.

I knew I wanted to be a painter from eight or nine.

Mum smiled as Clare back-announced me.

I simply drew and painted all the time. Painting's always been, in a way, my solace . . .

198

Mum glanced at me, and I saw a flicker of something like guilt pass across her features.

I like painting people who I feel are complex: I like seeing that fight going on in the face between the conflicting parts of someone's personality.

I realised that I often saw that fight going on in my mother's face – the glacial serenity beneath which I caught glimpses of the struggle with her deeper emotions.

Now Clare was talking about the complex nature of the relationship between sitter and artist. Then I heard myself speak again.

A portrait sitting is a very special space. It has an intimacy – painting another human being is an act of intimacy . . . I've never fallen for a human sitter, no . . .

Then there was some discussion of the influence of the BP award, and of how portraiture, once seen as safe and conventional, has become almost cool and cutting edge. Then the programme came to an end, and I turned the radio off.

'That was fascinating,' Mum said. 'You spoke well, Ella. But have you really never fallen in love with one of your sitters?'

'Never,' I lied.

'Well, I hope you do one day, because it must be a wonderful way to meet someone – think of how well you get to *know* them – and they must get to know you very well, too.'

'Yes – depending on who it is, and on how much I want to reveal about myself . . .' I was walking on quicksand. 'Now . . .' I peered at the invitation list. 'Why are you inviting the Egertons?'

'Well, because they're near neighbours, and because they asked us to Lara's wedding last year. In fact, they're about to become grandparents.'

'Really? How old is Lara?'

'She must be . . .' Mum narrowed her eyes. 'Twenty-four.'

'She's having her family young then.'

'Twenty-four is young,' Mum agreed. 'Especially these days: I think it's better to wait.'

'But . . .' I pressed the blotting paper down. 'You had me when you were twenty-four.'

Mum's pen paused in mid-stroke. 'That's true.'

'And you were very ambitious – it could have ruined your career. I've always been surprised that you had me when you did – in fact, I've sometimes wondered whether you really, well, *intended* to have me.'

Mum had flushed. 'Do you mean – were you an accident? Is that what you're asking me, Ella?'

I took another invitation. 'Well, yes – it's unusual for young ballerinas to have babies, isn't it, given how ruthlessly determined they have to be to succeed? And you got married in a register office: so, lately, I've been thinking about it all, and wondering whether or not I was . . . planned.'

'Oh, Ella.' Mum reached for my hand. 'I was so *happy* to be having a baby.'

'But . . . weren't you worried that you'd be unable to get back to fitness afterwards?'

She shrugged. 'I simply trusted that I would. As it turned out, I was on stage again within four months.'

'So . . . presumably my father looked after me in the evenings, when you were performing.'

200

'No.' Mum picked up her pen. 'He did very little in that respect.'

'Why was that?'

'Well . . . he travelled a lot for his work. At that time he was building a school in Nottingham.'

'But Nottingham's not far from Manchester.'

'Even so . . . he'd quite often be away: and so I had babysitters for you. Sometimes our upstairs neighbour, Penny, would help. And when I was on tour my mother would come and stay.'

'I see. So Grandma would have been there in the flat, with my father. That must have been awkward. Did they get on?'

Mum blinked. 'Not really.'

'Didn't he like her?'

'She didn't . . . like *him*.'

'Oh. Because she knew about his affair, I suppose.' Mum nodded, grimly. 'Well, that *would* have put a strain on the relationship.' I began to write another invitation, to a friend of Chloë's, Eva Frost. I glanced at Mum. 'What about *his* parents? I don't remember them at all – did we ever see them?'

Mum sighed. 'They lived in Jersey and didn't come to the mainland very often. They weren't really . . . involved.'

'Even though they had a grandchild?' She nodded. 'How mean – not to make more of an effort.'

'It *was* mean,' Mum agreed feelingly.

'But we could have gone there – *did* we?'

'No . . . as I say, it was hard for me to take time off.'

'I see. So I didn't do very well on the grandparental front, did I?'

201

My mother nodded regretfully. 'That's true. You only had my mother, my father having died two years before you were born. He was called Gabriel, as you know, and so I named you after him.'

'And . . . remind me how you met *my* father.'

At first I thought Mum wasn't going to answer; then she lowered her pen. 'We met in 1973,' she said quietly. 'I'd been with the company for two years and he came to a special fund-raising performance of *Cinderella*. I was the Winter Fairy and wore a costume that hung with "icicles".'

'How lovely.' I imagined them tinkling as she danced. 'So was my father interested in ballet?'

'Not particularly; he'd come along . . . with some other people. There was a cast party afterwards, to which some members of the audience were invited; your father and I were introduced – and we . . . just . . .'

'Fell in love?'

'Yes,' Mum answered quietly.

'So you were what, twenty-three?'

'I was. And he was twenty-nine.

'And was he artistic too?'

My mother's face tightened. 'Yes. He did a lot of painting and drawing, so I imagine . . . that's where you get it. Now,' she said briskly. 'We need to write the invitations for Nate's relations.' The conversation about my father was clearly over. Mum pushed back her chair. 'I've got their addresses on a separate list – if I can remember where I put it. Oh, I know . . .' She stood up and went to the dresser then opened a drawer. 'It's in here.' She pulled the list out, then studied it. 'There's quite a gang of them coming. Nate's organising their

202

accommodation – Chloë told me that he's paying for quite a lot of it too – he's terribly generous.' Mum returned to the table. 'Thank *God* she's made such a good choice. And she knows she has, because she keeps telling me how lucky she is. Yesterday I was on the phone to her and she suddenly reeled off a list of all his great qualities. It was very touching.'

'That's just what she did with me, last week.'

Mum smiled. 'Good. It's such a relief to see her so happy – and don't worry, Ella.' Mum laid her hand on mine. 'I know that *you'll* find someone just as wonderful.' I already have, I thought with a pang. Mum lifted her glasses on to her nose again then peered at my pile of finished cards. 'What letter are you up to?'

'G.' I wrote an invitation for Chloë's godmother, Ruth Grant, and I was about to address the envelope when I put my pen down, unable to bear it any longer. 'Mum . . . Can I tell you something?' My heart began to race.

She reached for another invitation. 'Of course you can,' she said absently. 'Tell me anything you like, darling.'

'Because there's something that I have to . . .' My voice trailed away.

Mum looked at me – her agate blue eyes magnified through the lenses of her spectacles. 'What is it?' She blinked, then took the glasses off and let them dangle against her thin sternum. 'Has something happened, Ella?'

'*Yes*. Something has.'

She looked alarmed. 'You're not in any trouble, are you?'

'No. But I have this . . . dilemma.'

'Dilemma?' she echoed. 'What dilemma?' I didn't answer.

'Ella . . .' Mum put down her pen. 'Would you please tell me what this is about?'

'All right . . .' I took a deep breath. 'I've heard from my father.'

My mother's cheeks instantly coloured, as though all the blood in her body had rushed to her face. 'When?' she whispered. I told her, then explained how the contact had come about. She inhaled sharply, snatching the air through her nose. 'I was appalled when I saw that piece in *The Times*.'

'I know you were, because you didn't say anything about it. I did ask the journalist to change it, but he refused.'

'I *immediately* worried that, were your father to come across it, he'd recognise you – and he *has* done. So . . .' She drew in her breath. 'What did he say?'

I'd already decided not to tell my mother that he was coming to London.

I shrugged. 'He just wrote that he'd like to be in touch. He said there are things he wants to explain.'

Mum's face spasmed with anger. 'There's nothing *to* explain! You and I *both* know what happened, Ella.' She blinked rapidly. 'He deserted us when I was twenty-eight and you were almost five – a little girl. A little girl who *adored* him! He was heartless.'

'Well . . . if it's any comfort, he said that he feels very guilty. He wants to make amends.'

My mother's eyes were round with contemptuous wonderment. 'It's too *late* to make "amends". He made his choice – to abandon *us* and start a new life with, with . . .' She seemed unable to utter the name of the woman for whom my father had left her. 'He has no

204

right to get in touch now.' Mum picked up her pen as though that concluded the conversation.

I could hear the low hum of the fridge.

'Of course he has that right,' I protested quietly. 'He's my father.'

My mother's face flashed with renewed fury. 'He *isn't* your father, Ella. He chose *not* to be.' She nodded towards the garden. '*There's* your father.'

I glanced through the French windows at Roy, in the far distance, his foot on the spade. 'Roy *is* my father,' I agreed. 'And he's been a wonderful one. But the man who brought me into the world, and who *was* my father, at least for the first five years of my life . . .' I felt my throat constrict. 'That man now wants to be in touch.'

Mum looked at me warily, her bird-like chest rising and falling. 'So . . . what are you going to do?'

I shook my head. 'I don't know. I feel torn, because a part of me *does* want to see him.'

She blinked. 'What do you mean – *see* him?'

'I mean, see him . . . one day,' I faltered. 'If I *do* get in touch with him.'

Mum stared at me. 'And . . . have you replied?'

'No. I've been in turmoil about it – so I've done nothing.'

'Good.' She laid down her pen. 'Because I don't *want* you to reply.'

'But it isn't *up* to you, Mum – it's *me* he's contacted.'

She flinched. 'But I felt that I *had* to discuss it with you – however painful that discussion might be – before coming to any decision.'

My mother looked away. When she returned her gaze

205

to me, her pale-blue eyes shone with unshed tears. '*Don't* answer him, Ella. I beg you not to.'

'But it was all *so* long ago! Why are you *still* bitter about him?'

'Because of what he *did*.'

'Okay, so he left you.' I threw up my hands. 'People get left every day, but they try and move on – *you* moved on: you've had a good life with Roy. So why can't you get over what happened with my father?'

'Because I . . . just . . . can't. I have my reasons. *Please*, Ella – let it lie.' She bit her lip. 'No good will come of it.'

I'd caught the note of warning in her voice. 'What do you mean?' Mum didn't answer. 'What are you trying to say?'

She shifted on her chair. 'Only that . . . if you *do* contact him, it could cause a lot of unhappiness. He's decided to get in touch – no doubt because he's getting older now, and wants to be forgiven. But we don't *have* to forgive him, do we?'

'*I* can if *I* want to!'

Mum's eyes flickered with pain, then she picked up her pen. 'We *must* get on with the invitations.' Her voice had been calm, but as she took another card out of the box I saw that her hand was trembling.

'Mum,' I said, more gently now. 'The invitations can wait. Because now that we're talking about my father, there are other things I want to ask you.'

She started to write. 'What things?' she said irritably. She was pressing on the pen so hard that her fingertips had gone red.

'Well . . . I've been having a lot of memories from

that time – memories that must have been triggered by my father's contact.'

My mother's hand stopped. 'So that's why you asked me about the holiday in Anglesey.'

'Yes. In fact, he e-mailed me a photo of him and me standing on a beach. He's holding my hand . . .'

My mother exhaled. 'Which is how you knew about the blue-and-white striped dress.'

'Yes. I was wearing it in the photo – otherwise I wouldn't have remembered it. But there are lots of things I *do* remember, and one particular memory is very confused. I've been trying to work it out, but I can't.'

Mum was looking at me warily. 'And what memory's that?'

'It's of you and him. You're walking along, with me in between you, holding your hands. It's a very clear, sunny day, and you're both swinging me up in the air, going one, two, three, wheee. And you're wearing this white skirt with big red flowers on it.' My mother flinched. 'But the reason I'm confused is because I would have been too young to remember it, because you can only swing children up like that when they're no more than two or three – yet I *can* recall it, vividly.'

Don't let go now . . .

My mother's already fair complexion had gone paler still.

Okay – let's do a big one.

'Why do I remember that, Mum?'

More, Daddy! More! More!

'All right,' she answered at last. 'I'll tell you. Then perhaps you'll understand why I feel as I do.' Mum laid her pen down, then clasped her hands in front of her.

'What you're remembering,' she began softly, 'is the day that I saw your father with his . . . with . . . his . . . *Frances*.'

This, then, was the 'traumatic' encounter. So I *had* been there.

'She lived in Alderley Edge, a few miles to the south of Manchester, in a very nice house. She had money,' Mum added bitterly.

'What was our flat like?'

'Very ordinary – it was part of a red-brick house on Moss Side, but it was convenient for the University Theatre, where the company was then based. And in September 1979, when you were almost five . . .' So, well past the stage of being swung in the air, I reflected. 'It was a Saturday afternoon,' Mum went on. 'I'd been waiting for your father to arrive.' She swallowed. 'He'd had to go in to the office that morning. We were due to go for a picnic with him after lunch – the weather was wonderfully clear and sunny – but by three o'clock he still hadn't turned up, and I had to be on stage that night – I was dancing Giselle – so there wasn't much time. I guessed that he must be with *her*, and I was . . . angry and *hurt*.' Mum looked at me beseechingly. 'He'd done this to me *so* many times and I couldn't stand just waiting for him, feeling wounded and disappointed. So I decided to go and find him.'

'In order to do what? Confront him?'

She exhaled wearily. 'I didn't know *what* I was going to do. There was a football match on – we could hear the roars from Old Trafford. I told you that we were going for a ride in the car, so I put you in the back and we drove to Alderley Edge.'

'How did you know where she lived?'

'I just . . . did. Women are good at finding these things out, Ella. So I went past . . . the house.' Mum stared straight ahead. 'There was your father's blue car, in the drive.' So he wasn't even discreet about it, I reflected dismally. 'I parked about fifty feet away then sat there, sick with misery.'

My heart contracted with pity. 'How horrible for you, Mum.'

She closed her eyes for a moment. 'It was . . . *hell*. You were chatting away in the back, asking me what we were doing – but I couldn't explain. I then decided that there was nothing that I *could* do – we'd simply have to go home. And I was about to start the car again when you suddenly said that you were hungry. There was a newsagent's a few yards behind, so we got out of the car and went in, and I bought you some chocolate. But as we were walking back to the car I looked up and, in the distance, I saw your father walking along with *her*, and . . .' My mother swallowed. 'With her and . . .'

Ready, sweetie? One, two, three . . .

'And *what*, Mum?'

U-u-u-u-p she goes!

Mum's face was perfectly still – like a frozen waterfall. 'And this little girl,' she answered softly. 'She was holding their hands. She was about three.'

More Daddy! More!

'They were swinging her up in the air and they were all laughing.' Mum paused. 'And then I understood . . .'

I tried to speak, but my mouth had gone dry. 'So . . .' My heart was banging in my chest. 'You're saying that

209

my father had a child with his mistress? And that he'd never told you?'

'Never.'

So this was why the encounter had been 'traumatic'.

'What a shock,' I breathed.

'It was more than a shock. It hit me like a blow from a hammer.' Mum was still staring ahead. 'They hadn't spotted us, but by now I was in a panic, not knowing what to do. I decided that we had to leave before we were seen, so I hurried towards the car, but you were trying to pull me in the opposite direction. I told you to come with me, but you refused. Then you turned and called out, "Daddy! *Daddy!*" He glanced up. And when he saw us, he looked *so* . . .'

I saw my father's face, his mouth an 'o'. 'Startled . . .' I whispered.

'Yes. He also looked ashamed and confused. I tried to hold you, but you wrenched your hand free and you ran towards him. I called you to come back, but you wouldn't stop. I had no choice but to follow you and so . . .' She blinked again. 'There I was, face to face with him, and her, and this . . . little girl.'

'A little girl,' I echoed, still trying to take it in.

Mum nodded. 'He'd concealed her existence from me. I knew about the . . . relationship.' I thought of the hotel bill that Mum had found in my father's pocket, and the love letter. 'But I tolerated it,' Mum went on bleakly, 'because I believed that it would end.' She exhaled. 'But I had no idea that Frances had had . . .' Mum looked at me in bewilderment. 'It didn't seem *possible*.'

'Why *not*?'

'Because . . . John had told me that she was unable

to have children – and she was ten years older than he was.'

'Really?' I adjusted my mental image of the woman who'd so beguiled my father.

'So for her to have a child was the *last* thing I expected. She would have been forty-two when that baby was born.'

'But . . . I still don't understand why you *stayed* with him. There he was, having this long affair – an affair you knew all about, such that you even discussed with him your fears that the other woman might get pregnant? How horrible!'

Mum looked stricken. 'It *was* horrible – it was *awful*!'

'Then why didn't you *divorce* him? You were young – and beautiful. You could have found someone else. Why didn't you leave him, Mum?'

Her blue-grey eyes were shimmering, like melted ice. 'Because I loved him,' she answered softly. 'I didn't *want* to leave him.' She drew in her breath, slowly, as if in physical pain. 'But . . . there we all were. And Frances looked at me with utter *hatred*.'

'But . . . why should *she* hate *you*?'

Mum gave a helpless shrug. 'She just . . . did. Then you said, "What are you doing, Daddy? Are you helping this lady?" Then Frances gave you this penetrating stare that I've never forgotten.'

'The skirt,' I said quietly. 'The white skirt with the big red flowers. It was *hers*, wasn't it? Not yours. *She* was wearing it.'

Mum nodded. 'Then she picked up the little girl and carried her inside. John looked at me furiously, then he told me that he'd never forgive me.'

'But – this all sounds the wrong way round – *you* were the wounded party.'

'Yes,' Mum said hotly. 'I was!' She banged her hand down on the edge of the table. 'I *was* the wounded party!' Her chin dimpled as she struggled not to cry. 'But I suppose he was confused and ashamed – his double life had been exposed.' She blinked away a tear. 'But as I walked away with you, I felt as though my whole world was sliding off a cliff. Because there was a child, and I knew that this would change my life for ever.'

'But . . . you're telling me that I had a *sister*.' I stared at my mother. 'What was her name?'

'Lydia,' she answered after a moment.

'Lydia,' I echoed blankly. 'And you've never *told* me?' Mum didn't respond. I glanced into the garden. 'Is *Roy* aware of this?'

She shook her head. 'I knew that he'd only tell you – or make *me* tell you. And I didn't want you to know.'

'But . . .' I felt anger and indignation rise up, like magma. 'What if I'd wanted to meet Lydia – or get to *know* her?'

A muscle at the corner of Mum's mouth twitched. 'That's precisely what I wanted to avoid, because if you had done then we'd have to have had contact with John again, which was the *last* thing I wanted.' Her hands were curled into fists. 'I was determined to preserve the integrity and stability of my *family*.'

'So you hid my sister's existence from me – all these years? How *could* you? How could you *do* that, Mum?'

She gave me a blinkless stare. 'It surely must have occurred to you, Ella, that your father might have had other children?'

212

'Well . . . of *course,*' I answered faintly. 'I guessed that he'd probably had another family, in Australia – but that's an *abstract* thought. You're telling me that he had a child *here,* in the UK, just a few miles from where we lived – a child who was only two years younger than me – a child I'd actually *met* – and might have *known*?'

Mum smiled bitterly. 'Oh, that would have been cosy. The daughters of the wife and mistress being playmates? Would *you* want that, Ella, if you were ever in the situation that *I* was suddenly in?'

I imagined myself in my mother's shoes. 'No,' I conceded. 'I wouldn't. It would be very awkward, even today; and yes, thirty years ago it would have been . . .'

'*Unbearable,*' Mum concluded. 'You can imagine the gossip and speculation.'

'All right.' I exhaled, sharply. 'Even so . . . the idea that you never, ever *mentioned* her to me – my God . . .'

'I *couldn't* . . .' She heaved an exasperated sigh. 'Because if I *had* done, then you might have wanted to contact her, which would have put us back in John's orbit, which, I repeat, I did *not* want.'

I glared at Mum. 'Everything's been about what *you've* wanted.'

She blinked. 'No, Ella. No. I was thinking of *you.* Because the point is not that your father got himself into that situation. The *real* point is that you were almost five years old by then, and your father had seemed devoted to you, but—'

'What do you mean "seemed"?' I interrupted. 'He was! He *was* devoted to me! That's why my memories of him are only happy ones. I remember him playing with me, and pushing me on the swings, and watching children's television with me, and taking me to the theatre to see you dance. I remember him putting me to bed, and reading to me and doing painting with me; I remember him hugging me, and holding my hand . . .' My throat ached. 'In *all* my memories of him, he's holding my *hand*!' I felt my eyes fill. 'So don't tell me that he wasn't devoted to me – because he *was*!'

Mum clasped her hands in front of her again, then inhaled. 'You still don't understand. You *still* haven't got there. So now I'm going to tell you.'

'Tell me *what*?' I fumbled in my pocket for a tissue. 'What are you going to tell me?'

'The truth,' Mum answered bluntly. 'I've never *wanted* to tell you the truth, Ella. I've sheltered you from it. But now I will.' My mother's slender chest rose, and then fell. 'Ella,' she said softly, 'your father chose to be with this *other* child. He chose to spend his life with *her*, and not with you.' Tears glimmered in her eyes. '*That* is what I've never wanted you to know.'

As my mother's words impacted on me I imagined feeling my father's hand in mine, his grip firm and strong, then his fingers suddenly loosening, and letting go.

Mum swallowed, painfully. 'But that's not *all* he did.'

'What do you mean?'

She inhaled, shudderingly, as though suddenly cold. 'That day, you and I then walked back to the car, and I drove home. I was in shock – how I managed not to crash, I don't know. You were asking me why Daddy was playing with that little girl and who that lady was. I didn't answer – I didn't know how. Nor did I know how I'd be able to go on stage that night and dance – but I did and *as* I danced I felt that Giselle's suffering

214

was my own: and afterwards everyone said that it was the best performance of my life. What I couldn't have known was that it was to be the *last* performance of my life.'

'The last . . .?'

Mum laced her fingers together. 'At eleven, I got back to the flat. The babysitter left, then I just lay on the bed, in the darkness, watching the headlights from passing cars strobe across the ceiling. After a while I heard the key turn in the front door – John was back. Despite what I'd discovered that day, my reaction was one of relief. He'd come *back*. I ran downstairs to greet him. But his face was white – he was trembling with emotion.'

'What did he say?'

Mum was staring ahead now, as if reliving those moments. 'He said that he couldn't stand it any more. He said that he'd prevaricated for three years and it had driven him *mad*. He said that he was finally being forced to choose. I felt myself start to panic, but then he went wearily upstairs and I felt *so* relieved – he was going to bed. We would sleep, then work things out in the morning – I was certain that everything would be all right, just as long as we stayed together. But as I went into the bedroom I saw him pulling his suitcase down from the top of the wardrobe; then he began opening drawers and taking out his clothes and putting them into it. Then he looked at me . . . and he said . . .' Mum's voice had caught '. . . that he'd decided to be with Frances. He said that he didn't want to lose her. He said that he loved her . . .' Mum wiped away a tear. 'So this was the second hammer blow that day. I begged him *not* to leave us, but he carried on taking his things out of the drawers, quickly putting them in his case. Then he snapped the clasps shut, picked the case up and, without even glancing at me, went down the stairs.'

My hand flew to my chest. 'Didn't he say goodbye to me? Surely he wanted to say goodbye to *me*?'

'He *did* want to – but you were asleep and I wouldn't let him wake you. I didn't want you to know what was happening. So as I followed him down I told him that he'd *have* to come the next day, to reassure you. But he didn't answer. He opened the front door and then, without a backward glance, he went down the steps.' As my mother said this I remembered the steps – they were steep, with smooth black tiles. Mum exhaled. 'As I followed him out I saw him throw his case into the back of the car. I called to him, but he didn't answer – it was as though he was sleep-walking. Then he got behind the wheel and turned the ignition. The car was moving away. So I ran down the steps after him . . .' Mum paused. 'But I was so distraught that as I reached the last step I slipped, and felt my ankle buckle. Then I was in agonising pain.'

'Oh, Mum . . .'

She was shaking her head. 'I must have screamed, because our neighbour, Penny, came running out. She called the ambulance then stayed with you until my mother got there in the early hours. I'd broken my ankle – the surgeon who operated on it told me that it was a very bad break – a "complicated fracture".' Mum looked at me in despair. 'So that was the *third* blow of the hammer on that terrible day, by the end of which I felt that everything in my life was . . . shattered.' She laid her hand on mine. 'But I consoled myself that I

216

still had you. You were my only solace in those dark days, Ella.'

I stared at Mum. 'I remember how sad you were. You used to sit in the kitchen, for hours, barely speaking, or you'd lie on your bed, your face to the wall.'

Mum turned up her palms. 'I felt as though I'd been hurled into an abyss. What I would have done without my mother, I don't know. But it remained my belief that John would come back, because he'd always come back, and I'd always forgiven him – and I would have forgiven him again, *even* then.'

'Oh, Mummy . . .' Now I understood the depth of her feelings for my father.

'But this time there was no word from him. And when I at last felt composed enough to phone his office, his colleague Al said that John wasn't there. Al seemed embarrassed,' Mum went on. 'I presumed that this was because he knew that John had left me.' She pursed her lips. 'But that wasn't the reason at all. It was because Al realised that I had no idea that John no longer worked there. When he told me this I was . . . stunned. I asked him *why,* and where he'd gone – it was so humiliating, not knowing where my own—' Mum drew in her breath, shudderingly. 'Then I heard Al say, "You don't *know,* Sue? That he's gone to Perth?" By now I was in turmoil, but desperately trying not to show it, so I asked him if John had gone there for work, adding that I knew he'd once done a project in Dundee. There was a pause. Then Al said, very quietly, "Perth in Australia. He left ten days ago. He's gone there for good."' Mum closed her eyes as if to shut out the memory.

'But . . . it takes *time* to emigrate,' I protested. 'All the bureaucracy – and the interviews.'

'It takes a *lot* of time,' Mum agreed. 'So he would have known for at least eighteen months beforehand, probably more.'

'But how had he managed to *hide* it from you?'

She rested her face in her hands. 'I've *no* idea – but he did.'

'He must have kept all the papers at work.'

Mum shrugged. 'But this is where he was *so* cynical, Ella.' She looked at me bleakly. 'He'd been planning it with *her*, all those months, while continuing to talk to me about all the things that *we* were going to do, the three of us: he'd talk about the lovely house we'd buy, and the life that we'd live, the holidays we'd have, when *all* the time . . .' Mum's mouth quivered as she tried not to cry: then she looked at me with an air almost of triumph. '*Now* do you understand why I feel as I do?'

'Yes,' I said quietly.

'You were almost five,' she said. 'Now you're *thirty-five*. And your father says that he'd like to make amends – as though he believes that he can wipe the slate clean with a few e-mails. I don't think he *can*. So . . .' Mum looked at me imploringly, then she reached out her hand. 'Are you going to answer him?' I didn't answer. '*Are* you, Ella?' I felt her fingers close around mine.

'No,' I said, after a moment. 'I'm not.'

'So that's that,' I said to Polly, over lunch, a few days later. I'd already told her the bare bones of the story on the phone. Now, sitting in a quiet corner of the Kensington Café Rouge, I'd related it to her in more detail.

She sipped her mint tea. 'So the memory that you

218

had was of him swinging *Lydia* through the air; but you'd thought it was you.'

'Yes. And now I know *why* I'd remembered it – because I was almost five, not three: and because of the emotion of it all, I suppose.'

'But what a *mess* your father got himself into.'

I nodded bleakly. 'I keep thinking of myself, aged six, seven and eight, asking my mother when I'd see him, not knowing that he was on the other side of the world with his other family – his other little girl.' The pain of this was so sharp that it was almost like a physical injury. The fact that Lydia had been born two years after me was an additional stab.

'It does make your mother's attitude easier to understand.' Polly shook her head. 'Even so, for her to have *kept* all this from you . . .'

'And now I feel *confused*; because, on the one hand, I feel angry with her for concealing something so . . . enormous, but on the other hand, I guess she was right. As a child, I don't think I *could* have coped with knowing that my father had left me in order to live with his other child, thousands of miles away. It would have felt like the most terrible rejection – it feels like that now.'

'But he didn't leave you in order to live with his other child, Ella. He left you in order to live with his girlfriend. It was your *mother* he was rejecting – not you.'

'No – he was rejecting me too, because if he'd loved me enough then no one could have seduced him away from my mother. Instead he went to Australia, leaving behind utter heartbreak – a complicated fracture,' I added bitterly.

219

Polly lowered her cup. 'You said that Frances was Australian.'

'She was: "was" being the operative word.'

Polly looked puzzled. 'What are you saying? That she's . . .?'

I nodded. 'Last night I Googled "Frances Sharp"; the first thing to come up was her obituary.'

'I see . . . that must have been a shock.'

'It was – he'd said nothing about it.' I reflected that my father had said nothing about himself in any of his e-mails – only that he hoped that we'd meet. 'It was in the *Western Australian*, from last December; it said that she'd been ill for some time. She was seventy-six – ten years older than my father.'

'That's a big gap. So he must have really loved her.'

'He clearly did. Mind you, Mum said that the fact that she had money would have featured in his . . . calculations.'

'Your mother probably would say that, whether or not it was true,' Polly pointed out. 'But what did Frances do, that she had an obituary?'

'She owned a winery near the Margaret River, south of Perth – it's called Blackwood Hills. I then did a search on it and on the website it said that Frances's parents had started it up in 1970 when that part of Australia was first being cultivated for wine. It explained that in 1979 she'd gone back to Australia to help them run it and that she inherited it in 1992, on her father's death. The site briefly mentioned *my* father, but it was clear that the estate was managed primarily by Frances.'

'So who runs it now? Lydia?'

'Yes. With her husband, Brett – they got married last

220

year. There was a photo of them standing in a vineyard with the river in the background.'

'Does she look like you?'

'She does.' I paused. 'It was *weird*, Polly – recognising my own face in the face of a stranger.' I felt a shiver run down my spine.

'And . . . have you told your mother any of this?'

'No. Because now that I know what my father did, I feel there's nothing more to say.'

Polly stirred her mint tea. 'A few weeks ago I said that perhaps there was another side to the story – that it might somehow be better than you thought: but it was worse.'

'Yes – and the fact that he's only contacted me now that Frances has died is another mark against him. Perhaps he promised her that he wouldn't look for me while she was alive,' I added bitterly.

'But he didn't know where you *were* until he saw that piece in *The Times*.'

'I'm sure he *could* have found me, if he'd wanted to. So if I choose to reject him now, it's no more than he deserves.'

'And . . . would you want to get in touch with Lydia?'

I didn't answer for a moment. 'I'm still trying to get my head around the idea that she *exists*. It's like discovering that I've got another arm – I can't quite cope with it. But I can hardly contact her if I'm refusing to see him, so I guess the answer to your question has to be no.'

Polly sighed. 'It seems . . . sad.'

'It suppose it does, but lots of people have half-siblings that they never get to see. But at least my mother's finally told me everything.'

'Well . . .' Polly grimaced. 'Let's hope she *has*.' I glanced at her. 'And presumably she's told Roy too?' I nodded. 'What did he say?'

'Not very much – he was shocked. But he texted me afterwards to say that he'd like to have lunch with me next week.'

Polly nodded then glanced at her watch. 'We'd better go, Ella, or we'll miss our appointment.' She waved at the waiter.

I opened my bag. 'So we're having a pedicure?'

'We are,' she said as the waiter brought the bill.

'But why would you ask me to have a pedicure with you when you've never wanted to have one with me before? In fact, I thought you *never* have professional pedicures in case they cut your nails all wrong and put you out of work.'

'*This* pedicure's different.' Polly flashed me an enigmatic smile. 'You'll see.'

'You're being very mysterious,' I said as we crossed Kensington Church Street. As we turned into Holland Street I remembered that this was where Iris had lived before she moved to her flat. I was looking forward to our next sitting.

We passed a patisserie and an art gallery then Polly stopped outside the last shop in the terrace. 'We're here.'

I read the sign. 'Aqua Sheko?' Through the window I could see a row of large clear tanks in each of which was a shoal of tiny dark fish. 'What *is* this? A sushi bar? We eat fish while we have our feet done?'

'No,' she said brightly. 'The fish eat *us*. My treat, by the way.'

'Thanks,' I said uncertainly.

We went in, and the proprietor, a young Chinese

woman, took our shoes, then we sat down while she washed and dried our feet.

'Okay,' said Polly. 'Up we go.'

We climbed on to the green leather bench. Polly dipped her perfect feet into her tank and I shuddered as the fish swarmed towards them in a writhing black mass.

'Come and *get* it,' Polly crooned at them.

'They're not baby piranha, are they, Pol?'

'Nope – they're tiny carp called Gara Rufa. They don't even have teeth – they just suck.' She nodded at my tank. 'Your turn.'

'Do I have to?'

'Yes – they're hungry.'

I peered at the wriggling black shapes then, grimacing, lowered my feet into the lukewarm water. The fish darted towards them and I felt their mouths dock against my skin. I shivered with distaste. 'Ooh . . . It tickles. But . . . it's *okay*, actually: in fact it's quite nice.'

'I thought you'd say that,' said Polly. 'In the wild they clean the scales of bigger fish, which is what human feet look like to them. They'll nibble the dead skin off your soles and heels, then they'll go between your toes and around your nails.'

'Yum.'

'And there's some hormone in their spit that's good for stress.'

'I could certainly do with *that*.'

I was surprised at how quickly I was able to forget about the fish as Polly and I sat there, quietly chatting, sipping green tea. Occasionally a passer-by would stop and gawp at us through the window.

'Have you had much work, Pol?' I asked her.

223

'I did a shoot at the British Museum last week. I had to hold this Ming vase. It was worth thirty-two million pounds, so they had security guards there to make sure I didn't run off with it and a thick mattress underneath, in case I dropped it, but luckily I've got very steady hands. Then I've got a booking this Friday – I've got to run my hands up Pierce Brosnan's naked back.'

'Sounds nice.'

'No,' Polly protested. 'It's *dull*. These jobs always are. I've stroked Sean Connery's chin, Sean Bean's chest, Jude Law's legs, David Beckham's pecs, Clive Owen's *face*,' she added in a sing-song. 'It's *so* boring – especially when we have to do twenty-five re-takes.' She stifled a yawn. 'I'd love to *stop,* or maybe not stop, because the money's quite good, but I'd like to do something *new* as well – something a bit more *stimulating* – not that I've any idea what.'

A woman walked, or rather wobbled past the window – teetering along on five-inch platforms.

'See that?' I said to Polly. '*Why* do women wear big platforms? They're not even attractive – they're just clumpy and ugly – and dangerous.'

Polly sipped her tea. 'Well, originally they were very practical shoes, designed to lift the wearer out of all the muck and filth on eighteenth-century streets.'

'I see . . .' I peered at 'my' fish, which had now encircled my lower shins like feathery anklets. 'And have you had any luck on the man front?'

Polly cocked her head to one side. 'There's a very nice divorced dad at Lara's school – we've chatted at drop-off a few times and I *think* he's interested. But if he asks me out I'm *not* going to tell him what I do. I want a man who's attracted to my face – not my feet,' she added firmly. 'What about your love life?'

I thought of Nate. 'Nothing.'

'Are you still painting Nate?' Polly asked, as though she'd read my mind.

'Yes. We've got a couple more sittings – then that's it.' Only two more 'dates with Nate', I reflected regretfully.

'Are you happy with his portrait?'

'It's . . . fine. In fact I think it's going to be *more* than fine.' The work I'd done to it after the engagement party had been good, despite the fact that I'd been painting by electric light, and had had quite a lot to drink. But now I felt that I could see more of Nate's soul.

'That's great.' Polly sipped her tea. 'I'm glad you came to like him, Ella – and it must have made him much easier to paint.' I didn't tell Polly that it had made it infinitely harder. I'd never told her what I felt for Nate. There were times when I'd been tempted to, but I felt ashamed to admit it, even to her. I suspected that Polly had guessed, but she'd been too tactful to say anything.

She took her feet out of her tank. 'So how's it going with the wedding?'

'Oh . . . pretty well, I think. Despite last week's emotional upset, it all seems to be under control. Chloë's asked me to do a reading.'

'That's nice – what are you going to read?'

'I don't know – she's still choosing.'

Polly dried her toes. 'It's very nice of her to invite me and Lola.'

'Well, she's known you all her life – and my parents want you to be there too, as do I. It's going to be a huge do.'

225

'So how's Chloë feeling?'

'Pretty nervous.' I thought of her tearful anxiety at the engagement party.

'That's normal,' Polly remarked. 'Remember how terrified I was before I married Ben?' I nodded. 'Though it was with good reason, now I come to think about it. I knew, even as I walked up the aisle that I was making a mistake. It was an awful feeling. How I managed to make my vows I don't know. But Chloë's happy?'

I shrugged. 'She seems to be. She keeps saying how wonderful Nate is – in fact she constantly eulogises him and so . . . what's the matter?'

'Erm . . . nothing.'

'You were frowning, Pol – tell me what you're thinking.'

For a moment Polly looked as though she might, but then I felt my phone vibrate. 'Just a second,' I said as I took it out of my pocket. I peered at the screen.

Seeing my father's name, in light of what I'd recently learned about him, gave me a sick feeling. 'I've had another message from my father.'

'Really? What does he say?'

I began to read it. 'Just more of the same. He says that he understands my reticence blah blah blah, but – oh, this is new – he refers to Mum. He says he hopes that she isn't discouraging me from responding to him. He says he hopes that I'll make my own decision, and that we'll meet when he's in London.'

'Which will be when?'

'A week on Sunday . . .'

'Gosh – soon.'

'Yes. But I *am* making my own decision about it,

226

which is that I'm having nothing to do with him. What does he expect after what he . . . *oh*.'

Polly looked at me. 'What?'

I stared at the screen. 'He's spotted that I say on my website that my studio's near to World's End.'

'He's not planning on coming round, is he?'

'No – he wouldn't know the address – I don't put it on the site. But he says that if he *doesn't* hear from me he's going to go to a café on the King's Road every day of his stay. It's called Café de la Paix, and he says that he'll sit there between three and six on the Monday and Tuesday afternoons, and between nine and twelve on the Wednesday morning, in the hope that I'll come. He says his flight back is at four on Wednesday afternoon.'

'He's certainly determined,' said Polly.

'He is.'

'So . . . *will* you do that, Ella? Maybe you could?' she added tentatively. 'What do you think?'

I went to 'Options', then hit 'Delete message'. 'No.'

EIGHT

'Haven't seen you for a while,' said the taxi driver three days later. He put my easel in the boot of his car. 'You been okay?'

'Erm . . . more or less. And you?' I asked as I got in the back.

'Can't complain.' He got behind the wheel. 'So we're off to Barnes again, are we?'

'Yes – to the same address on Castelnau, please.'

He started the car and we drove away, passing the Harley Davison showroom, then the Wedding Shop with its displays of Wedgwood and Waterford. As we waited to turn left, I gazed into the window of Artiques with its weird selection of fossils, crystals, conch shells, bleached animal skulls, sunburst mirrors, and stuffed fish. On the walls were frames containing huge mounted butterflies with wings of yellow, orange and blue.

As we pulled up at the lights the driver nodded at the railings. 'Lots more flowers.'

I glanced at the many new bouquets and at the two

pink balloons bobbing on their silver ribbons. 'That's because it's her birthday today.'

The driver looked at me in his rear-view mirror. 'How do you know?'

'I was told – in fact, I'm painting her.'

'Even though she died?'

'Yes. I'm doing it from photos.'

'Right . . . I suppose that's easier.'

'No – much harder.'

As we drove on I thought about how unhappy I was with Grace's portrait. I spent most of the journey torturing myself with thoughts of how let down her family would feel when they saw it.

We turned into Celine's drive. I got out with my stuff, paid the driver then pressed on the big brass bell. To my surprise the door was opened not by the housekeeper, but by Celine's husband – a tall, silver-haired man in a city suit.

He beamed at me. 'You must be Ella.'

'I am, and you're Mr Burke?'

'Do call me Victor – how *nice* to meet you. Let me take that.' He took the easel, tucked it under his arm then crossed the hall, pausing at the foot of the stairs. He put his hand on the newel post and looked up. '*Dar*-ling! Ella's here to *paint* you.' He turned to me. 'She'll be down in a tick.'

I followed Victor into the drawing room where the dustsheets were already in place. He put the easel down and I opened it up and positioned it in its usual place. 'So how's it going?' Victor asked as I got out my palette and brushes. 'Could I have a peek?'

'Of course.' I took the canvas out of the canvas carrier and put it on the easel.

Victor rested his hands on his hips. 'Yes . . .' He cocked his head to one side as he studied it. 'It's definitely Celine.'

'We've only had two sittings, but the basic shapes are there, so now it's a matter of building up her face.'

'I do hope you'll do her justice.'

'I'll do my best. The sittings are going well,' I added disingenuously, then wondered if he had any idea what a nightmare his wife had been.

'*Here* she is.' Victor beamed at Celine as she came in. 'Your picture's *really* taking shape, darling.'

'Good,' she said absently. 'Hello, Ella.'

'Hi,' I responded warmly. For all our difficulties, I had come to like Celine and was pleased to see her.

Victor turned to me. 'So today's what – the fourteenth of May? Celine's birthday is on the twelfth of June.'

'The portrait will be finished at least a week before,' I reassured him.

'Terrific. Now . . .' He glanced around the room. 'Where will it hang . . .?'

Celine's face spasmed with alarm. 'Not in *here*, Victor.'

'Why not?' he asked.

'It's too . . . *public*.'

'Oh, I don't know . . .' He was eyeing the space above the mantelpiece. 'I'd rather like it to go there – instead of the mirror.'

Celine looked appalled. 'Absolutely not! And if that's what you're planning, I won't do any more sittings!' Her vehemence took me aback. I wondered if there was about to be a full-scale row.

'All right, *not* there,' Victor placated her. 'We can discuss it when it's finished.' He glanced at his watch. 'But I'm going to leave you both to it, as I'm running late . . .' He straightened his yellow silk tie. 'Bye, darling.' He made to kiss Celine's cheek, but she turned her head and he ended up kissing her ear. He gave a bemused shrug then turned to me. 'Goodbye, Ella. *Very* nice to meet you.'

'You too, Victor.' He went out of the room then we heard his shoes snap across the hall, then the front door slammed.

Celine went over to the red velvet chair. 'I'm sorry about that,' she muttered as she sat down.

'Oh, don't worry.' I tied on my apron. 'Your husband's charming.'

She put her bag down on the floor. 'He is.'

'He's obviously devoted to you.'

'Yes,' she said wearily.

I began to squeeze out the paint, mixing yellow ochre with cadmium red to make the base for the skin tone. 'And he's very good-looking.'

Celine heaved a regretful sigh. 'That's true. My husband is charming, devoted and good-looking: he's hard-working, honourable and *very* generous. He's wonderfully thoughtful,' she added. 'Oh – and he's a marvellous father.'

I was reminded of Chloë's recitation of Nate's good qualities. 'Well . . . then you're very fortunate.'

Celine chewed on her lower lip. 'Yes . . .'

'And will you have a birthday party?'

She nodded. 'Victor is giving me a dinner for forty friends.'

I thinned the paint. 'How lovely – where will it be?'

'At the Dorchester,' she replied flatly.

'How fantastic.' I selected a medium-sized brush.

231

'We're then going to Venice for four days. He's booked the Cipriani,' she added without enthusiasm.

'Lucky you!'

'And for my present, he's taking me to Graff, where I'm to choose a diamond ring – four carats.'

'Good *God!*' I wanted to laugh. 'What an amazing husband you've got.'

Celine looked at me bleakly. 'He *is* amazing. Yes. *But . . .*' Suddenly her ring tone sounded. My heart sank as Celine fished her phone out of her bag, peered at the screen, then slid it open. '*Oui, chéri?*' She stood up.

'*Celine,*' I mouthed. '*Please . . .*'

She flashed me an imploring smile. 'This is *very* important.' She resumed the call. '*Il faut que je te parle. Oui, chéri. Je t'écoute . . .*'

As I watched her walk to the door, whispering endearments, I suddenly realised what Celine's situation must be. During the first two sittings I'd noticed that there was one caller to whom she expressed particular affection. The intense, covert nature of these conversations reminded me of how Chloë used to be when she was seeing Max. Celine was having an affair. That would explain why she didn't want to be painted. Victor had commissioned a portrait of her, but she was in love with someone else. It would also explain her irritability with Victor.

After four or five minutes she returned, looking slightly flushed, as though the call had affected her. 'Sorry about that,' she said as she crossed the carpet. 'I'll put the phone on "answerphone".' She did so then returned it to her bag. '*Alors . . .*' She sat down again. 'Let's continue.'

We chatted for a while, but Celine was clearly in an

agitated mood. In her eyes was a kind of anxious longing, and from time to time she would sigh.

My brush slapped across the canvas as I painted her dress – it was a pure mid-blue, like the blue of rosemary flowers. As I loaded the brush again I heard another deep sigh.

I looked up. 'Are you okay, Celine?'

'Am I okay?' she repeated after a few moments. 'Well . . . I suppose it depends on what you mean by "okay".' I swapped the brush I'd been using for a finer one and began to outline her mouth. 'I am in good health,' she went on. 'I'm not hungry or cold. I have comfortable accommodation, and clothes on my back, *but* . . .' Her eyes were suddenly bright with tears. 'No,' she whispered. 'I am *not* okay.'

'Celine . . .'

She fumbled in her sleeve then pressed a tissue to her face. 'Excuse me,' she murmured.

'Don't . . . worry.' I lowered my brush. 'We'll wait until you feel . . . better.'

She pursed her lips. 'I am not *going* to feel better. I shall only feel worse.'

'Well . . . is there anything *I* can do?'

'No.' She swallowed. 'Thank you.' She balled the tissue in her hand, clenching it so hard that her knuckles were white.

I wanted to ask Celine what the matter was, but didn't feel that I could. In any case, I reflected, she was unlikely to tell me. I dipped the brush in the jar of turps and stirred it around.

'I want to leave my husband.' I glanced at Celine. She looked at me desperately. 'I want to leave Victor,'

233

she reiterated fervently. 'I've wanted to leave him for a long time, but now it's all coming to a head, because of my birthday.' She dragged the tissue under her left eye. 'It's very difficult.'

'Well . . . is there . . . anyone you can talk to about it?'

She swallowed, painfully. 'I *have* just been talking about it – to my friend. That's why the call was so important.'

'I see.'

'And this friend of mine – Marcel . . .' Her boyfriend, I decided. She sighed with frustration. '. . . I *love* Marcel.' So I was right. 'But . . .' Celine's voice had fractured with emotion, '. . . she will not *support* me!'

'Ah.' *Marcelle.*

She sniffed. 'Marcelle thinks I'm . . . "insane". She told me so when I saw her in Paris last week, and she said it again just now. She says that if I leave Victor I will never, ever find a man who will be as good to me as he has been.'

'He does seem . . . very nice.'

'He *is*. He's a wonderful husband. I know that I am *lucky* to have what I have, and that to be discontented in *any* way is horribly ungrateful – and *yet* . . .' Celine's mouth quivered. 'I am *so* unhappy.'

'Why?'

Celine looked at me, her eyes wet-lashed. 'Isn't life supposed to *begin* at forty?' I remembered her saying this, with an odd bitterness, the first time we'd met. 'Well, I feel that *my* life is going to *end* at forty.'

'Why . . . should it?'

'Because . . .' She sniffed again, then tugged another tissue out of her bag. 'I've been with Victor since I was twenty-two. I'd known him for only a few months when

234

I got pregnant. It was an accident,' she went on. 'I had *no* desire to have a baby at that stage of my life. But I couldn't bring myself to . . . *not* have it, and Victor was thrilled. He vowed to make me and our baby *very* happy and I suppose I got carried away by his enthusiasm and his optimism.' Celine pressed the tissue to her eyes again. 'So we got married and four months later I had Philippe; then not long after that Victor bought this house . . .' Celine's eyes had filled again. 'Which is where I've been ever since!' She bit her lip. 'But now I need to *leave*.'

'Does Victor know?'

'Yes – but he refuses to discuss it.'

'Well . . . he clearly adores you.'

She gave a weary sigh. 'He does. But he is *so* much older than me.'

'Does that matter? After so long?'

'In some ways it doesn't.' She let out her breath. 'But the fact is, I got married too *young*. So whenever I meet a woman like you who has waited a long time to settle down I feel so . . . *envious*.'

'Envious?' I repeated. 'I thought you felt sorry for me.'

Celine looked at me in bewilderment. 'No. Because women like you have had years of fun – changing lovers, changing jobs, changing apartments, changing cities, changing your very *selves* – and then you can *still* marry and have children – while I have led just the same exist-ence, for seventeen years. Much of it has been taken up with Philippe, who of course I adore, but he will soon be making his own way in the world. So now I want to live a *different* sort of life.'

'I see . . .'

She blew her nose then looked at me desolately. 'There's no one else – in case you thought that.'

'No, no.'

'I've *never* had an affair.' Celine had said this not with pride, but with regret. 'I wish I *had* done,' she added. 'Then I might feel less discontented now. But I've told Victor that I'm unhappy and that it's my wish to leave.'

Poor man, I thought. 'So . . . what did he say?'

She swallowed. 'That he wants me to stay – that he can't live without me. He said that I'm having a crisis, because of turning forty: so I said, "Yes, Victor, I *am* having a crisis because of turning forty – precisely – because I want to do *more* with my life." Then he said that he would retire early so that we can spend more time together, travel, perhaps learn new languages, take on new challenges.'

'Then . . . why don't you take him up on that?'

'Because I want to do these things on my *own*.'

I felt a pang for Victor. 'I see.'

'I only ever meant to be in England for a year or two. After that it was my plan to travel to South America, Africa, or Indonesia. I got no further than Barnes! And as my birthday has approached I've been feeling so . . . boxed *in*.' I remembered how Celine had sat in the corner of the Knole sofa at the first sitting. *I am, as you say, boxed in.* 'So now I want to try and get back some of the freedom I had when I was a very young woman – before I am an old one.'

'But . . . how will you do that? Will you get a job? Retrain?'

'I do want to work, yes, but first I intend to find an apartment, then take things from there. I've already

started looking. I told Victor that, about a month ago.'
Celine looked at me. 'So what does he do?'

I shrugged, taken aback. 'I don't know.'

'*What* does Victor do?' she demanded again.

'I've . . . no idea.'

Celine was blinking at me furiously. 'He commissions a *portrait* of me!'

'But . . . it's your birthday present.'

'No! It *isn't*. It's a trap!'

'A trap?'

She leaned towards me. 'Can't you *see*? He's trying to fix my image in this house. He's worried that I'll leave, so he's trying to pin me to the wall.'

I nodded slowly. 'I understand . . .'

'*That's* why he's so enthusiastic about the portrait. *That's* why he wants to put it there – right *there* . . .' Celine's left index finger jabbed at the mirror. 'At the very heart of this house, because I think he believes that it'll work like magic – like *voodoo* – keeping me here, with *him*!'

'Do you still . . . love Victor?'

Celine gave a despairing shrug. 'I am very *fond* of him, but I don't want to regret, when I'm on my death bed, in perhaps *another* forty years, that I chose to remain in my safe, comfy box, with my safe, comfy husband. There . . .' She pressed the tissue to her eyes. 'You asked me whether or not I am okay. *That* is the answer.'

I sighed. 'You said you found the sittings frustrating – but I knew that wasn't the real reason why you didn't want to be painted. It was as though you were poised for flight.'

She nodded bleakly. 'I was – I still *am* . . .'

I exhaled. 'It'll take a lot of courage to do what you say you want to do. You may find you don't like it,

237

but that you can't then go back because you've burned your—'

'Bridges,' she concluded. 'I know. Well, I'll take that risk. But seeing Victor get so excited about the portrait made me feel very upset. Then Marcelle phoned, so I told her about it, but she wasn't *sympa*. So I decided to tell you.' She reached for another tissue. 'I hope you don't mind.'

'No. I'm glad you have, because at least now I understand what's been going on. But . . . what about counselling?'

'I've suggested it to Victor. But he insists that we don't have a problem. And the more I tell him that I want to leave, the more lavish his plans for my birthday become.'

'I see . . .'

'I don't *want* a big, expensive party,' Celine said bleakly. 'I don't *want* a diamond ring: I don't even want to go to Venice – it's such a romantic destination that it feels quite wrong. In fact, I don't want to celebrate my birthday at *all* because I feel so unhappy and unsettled that I think it would be dishonest. But Victor's been making all these arrangements as though nothing's amiss. So I'll be sitting there at the Dorchester, a month from now, feeling that I'm taking part in some lavish charade! I keep asking Victor to cancel it, but he refuses. So for weeks, the pressure has been building up inside me and I feel that I'm going to go . . .' Her eyes widened. '*Boom!*'

'I'm . . . sorry,' I said again, impotently. 'I wish I could say more than that, Celine – but I can't.'

'I know you can't. But I'm glad I've told you.' She sighed. 'And now we'd better get on.' She stood up, went to the mantelpiece, and checked her reflection in the mirror. Then she returned to the chair. 'I must let you do your job.'

238

'Okay . . .' I went back to the easel and picked up my palette and brush.

Then Celine lifted her head, and resumed the pose.

As I waited for Mike Johns to arrive three days later, I thought about Celine. Our conversation had been going round and round in my head. Now I understood why she hadn't wanted to be painted and why she just wouldn't sit still. I toyed with the idea of painting an open window into her portrait, or a mounted butterfly in a gold frame.

Since then I'd spent much of the time working on the picture of Grace – I had it on the easel now; and though it was almost finished I could see that it still wasn't *her*. It caught a good likeness but conveyed little sense of who Grace had been. Now I bitterly regretted having accepted the commission, and imagined the disappointment of her family and friends.

Remembering the anguished conversation that I'd had with Mike about Grace, I decided I'd put her painting away before he arrived, and I was about to take it off the easel when the phone rang.

I picked up. 'Hello?'

'*What* do you think of personalised champagne labels?'

My mother had clearly recovered from the emotional upset of the previous week and was once again fully focused on the wedding preparations. But *I* had not recovered and felt a bewildered distrust of her that was seeping into my soul like damp.

'Don't you think it would be nice?' I heard her say.

'I've no idea,' I answered. 'I didn't know that you could personalise them.'

'You can – and I think it would be rather fun for the

239

bottles to say "Chloë and Nate" with the date of the wedding. But Chloë's not keen – so I thought I'd discuss it with you.'

'Why? It's not *my* wedding – it's hers; so if Chloë doesn't like personalised champagne labels then I suggest you don't *get* them.'

'All right,' Mum said. 'No need to snap.'

'I didn't snap – I just told you what I think. And if you don't want my opinion about something, then don't ask me.'

There was a frosty silence. 'Ella – I hope you're not upset about the wedding.' I bristled at my mother's solicitous tone. 'You've been *quite* tetchy at times, darling, so it's crossed my mind that, as you're a few years older than Chloë, you might not be entirely hap—'

'Of course I'm happy for her! As happy as I possibly *could* be,' I added more truthfully. 'But . . . I'm still trying to get my head round what you told me about my father and about Lydia, and so I'm *not* in the mood to discuss wedding trivia!'

'Of course . . . I'm sorry, darling.' I heard my mother sigh. 'I should show more understanding, because it *is* hard for you. I always knew it would be. Which is precisely why I protected you from it for so long.'

'You protected me?'

'Yes. Of course.'

'You call concealing things of such huge personal significance, "protecting"?'

'I *do*. I'm not even sure that they *are* that significant. John and his daughter are, of course, your relatives, but they're relative *strangers* in that you don't know them.'

'Thanks to you, I *don't* know them – that's right!'

240

'Thanks to *him*!' she flung back. I heard her inhale, as though trying to calm herself. 'Ella,' she went on quietly, 'John and his daughter are *not* in your life. They live nine thousand miles and eight time zones away. Forget about them.'

'How *can* I, when they're my own flesh and blood? And isn't blood supposed to be—'

'Blood is *not* thicker than water,' she interjected. 'If it were, your father could *never* have done what he did!' I had to acknowledge the inescapable truth of this. 'Nor could Roy have done what *he* did,' Mum added with an air of triumph, 'which was to treat you as though you were *his*. He's never made the slightest difference between you and Chloë. You do realise that, don't you?'

I exhaled. 'Of course I do. He's been lovely to me.' *How's our Number One Girl?* 'I've never said otherwise, but—'

'Ella, I'm very worried,' I heard Mum say. 'Because you told me that you *weren't* going to contact John, but now I feel you're wavering. So let me say that *were* you to do so it would be very hard for Roy – I hope you've thought about that.'

'I have – of course I have, but . . . I'm *not* going to discuss it now.' I suddenly remembered what Polly had said. 'I just hope to God you haven't concealed anything *else*!' During the affronted silence that followed I glanced out of the window and saw Mike's car pulling up. 'But my sitter's here – I must go.'

After I'd ended the call I had to take a moment to calm myself. I splashed cold water on my cheeks then went to the mirror. As I looked at my reflection I imagined Lydia's face transposed on to it.

Drrrrrnnnngggggg!

I went downstairs and opened the door. 'Hi, Mike.' I was relieved to see that he looked a little less sombre than he had done previously. 'Congratulations, by the way.'

'On what?' He touched his chest. 'Finally remembering to wear the blue jumper?'

'No – though I *am* glad about that. I meant on the election – you increased your majority, didn't you?'

'Yes – that was a huge relief. It's been a tough time,' he added. As I followed him into the studio I saw Mike register the picture of Grace, still standing on the easel. He was staring at it.

'I'll just put that away,' I said breezily; I wished I'd done it before he got here. I quickly put it in the canvas rack then got out Mike's painting. 'Here's yours . . .' I placed it on the easel then quickly tied on my apron while Mike put his briefcase down by the sofa; then he sat in the chair. 'Right . . .' I smiled at him. 'This is our final sitting, so let's just go for it.'

I began to paint Mike's jumper, then I worked on his hair, blending a touch of grey into the sideburns; then adding some blue into the texture of his jaw. And all the time we chatted about the election and about how fraught it had been.

'But I'm glad to be part of the coalition,' he said.

'You've got a government job?'

'Yes – I was made a junior transport minister.'

'How brilliant.'

I asked Mike what he thought about Boris's bikes, and about the proposed reintroduction of the Routemaster bus. And so the time passed.

I worked intently, enjoying the scent of the paint and the

linseed. Then it came to the moment when I put in the very last thing I ever add to a portrait – the light in the eyes. That's when I feel like Pygmalion, having life breathed into his statue; because it's that little flick of white in each pupil that finally – 'ping!' – brings a portrait *alive*.

'There.' I took a few steps back. The touch of titanium white in Mike's pupils had given his portrait vitality. I put down my brush. 'We're done.'

Mike got to his feet then came and stood beside me as we studied his canvas. 'That's me,' he said wonderingly. It was as though he was seeing the portrait for the first time.

'I hope your constituency association like it,' I said. 'Above all, I hope you do.'

'I . . . do like it – but I look so *thin*.' It was as though he hadn't realised how much weight he'd shed.

I nodded. 'That was quite a challenge. Your weight loss changed so many things about you: it altered the planes of your face. I was worried that you'd appear less friendly than before, but I think you still look very approachable and warm and . . .'

'Sad,' he said.

I gazed at the portrait. 'You do look a bit – thoughtful, perhaps.'

'I look sad,' he insisted softly. 'That's what everyone will say.'

My heart sank. He was unhappy with the picture. 'If you're concerned about it, Mike, there are things I can do. I can tweak the corners of the eyes and mouth – less than a millimetre would lift your expression: but I painted what I saw. And you *did* look pretty serious a lot of the time.'

I now saw in the painting the air of tragedy that I'd noticed in Mike. I'd tried to avoid it but it had crept in. 'It'll need at least a month to dry,' I pointed out. 'Then I'll take it to be framed but—'

'Could I see it?' he asked.

'The frame? Well . . . I go to Graham and Stone on the King's Road; I was going to suggest that you go and look at their mouldings – I could come with you, if you'd like –'

Mike was shaking his head. 'I meant could I see the painting that was on the easel when I got here.'

'Oh. Sure . . .' I kicked myself again for not having put it away before he arrived. If only Mum hadn't distracted me with her maddening phone call.

I took Mike's canvas down and laid it on the floor, face up, so that it wouldn't drip. Then I went to the rack, lifted out the painting of Grace and put it on the easel.

Beautiful, sparkling, funny, warm . . .

None of those qualities were evident, I realised dismally.

Happy, loyal, brave, strong . . .

All I'd done was to replicate her features.

I heard Mike exhale. 'So is it finished?'

I chewed on my lower lip. 'It's as finished as it'll ever be. I've worked on it *so* much; I keep pushing the paint about, but I'm not happy with it. It's not . . .'

'*Real*,' Mike interjected softly as he stared at it. 'It's as if you've painted a waxwork.'

I suppressed a frustrated sigh. I didn't much like Mike's views on my portraits. I remembered what he'd said about Mum's – *she looks guarded . . . as though she's hiding something.* And he'd been right.

I folded my arms as we stood side by side, studying the portrait. 'The problem is that I never *met* Grace. So I have no memory of how she talked, or moved, or laughed – or how she felt about anything. If I'd been able to see some close-up video footage of her, that would have helped, but there isn't any – I've asked – and it's hard making someone look three-dimensional when you've only got two dimensions to go on.'

Mike was still staring at the portrait. 'It's life-like,' he said. 'But not *alive*.'

'Exactly.' I heaved a frustrated sigh. 'But I think it's as good as it gets. I'm going to have to accept that this portrait is *not* going to be my finest achievement.' I was about to put it back when, to my surprise, Mike lifted his hand to the canvas.

He pointed to the area below Grace's bottom lip. 'She had a tiny scar,' he said quietly. 'Just here. It only showed when she smiled, but as you've painted her smiling, it needs to be there.'

'Oh . . .'

'And her eyes aren't right.' He put his head to one side. 'The shape's correct, but they weren't such a pure blue – there was a lot of green in them, and the rim of the iris was a darker shade, like wet slate, which gave her gaze an intensity that you haven't caught. And she had this funny little hole, just here, on her forehead. It was tiny – smaller than a pin-head – but you could see it, if you were standing close enough – and there was a mole, just here.' He pointed to the place, his hand hovering over her cheek.

'I see . . .' I said softly. 'But—'

Mike continued to stare at the painting. 'She was

245

beautiful,' he murmured. 'She was really . . . beautiful. And if it weren't for me, she'd still be alive.'

It was as though I'd been plunged into a bath of ice water. 'What do you mean?' I stammered.

Mike blinked. 'That it's my fault that she died.'

My heart was thudding in my ribcage. 'But . . . *how*?'

He went to the sofa then sank down on to it. 'My life's been hell,' he murmured. 'It's been hell since January twentieth – since it happened. The *shock* of it . . . Then not being able to *talk* about it, all these months. Not being able to confide in anyone.' He closed his eyes as if he was exhausted. 'Let alone confess.'

'Confess . . .?' I echoed faintly. 'Confess . . . *what*?'

Mike didn't at first respond. Then he heaved a sigh so profound it seemed to come from his very depths. 'That her accident was *my* fault.'

My heart plummeted. Why was he telling *me* this? If his had been the car that had hit Grace, then he should be telling the police, not me. 'Was it *your* car?' I asked after a moment. My mouth had dried. 'Was it *your* black BMW?'

Mike looked at me in bewilderment. 'No . . . I didn't knock her off her *bike* – that's not what I mean.' Relief flooded through me. 'I only mean that if it hadn't been for me, Grace wouldn't have been cycling through Fulham Broadway that morning.'

'But . . . why *was* she?' Mike didn't reply. 'Her uncle said that they think she must have been staying with someone – but they've no idea who, as that person hasn't come forward.'

Mike closed his eyes. 'She was staying with me.'

I stared at him, dumbfounded. I'd been so taken aback by the turn the conversation had taken that my brain had simply failed to keep up. 'You were in love with Grace,' I said wonderingly.

How else could Mike have known about the tiny scar under her lip, or be able to describe the precise blue of her eyes? How else could he have known about the little hole in her forehead that could only be seen by anyone standing very close to Grace, as he must have been? 'You loved her,' I reiterated.

'Yes,' Mike said softly. 'I did.'

I sank on to a chair. 'And no one knew?'

'No one,' he confirmed blankly. 'Neither of us told a soul.'

'That's why you cancelled the sittings.' He nodded. And that's why he'd lost so much weight, and why he'd become upset when he'd talked about what had happened to Grace. That's why he'd wept when he heard 'Tears in Heaven'. 'How did you know her, Mike?'

He exhaled. 'She was a member of the London Cycling Campaign. Last September she and two others came to talk to the cross-party transport committee that I'm on. We discussed cycle lanes and whether there should be more red routes on busier roads – extra mirrors on lorries – all those issues. But I found it almost impossible to focus on anything other than Grace. She was so beautiful,' he went on quietly. 'It was as though there was a light on inside her – a sort of dancing light that spilled in all directions.'

I glanced at the portrait: now it seemed all the more flat and dull.

I heard Mike sigh. 'After that meeting I couldn't get

Grace out of my mind; so I phoned her, and asked her if she'd have a drink with me sometime. To my delighted surprise, she said yes. Then we met again and we realised that we were very drawn to each other.' Mike clasped his hands in front of him. 'Sarah and I had been unhappy for a long time: we'd been trying to decide whether to stay together or call it a day. Then I met Grace,' he added with a kind of wonderment. 'And I was happier than I've ever been in my adult life.'

'I remember how happy you seemed – when you first came here, last December.'

Mike nodded. 'Now I'm still trying to take in the fact that I'll never see Grace again, or talk to her, or hear her laugh, or hold her . . .' His voice caught. 'And I haven't been able to talk to anyone about it; so I've felt completely . . . alone. I wondered about going to a bereavement counsellor, but I was worried that it might get out – it would have ended up in the papers.' He looked at me. 'Though that's *not* why I'm telling you. I'm telling you because your painting isn't right, Ella – and I *want* it to be right.'

'But . . . what actually *happened*? That morning?'

Mike put his hands on his knees, as if bracing himself against some impact. 'Grace had stayed with me the night before,' he began quietly. 'Sarah was in New York and wasn't due to return until the Thursday morning, but early on the Wednesday morning I saw that a text had come in from her to say that she was flying back a day early. I realised that she'd be home within two hours; so I told Grace this, and she said that she'd leave straight away. I asked her to wait until it was light, but she said she wanted to go back to her flat so that she could change.'

Mike swallowed. 'I urged her to be careful, because there'd been a hard frost. She told me that she was always careful, then she put on her helmet and I kissed her goodbye . . .' Mike smiled. 'It's not easy kissing someone when they're wearing a bicycle helmet, and we were laughing about it.' He paused. 'Sarah had texted me that she didn't have her keys, so I waited until she arrived, at about nine, then I set off for the House of Commons.

Mike heaved a deep sigh. 'As I drove up to the New King's Road I saw that the right-hand turn to Fulham Broadway was blocked off. I assumed that this was because of roadworks and so didn't think anything of it as I followed the diversion. Then – I had London Radio on – I heard a report about a woman cyclist who'd been injured following a hit-and-run incident at Fulham Broadway. I immediately worried that it might have been Grace, so I called her on my Bluetooth, but she didn't reply. I told myself that this was because she'd be in class, but to reassure myself I phoned her school, without saying who I was. They said that Grace hadn't yet arrived. By now I was in a panic. When I got to work I phoned the Chelsea and Westminster Hospital, as that's where anyone injured at Fulham Broadway would be taken. The nurse in the intensive care unit wouldn't confirm or deny that Grace was there; so then I knew that it *was* her.'

'How terrible . . .'

Mike's eyes were shining with tears. 'It was . . . *hell*. I had a meeting to go to, then a lunch; after that, there was a debate. I don't know how I got through that day. All I wanted to do was to rush to the hospital, but I knew that I couldn't even if I'd been free, because Grace's parents would be there. All I could do was to keep checking the news, which I did, every other minute. By now there was a photo of Grace, and a brief biography of her on a number of news websites. And I was annoyed, because they'd all got her surname spelt wrong, without the "e", and I was staring at it, furious that they couldn't have got something as basic as that right, when the piece was suddenly updated to say that . . . that she'd . . .' Mike's head dropped to his hands.

'I'm sorry,' I breathed.

'It was *my* fault,' he said. 'If she hadn't been with me, then she wouldn't have been rushing away from my house in the icy darkness because my wife was coming home. Then she wouldn't have been hit by a car: then she wouldn't have struck her head on the kerb: and then she wouldn't have been in hospital . . . *dying*.' He covered his eyes with his left hand. 'So *that's* why I feel responsible for what happened to Grace. And I've spent the last four months pretending that everything's normal, when my life's been a living hell. I hardly eat. I can't sleep. Work's been my only distraction from the pain and stress of a bereavement that I can never admit to.'

'So your wife doesn't know?'

Mike shook his head. 'She thinks I'm like this because of the problems we've had.' He let out his breath. 'There's no one in the world that I can tell. But when I realised that you were going to *paint* Grace, I was . . . shocked.' He blinked. 'I wanted to talk to you about her then; I wanted to tell you everything I knew about her, but I bit my lip, because I was afraid. But when I saw the portrait just now, and saw how much is . . . *missing* from it, I knew I *had* to tell you, whatever the consequences.'

I nodded slowly. 'I won't tell anyone, Mike.'

'Please . . . don't.'

'But her parents – they'd surely want to know; they need to understand why she was where she was.'

'No,' Mike said bleakly. 'I couldn't face them. They'd say that I was a sleazy married man who'd messed about with their daughter. They'd blame me for her death. And I don't need them to do that, because I'm going to be blaming myself for the rest of my life.'

'But you urged Grace to stay until it was light – she chose to leave. It's not your fault that she was knocked off her bike – that could have happened to her in broad daylight, in good conditions – she was . . . unlucky. But . . . didn't she even tell a best friend about you?'

'She simply told her closest friend that she'd started seeing someone called Mike, and that she was happy – which she was.'

'Wouldn't your number have been on her mobile phone?'

'Her mobile was never found. It might have gone down a grating or been crushed by a van or lorry and the pieces swept up. But yes, my number was on it – and all my messages.' Mike inhaled. 'And I've got all her messages on mine.' He put his hand into his pocket, pulled out his phone and looked at it. 'I read them over and over again. And I listen to her voicemails to get that momentary illusion that she's still alive, and I . . .' Mike was pressing the buttons now, and I realised that he was going to play me Grace's voice messages. I didn't want to hear them.

'Mike. I really don't—'

'No, please . . . you *must*.' As he handed me the phone my heart sank. Then, as I saw what was on the screen, it lifted again . . .

251

There was Grace. She was leaning against a kitchen counter, laughing into the lens. *Why are you filming me?* I heard her say. *Because I'm nuts about you*, Mike answered. Grace laughed, then picked up a bowl of something and offered it to him. *Then have a Brazil*, she giggled. *I hope this isn't going on YouTube*, she teased. *Certainly not*, Mike said. *It's so that I can take my phone out from time to time during the day and look at you and feel that I'm with you, because that's a wonderful feeling.*

Now, as Grace turned, I could see her profile; I could see the prominence of her cheekbones, the slight flare of her jaw, the curve and shape of her ear and the length and angle of her throat. *Smile, Grace* I heard Mike say. She turned back to the lens, smiled shyly and blew him a kiss. Then the screen went dark.

Mike got to his feet and picked up his briefcase. For a moment I thought he was going to leave. But now he was opening his briefcase and pulling out a charger. He inserted the jack into his mobile then handed the whole thing to me. 'You can copy this on to your hard drive while I wait.'

'Yes. I can. Of course I can. Thanks, Mike. *Thank you . . .*' I plugged the cable into my computer, opened a file then downloaded the video and clicked on 'Save'. *Saving . . .* Then I hit 'Play'. There, enlarged to the full width of my screen was Grace's living, breathing, moving, talking, laughing, smiling face. I could see everything I needed to see – the form and depth and mobility of her features and, most importantly, the life in them.

Then I looked at the portrait and knew what to do.

NINE

I spent most of Saturday engrossed in Grace's painting – replaying Mike's footage of her over and over again, and wondering whether he'd ever be able to tell anyone about his relationship with her: I wondered whether he'd ever be able to tell his wife – after fifteen years of marriage, perhaps he wished that he could. I wondered whether Mike would go to Grace's memorial service or whether he'd feel that he should stay away. Then I wondered what one word *he* would have chosen to encapsulate his feelings about her. As my brush moved across the canvas I thought about my mother and about John; within twenty-four hours he'd be in London – my heart began to pound. Now I thought about Lydia, and then about Iris and Celine, before my thoughts returned, as they always did, to Nate.

He'd messaged me earlier in the week to say that he'd be returning from Stockholm on Saturday so wouldn't be able to make this week's sitting. I consoled myself with the thought that the delay would at least mean that the portrait process would continue for longer. I was tempted to make deliberately slow progress in order to justify asking him for a few extra sittings.

On Sunday I got up late, showered, pulled on jeans and a T-shirt and went out. I intended to power-walk up to Sloane Square and back, but as I crossed the railway bridge I decided to turn down Lots Road and have a look at the auction house. *Previewing Now* announced the sandwich board on the pavement outside. I pushed on the swing doors and went into the huge, hangar-like room. I looked at the Persian carpets hanging on their rails, and the suites of modern furniture and the assortment of silver plate. There was a big leather rhinoceros, a footstool upholstered with a Union Jack, and a rather lovely silver ink well in the shape of a shell. I peered at it in its glass case, tempted to leave a bid for it.

'That's George the Third,' said a familiar voice. As I turned and saw Nate I felt my face flush with pleasure and surprise – and discomfiture. I wished that I'd worn something nicer, or at least put on a little make-up.

'What are *you* doing here?' I glanced round, half-expecting to see Chloë amongst the people inspecting the lots.

Nate shrugged. 'I just came out for a walk. I sometimes come down here on Sunday mornings for the interest of it – occasionally I buy something. Anyway, that inkpot . . .' he flipped through the catalogue in his hands, '. . . is London silver, circa 1810, made by Thomas Wallis.

'Right . . . and . . . is . . . Chloë here?'

Nate shook his head. 'She's gone to see your folks.'

'Really? I haven't spoken to her for a while.'

254

'I only got back from Stockholm last night: so she said that she'd let me off coming with her because she just wants to talk to them about wedding things . . . Anyway, . . . I'm at a bit of a loose end.' I nodded. 'And . . . what are you doing now?'

'Erm . . . nothing much.'

'Good – because I was just about to go and find myself some lunch. Will you join me?'

'Yes.' I looked at my jeans. 'As long as it's not anywhere smart.'

Nate smiled. 'You look great. So . . . where shall we go?'

'Megan's Deli?' I suggested. 'Though that gets busy on Sundays. Or there are a couple of places on the river . . .

'Let's try that,' Nate decided.

So Nate and I walked down Lots Road in the shadow of the power station, then we turned on to the Thames Path and strolled along the embankment, past the house-boats and barges, towards Albert Bridge. Terns wheeled and dived above the water. The day was warm, so we just walked on, talking about politics, and the weather, the price of groceries and the last film we'd each seen.

'What about this?' Nate said as we came to the Cheyne Walk Brasserie.

'Looks good.'

We managed to get a corner table and sank on to the blue leather banquette.

'Would you like a glass of wine?' Nate said as we looked at the menu.

'Yes – please.'

'How about a bottle?'

'No – I couldn't manage a whole bottle.'

'To share, I mean. With me.'

'Oh – a much better idea.'

Nate laughed. 'It's funny seeing you outside of the studio,' he said. 'You're so much more relaxed, though I miss having you staring at me in that insane way of yours.'

'I don't stare on Sundays. I give my eyeballs the day off.' Nate placed our order and the waiter quickly returned with the wine and filled our glasses. 'So . . .' I raised my glass. 'Cheers.'

Nate lifted his. '*Salute.*'

Over the smoked salmon starter the conversation turned to Nate's father – I thought, with a rush of adrenalin, about my own father, who would perhaps even now be landing in London, if he wasn't already here. I tried to push the thought away.

'Ella,' said Nate, 'can I ask you something?'

'Sure. What?'

'It's a bit personal.'

'Really? Like – what's my favourite colour? Well, if you must know, it's phthalocyanine turquoise, with transparent oxide yellow coming a close second. What's yours?'

'Er . . . green. But that's not what I was going to ask. I was going to ask you . . . tell me to get lost, if you want to, but how could your mother . . .' Nate gave a bewildered shrug. 'How could she *not* have told you something so huge?'

'Chloë's obviously mentioned what's happened.'

He nodded. 'Your father . . . *did* contact you.'

'Yes. In fact he'd already done so when I talked to you about him that day.'

'Ah . . .'

'But I didn't tell you because, well . . . I was worried that you might tell Chloë, who might have told Mum.'

'I know how to keep a secret, Ella,' Nate said gently. 'But *now* I understand why you were so upset that time . . . I just . . . *hated* seeing you like that.'

I realised that Nate *had* simply been consoling me when he'd held me in his arms that day. As my mother had correctly identified, he was a compassionate sort of man – and a tactile one, not afraid to give someone a hug if they were feeling low. I banished my dangerous, deluded and futile fantasy that his touch had ever meant anything more.

'So . . . do you think you'll want to see . . . John?' Nate asked. 'And your sister?'

My sister . . . ? 'My sister' had only ever meant Chloë. Now it meant another woman, who I'd met just once, for a few moments, when we were both very young children. 'I . . . don't *know*. I'm still really confused . . . so . . . I'd rather not talk about it, if that's okay.'

'Of course,' Nate murmured. 'I didn't mean to intrude.'

'You weren't intruding.' I sipped my wine. 'How could I possibly think you were when I've already told you so much about it. But there's enough going on in the family at the moment, with the wedding, so I just want to . . . park it all for now.'

Nate nodded. 'I understand,' He deftly turned the conversation to other things and the awkwardness of the moment passed. I felt so happy just being with him, in this unexpected way, that I had to stop myself from smiling too much. *I've had an extra three hours with*

257

him, I reflected. As the waiter brought the bill. I reached
for my bag.

Nate shook his head. 'Put that away, Ella.'

'But . . .'

'I'm Italian – I don't go Dutch; anyway, I invited you.'

'Well, I'm glad you did. It's been lovely Nate. Thanks.'

As we strolled back along the embankment, Nate's phone
rang.

He reached into his pocket. 'I'm sorry – I'd better . . .'

'It's okay.' I hoped the call wasn't from Chloë. A call
from Chloë would break the spell.

'Hi, Chloë,' Nate said. 'Yes . . . I'm fine.'

Her clear, light voice cut through the ether. '. . . still in
Richmond,' I heard her say. '. . . so where are you, then?'

'Well . . .' Nate had flushed. I wondered whether he'd
tell Chloë about our lunch. 'I've just bumped into Ella.'

'How *funny* – well, give her my love.'

He glanced at me. 'Sure. So . . . see you later, Chloë.'

'Yes,' she said warmly. 'I'll see you later, darling. I
can't *wait*.'

When I got back to the house there was a message from
Roy on my answerphone.

'I'm sorry I haven't been in touch with you about our
lunch,' he said when I called him back. 'I've been covering
for a colleague, so life's been frantic; but now I've got
a few days off, so would tomorrow be okay?'

'Yes – where shall we meet?'

'I thought somewhere close to you. How about that
pub on the King's Road – the Chelsea Potter? I'm sure
you know it.'

258

'I do.' It was dangerously close to the Café de la Paix. 'I'm . . . not sure about meeting there, Roy.'

'Well . . . it would be convenient for us both as I can just walk up to Sloane Square tube afterwards, but it doesn't matter – we can go somewhere else. What about—'

'It's okay,' I said suddenly. 'The Chelsea Potter's fine.'

'Good. So I'll see you there at, what . . . one?'

'Could we make it half past twelve?' Then we'd easily be out by two-thirty, which would give me time to leave the danger zone before three o'clock.

'Half twelve it is then,' said Roy.

I went up to the King's Road an hour beforehand as there were some things I needed to do. First I went into Graham and Stone and bought lots of oil paints, some canvas stretchers, and a few brushes. I also looked at frames, and decided that the Dutch Black with the brass scrolling would suit Mike's portrait. I took a photo of it to e-mail to him. Then I went up to Waterstone's as there was a new book about Whistler that I wanted to buy. On the way there, I passed the Café de la Paix. I looked through the full-length glass window at the simple interior. How strange to think that in three hours time my father would be seated at one of those tables. I quickened my step, and walked on.

Now I wondered whether I should send him a text to say that I wouldn't be coming. I hadn't replied to any of his e-mails, because to do so, if only to say that I didn't wish to see him, would have been to begin a dialogue with him that I just didn't want. Even so, I felt guilty at the thought of wasting his time. Then I decided that there was no need for me to feel guilty about anything vis-à-vis my father. If he chose to spend a few hours in a café on the King's Road, then that was a matter for him.

In Waterstone's I looked for the Whistler biography but couldn't find it. As the assistant went to see if there might be a copy in the stock room, I browsed through the fiction on the tables; I was about to pick up the new Kate Atkinson when I noticed several piles of Sylvia Shaw's latest novel, *Dead Right*.

I read the back with its gushing hyperbole: *Riveting . . . Daily Mail; Thrilling . . . GQ; It's Shaw good! . . . Express*. Now I studied the author's photo. It was more flattering than the one in *Hello!*, but she still looked rather grim-faced, as though she thought it inappropriate for someone who wrote about murder and mayhem to smile. I turned to the dedication page – *For Max* – and marvelled that she'd never known about her husband's affair.

The bookshop assistant reappeared and told me that they didn't have the Whistler in stock, so I ordered it then had a quick look at the greetings cards. There was already a selection for Father's Day so I bought one to give Roy – *I've Got the World's Greatest Dad:* as I left the shop I reflected that I pretty much had. It was Roy who'd taken me to the park and taught me to ride a bike. It was Roy who'd helped me with my homework and who'd turned out to watch me in school hockey matches, concerts and plays. It was Roy who'd coped with my teenage years, and who'd regularly come out at two in the morning to get me safely home from parties and clubs. It was Roy who'd paid my art school fees and who'd lent me half the deposit to buy my house.

I pushed on the door of the Chelsea Potter and there he was, on the other side of the wood-panelled saloon, waving at me.

I went over to his table, greeted him with a kiss, then hung the carrier bag containing my new paints and brushes on the back of my chair. As I sat down he asked me what I'd like to drink then handed me a menu. I glanced at it. 'I'll just have some soup.'

'Have more than that, Ella.'

'I'm not hungry, thanks; I'm a bit . . . stressed.'

'Well, that's hardly surprising. Right . . . I'll go and order.' Roy went to the bar and returned with a pint of lager for him and my diet Coke.

We sipped our drinks then he lowered his glass. 'Ella, I just wanted to talk to you,' he said. 'Because I felt it was important, firstly, that I should tell you, face to face, that I had *no* idea about, well . . . what you've at long last learned. If I *had* known, I'd have compelled your mother to tell you.'

'Which is why she concealed it from you too. Mum's good at keeping secrets, isn't she?' I stared at the island of ice in my drink. 'I keep thinking that she should have been a spy, not a dancer.'

Roy laughed softly. 'I love your mother, Ella, but she's handled things with you *so* badly. I'm appalled at the degree to which she's . . . *manipulated* things.'

'Oh, she has.' *I know how I want things to be.* I looked at Roy. 'But did you ever guess? About Lydia, I mean?'

He shook his head. 'I did once ask your mother whether she thought that you might have any siblings in Australia. She replied that she didn't want to think

261

about whether or not there were – which wasn't a lie, and wasn't the truth, as we now know. But the second, more important, thing I wanted to say to you today was that I feel your mother's putting pressure on you *not* to reply to . . . to your . . .' Roy's voice had caught.

'To John,' I said gently.

'To John. Yes . . .' He cleared his throat, then paused. 'She's saying that you shouldn't have anything to do with him – on *my* account. But I just want you to know that, if you do decide to contact . . . John, then, I'd be . . . fine about it. I'd support you, Ella.'

'Well . . . that would make you very unpopular with Mum.'

He shrugged. 'So be it. You must put your own feelings before hers – or mine.' He paused while the barman brought my minestrone and Roy's fish pie. 'Anyway,' he exhaled painfully. 'You need to give it careful thought.'

'Thanks, Roy, but I already have.' He glanced at me anxiously. 'And I've decided that I'm *not* going to get in touch with him.'

A flicker of relief passed across Roy's features. 'Well . . . it's not long since you found out. Your feelings may change,' he added fairly.

'I don't think they will. So I'm not going to answer his e-mails, and I'm certainly not going to see him.'

'See him?'

I broke my bread roll. 'I wouldn't see him even if he was in London right now. I wouldn't see him even if he was in *this* part of London, just a few minutes away from where we're sitting. I'd walk *right* past him, without giving him so much as a glance.'

Roy looked surprised. 'Well, I think that would be . . . *sad*.'

'*He* caused enough sadness, didn't he?' I began to eat my soup.

Roy picked up his fork. 'People make mistakes, Ella.'

'They do.' I lowered my spoon. 'But what he did wasn't a "mistake" – it was a calculated choice. That's why I can't forgive him.'

'Well . . . please *try*. Not least because the negativity you feel will only weigh you down, spoiling a part of your life.'

We ate in silence for a while. I looked at Roy. 'And has Chloë said much about it to you? She's said nothing to me.'

'She just said that she wasn't surprised, though I think that she was quite upset. I know she doesn't like the idea of you having another sister any more than she ever liked the idea of you having another father. When she was about five and had worked everything out, she used to tell me, when I was putting her to bed, that she was afraid that John would come to the house one day and take you away.'

I laughed darkly. 'An unlikely scenario, given that he was nine thousand miles away and not remotely interested in me.'

'You don't know that he wasn't.'

'I *do* – because he never got in touch. It was as though I was suddenly . . . *nothing* to him.' I pushed my soup bowl aside. 'But now that we're talking about all of this, Roy, there's something I've long meant to ask you – about my adoption.'

Roy looked at me. 'And what's that?'

'Whether, when you applied to adopt me, John had to give his consent.'

'Let me think . . .' Roy narrowed his eyes. 'When your mother and I first saw the solicitor about it, he *did* say that John would have to agree to it, yes, presumably because his name would have been on your birth certificate. But your mum handled the application herself. All I had to do was to go along to the court one morning and satisfy the judge that I wasn't insane, didn't have a criminal record, was indeed married to your mother – she'd already submitted our marriage certificate – and that I was, as stated in the application, employed as a surgeon and would be able to provide for you. I do remember the judge asking your mum about John's whereabouts: she said that she had no idea where he was.'

'But that wasn't true. She knew that he was in Australia. Didn't she tell the judge that?'

'No. If she had done I'd definitely have remembered it, as I didn't know that myself then – any more than you did.'

'That's right. I only got *that* out of her when I was eleven.'

'Well, as you say, your mother's good at keeping secrets.'

'But . . . surely she *would* have had an address for him, because he would have to have signed the divorce papers?'

'Well . . . I'm not sure whether or not he did sign them. In cases of desertion, the divorce is granted automatically, after two years, and I always had the impression that that's what had happened in their case.' Roy shrugged.

'But the fact that Sue was able to say that John had made no contact for three years, as it was by then, made adoption by me, as your stepfather, fairly straightforward. But why are you asking about it now?'

Because it's been puzzling me, and I didn't want to ask Mum as I don't want to talk to her about *any* of it at the moment. I don't think *she* does either; she's just carrying on as though everything's normal.'

Roy shrugged. 'She's probably blocked it all out – that's always been her way with anything she finds painful or unpleasant. Down come the mental shutters. And of course she's very preoccupied with the wedding, as am I. I want Chloë to have a really memorable day.'

'I'm sure it will be.' I thought again of Nate, standing at the altar, turning to look at Chloë. 'Not long now.'

Roy nodded. 'The RSVP's are arriving thick and fast – everyone's coming.'

'That's good.'

'Anyway . . . would you like a dessert, Ella?'

'Oh – no thanks – in fact . . .' A jolt ran through me as I glanced at my watch. 'It's half past two – I have to go. Right now.'

'Sure,' Roy said, looking slightly surprised. 'But I'm glad we've had this chat.'

'So am I, Roy.' As he went to the bar to pay I remembered what Polly had said. *He'd support you, Ella. I know he would.* She'd been right – but so had I, in predicting that he'd be upset. I was glad to know that I wouldn't be exposing him to any more painful feelings.

Roy had to wait a few minutes to be served, so by the time we left the pub it had gone twenty to three.

'Thank you for lunch,' I said to Roy. 'And thank you for everything you've said.' Roy smiled, then we hugged goodbye. As he set off for Sloane Square I went the other way, with a sick feeling gathering in my stomach at the thought of how close my father now was.

I tried to distract myself by thinking about work. I was going to see Iris again in two days' time. Then there'd be another sitting with Nate on Saturday morning. Then I was going to do Celine's last three sittings over three days as time was short. I'd also spoken to the couple in Chichester – Mr and Mrs Berger. They wanted the portrait for their silver wedding celebration in mid July, so I was going to go there in early June and get it done in a week. I was glad I'd bought the new paints – I was going to need them.

I stopped dead. I'd left the paints at the pub. I'd put the bag on the back of my chair and had forgotten it when we'd left. I'd have to go and get it.

I ran back to the Chelsea Potter, where the bag had already been handed in. I had to wait while someone went upstairs to the office to retrieve it, so by the time I left it was five to three. My father would be arriving. My heart banging, I began to walk down the road, fast: and there the café was, just a hundred yards or so ahead. What if he was there already and saw me go by? What if he rushed out and pleaded with me in the street? What had I been *thinking* in agreeing to have lunch within five minutes of where *he* was going to be? Had it been raining, I could have concealed myself beneath an umbrella, but it was a bright, sunny day and I'd only have made myself more conspicuous.

Now the Café de la Paix was less than fifty yards

away. I decided to cross to the other side of the road. I stopped at the kerb and waited for a number 22 bus to go past and was momentarily distracted by the sight, all the way up the back of it, of Polly's massively magnified thumb and forefinger, holding a memory card. Then I realised that crossing the road was hardly going to help as I'd be no less visible from the other side.

Suddenly I saw a taxi coming towards me, its carriage-work gleaming like treacle in the sunshine. I hailed it, climbed in, then sank right back into the corner of the seat as we drove past Starbucks, Sweaty Betty and India Jane. Now we were within ten yards of Café de la Paix. With its full-length glass windows it was as transparent as a fish tank.

I could see the barrista making coffee, and a man of about sixty standing at the counter, but he was too tall and thin to be John. Waiting behind him were a couple of smoochy-looking teenagers. At a table in the window was a forty-something woman in a blue sleeveless dress, reading the *Independent*. I felt heat flood into my cheeks. For there, at the other window table, was my father. His face looked weathered and lined, but he was otherwise quite recognisable from the photo he'd sent. He was still handsome and broad-shouldered, though his hair was iron-grey now, and swept back, giving him a leonine appearance. He was wearing a light-coloured suit over a white shirt.

By now we had drawn almost level with the café. I pressed myself further back into the seat and hoped that he wouldn't spot me through the taxi's quarter-light window. There was a large 'thank you for not smoking' sticker on it, so I sunk right down so that it would at least partly obscure me, and lifted my hand to the side of my face. Through my splayed fingers I could see that my father wasn't looking at the taxi at all; his eyes flickered over the passers-by, his head turning subtly from side to side. Now he'd spotted a dark-haired woman of about my age, but as he saw that she wasn't me, he glanced away. I expected the taxi to crawl past the café, but to my dismay we'd stopped – there was a red light ahead. We were right outside now, the full length of the taxi reflected in the window. All that separated me from my father were two panes of glass. As I saw the anxiety on his face my heart contracted. I imagined jumping out of the cab then going into the café.

How can I *not* do that, I asked myself miserably, when he's sitting there, *right* there, in that window, looking out for me? Then I thought of myself, aged five, sitting at the window in our flat looking out for *him*. Hoping to see *him*. I'd sat there not just for a few hours, but for months . . .

I saw the traffic light change. We moved forward, quickly picking up speed, and my father was behind me now, as the taxi drove on.

'It's so nice to see you again,' Iris smiled as she opened the door of her flat to me two days later. 'This is our third sitting, isn't it?' she asked as I stepped inside.

'It is: we had a gap because you were away for a while, and then you had that cold. But it doesn't matter,' I added, as I followed her down the hallway. 'I once had a sitter who was so busy that her portrait took a year to complete.'

Iris gave me a rueful smile. 'Given my age, I don't think we can risk it taking *that* long.'

We went into the sitting room. 'You look in fine fettle, Iris.'

'I'm not doing *too* badly.' She sat on the sofa, leaning her stick against the arm. 'I was thinking this morning that I've already outlived my mother by twenty years. But then she'd been worn down by the war and her life wasn't easy afterwards.'

I put my equipment down. 'What about your father? Did he reach a good age?'

Even as I asked the question I remembered that Iris hadn't told me anything about her father – she'd only ever mentioned her stepfather.

'My father died at thirty-seven,' she replied quietly.

'So young . . .'

I wondered if Iris would explain what had happened to him, but she didn't seem to want to say anything more. Now, as I opened the easel, I thought about my own father. He'd be getting ready to leave London; he'd probably be making his way to the airport right now . . .

I got out my palette and began to mix the colours.

'Was I sitting like this?' Iris asked.

I looked at her, then at the canvas. 'You were. But if you could just fold your right hand over your left – you've got your left over your right, and if you could lift your chin a little . . . and look *this* way . . . That's lovely.' I picked up a medium-sized brush.

As I began to paint we chatted about what was in the news. Then Iris told me that Sophia had gone to the Chelsea Flower Show this morning, but that she herself had always preferred the flower show at Hampton Court. Then she asked me whether I ever held exhibitions of my work.

'No. The Royal Society of Portrait Painters have an annual show and I might take part in that next year, otherwise I don't exhibit my work, because I'm painting to commission.'

'You *should* have an exhibition of your own,' Iris said.

'Well . . . maybe I will. I could ask a few of my more recent sitters to lend me their portraits; they could all come in the clothes that I'd painted them in. Would you come if I did that, Iris?'

'I'd be delighted to.'

I could do it in September, I reflected, on my birthday. 'I'll give it some thought,' I said. Then I asked Iris about the paintings on her sitting-room walls: there was a very fine Scottish landscape, a couple of beautifully executed botanical paintings and a geometric-looking nude that she told me was by Euan Uglow. All I really wanted to talk about was the picture of the two little girls.

'Iris, I hope you don't mind my asking,' I said at last, 'but when I first came here you started telling me about the painting in your bedroom – the one by Guy Lennox?'

She nodded. 'I remember. I didn't finish telling you the story, did I?'

'No, though I'd . . . love to hear it – if you're happy to tell me.' It had occurred to me that she might have changed her mind for some reason.

'I *am* happy to tell you – in fact, it was on my mind to do so. But I'm a little stiff today, would you mind fetching the painting for me?'

'Of course.'

I put down my palette and brush then went out of the sitting room and along the hallway to where I remembered Iris's room was. There was the picture, in its usual place by her bed. I looked at it for a moment, captivated, as before, by the tenderness of the composition: and now I could see that there was somehow an elegiac mood to it. I lifted it off its hook, leaving a ghostly rectangle, then took it to Iris.

'Thank you,' she said. She placed the painting on her lap. 'I can't recall where I had got to.'

I went back to the easel. 'You told me that Guy Lennox was commissioned to paint a very rich man called Peter Loden, who then started an affair with his wife.' I picked up the palette and brush.

Iris nodded. 'That's right. It must have been dreadful for Guy. But – and *this* was where I left off, I remember now – far worse was to come. Edith told Guy that she wanted a divorce – that was a bad enough blow; but she added that she was not prepared to admit to having committed adultery.'

I began to paint Iris's hair. 'I see.'

'She argued that to have her name besmirched in a "scandal" would damage the girls socially in years to come. She said that in order to protect them from this *he* would have to be the adulterous party.'

'Oh . . .'

'She added that if he didn't consent to this, then she'd make sure that he never saw them again. So, caught between a rock and a hard place, Guy agreed.'

'Poor man.'

'Poor man, indeed,' Iris concurred. 'So he went to a hotel somewhere on the south coast, where he met a young woman who'd taken part in this kind of charade before – for a fee, naturally. The chambermaid duly opened the door the next morning to see them sitting up in bed together, and within three months Edith had her divorce. But it turned out that Guy had fallen on his sword for nothing. When, a short time later, Edith married Peter Loden, she changed the girls' surname to his. Guy, outraged, went to court to contest it, at which point Edith carried out her earlier threat. She got an injunction, barring him from having any contact with his children, who were then just over two years, and twelve months.'

I mixed a little more zinc white into the hair tone. 'But how was Edith able to do this?'

'She made all sorts of claims against Guy – the main one being that he was mentally unstable, due to having been gassed during the war. But she must have convinced the judge, because the injunction was granted. For a period of five years Guy was not to contact, or attempt to contact, his children.'

I lowered my brush. 'How terrible.'

'It was . . . *inhuman*. But he went on working – he needed the distraction of it almost more than the money. And three years later, in the summer of 1934, he was walking through St James Park. He was carrying his easel because he'd just been doing a sitting. As he approached the lake, he saw two little girls of about five and four. He knew at once that they were his daughters. He stood and watched them for a while. They were playing with a red ball, and they had a dog with them, a Norfolk terrier called Bertie.' I wondered whether Iris also knew the names of the girls, but I didn't like to stop her in mid-flow to ask.

She narrowed her eyes as she continued. 'Their nanny was sitting on a bench nearby, knitting. Guy didn't at first know what to do. He didn't speak to the girls – not just because he was forbidden by law from doing so, but because it was clear that they didn't recognise him. So he spoke to the nanny: he explained that he was a portraitist and asked whether he might have her permission to paint this charming scene. Knowing exactly who he was, she agreed.' Now I understood the nanny's expression in the picture – it was one of complicity. 'So . . .' Iris shifted on the sofa a little. 'Guy set up his easel a few yards away, and painted the girls while they played, occasionally chatting to them. This was the first contact that he'd had with his children for more than three years.'

'How sad,' I murmured.

'It was tragic.' Iris heaved a deep sigh. 'He came to the park every morning for the next four days and continued to paint them. But when he went there the fifth day, they'd gone. He later discovered that their mother had found out – the girls must have said something – and their visits to the park had been stopped.' She paused. 'Guy Lennox never saw his children again.'

'Not even when the injunction ended?'

'No. Because by then it was too late.'

'Why? Didn't his daughters *want* to see him after so long?'

'No – that wasn't the reason.' Iris shook her head. 'In the spring of 1936 the Spanish Civil War started. In August of that year Guy joined the International Brigade and went to Spain. He survived fierce fighting near Madrid . . . But in March 1937 he was killed at Guadalajara . . .' Tears shone in her eyes.

'Poor man,' I murmured. '*Now* I understand.'

Iris looked at me, sharply. 'What do you understand?'

'Well . . . why the painting makes you feel so sad. It's a . . . heartbreaking story.' Iris nodded slowly. 'But, you said that you bought the painting on an impulse, knowing nothing about it – not even who it was by; so you obviously researched its background very thoroughly.'

'I did. Most of it I learned in 1963 from my husband's friend, Hugh, who took it to show to his uncle.'

'You said that his uncle had known Guy Lennox.'

'Iris nodded. He'd known him quite well. And when Hugh brought the painting back and told me what his uncle had said about it, I was . . . shocked.' She paused. 'I then took it back to the antique shop where I'd bought it, and I asked the man there about the woman who'd sold it to him. He found her name and address in his purchase book and as she lived close by I went and knocked on her door. She was happy to talk to me and confirmed that she'd found the picture in her late brother's attic. He'd never married or had children, so she was clearing his house.'

'You said that he'd worked for Guy Lennox.'

'That's right – he'd been his studio assistant, and an artist himself. She'd thought that the painting might have been by her brother, but since she already had a number of his pictures she'd decided to sell this one. When I told her what I had found out about it she guessed that her brother had taken it to his own home, after Guy's death, in order to look after it.'

'Would Guy necessarily have told him who the girls in the painting were?'

'Perhaps not – it was so very personal; but she thought it likely that her brother *had* known as the two had got on very well. She thought that it might have been his intention to try and give the picture to the girls. But then the war started and everything was in chaos, so it had just stayed in his attic until he himself died.'

'You went to so much trouble about the painting, Iris.'

'I did.' She looked at me for a moment or two. It was an odd, penetrating sort of look and I suddenly realised that she must be tired and was hoping that I'd go. I glanced at my watch. It was ten past three. The sitting was over.

I began to pack up my easel and paints. 'Thank you for telling me about it, Iris. I'm glad to have heard the story, sad though it is.' I clipped her portrait into the canvas carrier then gathered up the dust sheet. 'So . . . is the same time next week okay for you?'

'Yes,' she answered. 'It's fine.' She pushed herself to her feet. 'So . . . I'll see you then, my dear.'

I picked everything up and we walked to the door. I smiled goodbye, then went out, pulling the front door closed behind me. I walked to the lift and pressed the button. I heard it grind upwards, then it clanked to a halt. And I was about to pull back the grille, when my hand stopped. I turned and looked at Iris's front door: then, with a fluttering in my gut, I walked back down the corridor and knocked on it.

After a moment or two I heard the chain being taken off. As she opened the door Iris looked at me expectantly.

'Iris,' I said, 'I've come back because I'd been wondering what the girls in the painting were called. And I've just realised – they were called Agnes and Iris.'

Iris nodded slowly. 'Yes.'

'It's you in the painting – you and your sister.' She nodded again. 'And Guy Lennox was your father.'

275

'He was.' She pulled back the door and I stepped inside. 'I was waiting for you to understand, Ella. I knew you would.'

'I was so absorbed in the story that I didn't . . . make the connection. Then it suddenly came to me with this little "thud", here.' I laid my hand on my chest. 'But *that's* why the painting makes you feel so sad.'

'Yes. That's why. Please come . . .' I put my easel and the canvas carrier down then followed Iris to the sitting room. She sat down, propped her stick against the arm, then picked up the painting. I sat down next to her and we held it between us. As I looked at it, I felt the intense sadness and yearning that lay behind its surface charm.

'So that's why you said you were "shocked" when Hugh told you the story,' I said.

'I *was* shocked,' Iris responded softly, 'because he'd said the name Edith Roche. I'd never known either that my mother had been an artist's model, or that she'd been married before. But she was, to Guy Lennox.'

I lifted my hand to the darting figure of the younger girl then glanced at Iris. 'I can see now that it *could* be you, though it's hard to tell because she's painted in profile, and it's slightly blurred to give the impression of movement.'

'That's why I didn't recognise myself – but then, I didn't expect to see myself in a portrait. Nor did I recognise Agnes.' Iris pointed to the older figure. 'Here her hair's very long; when the war started she had it cut short, which is how she always wore it after that. There *were* times, before I knew the truth about the picture, when I fancied the older girl *did* resemble Agnes, but I dismissed it as coincidence. Again, the nanny's features are painted in an impressionistic way – added to which this was a model for a larger picture, so Guy hadn't put in the detail that he would have done, had he been able to continue the painting.'

'When I first came here, Iris, I asked you if you'd ever had your portrait painted before. You replied that you had, but a long time ago.' I looked at the painting. 'This is that portrait.'

She nodded. 'And when I saw it for the first time, in that shop, I felt as though I'd been not just drawn to it, but almost *guided* to it. I had this overwhelming sense that I was connected to it, but I couldn't have known how or why.'

'But you said you showed it to your mother.'

'I did – because I was staying with her at the time. She reacted to it negatively. I assumed that this was because she thought I'd been extravagant, but I was wrong. It was because she knew at once what the picture was and who had painted it. It must have made her feel guilty, because after that an enduring sadness seemed to descend on her.'

'So you didn't know, all that time, that Guy Lennox was your father?'

'I didn't know.' Iris paused. 'Agnes and I were only twenty-one months and six months when our parents divorced. We had no idea, as we grew up, that the man we called "Daddy" was really our stepfather, or that our names had been changed from Lennox to Loden.'

'But you must have asked your mother how she met your "father".'

'We did: she just told us that they'd met at a party

277

that Peter gave – which wasn't a lie.' Iris shrugged. 'But wasn't exactly the truth.'

'What happened when you found out the truth? Did you ever confront your mother about it?'

'I never had the opportunity, because she'd died a few months before. It was during the dreadful winter of 1963 when the country was snowbound. Agnes lived in Kent and couldn't get up to London. I was in Yugoslavia. Our mother, who was already frail, caught pneumonia.'

'So . . . she *never* talked about your father to either of you?'

'Never – not *even* when she saw this painting, which must have taken considerable self-control. But she'd concealed the truth for so long that she probably found it impossible to reveal.' I thought of what my own mother had concealed from me. 'But it's just as well,' Iris went on. 'Because if I *had* known the truth while my mother was alive, then I don't think I could have forgiven her. My sister still hasn't, nearly fifty years on.'

'Did Agnes remember your father painting you both?'

'She did, because she was nearly six. She told me that that's how she always thinks of him – standing behind the easel, chatting to us and smiling. But I have no recollection of him at all – though I'm sure it *was* some deeply buried memory that led me to notice the painting in the first place; I do remember feeling this sense of . . . *familiarity*.' Iris sighed, then ran her fingers lightly across the top of the frame. 'I often think about how much my father must have missed us, and longed to be with us. He was deprived of us, as we were of him.' She looked at me in surprise. 'But there are tears in your eyes. Don't

278

cry, Ella, please.' She laid her hand on mine. 'I didn't mean to make you cry.'

I fumbled for a tissue. 'It's just so sad – to think how *near* you were to him.'

She exhaled. 'We *were* near – and at the same time . . . so far. But Agnes and I would give anything to have known him.'

I thought of my own father, wanting to know *me*. I thought of him sitting in that café for hours, anxiously looking at the passers-by. I let out a sigh. 'So now I know why this painting's priceless.'

Iris nodded. 'It *is* priceless – to my sister and me. I asked Agnes whether she'd like to have it for a while, but she said she didn't want to because it upsets her so much. So I keep it close to me, beside my bed, and every day I look at it and try to imagine what my father was like. Agnes and I were fortunate in that we were able to visit Hugh's uncle. We talked to him about Guy and heard his recollections of him, and even looked at some photographs of Guy that he had, so that was at least some comfort.'

'But . . . there must have been people who knew that Peter Loden wasn't your father.'

'There were – but they wouldn't have discussed it in front of us. They probably assumed that we knew, or that we'd been told that our father had betrayed our mother and that we didn't see him any more. Guy's name was simply never mentioned. But after I knew the truth, I stopped referring to Peter Loden as my late "father", and referred to him as my late "stepfather".'

'And . . . what happened to him?'

'He was a very busy, and powerful man.' Iris gave a

shrug. 'He was nice enough to Agnes and me; how much he ever thought about Guy Lennox, and the way he'd destroyed Guy's life, I'll never know. But my stepfather lost everything after the war. I told you that he laid the first oil pipeline to Romania?' I nodded. 'When Romania became part of the Eastern Bloc, the pipeline was nationalised. My stepfather's losses were catastrophic. He had to give up his offices in the City. The house in Mayfair had to go . . .'

'You said that it was very grand.'

'It was – it was just off Park Lane. It was lovely – like something out of the—'

'*Forsyte Saga*,' I interjected. 'That's what you said when you first started to tell me the story. I wondered how you could have known that – it was because it was your home.'

Iris nodded. 'We lived there until 1941; then my sister and I were evacuated. But in 1948 it was sold and my mother and stepfather moved to a small house in Bayswater. Their later years were very hard. After he died in 1958, Agnes would come up to town and help my mother, who was by then already quite frail. I'd spend time with my mother when I was back in London though, as I say, she never told me the truth. Then I chanced upon the painting and found out the truth – or perhaps it wasn't chance. Perhaps my father guided me to it. But it's a story I've told very few people, Ella. Only my two girls and their families know it. Now you do too.'

I clutched the tissue. 'I'm very touched that you've shared it with me – but, why *have* you, Iris?'

'Because you're a portraitist, just as he was – and because I saw that you were drawn to the painting: I think you instinctively recognised the intense longing that went into every brushstroke.'

'I *did* recognise that longing . . . yes . . .' I felt my eyes fill. 'But . . . I ought to go now.' I didn't want to cry again in front of Iris, or have to explain to her that my tears were prompted not just by her story, but by my own. I stood up. 'So . . . I'll see you next week.'

'I look forward to it, my dear.' Iris got up and came with me to the door. I picked up my easel, bag and the canvas carrier, smiled goodbye, then left.

I didn't wait for the lift, but walked down the stairs, my mind filled with the image of my father looking through the window of the café. I imagined his sorrow when he realised that I wasn't going to come. I thought of him waiting there again yesterday, then going back there this morning.

I left the building and hailed a cab. As it turned off Kensington High Street I saw the sign for my father's hotel, and was about to ask the driver to stop, when I realised that my father wouldn't be there. His flight was leaving in less than an hour. He'd be in Departures or making his way to the gate. I got out my phone and re-read his last message.

I hope you'll find it in your heart . . .

I hadn't done so. Now, because of Iris's painting, I felt that I could. I looked at his mobile number then, with no idea of what I would say or how I would even find the voice with which to say it, I began to dial. 07856 53944 . . . I pressed the last digit.

Call?

281

I stared at the screen, my hand shaking. Guy Lennox hadn't abandoned his children. He'd fought to keep them, and had suffered injustice in his attempt to remain close to them. My father had simply left me, and had never looked back.

With a sinking feeling I realised that my mother, for all her bitterness, had been right. It *was* too late. I pressed the red button then put the phone in my bag.

I'd made my decision, I reasoned as I arrived home: my father was now leaving, and after all the agonising and the tears it was time to let things lie.

Which is what I would have done, but for the e-mail that I received two days later . . .

It was Friday night, very late. I'd been to see a film with Polly, then we'd had a drink. I'd just got home and was in the studio, thinking about my sitting with Nate, who was coming in the morning, when I heard an e-mail drop into my inbox.

I went to the computer and saw that the message was from my father. I didn't *want* to hear from him again. I'd made it clear that I didn't wish to be in touch with him. What could there be to say? For a moment I toyed with the idea of deleting it without reading it. Then, with a weary sigh, I opened it. I was surprised to see that he'd written at length.

Dear Ella
I'm very sorry that we didn't get to see each other in London. I felt so sad as the plane took off, but consoled myself by deciding that I'd write to you, so that I could convey to you at least some of what I would have said, had we met.

Firstly, I'd have asked you about yourself – about
your career, your family and your friends. It would
have felt strange, having to ask my own daughter
such basic questions, but I know so little about
your life. Then I'd have told you a bit about me –
in particular, that I was widowed six months ago
and am still adjusting to that sadness. I'd have told
you that I live near a small town called Busselton,
not far from Perth, on a winery that was started
by my wife's parents, and to which it had always
been her intention to return. I never entirely shared
her enthusiasm for this plan, but in the end,
coming here became a means by which to escape
an intolerable situation. Because, as you know only
too well, I'd made a dreadful mess of my personal
life.

'Of course,' I muttered. 'I know the whole story.'

When I first contacted you, Ella, I said that I
wanted to try and explain. I hoped to be able to sit
down with you and tell you why I behaved as I did
all those years ago. I also wanted you to know that
I did try to remain in touch: but all my airmails
came back, unopened, with 'return to sender'
written on them in your mother's neat hand.

I felt my insides coil.

I wrote to you many, many times. In these letters I
told you that I was living in Australia, but didn't
say why, because you were too young to understand

the circumstances that had led me here. I knew that your mum would have told you that I'd simply abandoned you both, which, to my eternal shame, is true. But I wanted you to know that I still loved you, and missed you, and wished with all my heart that it had been possible for me to be with you.

Of *course* it would have been possible – if he hadn't run off with someone else!

I must say I didn't have my wife's blessing in any of this. She was very upset at what had happened.

I wanted to laugh. *She* was upset?

Frances said that if I wanted to ease my conscience I should simply open a bank account for you that your mother could access. I did so, but your mum ignored my many requests for her to sign and return to me the forms that I'd sent her. So then I began sending cheques to her, but she'd send them all back.

Her pride wouldn't allow her to take his money. Perhaps her pride had also made her refuse to seek maintenance from him after they divorced. I read on.

Then I heard that your mother was leaving her flat –

What did he mean 'her' flat? It was their flat.

I discovered this from my old colleague Al, with whom I'd stayed in touch. Al bumped into your mother in the centre of Manchester a couple of years after I'd left. She told him that she'd recently married, and was moving to London. She mentioned that she was no longer dancing – Al assumed that this was because she was very obviously having another baby.

So my father knew nothing about her accident.

I was glad to know that your mother had found happiness with someone else, and I prayed that he'd be a good stepfather to you, Ella. But I still wanted to be in touch with your mum, not just because I intended to provide for you, but because it was my dearest wish to see you again one day. I hoped that you'd be able to come and visit me when you were old enough, though I'd have to have handled that very carefully, as Frances, had found the whole situation so painful.

She'd found it painful? Having seduced my father away from his family and dragged him Down Under?

So when Al told me that your mother was moving to London, I wrote to the Northern Ballet Theatre asking them to forward to her a letter that I enclosed – but I didn't hear from her. I then placed an ad in The Stage, *with a box number, but she didn't respond. Your mother was clearly never going to forgive me for the way our relationship had ended.*

285

Their 'relationship'? What a weird way of putting it.

*I'm sure she must have told you how she and I
met. It was after a performance of Cinderella, in
which she had danced the role of the Winter Fairy,
in a beautiful tutu that sparkled with 'ice'. Frances
loved ballet and had bought special tickets that
included an invitation to the cast party afterwards:
so we went along . . .*

My father had gone to see Cinderella with Frances?
Mum had said only that he'd been there with 'a few
other people'. So *that* would explain why Frances had
hated Mum – because she'd liked John too, but it was
my mother who he fell in love with.

*I'd gone to get Frances a drink, and when I came
back with it she was chatting to your mother; so
Frances introduced us.*

This all tallied with what Mum had told me.

By then Frances and I had been married five years.

I stared at the sentence.

I loved Frances. I'd never been unfaithful to her.

It was my mother who was 'the other woman'.

*Ella, this will be hard for you to read, but it's
important that I tell you the truth, which is that I*

never meant to become as deeply involved with
your mother as I did. But she was captivating, and
I was weak.

Now I thought of the hotel bill that she said she'd found
in my father's pocket, and the love letter – it had been
the love letter of a wife to her husband.

I'd often try to end the affair, but she'd become so
distressed that I couldn't bring myself to hurt her.
Six months after we'd met, I told her that it had to
stop. It was then that she told me she was
pregnant.

I closed my eyes, then opened them again.

I was distraught, because I didn't want to hurt
Frances, or lose her. I was also shocked – which
you'll think is naïve; but I'd never imagined that
Sue would risk her career by having a baby; she
was young, and very ambitious. It was only then
that I realised just how powerful her feelings for me
were. I told her that I would never leave my wife.
But Sue knew that Frances couldn't have children,
and she must have believed that once I'd bonded
with the baby then my love for Frances would fade.

Mum had me in order to get John to leave his wife.
That's why she'd said she was 'so happy' to be having
a baby. Now I remembered her fury when Chloë had
contemplated getting pregnant in order to force a
commitment from Max. Mum clearly knew, from her

own experience, that to do so would be – how had she put it? 'Too big a risk.' I read on.

Despite my huge anxiety, Ella, I was thrilled when you were born and immediately felt a deep love for you. But your birth marked the start of a double life that was so stressful that at times I wondered how I'd survive it. In saying that, I'm not appealing for sympathy; I'm just trying to explain how I ended up causing so much hurt.

So much, I reflected.

Your mother urged me to tell Frances the truth: but I refused to do so because I was terrified that Frances would leave me. I loved her. I loved all three of you – my wife, your mum, and of course you, my precious baby. I simply didn't know what to do. So, like many men in that situation, I did nothing. I'd visit Sue and you after work during the week, and at weekends, whenever I could. I'd drive down West Street and I'd see your mother standing at the window of her flat, looking out for me.

I remembered how she used to call out to me, 'Daddy's here!' Now I realised why she always referred to my father 'arriving'; because he didn't *live* with us. So many of her elliptical remarks suddenly made sense.

You had no idea that your mum and I weren't like any other parents. I'd push you on the swings and take you swimming; I could easily have been spotted by someone that Frances and I knew, but I loved you so much that I was willing to take the risk: sometimes I'd take you to the theatre to see your mum dance. I'd read to you and paint and draw with you. I became so deeply attached to you that I decided, many times, that I would leave Frances. But then I'd agonise all over again, because I didn't want to lose her.

So, instead, he lost *me*.

Then Frances began to feel unwell. When she discovered that she was pregnant, it seemed a miracle, not just because she'd been told that it could never happen, but because by then she was forty-two. We were both so happy but I was terrified of telling Sue. So I didn't tell her. I hadn't even told my parents about you, because I was worried that they'd tell Frances.

So that was why I never met my paternal grandparents. And that was why Grandma was around so much – because my father wasn't in a position to look after me, given that he had to get back to his wife every night.

Then in 1978 Frances began to plan for us to return to Australia. At that point my life became hell. How could I go there, when I had you? But how could I not go when I had Lydia, who was by then eighteen months? I was so stressed at the thought of having to choose between my two

*families that I'd often want to kill myself or just
disappear into the bush – anything not to have to
face up to such an awful situation.*

By now I felt only pity for my father.

*Your mother increasingly demanded to know why I
was still with Frances. It was to be another year
before things came to a head. I'd told Sue that I'd
take her and you for a picnic – it was a beautiful
Saturday in early September. But I couldn't get
away and instead went for a walk with Frances and
Lydia. Perhaps you know what happened next,
Ella. Perhaps you even remember it.*

'I do,' I whispered.

*Suddenly there you were, running towards me,
looking so delighted and surprised. I remember you
chatting to me, then peering at Lydia with innocent
curiosity. Then your mother caught up with us,
clearly distressed. Frances was staring at you, Ella,
then, as she took in the situation, she gave your
mother a look of utter loathing, picked Lydia up,
and went into the house.*

So the situation wasn't the wrong way round at all.
Frances had had every reason to hate my mother.

*In that moment all the complexity of my life fell
away. Awful though it was, I felt a huge relief that
from this moment there were no secrets – only the*

terror of the decision that I would now have to make.
Even up until then, with many of our possessions
already being shipped to Australia, I'd been torn as to
whether I'd actually go. Some days I'd imagine myself
staying in Manchester with Sue and you. At other
times I'd see myself boarding the plane with Frances
and Lydia. But the events of that day meant that I
would finally have to choose. So I chose . . .

'To desert Mum and me.'

. . . to stay with my wife. That choice – and the
terrible way I handled it – has haunted me ever since;
because the truth is I didn't have the guts to tell your
mother what staying with Frances would actually
mean. I didn't know how to tell her. So, to my shame,
I didn't. I just collected my things from her flat, and
then left, because I knew no other way to do it.

'You ran away,' I murmured.

So it's not hard to understand your mum's bitterness
towards me, or her determination to cut me out of
her life. This, of course, suited Frances. She
forbade me from telling Lydia about you, because
she didn't want Lydia contacting you in years to
come, in case that should bring Sue back into our
lives. So Lydia grew up knowing nothing about
you, Ella. I wonder at what stage of your life you
were told about her. Perhaps you've known for a
long time.

'A *very* long time – three weeks!'

Lydia found out about you a year ago. It was only then that Frances, knowing how very ill she was, at last told her the story. Lydia said nothing about it to me at the time, but a month or so after her mother had died, she told me that she wanted to find you. I felt a kind of euphoria, swiftly followed by dread, because I believed that you'd want nothing to do with me. Who could blame you, if you didn't?

'Who could blame me?' I echoed dismally.

So I resumed the search. But none of the Gabriella Sharps that I found online were you, and so I assumed that your name had been changed. But without knowing what your name was, or what you did, it was impossible. So then I tried to trace you through your mum, but could find no reference to Sue Young and assumed that she used only her married name – a name I had no reason to know. And then I happened to click on an article in The Times. *For a split second I was confused, because I thought I was looking at a photo of Lydia. Then I saw that it was you, and I was . . . overcome. Lydia was so excited that she wanted to e-mail you herself, there and then; but she quickly realised that she couldn't do that until you and I had re-established contact. I warned her that this might very well not happen, but told her that I'd write to you, via your website. But when I sat down to*

292

*do it, I found it impossible. The words just
wouldn't come.*

I felt a pang of sympathy for him.

*So Lydia said that I should go to London: she
believed that you might agree to see me if you knew
that I was close by. So I booked my trip then sent
you my first message. There was no answer, so I
e-mailed you again. As each message drew a blank,
I'd tell Lydia that it wasn't going to work. She then
said that I should suggest a specific meeting place,
near your studio, and she found the Café de la Paix
online. So that's where I waited – I waited right up
to the very last minute, but you chose not to come.
Lydia's desperately sad about it, as am I.*

'As am I,' I echoed.

*Now I feel both better and worse – better for
having at least tried to see you, and worse for being
rejected. Ella, when I first got in touch with you I
wrote that I wanted to 'make amends'. Of course I
can't. All I can do is to tell you how sorry I am for
all the pain and hurt I caused you: I only wish that
I'd been able to say it to you face to face.
With every loving wish,
Your father, John*

TEN

I read my father's e-mail again and again. As I finally closed it, a wave of anger with my mother rose up, but then, to my surprise, quickly subsided, leaving only an intense pity for her that she'd felt she had to conceal her true place in my father's life. Unhappy with the role she'd ended up with, she'd re-cast herself as the wronged wife, a part she'd played with such passionate sincerity that I'd never questioned it. I almost admired her for having maintained the illusion for so long. She'd achieved this, I reflected, not so much through lies – though I now knew that she had lied – as through evasion and deflection. She'd either refused to talk about her relationship with my father, on the basis that it was too painful for her to do so, or she'd cleverly equivocated, allowing false impressions to stand.

I realised that my mother had never used the words 'husband' or 'wife' but had constantly referred to Frances as 'the other woman' – which, in one sense of course Frances *was*. She'd also avoided giving direct answers, responding instead with statements that weren't exactly lies, but weren't the truth. She'd suggested that what I'd innocently referred to as her 'first marriage' hadn't taken place in church because my father wasn't a 'believer', rather than admitting that they hadn't been married at all. She'd never spoken to me of her 'divorce', but had let *me* refer to it without ever correcting me.

Now I understood how my father had been able to hide the emigration papers from her, because they would have been sent to his home address. I understood why there'd been no maintenance order, and no wedding photos – not, as my mother had claimed, because the photos had got lost, but because there'd been no wedding to take photos *of*. I also understood the real reason why we couldn't take proper holidays with my father: because he'd been unable to get away from his wife and daughter for more than three days.

My mother had inverted the love triangle with tremendous subtlety and, at times, audacity.

That would have been cosy, wouldn't it – the daughters of the wife and the mistress being playmates! Would you have wanted that, Ella . . . ?

I marvelled at her mental complexity: or perhaps she'd convinced herself that she *had* been married to my father, and this is what had enabled her to carry on the charade with such vehement commitment.

I was the wounded party! I was!

As I went wearily down the stairs to bed, I thought about my mother's apparent familiarity with the frustrations of being a mistress. It was here, I now realised, that she'd nearly slipped up. She would often warn Chloë that married men 'never' leave their wives. Yet this was an odd thing for her to say, given that she, supposedly, *had* been left. Most of all, I understood why Mum had had it in for Max – not because he'd betrayed his wife, but because he'd stayed with his wife, just as John had chosen to stay with his.

He'd tell me about the lovely house we'd buy, the holidays we'd have and the life we'd lead – when all the time . . .

This I realised was the real reason why my mother had always been so censorious about adultery – because it hadn't worked out for *her*. Or was her indignation simply part of the performance, because it strengthened the impression that she herself had been a wronged wife?

As I got into bed, I tried to work out what I felt about my father. The fact that he hadn't been married to my mother didn't make what he'd done any less inexcusable. He'd had two families and had abandoned one of them – and that would never change. But I now realised that Polly had been right: there *had* been another side to the story. My father hadn't left us in a cold, calculated way, but in a blind panic. He was a weak man who'd got himself in a mess. And he *had* tried to keep in touch – that he hadn't was one of my mother's few overt lies, but it was a lie that had been essential to the case she'd built against him.

As I turned out the light I thought of my father's letters going out, then coming back to him, like boomerangs. Then I went to sleep and dreamed of my mother, in her long white tutu and bridal veil.

When I woke the next morning to the sound of my mother's voice I thought I was still dreaming.

'Ella?' I heard her say. '*El*-la . . .?' I'd slept fitfully and was so exhausted that I half-expected to see her standing by my bed. '*Please* pick up, Ella – I need to talk to you.'

I threw off the duvet then stumbled downstairs, clutching the handrail. As I picked up the phone the answerphone clicked off, the red light flashing angrily.

'Thank goodness,' said Mum. 'I was worried that you weren't there. Ella? Answer me – *are* you there?'

'Yes. I am . . .' Fury welled up inside me as I remembered her lies and her deception. I wanted to challenge her about it there and then, but every instinct told me to wait. I bit my lip. 'What's the matter, Mum?'

'Chloë's driving me *mad*.'

'In what way?'

'She's being *so* interfering.'

'Why shouldn't she interfere – it's *her* wedding.'

'Yes – but I can't have her trying to alter everything at this late stage. She's unhappy with the cake – she wants it to have forget-me-nots on it to match the ones on her dress, not pink roses.'

'Has it been iced yet?'

'No – but it means having to phone the cake shop to change the order when I'm already *so* busy. Then she's being difficult about the menus – she now says that she doesn't want *pot au chocolat*, she wants a tower of profiteroles.'

'Well, why not? Or would you have to get planning permission for it?'

'Don't be facetious, Ella. Worse, she won't make up her mind about the hymns, which means that we can't get the Orders of Service printed – oh, one good thing though – she *has* now chosen your reading: it's "The Good Morrow" by John Donne.'

'Right . . .' I reached for a pen and scribbled it down on a scrap of paper.

'Then she wants to change the crockery that we're hiring – I'd ordered the thin, plain white with a fluted edge, but now she wants the pale blue with the gold rim. She's suddenly become terribly demanding.'

'Well, that must be hard.'

'It's infuriating – although in *one* way it's a good sign that she's now so involved; between you and me, I think she had a little wobble a while ago – but then, brides often get jittery before the big day.'

'You would know.'

There was an icy silence. 'What do you mean?'

'Well, only that you've been a bride *twice*,' I said innocently. 'So you would know.'

'I can't *bear* wrangling with her,' Mum went on smoothly. 'Chloë and I often rub each other up the wrong way – I suppose because in some ways we're rather alike.'

'Oh, you are.' I suddenly realised how much Chloë's life had mirrored Mum's.

'Anyway, I hope she'll calm down and leave everything to me, otherwise the wedding will be a disaster.'

'I'm sure it won't be.' I glanced at the kitchen clock. 'But I have to go.'

I quickly ended the call, realising that if I didn't do so I'd be opening the door to Nate in my nightie. A part of me *wanted* to open the door to him in my nightie. A part of me wanted to open the door to him stark naked, pull him inside and hold myself to him.

I went upstairs and had a cool shower, after which I didn't blow-dry my hair – I left it damp and unbrushed, my face bare of make-up. I put on a shapeless shift in a bilious shade of custard and a pair of hideous sandals that gave me fat calves. I wanted to make myself look, and feel, plain and frumpy in order to extinguish any sparks that had ever flared between Nate and me. But as I placed his canvas on the easel I felt the sparks glow.

It was as if the portrait *was* Nate – as though there'd somehow been a fusion of person and picture. I kissed the tip of my finger then placed it gently on his painted mouth. I stroked his cheek then touched his hair. I suddenly decided that I wouldn't give the portrait to Chloë – I'd keep it, like Goya kept his portrait of the Duchess of Alba because he'd fallen in love with her and wouldn't part with it.

Drrrrrrnnnnngggggg!

I took a deep breath, walked slowly downstairs, then opened the front door. There Nate was, in jeans and a pale-blue Polo shirt, the green jumper slung around his shoulders. I gave him the kind of neutral smile that I'd give the plumber or the postman. 'Hi there.'

He smiled warmly in return and I felt my stomach flip-flop. 'You look great,' he said as he came in.

'No I don't.'

He looked taken aback. 'You do: it's a – nice dress.'

'It *isn't*,' I protested. 'The colour's vile and it's completely shapeless.'

Nate gave a bewildered shrug. 'Then why are you wearing it?'

'Because . . .' I could hardly tell him the truth. 'Because I'm going to be painting in it, so it doesn't matter.'

'Well . . . I guess that makes sense.' We went upstairs

into the space and light of the studio. I adjusted the blinds, rearranged the screen then tied on my apron. Nate pulled on the jumper then came over to the easel and looked at the canvas. 'You've done a lot more to it since I was last here.'

'I have – but only because time's getting short now. In fact this is the penultimate sitting,' I added cheerfully, as though I didn't mind that the portrait process was almost over.

'And will the last one be next Saturday?'

I twisted my hair into a scrunchie. 'The Saturday after, if that's okay, as I have to go to Chichester.' I told Nate about the silver wedding portrait commission. 'They need it very quickly. It's an emergency,' I added seriously.

Nate smiled. 'Do you charge more for emergency portraits?'

'I do. I have a twenty-four hour call-out, with an 0800 number.'

'And a blue flashing light on your easel?'

'Of course. And a siren.' I felt myself smile. 'Anyway . . .' I took the lid off the jar of turps. 'Today I'm going to be working on your eyes, so I'm just going to stare right into them, if that's okay.'

'Be my guest.'

I went over to Nate, put my hands on my knees, and gazed into his eyes. I was so close to him that I could see my reflection in his pupils and, behind me, the square of the window, its sides curved across the convexity of his cornea.

Nate gave me a suspicious glance. 'What are you muttering?'

300

'I'm counting your lashes. Now you've distracted me I'll have to start *all* over again. Right . . .' I narrowed my eyes. 'One, two, three, four . . .' I could smell the scent of Nate's vetiver and the faint tang of his sweat.

He smiled and his laughter lines deepened into small creases. 'I can see myself,' he said. 'In *your* eyes.'

'Well . . . that's what happens at this distance.'

'Can you see yourself in mine?'

I looked into his pupils. 'Yes – my hair's a mess.' I pulled at my fringe. 'Hey, don't blink. Right . . . that's enough eyeballing.' I went back to the easel and began to fill in Nate's irises with a myriad dots of lamp black and viridian green.

'I wonder how many times you look at the person while you're painting them,' I heard Nate ask.

'Oh – *so* many.' I wiped a drip of paint off the back of my hand. 'A portrait consists of many thousands of glances. But you're a terrific sitter, Nate. I'm going to nominate you for a Golden Behind award.' I felt my face flush. 'I mean . . . a Golden Chair.'

He grinned. 'So have you worked out who I am yet?'

'Hm . . . getting there.'

'Let me know, won't you? It's been driving me crazy.'

'I hope you'll see it for yourself, in the portrait. And I hope you'll be happy with it.'

'Are *you*?'

'I *love* it,' I said unthinkingly.

Nate blinked. 'You love my portrait?'

'Yes . . . I just mean . . . that I feel a creative satisfaction with it. I think the composition's worked really well – having you looking straight out of the canvas, eye to eye with the viewer – it's dramatic and engaging and—'

'In your face?' Nate suggested.

I smiled. 'It's certainly very direct. I hope Chloë likes it,' I added with a pang.

'I'm sure she will.' At that, Nate's phone began to ring. He got it out of his pocket and peered at it. 'In fact, that's her now. Do you mind, Ella . . . ?'

The skewer turned in my heart again. 'That's fine. We'll have an early break.'

'Hi, Chloë,' Nate said as I filled the kettle. 'No . . . you're not interrupting.' I could detect the enthusiasm and happiness in Chloë's voice. 'Er . . . I do like profit-eroles,' I heard Nate say as I spooned coffee into the pot. 'No, I don't mind *what* colour the crockery is . . . We'll talk about the hymns – sure . . . I'll see you later.' He put the phone back in his pocket. 'Sorry – Chloë's getting all worked up about the wedding.'

'But she seems very happy.'

He shrugged. 'I think she is.'

'And you must be too.'

He gave a bewildered laugh. 'I guess I am. It's pretty close now.'

'Yes – so there's *no* getting out of it,' I declared cheerfully as I handed him his coffee. 'Not that you'd want to,' I added hastily. Then I asked Nate when his sisters and mother would be arriving, and how long they'd be staying, and whether his friend James was looking forward to being best man.

'He can't wait – he says he's already written the speech.' Nate went back to the chair and sat down.

I picked up my tiniest sable brush and started to paint the fringe of Nate's eyelashes. When I'd done that I worked on the hollow at the base of his throat, on the

302

swell and curve of his Adam's apple, then on the blue shadow beneath his chin. We were in silence now, except for the rumble of traffic and the somehow incongruous trilling of a blackbird.

I put down my brush. 'That's it, I think – for today.'

Nate stood up and stretched, then he took off his jumper. As he did so his shirt rode up, revealing his abdomen with its covering of dark, fine hair. I was almost felled by a wave of desire.

I put the palette back on the table, took off my apron, then we went down the stairs. I opened the front door. 'So . . . we're almost there.'

'Almost there,' Nate echoed quietly. '*Ciao*, Ella.' He kissed me on the cheek, and as his skin grazed mine it was all I could do not to put my arms round his neck.

Instead I gave him a bright, impersonal smile. 'Bye, Nate.' I opened the door.

'*Ciao*,' he murmured. He was still standing there.

'You've already said that.'

'Have I? Oh . . .' He kissed me again. 'And had I done that?'

Heat spilled into my face. 'Yes.'

'Ah.' He gave me a rueful, crooked smile. 'I got confused.'

'Well, please . . . don't.'

'I won't,' he responded firmly. 'I mustn't.' Then, to my despair, he kissed me a third time, and left.

'You've got that look on your face again,' Celine said the following week. It was her final sitting.

I picked up my palette knife. 'And what look's that?'

303

'A wistful one – as though you're thinking about someone – a man.' I didn't answer. 'I do wish you'd tell me about him,' she added. 'You know so much about me, after all.'

'There's nothing to tell.' I put a few red-gold highlights in Celine's hair.

'But there *is* someone . . .'

'No. At least, no one that it could ever work out with.'

'Why not? Is he . . . otherwise engaged?'

'Yes. "Engaged" being the operative word.'

'Ah.' She sighed. 'That's hard.'

'Yes.' I put down the palette knife. 'But there it is. Anyway . . . I've almost finished your portrait.'

'You have?'

'Just one more thing to do . . .' I picked up a fine brush.

'I shall miss the sittings,' Cecile said. 'I've come to enjoy them. I'm only sorry that I made it so tricky for you at the beginning.'

'That's okay.' I dipped the brush in the titanium white. 'I'm sure it helped the painting to have had that initial . . . tension,' I said carefully. Celine smiled. Now I looked at her, then placed a touch of white in each eye. I stood back from the canvas. 'That's it.'

'Let me see.' Celine came over to the easel and stared at the painting. 'It's lovely,' she said after a few moments. 'Thank you, Ella.'

I'd worried that Celine would look anxious and unhappy in the painting, but she looked calm and composed, though there was an air of determination about her.

She tilted her head. 'I look as though I'm about to

304

get up and go somewhere. I think that's what people will say.'

'Perhaps some will, but we all see different things – it's very subjective. Sometimes people see things in my portraits that I haven't even seen myself.' I picked a stray bristle off the canvas. 'It'll be a few weeks before it can be framed, but at least you'll be able to display it in the meantime.'

She sucked on her lower lip. 'I'm still not sure where: definitely not in *here*,' she added wryly. I thought of her fury with her husband when he'd suggested that it should go above the mantlepiece. 'Maybe in the study,' she mused. 'In fact, if you wouldn't mind putting it in there now for me . . .'

'Sure – that'll be a good place for it to dry.' I lifted the portrait off the easel and followed Celine across the hall into the study, then laid it on a corner table.

'I hope Victor will like it,' I said, as we returned to the drawing room.

'I know he will.'

'But a portrait's a lovely thing to have and it will last for a long, long time.' I began to pack up. 'Barring fire, catastrophic flooding or nuclear attack, your portrait will *still* be being looked at in two or three hundred years, Celine.'

She smiled. 'Which rather puts forty years into perspective.'

'It does. So . . .' I put the brushes in the box. 'Are you looking forward to your birthday a bit more?'

'I *am*,' she answered carefully. 'Not least because I've reached a compromise with Victor. We *are* going to have the party, because it would be disappointing for our friends if we cancelled it.'

I collapsed the easel. 'Of course.'

'But I've told him *not* to buy the diamond ring.'

'I see.'

'It's far too extravagant a gift when things between us are so . . . unsettled. Instead I've asked him if he'll make a donation to a charity.'

'That's nice,' I said as I gathered up the dustsheet. I straightened up. 'Any particular one?'

'Yes. I was at a lunch a week ago,' Celine said. 'Sitting next to me was a man who runs a clean-water charity, Well-Spring.'

'Max Viner?'

'You know him?'

'I do – a little.' I wasn't going to say how. 'He's married to the crime writer, Sylvia Shaw.'

'*Was* married to her,' Celine corrected me. 'He told me that they separated three months ago and are divorcing.'

'Really?' I wondered if Chloë knew.

'He talked about it briefly; he seemed sad, but said that it was mutual; it appears she's involved with her publisher now.'

'I see.' The photo of Max standing proudly beside Sylvia at her book launch took on a different complexion.

'Anyway, I was very impressed with what he told me about the charity, and so, having now talked to Max himself, Victor's agreed to make a donation that will fund forty new hand-dug wells in Mozambique.'

'How wonderful. What a fabulous birthday present!'

'It is. He said that he still wants to give me something for myself – something memorable, he said, which is typically kind of him, but I can't think of anything.'

306

I collapsed the easel. 'I've decided that I'm going to do something for *my* birthday, Celine – it's in mid-September. I want to have an exhibition of my recent portraits. I'll hire a gallery for a few days and I'd like to borrow your portrait back, if you'll lend it to me; and I'd love you to come – preferably wearing what I painted you in. Will you do that?'

Celine smiled. 'I'd love to.'

I'd come to think of my forthcoming stay in Chichester as a working holiday, but it became clear from further telephone conversations with the Bergers that it was to be far more work than holiday, given that they now wanted the portrait to include their grown-up son and daughter, their three dogs and their two Siamese cats. I wasn't about to complain – a big group portrait like that would boost the bank balance, but it would be a challenge to do it in a week: it would also need a large canvas; and I was just wondering how I'd transport it down there when Roy phoned to ask me if he could give my number to a colleague who wanted to have his daughter sketched.

'Of course you can,' I answered, cheered at the prospect of more work. 'I'll chat to him about the different options, so ask him to call me – thanks for that, Roy.' I told him about my trip to Chichester.

'That's a big commission then.'

'It is – with a correspondingly big canvas; I don't know how I'll get it down there.'

'Surely you could buy the canvas in Chichester?'

'I could, but I have to prime it with emulsion first, which takes two days to dry, so I want to take one from London, ready prepared. I'll have to hire a car.'

'You can borrow mine.'

'Don't you need it?'

'I'm only at the hospital one day next week, and I'm sure your mother will lend me hers, or drop me there – it's not a problem.'

'Well, that would be great.'

So I went to collect the car on the Saturday morning. 'This is really kind,' I said to Roy as he unlocked the garage.

He pulled back the green painted doors. 'Glad to help my Number One Girl.' He went in and backed his silver Audi out on to the drive. He got out then gave me the keys. 'Are you going to come in for a cup of something, before you go?'

'Erm . . .' I was worried that if I saw my mother, there might be a scene. 'Is Mum here?' I asked casually.

'No.' I felt a wave of relief. 'She's gone to collect her wedding outfit – it was being altered.'

'Right . . . well, I'll have a quick coffee then.'

We went into the house. It was the first time I'd been there since Mum had told me about Lydia. I sat at the same place at the kitchen table and remembered her eyes shimmering with tears, her face a mask of suffering.

I've never wanted to tell you the truth, Ella, but now I will.

She *hadn't* told me the truth – just her own twisted version of it.

What you're remembering is the day I saw your father with his . . . with . . . his . . .

Wife, I thought balefully.

'Are you all right, Ella?' Roy asked. 'You look a bit . . . troubled.'

308

'Oh . . . I'm fine.' I was tempted to tell him about my father's e-mail, but it felt wrong to do so before I'd had a chance to confront Mum about it, and as she was so busy I had no idea when that would be.

Roy filled the kettle. 'I'll have to hire a penguin suit,' he said as he got down two mugs. I wondered what I was going to wear – I saw myself in funereal black.

The French windows were open. I went and stood by them and looked at the huge, luxuriantly green, lawn, fringed by the herbaceous border, with Chloë's Wendy house, long since turned into a tool shed, at the far end, by the horse chestnut tree. I imagined the massive white tent with its awnings and ropes and gathered drapes. I imagined the guests drifting in and out of it in their formal suits and silk dresses and wide hats, and the cohorts of caterers, musicians and entertainers, all presided over by my mother with her glacial charisma and her ineffable poise.

Roy made the coffee. 'So how do you think the garden's looking?'

'Wonderful.'

'I'm just doing it bit by bit, with endless mowing and feeding and sprinkling – I'm praying there won't be a hosepipe ban.'

'Fingers crossed.'

'And no freak winds – we don't want the marquee ending up wrapped round the tree.'

'That *would* be inconvenient. But it's going to be a huge event.'

'It is,' Roy said wearily. He put our mugs of coffee on the table. 'One hundred and *eighty* people are coming – and that's without all the replies in yet.'

'Good God.'

He sat down and sighed. 'It's too *much*. I tried to get your mother to agree to half that number, but she said she wanted a wedding that everyone would remember – and that's what she's going to get.'

We've got a huge cast list.

'You'd think it was her *own* wedding that she was organising,' he added wryly.

I've been thinking about confessi—

'Roy—' I said suddenly.

'Yes?'

I went and sat opposite him, my heart thudding. 'Roy, there's something I want to tell you, even though I'm not sure that I should.'

He blinked. 'Tell me what?' His brow furrowed as he peered at me. 'Are you sure you're okay, Ella?'

'Yes – more or less, but . . .'

'But what?'

'It's just that . . .' I realised that I couldn't tell Roy what I now knew – after all, Mum was his *wife*: he might not want to hear it. And was it my story to tell? 'That Max is getting divorced,' I blurted.

'I saw that.' Roy sipped his coffee. 'In a newspaper – can't remember which one – but it was in the gossip column. His name leaped out at me.'

'Does Chloë know?'

'Yes. I wasn't going to say anything about it to her, of course, but then she mentioned it to me.' He shrugged. 'She said she felt fine about it.'

'Well, that's . . . good.'

'She said that she's looking forward to marrying Nate. Which is all as it should be,' he concluded.

310

We drank our coffee in companionable silence, then I stood up. 'I'd better get going. I said I'd be in Chichester by three and I have to go and get my stuff first. Thanks again for the wheels.'

We went out to the front, I got in Roy's car, gave him a smile, then drove away.

I went home, got my equipment, my laptop and my suitcase, stowed everything in the back of the car, locked up the house, then set off towards the A3.

As I sped on to the motorway twenty minutes later, I felt a surge of relief to be having a week out of London. It would provide a welcome respite from the wedding preparations. Seeing the South Downs rise up in the distance I felt myself begin to relax. Most of my recent commissions had been stressful in one way or another, so I was glad to have one that would be reasonably straightforward – dogs and cats allowing.

Frank and Marion Berger lived in Itchenor, very close to Chichester Harbour. I drove down their tree-lined lane, catching my breath at the sail-dotted water glinting in the distance. Then I saw the sign for 'Woodlands' and turned into the drive. The house was Edwardian, low and wide, fringed by a fuchsia hedge that dripped with pink flowers. It was set in a large garden at the back of which was the turquoise glimmer of a pool.

As my wheels crunched over the gravel the front door opened and the Bergers came out, followed by three black Labradors who heralded my arrival with a volley of good-natured barks.

I parked where Mr Berger indicated me to, then got out, shook hands with him and greeted his wife. They were much as I'd imagined them – a pleasant-looking couple in their mid-fifties. I already knew that Frank was a local GP and that Marion worked in the Dean's office at the Cathedral.

'You'll be staying in the guest cottage,' she explained as her husband helped me get my equipment out of the boot. 'That way you'll have privacy – but we hope you'll join us for meals.'

'Thank you, I'd love that.'

The cottage had an open-plan ground floor on which I'd be able to put the easel if I needed to, and a prettily decorated bedroom and bathroom at the top of a narrow box staircase. From the bedroom window I had a clear view of the sail-dotted harbour and in the distance the shining expanse of the Solent.

Frank put my case down. 'Now, we've got Wi-Fi in here if you want to e-mail. There's a radio, a small TV . . . lots of books.' He nodded at the shelves. 'But let's go and have a cup of tea.' I followed him down the stairs and back to the house.

'Have you any thoughts on where you'd like to be painted?' I asked them as we sat in the sunny kitchen.

'Perhaps in here?' Marion asked.

'Maybe.' I could paint them at the table, perhaps with the children standing by the Aga. 'Could I have a look at the rest of the house?'

Frank nodded 'Sure.' He and his wife gave me a tour, first showing me the blank wall in the dining room where the portrait would hang. Then we went into the sitting room.

'You could paint Frank and me standing on either side of the fireplace,' Marion suggested, 'with the children on the sofa.'

I appraised the mantelpiece with its large mirror. 'Perhaps . . . but standing up all that time is going to be hard work, plus it's going to look very formal – do you really want that?'

'No,' said Frank as one of the cats came in through the open French windows. It began to wind itself in and out of his legs. 'We want to look relaxed and casual, don't we, Katisha?' he crooned as he picked the cat up.

'Could we go outside?' I asked. I followed the Bergers through the garden doors on to the patio where the other cat was lying on a low stone wall, blinking in the sunshine. 'How about in the swimming pool?' I suggested as we walked towards it, the dogs ambling along beside us.

'Are you serious?' Frank asked.

'I am. I did once paint a family in their pool and they loved it – it's on my website; you could have a look.'

Marion grimaced. 'I'm not sure I'd want to be painted in my swimsuit – but how about in our boat? It's moored in the harbour – you could put your easel on the pontoon.'

'That could be tricky with the movement of the water, and would the dogs and cats cooperate?'

'Ah. No. Forget that then,' she said with a laugh.

In the end we decided that Marion and Frank would sit on a white wrought-iron garden bench, on the lawn, the cats on their laps, their children lounging on the grass in front with the dogs, with the harbour in the background.

'That will be lovely,' Marion said. 'And how long will we sit for you each time?'

313

'If I'm to get the picture done in a week, then I'll need you to do three hours a day.'

'That'll be fine,' said Frank. 'We'll just chat – or look at the boats.'

I made a start that afternoon. I tied the canvas to the easel because it was slightly breezy, then I began to block in the main shapes with charcoal marks. It was a pleasure being in the sunshine hearing the wind blowing through the trees and with the views of the fields rolling down to the sea.

The Bergers' children arrived from London that night – twins of twenty-three; Hannah, a pretty red-haired girl who was a graphic designer, and Henry, a tall boy with brown curls who worked in IT. They could only spare three days, so we agreed that I'd paint them first.

The week passed quickly because I was working so intensively. Sometimes thistledown would drift on to the canvas and I'd have to tweeze it off. Several times I had to extricate a ladybird or a mayfly from the paint, and I had to watch out for the dogs' wagging tails. Apart from these hazards, the composition flowed. It was a relief to have a break from the emotional intensity of painting a lone sitter, one on one.

I'd spend the afternoons working on the background landscape. At night I'd be so exhausted that I'd go to bed early and read: amongst the books on the shelf was a poetry anthology in which I found 'The Good Morrow'. I'd forgotten how beautiful it is – a tender *aubade* in which, for the lovers, their 'one little room' is 'an everywhere'.

I gave myself a few hours off; on one afternoon I drove into Chichester and looked at the cathedral. On another I walked down to the beach and lay amongst the dunes beneath the blue bowl of the sky, watching the dinghies and windsurfers rip past.

On my last night the Bergers set dinner in the dining-room and we drank champagne to celebrate the fact that the portrait was done. They were to have it framed, locally, the week before their silver wedding party.

Marion couldn't stop looking at the picture, propped against the wall. 'It's full of warmth and happiness.'

'That's because your family is,' I told her. 'I just paint what I see.'

Afterwards I went back to the cottage and sat by the bedroom window watching the midsummer sky turn from orange to crimson, to a deep indigo, against which the first stars were beginning to shine. I thought about Celine, who would be at the Dorchester now, mid-party. I wondered if she really would leave Victor and, if she did, where her life would take her; I wondered how Mike was coping, and how Iris was. Then I opened my laptop to check my e-mails: there was one from Chloë to say that Nate's final sitting would have to be post-poned as he had to go to Stockholm again. *I can't wait to see the portrait*, she'd added in a PS. I sent her a quick reply and was about to close my inbox when, instead, I clicked on 'Create', and in the 'To' box I typed *John Sharp*.

315

ELEVEN

'So you had a good time?' Roy asked when I returned the car to him the following afternoon. He shut the garage doors.

'I did. It was a wonderful break and they were nice people.' I handed him the keys. 'I've filled the tank.'

'That's kind.'

'It's the least I could do. So how's everything been here?'

'All right.' He grimaced. 'Actually, that's not true – there've been rows.'

'About what?'

'Oh, about the seating plan, inevitably, and the choice of hymns, and whether or not we should have fireworks – your mother wants them because it's the Fourth of July the next day, but I say absolutely *not* as there won't be enough space to let them off safely. There was a spat about whether the chairs should have white tie-on covers – Chloë likes the idea, but your mother doesn't.'

'I see.'

316

'Anyway, I'm glad you enjoyed your week away. What did you do in the evenings?'

'I listened to the radio or I read. I had my laptop with me. In fact . . . there's something I wanted to tell you.'

Roy looked at me apprehensively. 'And what's that?'

'Well . . .' My heart began to pound. 'I've decided that I *do* want to get in touch with John.' Roy's face flushed. 'I'd been thinking about it, but then last night I decided to send him a short message; so I just wanted to tell you about it, and to say that I hope you're okay with it.'

'Yes . . .' He gave a shrug. 'Of course I am.'

'Because you see—'

'It's all right. You don't have to explain.'

'I feel I *do*, because I told you that I *wasn't* going to contact him and now I have.'

Roy put up his hands. 'So you've changed your mind, Ella. That's fine.'

'But there's a reason *why* I've changed it, which is that—'

'Ella,' Roy interrupted. 'You're thirty-five: you don't have to justify getting in touch . . . with your . . .' His voice had caught.

I felt my throat constrict. 'There are things I didn't know,' I said softly. 'And now that I *do* know them, it's changed my view of what happened – at least in. *some* ways,' I hurried on. 'Because you see—'

'I don't want to talk about it,' Roy said. 'So do what you want to do, Ella, but please don't *tell* me.' To my dismay, his eyes were glimmering.

I felt tears sting my own. 'You said you'd *support* me.'

Roy looked crestfallen suddenly. 'I did say that,' he conceded quietly. 'But . . . it's not easy. The truth is, I've always dreaded this. I've read about how hard it is for adoptive parents when their children contact their birth parents – even when they've encouraged them to do so. Now I'm finding out just how hard it is.'

'Mum never told me the whole story,' I persisted. 'But now I know it, and the point *is* that she's . . .' I froze.

Roy looked at me. 'That she's what?'

Over Roy's shoulder I saw Mum walking towards us, her arms outstretched. '*El*-la,' she crooned.

'Don't say anything to her,' I whispered. 'Please.'

Roy flashed me a puzzled glance, but nodded.

'How lovely to *see* you, darling.' Mum laid her palm on my cheek. It felt cold, and I shivered. 'What *were* you two talking about?' she added playfully. 'You looked quite engrossed.'

'I . . . was just telling Roy about Chichester.'

'Did it go well?' Mum's ice-blue eyes scanned my face. 'You've caught the sun, darling.'

'Yes. A bit. I was painting outside.'

'*En plein air*? How lovely. Now do come in and tell *me* about it too – I've just made a pot of coffee.'

We were already halfway to the front door. I pulled my hand away. 'Thanks, Mum, but I need to get back. I've got things to sort out.'

'That's a shame,' she responded softly. 'But I was just about to e-mail you to ask whether you'd come over next Sunday and give Roy a hand in the garden. I've got a rehearsal for my students' summer performance, so I have to be there all day, but there's a lot of last-minute planting to be done here. *Would* you be an angel and help Roy with it?'

'Yes – of course.' It would give me another chance to talk to him alone.

The week passed quickly. I took Mike's portrait to be framed and in the dress shop opposite found an outfit to wear to the wedding. I went to Peter Jones and bought a hat and bag to match, then went up to their wedding registry to order the soup tureen from Chloë and Nate's chosen dinner service. After that I walked down to Waterstone's, collected the Whistler biography, and bought the Everyman edition of John Donne's *Collected English Poems* to read from in the church.

On my way home I saw the Café de la Paix. I went in, bought a latte, then, as a small act of atonement, I sat at the table where my father had sat, looking out. Then I got out my phone and read again his delighted reply to my e-mail.

I spent the next couple of days working on the portrait of Grace, which, thanks to Mike's film of her, now had a luminosity and vitality that it had lacked.

On the Friday I went back to paint Iris again – she told me that she'd had an idea about what I might put in the background of her portrait.

Then, on the Saturday morning, Nate came for his final sitting.

He was very quiet, which suited me because I was worried that, if we talked, we'd inevitably flirt and banter, and it was too tantalising; but today there seemed to be an unspoken recognition that the bubble of exclusivity that we'd been in was about to burst.

I dipped my finest brush in the titanium white then, put a tiny stroke on to each of Nate's pupils. It was like throwing a switch – his face was suddenly vibrant, *alive*.

I stood back from the canvas. 'It's done.'

Nate stood up, came over to the easel but barely glanced at the painting before saying, simply, that it was 'very good'.

I wiped my paint-spattered hands on a rag. 'So . . .' I smiled. 'It's over.'

'Yes.' Nate nodded. '*Finita la comedia*,' he said quietly.

I untied my apron, then we went down the stairs. I hoped that Nate wouldn't make the kind of lingering goodbye that he'd made last time – it had left me with a melancholy ache that had lasted for days.

'Well . . .' I opened the front door. 'Thanks for being such a great sitter.'

He gave me a rueful smile. 'Funny to think that you hated me to start with.'

'Not hated.'

'All right then – loathed.'

'Erm . . . let's say "didn't much like".'

'Okay – I'm happy with that,' he said judiciously.

'But it was all a misunderstanding.'

'It *was* . . .'

'And . . . we're friends now, Nate. Aren't we?'

'We are. We ought to be,' he added. 'After twelve hours together. No – fifteen with our lunch,' he added brightly.

'Fifteen hours,' I echoed. 'That's more than half a day.' Put like that, it didn't sound very much. 'Anyway . . . I'm

320

looking forward to the wedding.' He nodded. 'So . . .' I smiled goodbye. 'I'll see you then, Nate.'

'I'll see you then.' The sittings, with their bittersweet intimacy were over. 'Bye Ella,' Nate whispered. He kissed me, holding his cheek against mine for just a moment too long, then he walked quickly away.

On Sunday, late morning, I put on some old clothes then cycled down to Richmond. As I rode through Fulham Broadway, I saw that there were perhaps twenty new bouquets tied to the railings. I realised that it was six months to the day since Grace had died and that her family and friends must have been there earlier to mark the anniversary. The yellow sign appealing for information had gone.

I cycled over Wandsworth Bridge, through Roehampton, then across Richmond Park to the house. In my basket was the card I'd bought for Roy and a big box of his favourite Belgian chocolates.

I locked my bike up by the garage then hung my helmet on the handlebars. Mum's car wasn't in the drive – I felt relieved. I walked round the side of the house and spotted Roy at the end of the garden, surrounded by trays of plants. As I approached him, he looked up and waved.

'Happy Father's Day.' I gave him the chocolates and the card.

'*Thank* you, Ella. You never forget. You always used to paint a card for me.'

'I remember.'

He sat on the bench that encircled the horse chestnut tree and took the cellophane off the chocolates. 'I've kept them all, you know.'

'You have?'

'Of course.' He grinned. 'I knew they'd be worth something one day.' He offered me the chocolates. 'Dig in – before *we* dig in,' he added with a baleful glance at all the plants. I took one and ate it, then Roy put the box down and opened the card. *I've Got the World's Greatest Dad*. 'That's lovely,' he said, his voice fracturing.

'Well it's true. You are. Did Chloë give you anything?'

'No – not that it matters. She's got enough on her mind.'

'And is she coming over to help too?'

'Not today – she did a bit yesterday, while you were painting Nate. Now, you'd better put some wellies on – there are some in the Wendy house – ditto gardening gloves.'

'Oh, my hands are always covered in paint, so a bit of mud won't matter.'

As I went into the Wendy house I remembered how, when we were children, Chloë and I spent hours in it. She used to have her toy cooker in there and I'd have to sit hunched over a tiny table in her 'café', eating triangles of plastic pizza with rapturous relish.

I took a pair of wellingtons outside, checked them for spiders then pulled them on. 'Right, I'm booted. What do I do?'

'We've got twenty white lavender bushes to plant—' Roy indicated them in their trays. 'There are also twenty phlox, thirty Achillea, forty Aquilegia and twenty-five sedums. This side of the tent will be open – unless it's pouring – so I want the border to be a joy to behold.'

I looked at the mass of delphiniums, peonies and acanthus. 'It's already looking gorgeous.'

'Well, this is the last lot to go in. Okay . . .' He handed

322

me a small spade. 'Let's start. Just follow the markers that I've stuck in the ground – and don't snag yourself on the roses.'

It had rained overnight, so at least the soil was easy to turn. I started at one end of the border, Roy at the other, and we worked towards the middle.

'We're doing well,' he announced after an hour or so. He straightened up then ran his hand across his brow. 'But let's stop for a bit of lunch.'

'I'm glad you said that.'

We left our boots outside and went into the kitchen. Roy washed his hands then opened the fridge and got out some ham and a bowl of salad while I set the table.

We didn't talk for a while, then finally Roy broke the silence. 'Ella . . . I'm sorry I was a bit . . . touchy last week. When you spoke to me about John.'

'It's all right.' I exhaled. 'I didn't mean to upset you. But I wanted to tell you about it, because . . . well, it wasn't as it's always been portrayed.'

Roy frowned. 'What do you mean?'

Now at last I talked to Roy about the long e-mail my father had sent me. I told him about the many letters that John had written to me when I was a child, and about the cheques and the notice that he'd put in *The Stage*.

Roy sat very still, until I'd finished. He pushed aside his plate. 'So this is very different from what your mother's always maintained.'

I nodded. 'She's always said that he behaved as though we'd never existed. But there's something else, Roy – something that I've never known, or even guessed at.' I told him what it was.

He didn't say anything for a few moments. He just

blinked, as though he was trying to work something out. 'Well . . .' he said at last. 'Things that have puzzled me for years now make *sense*.'

'That's just what happened with me, when I found out. I felt as though I had to . . . recalculate everything.'

He folded his arms. 'During the adoption process, I do remember that your mother seemed keen for me not to see our marriage certificate.'

'Because it would have said "spinster" by her name rather than "divorcée"?'

He looked at me. 'Yes. She insisted on submitting it to the court herself, even though it was my responsibility to do so. I also remember that she used to gloss over the way in which her marriage had ended. She just said, very bitterly, that your father had abandoned you both to be with this "other woman".'

'But you never guessed at the truth?'

'No . . .' Roy narrowed his eyes. 'Your mother was so *convincing*. And to be frank, I didn't *want* to talk about her relationship with John because I knew that she'd loved him. But . . . to think that you can live with someone for almost three decades and not really *know* them.' He gave a bewildered laugh. 'And her obsession with the horrors of adultery . . .' He shrugged. 'All part of the charade, I suppose . . . I really don't know what I feel. I think I mostly feel *sorry* for her.'

'That was my reaction too, but I also feel . . . *angry*.'

Roy let out his breath. 'Well, she's concealed so much from you. And she's lied to you. It's as though she's woven a web around her relationship with John – a tangled web,' he added balefully.

'The only reason I'm telling you all this is because I

hope it'll help you understand why I've changed my mind about replying to John.'

'Yes, I do understand that,' Roy said. 'This does . . . change things.'

'Because you see he was *here*.'

'Here?' Roy echoed.

'Yes. He came to London – to see me.'

'You *met* him?'

'No, no – I didn't.' I explained why.

Roy's jaw went slack. 'Are you saying that you went past that café in a taxi, and *saw* him there but didn't go *in*?'

'That's right,' I said faintly. I felt my throat constrict. Roy closed his eyes. '*Poor* man . . .'

I nodded bleakly. 'All he wanted to do was to sit with me for a few minutes, and tell me that he was sorry. But as I didn't give him the chance, he wrote to me, not realising that I'd never known the truth about him and Mum.'

'And . . . does it make what he did feel any . . . better?'

'Not much – but it does at least make it easier to understand. I no longer see him as Mum's always portrayed him – heartless and calculating: I just see him as weak and confused.'

Confused? Allowing men to be 'confused' gives them an excuse to just . . . string other women along, offering them . . . nothing.

'And where does his wife feature in all this?'

'Nowhere now – she died last December.' Roy looked surprised. 'She'd been secretive about the whole thing too, and only told Lydia about my existence a year ago. Then John began searching for me, and happened to see me in *The Times*.' I shrugged. 'The rest you know.'

'So . . . you're in e-mail contact with him now?'

'Yes. I explained that I hadn't known most of what he'd told me. I said that I didn't even know where he *was* until I was eleven.'

'Did you tell him about your mother?'

I shook my head. 'I said that I have a sister who's about to get married. And I told him that I have a wonderful father, whose name is Roy.' Roy flushed; his eyes were glimmering. 'You don't have to worry,' I went on. 'John's not going to become my *dad* again – even if I didn't have you. It's far too late for that – plus he lives nine thousand miles away, but . . . I'd just like to e-mail him from time to time – if you're okay with it.'

Roy hesitated. 'No. I'm not okay with it.' My heart plunged. 'Because I think you should do more.'

I looked at him. 'More? What do you mean? Phone him? I've got his number – I guess I *could* . . .'

'No. I mean that you should go and see him – see *them*.' My heart did a swallow dive. 'If you can't afford it, then I'll happily—'

'No, I *can* afford it – thanks. But . . . one step at a time,' I added faintly.

'Of course. You need to build up to it – send some more e-mails. But look – are you going to *talk* to your mother about all this?'

'I am – I need to; but I won't do it until after the wedding, because it's going to be a very upsetting conversation. So please *don't* tell her that you know what you do.'

'I won't say anything to her,' Roy agreed.

The next few days passed quickly. I went to see two or three art galleries with a view to hiring one for a week in September, and decided on the Eastcote Gallery, halfway down the King's Road. I might get a bit of press about the show, I reflected; it might even lead to a new commission or two but, most of all, it would be fun just to get my sitters together and have a party.

There was space for about twenty portraits, so I contacted everyone who'd sat for me during the past three years. To each I explained that I would personally collect the paintings, insure them, and safely return them.

I gave Celine the details when I went to collect her portrait to take to the framers.

'*Alors* . . .' She opened her diary. 'Fifteenth of September . . .' She flicked over the pages. 'That's a Wednesday.' She wrote it down. 'I shall be back by then.' Back from where, I wondered. 'At what time?'

'It'll be from six-thirty to eight-thirty. I'll invite Victor too.'

'Of course.'

'So how was your birthday party?'

She smiled. 'It was wonderful – Victor made a lovely speech, and Philippe said a few words. My friends and family were all there. It was a very happy occasion.'

'I'm glad.'

'And Victor is giving me the most *wonderful* present.'

'Really?'

'I couldn't think of anything I wanted, but yesterday he hit on a brilliant idea. He said that he'll give me a trip, on my own, lasting precisely forty days, during which I can go wherever in the world I'd like to go. I'm planning the itinerary at the moment.'

'How exciting.'

'It will be *liberating*. I have friends in the States, in

327

Argentina, in Cambodia, Ghana and Greece; I shall visit them all, with my round-the-world ticket, finishing my journey in Venice, where Victor and Philippe will meet me. We'll then spend three days there before flying back to the UK in time for Philippe's return to school.'

'It sounds fantastic.' We heard the doorbell ring. 'That'll be my cab – I'd better get your portrait ready.' The painting was still in the study, propped up on top of the desk. I clipped it into the canvas carrier that I'd brought with me, then went outside.

It was the usual driver because I'd asked for him. I put the painting carefully on the back seat, got in, then waved to Celine, who was standing in the doorway.

'Picture finished, is it?' The driver turned to look at it. 'Beautiful.' He glanced at Celine. 'It's just like her.' He started the car. 'Now don't forget . . .'

'I know. But if I painted you – what's your name, by the way?'

'It's Rafael.'

'Well, you'd have to come to my studio and sit for a total of at least twelve hours.'

'Oh.' He turned out of the drive. 'Can't see myself doing that, to be honest – I do more than enough sitting in my cab. Couldn't you do it from photos, like that poor—'

'No,' I interrupted. 'I couldn't. I paint only from life.'

'They've found the car, by the way.'

'Have they?'

'It wasn't a black BMW – it was a dark-blue Range Rover, but the number plate was so muddy that they hadn't been able to read it. Turned out the poor sod driving it had no idea. He hadn't even touched her, but he'd driven too close and she'd swerved into a pothole and got thrown off.'

'Poor girl . . .'

'I'm not sure I *do* want to be painted,' Rafael said as we drove over Hammersmith Bridge. 'Maybe you could just draw me.'

'I could – in charcoal, or crayon, or pen and ink.'

'So what does that cost then?'

'Well . . . perhaps we could barter? I used to do that when I first started out. I once painted my plumber in return for a boiler repair. So . . .'

'All right then – I'll give you some free cab rides – within central London, that is.'

'Fair enough. And how many would you offer?'

'Erm . . . would ten do it?'

'Ten would be great.' He could help me collect some of the portraits for the party. 'It's a deal.'

On the Saturday, the doctor colleague of Roy's brought his daughter for her sitting; she was an intelligent-looking girl of ten with long, glossy dark hair; she said that she wanted to be a violinist. Her father stayed while I sketched her in red crayon on brown paper.

On the Tuesday I went back to Iris: her portrait was very nearly done: in it she looked distinguished and serene, and the background that she'd chosen added depth and interest to the composition.

And now, the wedding was only two days away.

On the Thursday afternoon I cycled over to the house to write out all the place cards. In the drive was a big white van with *Pavillioned in Splendour* emblazoned on it; in the garden a team of men were slotting steel poles together and unrolling expanses of white canvas.

Roy came and stood next to me and we watched the tent rise up. 'Well . . . it's all happening,' he said. 'And Nate's family have been arriving.'

I glanced at him. 'When will you meet them?'

'We're going to have a quick drink with them tonight, tomorrow your mum and I will be very busy here all day; then we'll have a quiet evening with Chloë – she wants to sleep in her old bedroom one last time.'

'Of course – and how's she feeling?'

Roy shrugged. 'Absolutely fine.'

I turned and saw my mother walking towards us, shielding her eyes against the bright sunlight. She nodded at the men. 'I hope they're being careful with the plants.'

'I'm watching them like a hawk,' Roy assured her. 'I'm not going to let anyone trample my aquilegias.'

'I'm very worried about smoking,' Mum said. 'I just *know* that Gareth Jones will light up – he's still on forty a day, according to Eleanor.'

'Then I expect he will,' I said.

'As long as he doesn't light up in church,' Roy teased.

My mother ignored us as she considered the problem. 'I think I'll tell everyone that smoking *is* allowed – but after-dinner cigars only: I'll get a big box of Romeo y Giulietta.'

Roy groaned. 'That's another five hundred quid I can kiss goodbye to then.'

Mum looked at him reproachfully. 'Let's not spoil the ship for a ha'porth of tar.'

'Tar being the operative word,' he muttered.

Mum turned to me. 'Ella, will you come and write the place cards now? I've got them all ready on the kitchen table.'

'Sure.' I followed her inside. Once there, she opened the box of gold-edged white cards, handed me the guest list, then I got out my calligraphy pen and set to work. 'I feel like the official scribe.'

'Well, it's a great help that you're doing this,' she said. 'But everything's coming together very smoothly. We've got the rehearsal in the morning.'

'Do you need me for that?'

'No: it's really so that the soprano can practise and so that Chloë and Nate can go through their paces. Then in the afternoon the caterers and I will lay the tables.' She sucked on her lower lip. 'I don't suppose you could lend a hand with that, could you, Ella darling?'

'No – I'm sorry, I can't: Chloë's coming to see the portrait.'

'Oh, well then.' Mum frowned. 'But hasn't she seen it yet?'

'No – she insisted that she didn't want to see it until it was finished so she's coming to the studio at three.'

Mum smiled. 'So it'll be the moment of truth!'

At five past three the following afternoon the doorbell rang and I went quickly downstairs.

'Ella!' Chloë beamed at me then turned to the smartly dressed white-haired woman standing beside her. 'This is Nate's mother – Mrs Rossi. She said she'd like to see the portrait too – I hope that's okay.'

'Of course it is.' I held out my hand and Nate's mother took it. 'Hello, Mrs Rossi.'

'Please . . . call me Vittoria.' Mrs Rossi sounded very

331

Italian, and was less frail than I'd imagined. She had pretty, mobile features and large greenish-grey eyes that reminded me of Nate's.

'Nate looks like you,' I said as she stepped inside.

She nodded. '*Si* – more than his papà.'

'My studio's at the top of the house. I can bring the painting down, if you'd . . .'

'No, no,' she said. 'I can go up.' She followed Chloë and me up the stairs.

'Nate was a good sitter,' I said to Vittoria as we reached the first landing. 'He kept very still.'

'Ah . . . well, he is a good boy.'

We went into the studio. Vittoria smiled appreciatively at the paintings on the wall.

'How was the rehearsal?' I asked Chloë.

'Fine. I think it'll all go very well tomorrow. Are you happy with your reading?'

'Yes. I've been practising.'

'That's good. *So* . . .' She clapped her hands together, beaming. 'Let's see the portrait!' She turned to Vittoria. 'It's very exciting.'

'It is exciting,' Vittoria agreed.

I went to the rack, took out Nate's canvas and placed it on the easel.

Chloë and her future mother-in-law stood in front of the portrait, side by side.

In the silence that followed, I was aware of the soft roar of the traffic, and of the distant wail of a siren. After a few seconds had passed I began to think it would be nice if they said something. Of course, coming from Florence Vittoria would have high standards, I reasoned; but while I wouldn't claim to be up there with Raphael or Leonardo, I was pretty sure that I'd done a good job. But Vittoria and Chloë's continuing silence seemed only to confirm that they were disappointed. My heart sank.

Vittoria put her head on one side as she studied the picture. '*Piacevole*,' she said at last. 'Pleasant', I silently translated. She thinks the portrait is 'pleasant'. '*Molto piacevole*,' Vittoria added as she studied it. 'Very pleasant'. Great, I thought. '*È un buon ritratto* – a good portrait. *Brava*, Ella,' she concluded, and smiled at me.

I looked at Chloë's profile as she contemplated the painting. 'I agree with Vittoria,' she said after a moment. 'It's a . . . good portrait. Very good,' she added firmly. 'So . . . thank you, Ella. But . . . we have to go now.'

'Won't you have some tea?'

'Oh. No . . .' Chloë said. 'I'm afraid we don't have time – I need to take Vittoria back to her hotel, then I have to collect things from my flat and drive over to Richmond – and of course I want to have an early night tonight; But . . . *thank* you,' she said again, with this stiff, dignified air, which wasn't like Chloë at all. It was wedding nerves I told myself. She turned to go.

'Aren't you going to *take* the portrait?' I asked her. 'I thought you were going to give it to Nate tomorrow.'

Chloë glanced at the painting again, then coloured. 'Oh . . . no. I think I'll . . . wait.'

'Until it's been framed?' I said.

'Yes. Yes . . . that's right.'

'Fair enough.' We went down the stairs. 'So . . .' I opened the front door then smiled my goodbyes. 'I'll see you both tomorrow.'

'*A domani*,' Vittoria replied. She reached for my hand and squeezed it – as if to console me, it occurred to me;

then she smiled brightly. '*Brava*, Ella. So nice to meet you – *arrivederci*.'

'*Arrivederci*,' I said. Then they left.

The next morning I woke early and lay in bed feeling not just depressed at the thought that this was Nate's wedding day – but weighed down – as though someone had left a pile of bricks on my chest. I tried to distract myself by working – I finished the drawing of the doctor's daughter text; then I sent Chloë a 'Happy birthday' text; then I looked at Nate's portrait again, still standing on the easel. '*Piacevole*', I murmured balefully. Vittoria's verdict depressed me, and Chloë's response had been barely more enthusiastic.

I showered, did my hair and make-up and, having scrubbed the last traces of paint off my hands, I polished my nails then got dressed.

At 12.45 I heard Polly beep her horn – she'd offered to drive me to the wedding. I ran downstairs, opened the door then waved as she parked her silver Golf.

She got out then opened the hatchback so that I could put my hat on the shelf. 'Great dress,' she said, with a glance at my fitted silk shift with its deep ruffle across the front. 'I love lime green.'

'Well . . . it's suitably bright and joyous.' Not that I felt either. 'You look lovely, Pol.' She was wearing a pink linen suit with flat silver sandals through which her toes, lacquered with candy pink polish, showed to perfection. I smiled at Lola, sitting in the back in a sky-blue linen dress, her long, fair hair twisted into a bun. 'You look very grown up, Lola.'

'Eleven *is* quite grown up,' she pointed out gravely.

I went back into the house to fetch my bag and the book of poems. I locked up then, mindful of my tight seams, I lowered myself carefully on to the front seat of Polly's car.

She pulled on her driving gloves. 'Gorgeous day for it,' she remarked as we drove away.

As we went through Putney I told Polly about Chloë and Vittoria's visit.

'I bet they loved the portrait,' she said.

'Erm . . . I don't think they did.'

Polly glanced at me. 'What do you mean?'

'Well, Chloë said that it was very good.'

'Then that's *fine*. I'm sure it's wonderful,' she added loyally.

'But Nate's mother just said that it was *piacevole* – i.e. "nice" – as though she thought I hadn't done him justice.'

Polly put on her indicator. 'Look, Ella – she's his *mum*; she'd probably have said that if Michelangelo himself had painted him.'

'You've got a point there. I'm being over-sensitive.'

'That's okay – you're an artist.'

The traffic was surprisingly light, so we got to Richmond in good time. Polly parked outside the house, swapped her driving gloves for a pair of white lace ones, then we all got out. She opened the boot and passed me my hat.

'Let's have a quick look in the garden,' I said.

The tent looked magnificent, the canvas a pristine white, the 'ceiling' a lining of pale calico that spangled with tiny mirrors. The poles were swathed in cream voile and laced with long coils of summer jasmine. Bone china and lead crystal gleamed on the linen-covered tables on each of which was a huge centrepiece of belladonna lilies.

Polly gave a low whistle. 'It's spectacular – isn't it, Lola?'

Lola nodded. 'So many flowers . . .'

In front of each place setting was a gold-tasselled menu, and a silk mesh bag of pink and white sugared almonds. I wondered if Chloë and Nate would smash a glass.

Through the open side of the tent I saw four uniformed caterers crossing the lawn, carrying a huge ice sculpture of a swan, anxiously supervised by my mother. They came into the tent and lowered it on to the large side table from which the drinks were to be served.

Mum looked up and saw us. 'Polly!' she exclaimed softly. 'And Lola – *you've* grown since I last saw you. And what a terrific outfit, Ella – you all look beautiful.'

'So do you, Sue,' said Polly. 'But it's all . . . *wonderful*.'

'Thank you,' Mum gave Polly a gratified smile. 'I must say I think the intensive planning's paid off.'

'I thought you'd be helping Chloë get dressed,' I remarked to her.

Mum gave an odd little laugh. 'She said she didn't want me to. But as she's got her hairdresser and a make-up artist with her, I thought I'd leave them to it and get on with things here. But I'll walk to the church with Chloë and Roy.'

I glanced at my watch. 'I think *we'd* better go.'

'We'll see you there,' Polly said to Mum.

I put on my hat and we walked up the road to St Matthew's. Nate was standing outside, looking so hand-some in his morning suit and grey waistcoat that my heart contracted. As he saw me he smiled, and my heart flooded with longing. I walked up to him and congratulated him, then introduced Polly and Lola.

'Great to meet you,' he said to them. 'This is my best man, James,' he added as James appeared.

I smiled at him. 'I hear you've written a great speech.'

'Oh, it's a humdinger.' He clapped his hands. 'I'm looking forward to it – after all, you've made me wait long enough for this day, pal,' he joshed Nate. Nate gave him a good-natured grin.

'You're certainly going to have a big audience,' I said to James.

He nodded. 'There's gonna be a huge crowd.'

By now that crowd was beginning to materialise as the guests rounded the corner in knots of two and three, then congregated by the porch. A woman with a camcorder and a big black bag slung over her shoulder was filming us while a man in a cream suit snapped away with an SLR.

'Shall we go in now?' I said to Polly.

'Let's.'

As we entered the church we could hear the organist playing 'Jesu, Joy of Man's Desiring'. I spotted Honeysuckle, wearing a black-and-white houndstooth suit and wide-brimmed black hat, chatting to Kay, who was in a blue-and-white floral patterned dress. I smiled at them and hoped that they'd both forgotten my rather intense behaviour at the engagement party. Honey's husband Doug, who was an usher, handed Polly, Lola and I our Orders of Service, then we walked to the front of the church.

There were posies of sweet peas tied to the end of each pew; but as I saw the flowers on the altar I caught my breath – a tumbling mass of peonies, agapanthus, viburnum and tuberose – the overpowering scent of which brought to mind my mother's Fracas.

'Where should Lola and I sit, Ella?' Polly whispered.

337

'With me,' I answered. 'After twenty-nine years, you count as family.'

So the three of us sat in the second pew on the left-hand side, leaving the front pew for my mother and Roy. The soprano, Katarina, was already sitting there, looking through her music folder. The sun sliced through the stained-glass windows scattering coloured shards across the walls and floor.

Now Nate came and took his place at the front.

'Well,' said Polly as she looked at him. 'You did say he was attractive.' She glanced at me. 'You enjoyed painting him, didn't you?'

'I did,' I said neutrally.

'He looks nervous,' Lola observed.

'He does rather,' Polly murmured.

Nate didn't look so much nervous as troubled, I reflected.

Across the aisle, a number of women, who, I assumed, were Nate's sisters, were taking their places with their husbands and children; I could hear them chatting in a mixture of Italian and English.

– *Che bella chiesa.*

– I am so jet-lagged.

– *Che bei fiori.*

– *Si, sono magnifici*: I shoulda had lunch.

– *Mamma dice che il ritratto é un* disastro.

'Are those *all* his relations?' Polly asked me wonderingly.

'I think they must be.' I tried to work out *why* Nate's mother should think the portrait a '*disastro*'. It *wasn't* a disaster – it was a good, vibrant portrait. She and Chloë obviously hadn't liked the composition. Now here his mother was, in an emerald-green two-piece with a navy hat and shoes. As she stepped into her pew I smiled at her and she smiled back then fixed her gaze on the altar. I turned and had a quick look behind. The central part of the church was now full.

A friend of Chloë's, in a beige silk dress, teetered past on six-inch black stilettos: for a moment she looked as though she might fall.

'She needs stabilisers,' I murmured to Polly. 'Or maybe a Zimmer frame.'

Polly nodded. 'In the seventeenth century the aristocrats used to wear heels so high that they'd have a servant on either side, holding them up as they walked along.'

'How sensible . . .' I opened the book of poems.

Polly glanced at it. 'Are you nervous?'

'Very. I haven't read anything in public since I was at school: by the way, how's it going with the nice dad?'

'Fine.' Polly smiled. 'He's coming to lunch tomorrow.'

'Good. Have you told him what you do for a living yet?'

'I have, and it's not a problem. In *fact*—'

Suddenly the organ stopped and the hubbub subsided. The vicar, Reverend Hughes, had stepped out on to the altar. He lifted his hands and we all stood up.

He smiled. 'May the grace of our Lord Jesus Christ, the love of God, and the fellowship of the Holy Spirit be with you all . . .'

'And also with you,' we intoned.

I turned and saw, across the sea of hats, Chloë silhouetted against the west doors of the church, with Roy beside her, and behind her Mum, who was making some last-minute adjustment to Chloë's dress. Then the

'Arrival of the Queen of Sheba' sounded, and Chloë stepped forward.

As Chloë processed slowly up the aisle on Roy's arm, my mother walked quickly up the left side of the church and slipped into the pew in front of us. Now Chloë was passing us, gloriously beautiful in her forget-me-not scattered tulle, an organza stole shimmering over her slender shoulders, her hair wound into a chignon and dressed with a gardenia. In her hands was a simple spray of white roses. Nate's niece Claudia, in a pale-blue dress and matching ballet shoes, followed a few feet behind.

I glanced at Nate as Chloë approached the altar. I'd often tortured myself by imagining his delighted pride at this moment, but in his face I could see only tension and anxiety. As Chloë drew level with him he smiled at her, but his smile didn't quite reach his eyes. If Chloë had noticed this, her features didn't betray it. As she turned to hand Claudia her bouquet she wore an expression of ineffable serenity. Claudia took the flowers then clambered into the third pew to sit with her parents while Roy came and stood next to Mum.

The Handel drew to a thundering close. The vicar let the last reverberations subside, then he welcomed us all to St Matthew's to witness the marriage of Chloë and Nathan, to pray for God's blessing on them and to share their joy. Then he announced the first hymn – 'Praise My Soul the King of Heaven'. As we sang it, Katarina's exquisite voice soared above all of ours.

During the last verse I saw Nate lift his eyes to the altar. Chloë looked very solemn. Then the hymn ended and we all sat down.

'And now the first reading,' said Reverend Hughes, 'which is read by Chloë's sister, Gabriella.'

My heart pounding, I stepped out of the pew and went up to the eagle-shaped lectern. I placed the book on it.

'"The Good Morrow",' I said. 'By John Donne.' I lifted my head. The sea of faces was a blur. 'I wonder by my troth what thou and I did, till we loved. Were we not wean'd till then? . . .' As I read on, I could feel Nate's gaze upon me, but was aware that Chloë was staring straight ahead. 'And now good-morrow to our waking souls, Which watch not one another out of fear; For love, all love of other sights controls, And makes one little room an everywhere . . .' I paused. 'My face in thine eye, thine in mine appears . . .' At that I saw Chloë turn and look at me. 'And true, plaine hearts do in the faces rest. Where can we find two better hemispheres Without sharp north, without declining west? . . .'

I read on to the end, then returned to the pew, my knees shaking.

Polly put her gloved hand on mine. 'Well done,' she whispered.

Now the vicar was declaring the gift of marriage to be a way of life made holy by God, and a sign of unity and loyalty which all should honour and uphold. 'No one,' he went on, 'should enter into it lightly or selfishly, but reverently and responsibly in the sight of almighty God.' He lifted his hands. 'First, I am required to ask if there is anyone present who knows a reason why these persons may not lawfully marry, to declare it now.' I glanced at my mother. She was smiling serenely but her jaw was tight; then, as no one spoke, she relaxed.

341

The vicar looked at Chloë and Nate. 'The vows you are about to take,' he said intently, 'are to be made in the presence of God, who is judge of all and knows all the secrets of our hearts; therefore if either of you knows a reason why you may not lawfully marry, declare it now.'

There was a silence, then the vicar joined Nate and Chloë's hands. 'Nathan,' he said, 'will you take Chloë to be your wife? Will you love her, comfort her, honour and protect her, and, forsaking all others, be faithful to her, as long as you both shall live?'

Nate didn't respond. I felt a sudden rush of hope, followed by a stab of shame. 'I . . .' he began. 'I . . .' he faltered again. Now he exhaled gently, as though breathing on glass. Then I heard him whisper, 'I will.'

The vicar turned to Chloë. 'Chloë, will you take Nathan to be your husband? Will you love him, comfort him, honour and protect him, and, forsaking all others, be faithful to him as long as you both shall live?'

Now Chloë hesitated as well: I decided that this must be because Nate had hesitated and she didn't want to look too eager, or to show that she had listened to the question carefully and was giving it her fullest consideration, but by now ten seconds must have passed since she'd been asked it, then fifteen, then twenty . . . The silence in the church had intensified and thickened until it seemed to hum and throb. And by now at least a minute had gone by and the pews were creaking as people shifted in their seats.

'Will you?' Reverend Hughes tried again. His face was crimson, but still Chloë didn't reply. She simply stood there, immobile, head bowed. People craned their necks to see what was happening. Suddenly Chloë's shoulders began to shake. She was giggling – the emotion of the occasion had made her hysterical I thought. Then I realised that she wasn't giggling. She was crying.

The vicar, clearly used to seeing brides weep on their wedding day, ignored her tears. 'Chloë, *will* you take Nathan to be your husband?' he pressed on. 'Will you love him, comfort him, honour and protect him, and, forsaking all others, be faithful to him as long as you both shall live?'

Chloë's drew in her breath, brokenly. Then there was another pause that seemed to stretch forever. 'No,' she whispered.

There was a collective gasp. Mum's hand flew to her mouth.

'But . . . Chloë?' The vicar's face was beaded with sweat.

She looked at him imploringly, then her face crumpled. 'I . . . *can't*,' she sobbed; then she glanced at Nate, who was staring at her, his jaw slack. She let go of his hand. 'I'm . . . sorry, Nate.'

Reverend Hughes whispered something to them both, and they nodded. I heard Chloë sniffle. Nate reached into his top pocket and gave her his silk handkerchief, which she pressed to her face. Mr Hughes cleared his throat, loudly, then addressed us. 'There will now be a slight change to the proceedings,' he announced. 'Miss Katarina Sopuchova will sing "Ave Maria" while I go into the sacristy with Chloë and Nate for a brief chat. Thank you for your patience.'

The organist played the opening arpeggios of the Bach-Gounod as Katarina walked up the altar steps.

A-ve Ma-ri-a . . . she sang as Chloë and Nate

343

followed the vicar. *Plenum gratia* . . . Suddenly Chloë stopped and, to my surprise, turned and beckoned for me to come with her.

Dominus te-cum . . .

I stood up, and so did Mum, but Roy whispered to her to sit down again which, with clear reluctance, she did.

Benedicta tu in mulierbus . . .

I followed Chloë and Nate to the sacristy, which was down a short passage to the left of the altar.

Et benedictus fructis . . .

On the table the thick, leather-bound Marriage Register was open, awaiting Chloë and Nate's signatures. Chloë sat down, her cheeks gleaming with tears, while Nate sat next to her, staring at her in bewilderment.

. . . ventris tui, Iesus . . .

I closed the thick oak door and Katarina's singing faded.

'Chloë,' said the vicar, 'would you please tell me what this is about?' She didn't answer. He turned to Nate. 'Do *you* know?'

Nate gave a slow shake of the head. 'I have *no* idea.'

'Is it just wedding nerves?' Reverend Hughes asked Chloë. She shook her head bleakly. 'But yesterday, after the rehearsal, you told me that you were looking *forward* to marrying Nate, and so . . .' He turned up his palms. 'I don't understand.'

Chloë ran the handkerchief under her eyes. 'I'm *sorry*,' she croaked. I should have called it off last night – or even this morning – but I didn't have the guts. I told myself that it was too *late*, and that I'd simply have to go through with it, then decide what to do afterwards.

But now that I'm here, and I have to say those words in front of all our friends and family, not to mention God, I just . . . *can't*.'

The vicar blinked. '*Why* can't you?'

'Because . . .' Chloë sniffed. 'Because . . . yesterday I *discovered* something.' She swallowed painfully. 'I discovered something about my mother that—'

Suddenly we heard footsteps, then the door swung open, its hinges creaking, and Mum appeared, Roy just behind her.

Sancta Maria . . . we heard.

'Chloë!' Mum's eyes were blazing.

Sanc-ta Mar-i-a . . .

Roy shut the door.

'What *are* you playing at, Chloë?' Mum demanded hoarsely.

Chloë glared at her. 'Go away! You've done *enough* harm!'

Mum recoiled as though from a slap, then recovered her composure. 'No,' she said calmly. 'I *won't* go away – not when this wedding has cost *forty thousand* pounds—'

'Don't, Sue,' Roy interjected, but Mum ignored him.

'– and when I've *slaved* to make it an unforgettable day.'

'Well, it certainly will be now,' Roy said dismally.

'Whatever are you *thinking*, Chloë?' Mum persisted.

Chloë clutched the handkerchief in both hands. 'I'll tell you what I'm thinking.' She blinked away a tear. 'I'm thinking of how you've interfered, Mum, and manoeuvred and . . . *manipulated*.'

Mum pursed her lips. 'The word you should really

345

be using here is "helped"; you clearly have *no* idea what—'

'Please, Mrs Graham,' the vicar interrupted. He turned back to Chloë. 'Chloë, can you *please* explain what's happened since yesterday to make you do this?'

'Chloë nodded bleakly, then pressed the hanky to her eyes. 'What's happened is that late last night I found out something about my mother, something that . . . well, it *changes* everything.' At that Roy emitted a low groan.

'What do you mean, Chloë?' the vicar asked.

'I was once very happy with someone,' Chloë replied. 'He was called Max, and I *loved* him – and he loved me.'

'Not enough!' Mum spat.

Chloë ignored her. 'But the problem was that he was married.'

'Don't *tell* everyone!' Mum implored her.

Chloë glared at her. 'And my mother was *so* disapproving – as you've just seen. She kept telling me that I had to stop seeing Max because he *wasn't* going to leave his wife, and what I was doing was *wrong* and in any case I was wasting my time, because it would never, never, *ever* work out.'

'It didn't!' Mum said triumphantly.

'No it didn't,' Chloë agreed miserably. 'But it *would* have done if you'd just left me *alone*, because now Max and Sylvia have split up.'

But Chloë had known this for weeks: Roy had told me that she'd been fine about it, so why would it bother her now?

Chloë looked at the vicar her eyes red-rimmed. 'I'm not expecting you to approve of any of this,' she said quietly. 'I'm just trying to explain . . .'

346

Reverend Hughes's brow furrowed. 'So, you feel that your mother stopped you from being with Max.'

'She *did*.' Chloë's eyes had filled again. 'Because she persuaded me to end the relationship – and it broke my heart.'

'How old were you then, Chloë?' he asked her.

'Twenty-seven – so, yes, more fool me for listening to her at that age. But I *trusted* her, and believed that she was acting only in my best interests.'

'I *was*!' Mum protested. 'Of course I was.'

Chloë shook her head. 'But last night I discovered something about my mother that made me realise that she hadn't acted in my best interests at all.'

Mum blenched. 'Whatever are you talking about?'

Chloë stared at her coldly then turned back to the vicar. 'Over dinner, Mum and I had a row. She said, yet again, how happy she was about the wedding, and how thankful she was that I'd "seen the light" about my "awful relationship" with Max – and she was rude about him. I became very upset. But after she'd gone to bed, Dad tried to calm me down. And he told me where this obsessive attitude of my mother's comes from. He said that it was because *she'd* had a long affair with a married man – Ella's father, John.' Mum looked at Roy, aghast. 'Yet Mum's always made out that she was his poor abandoned wife.'

Mum sank on to a chair. 'What have you *done*, Roy?' she whispered.

'What have *you* done, Sue,' he countered quietly, 'in not being honest with us all these years? Ella learned it only very recently, from John, in an e-mail – he had no idea that she didn't know. A few days ago, she told me.

And last night *I* told Chloë.' He closed his eyes. 'And now I wish I *hadn't*.'

'I'm *glad* you did,' Chloë exclaimed.

Reverend Hughes heaved an exasperated sigh. 'I still don't understand why this should have such a bearing on *today*, Chloë.'

She looked at him desperately. 'It's because last night everything fell into place. I finally understood *why* my mother had been so relentlessly negative about Max – it was because my relationship with him reminded her of her own failed relationship with Ella's father. She was transferring all her stored-up bitterness about John on to *him*.'

'No!' said Mum. 'I was trying to protect you.'

'I was an adult!' Chloë retorted. 'I didn't *need* your protection, and now I realise how much damage your "protection" has done. Not just because you stopped me being with someone I loved, but because you've pushed and *pushed* for this wedding to happen.' I saw Nate incline his head.

Mum sniffed. 'You didn't have to agree to it – did you?'

Chloë stared at her. 'That's true – but you're *so* persuasive, and Nate's a *nice* man, and I was desperate to try and forget Max and move on and so I allowed myself to get swept up by your plans, and I wish to God I *hadn't*,' Chloë wailed. 'Because then there would have been enough time to avoid this . . . *mess* that I'm in now!' She buried her face in her hands.

'You've heard from Max again,' Mum said quietly. 'That's what this is about.' Chloë nodded. Mum's lips compressed. 'When?'

Chloë looked up, her cheeks shining with tears. 'The night of the engagement party,' she replied thickly. 'He phoned me to tell me that he and Sylvia had finally separated.' I realised that that was why Chloë had been so upset when she'd showed me out that night. 'Max knew that I was engaged, but he desperately wanted to see me again before it was too late. So I did see him.' Chloë looked at Nate. 'It was when you were in Finland. We only talked,' she added. 'Nothing else. *But* . . .' She twisted the hanky in her fingers. 'Seeing Max again made me wish that I *could* be with him.' So that's when Chloë had had her 'wobble' I reflected. 'I was dreadfully torn,' she went on. 'So I saw Max again: it was on that Sunday when you said that you'd bumped into Ella, Nate. I'd told you that I was going to see Mum and Dad – but I was with Max. I hated lying to you, but I knew that I had to see him just one more time, in order to decide. And I told him that it was too *late*: because I'd made a commitment to you.'

'You certainly *had*,' Mum said.

Chloë ignored her. 'I thought about all Nate's good qualities,' she went on. 'I'd repeat them to myself over and over. I'd tell myself how lucky I was to be with him.'

The vicar frowned. 'But you said that to me only *yesterday*, Chloë. After the rehearsal.'

Chloë looked at him desperately. 'I *did*. But there was a big problem that I didn't *know* about. Because the thing is that . . .' Suddenly the door opened and Nate's mother came in, with James and Honey. 'You see, the thing is . . .' She turned up her palms. 'That Nate doesn't love me.'

Mum gave a contemptuous snort. 'Of course Nate loves you. He asked you to marry him.'

'No.' Chloë shook her head. 'I asked *him*. We were in Quaglino's, celebrating my promotion – we'd had a bottle of champagne, and I suddenly said, "Why don't we get married?" I said it as a kind of joke – we'd only known each other four months – but to my surprise Nate said, "Okay – why don't we?" Then that night, at the auction, we told you about it, Mum, and before we knew what was happening you'd not only set the date, you'd made half the arrangements. You've controlled this wedding, Mum – you've controlled the whole show!'

'Why *shouldn't* you get married?' Mum countered. 'You're twenty-nine – Nate's nearly thirty-*seven*! And love isn't everything at the start of a marriage. Love *grows*.'

'That's what I told myself.' Chloë sniffed. 'But I knew that I didn't feel for Nate a fraction of what I'd ever felt for Max.'

'How *can* you say such hurtful things in front of Nate?' Mum demanded.

'Because I know I'm *not* hurting him,' Chloë replied. 'And that's not just because, as I say, Nate doesn't love me.' She swallowed. 'It's because I know that he loves someone *else*. And I had no idea until yesterday afternoon; it was only then that I realised that Nate loves . . .' She gave a bewildered little laugh. 'Nate loves . . .'

'Ella,' Vittoria said. 'Nate loves Ella.' She looked at him. 'Don't you, Nate? *Tu ami* Ella?' Nate didn't answer. My cheeks burned as everyone turned their gaze on me. 'I saw it,' Vittoria went on; 'I saw it in the *ritratto* – the portrait; it's there, Nate, in your eyes, in the way that

350

you're gazing at Ella as she paints you. I saw it at once. And I could see that Chloë had seen it too – but then it's quite *unmistakable* – no one could have missed it.' *I* had missed it, I realised. Still Nate didn't respond. 'And I felt very sad for Chloë,' Vittoria continued. 'I felt sad for you, too, Nate, because I knew it would be a *disaster* for you to marry Chloë when you were clearly in love with her sister. But I couldn't say so, because it was too late.' She shrugged. 'But you *do* love Ella.'

Mum turned to me. 'What have you done, Ella?' she demanded coldly. 'Were you so jealous of Chloë, that you had to use the sittings to try and—'

'Ella's done nothing,' Nate said sharply. It was the first time he'd spoken and we all turned to him. 'All she did was to paint me, and talk to me,' he said. 'But yes . . . we got on . . . well.'

Mum gave Nate a basilisk stare. 'Then *why* did you go ahead with the wedding if it's *Ella* that you love?'

'Because . . . I'm not a flake,' Nate answered. 'I wasn't about to cancel my wedding on the basis that I'd spent a total of fifteen hours with Ella – especially as I had no real idea what *she* thought of *me*!'

A silence fell, then Honey gave a little cough. 'She's nuts about you, sweetie.' We all looked at Honey. 'I didn't *tell* you that,' Honey went on. 'I didn't feel that I could, given that you were about to marry Chloë. But I saw it at the engagement party – in the close attention that she'd paid to everything you'd ever said to her; and in the little glances that she'd throw you.' I felt my pulse race. 'And I felt so sorry for her.' Honey turned to me. 'But I don't feel sorry for you now, Ella, because I think that everything's going to be all right.'

351

'Well . . .' said Reverend Hughes. 'I assume that the upshot of this discussion is that Chloë and Nate are *not* now to be married.'

'That's right,' said Chloë quietly. 'Isn't it, Nate?' She turned to look at him, and he nodded.

Mum's face crumpled. 'There are one hundred and eighty-*nine* people out there.' It was the 'nine' that seemed to bother her.

Roy straightened his shoulders. 'Then we need to tell them what's happening.'

He spoke to Reverend Hughes, then we all went back into the church, where by now Katarina had finished *Panis Angelicus* and was halfway through Rossini's '*Stabat Mater*'. The organist brought the piece to an end then Katarina returned to the front pew, her face pink with exertion from her unexpectedly lengthy recital.

The vicar cleared his throat. 'We're sorry to have kept you all waiting,' he said. 'But we've been having a very important conversation, the conclusion of which is that Chloë and Nate have decided that they're *not,* after all, to get married.' There were whispered exclamations as everyone reacted to this news. 'They both recognise that marriage is too profound a commitment to make where there are doubts,' the Reverend went on. 'However, Roy has asked me to point out that today is Chloë's birthday, and he hopes you'll all come back to the house, as planned, and celebrate that instead.'

Everyone was shifting in their pews, some were laughing, out of shock. 'What *happened*?' Polly whispered as everyone stood up to leave. 'Did Chloë just get cold feet? But what a disaster,' she added.

'No it's not a disaster,' I said, my spirits soared.

As I walked out of the church into the bright sunshine Vittoria approached me. She touched my arm. '*Now* I can tell you what I *really* think of your portrait of Nate,' she said quietly. 'I think that it is . . . *fantastico!*' I wanted to kiss her, but simply gave her a grateful smile. I glanced at Honey, and wanted to kiss her too. Then I looked at Nate, and felt my heart expand. But I left him to walk to the house with Honey and James, who looked disappointed not to be making his speech. My mother walked beside Roy, doing her best to retain an air of dignity, but her face was a mask of shock and dismay.

When we reached the house Mum didn't come into the garden with everyone else – instead she opened the front door and went in, closing it behind her: through the hall window I saw her walk slowly upstairs, leaning on the handrail.

I went into the tent where Roy was pouring the champagne. Next to him the ice swan was dripping into its tray. Then I went into the kitchen to help the bemused-looking caterers. Chloë was standing by the French windows, next to the trolley on which was the five-tiered wedding cake. She gazed at the guests milling in and out of the tent, then she went to the dresser and picked up the phone. As she began to dial, I knew who she was calling. And I knew too why she'd chosen the forget-me-not-scattered dress: because she'd been drawn to its story of a love that had been ruptured and then restored.

EPILOGUE

15 September 2010

I am at the Eastcote Gallery, on the King's Road, putting the finishing touches to my exhibition, which will open in five minutes' time. The twenty-five paintings are all on the white-painted walls; most of them collected with the help of Rafael, whose red crayon portrait hangs next to that of David Walliams. There are pictures of P. D. James, Cecilia Bartoli, and, courtesy of the National Portrait Gallery, the Duchess of Cornwall. The biggest painting is the one of the Berger family, which takes up most of the back wall. There are portraits of Polly and Lola, of Roy and Mum, Celine, Mike, Chloë, and a dozen more. Surrounded by their faces, I feel that the party has already begun.

The gallery assistant, a pretty dark-haired woman called Lucy, is pouring the wine – just in time, as my first guest is arriving. Iris stands framed in the doorway, leaning lightly on her stick; she is wearing her blue suit and her lapis beads. I cross the pale wooden floor and greet her with a kiss.

'Many happy returns, Ella,' she says. 'And many congratulations!'

'Thank you, Iris. I'm glad you're the first – this was your idea, remember.'

'I do.' She looks around. 'What lovely paintings – I shall enjoy looking at them and meeting the people behind them.'

'You're over there, on the other side of that screen.' I take Iris to her portrait, which I collected from the framer only yesterday.

As we study it, Iris tilts her head. 'I like it. I feel that it's . . . me. I loved being painted,' she goes on. 'It made me really think about who I *am*, and how I've lived my life. And I didn't cry, did I?'

'No. *I* did though.'

'You did,' says Iris thoughtfully. 'I'm glad that in our later sittings you chose to tell me why.'

Lucy brings us both a glass of wine. She looks at Iris, then at the canvas. 'It's a lovely likeness – and you look very distinguished.'

'Thank you,' Iris says.

'But what's this?' Lucy points to the corner of a painting that is included in the background of the portrait.

'That,' says Iris, 'is a fragment of a picture of my sister and me when we were children.'

Lucy looks at it more closely. 'So that little girl chasing the dog – is that you?'

'Yes, it is.'

'So who did *that* painting?'

'My father – his name was Guy Lennox.'

'Oh, I've heard of him,' Lucy says. 'So it's a way of having him in your portrait with you?'

Iris smiles. 'Exactly.'

Lucy glances at the door. 'People are arriving – excuse me – I'm on duty.'

In comes Polly with Lola, who's gripping a silver balloon.

'Happy birthday, Ella.' Polly hugs me, then I introduce her and Lola to Iris, then Polly takes off her jacket to reveal the green T-shirt that she's wearing in her portrait. 'I'm afraid Lola's outgrown the yellow dress that she wore when you drew her, but she's put on something very similar.'

Lola ties the balloon to the back of a chair, then goes to look at her red crayon drawing, which I've hung next to that of the doctor's daughter.

Lucy offers Polly a glass of wine. Polly takes it and has a sip. 'This is nice,' she says. 'What is it? Prosecco?'

'It's a sparkling chardonnay,' Lucy replies.

'From the Blackwood Hills estate in Western Australia,' I add.

'So it's from John?' Polly says.

I nod. 'I told him about the party, and he and Lydia kindly sent me six crates.'

'How nice,' Iris says. 'At our last sitting you said that you might go and see him.'

'I am going to – next month. I'm planning to spend a week there.'

'Will you go on your own?' she adds.

'No. Nate's coming with me.'

Polly glances around. 'So where is he?'

'On his way from the airport. He should be here soon – oh, he's here's Chloë. Hi!'

Chloë hugs me, then hands me the gift bag that she's holding. 'Happy birthday, Sis.'

'Thanks – let me get you a drink.'

'Just half a glass,' she adds as Polly and Lola chat to Iris. 'I can't stay long. Max is giving a talk about the charity at the Wellcome Trust. He sends his apologies,' she adds as we walk to the drinks table. 'He'd love to have been here.'

'That's a shame – but never mind.' I hand her a glass of wine.

She takes a sip then looks around. 'So where am I, then? I hope you've hung me next to someone I *like* . . .'

'I've put you next to Cecilia Bartoli.'

'That's nice – perhaps her portrait will sing to mine – as long as it's not "Ave Maria".' Chloë grimaces. 'I don't want to hear that ever again.' At that we both laugh darkly, then walk over to Chloë's painting. Chloë cocks her head to one side. 'It's funny seeing it here. But I *do* look grim, don't I?'

'Well, you were feeling grim.'

Chloë nods. 'I wanted to be with Max so much I thought I'd go *mad*. I look mad,' she adds cheerily.

'I didn't *want* to paint you like this, remember?'

'I know – I insisted on it. But I've been thinking – I *would* like you to paint me again, Ella.'

'Oh, I'd love to. I could paint you and Max together – gratis, of course. After all, I owe you a picture, don't I?' I nod at my portrait of Nate, which, under the circumstances, Chloë hadn't wanted to keep.

Her face lights up. 'Okay then – you're on. We could sit for you when you're back from Oz. Oh, there's Dad.'

357

Roy walks in, wearing the same tweed jacket, checked shirt and blue speckled bow tie that I painted him in three years ago. He beams at us. 'My two girls!'

'Hi, Dad,' says Chloë.

He kisses Chloë, then me. 'Happy birthday, Ella.' He glances around the gallery. 'This is rather fun. So . . . where am I?'

I laugh. 'That's what everyone wants to know first. You're over here.' I lead Roy to his portrait.

He stands beside it. 'Spot the difference!' he challenges us.

'Well . . .' Chloë narrows her eyes. 'Your hair's quite a bit greyer now, Dad. And you're thicker round the middle.'

'All *right*,' he says good-naturedly. 'I asked for that. But this is very nice, Ella. I can imagine the portraits all chatting to each other after we've gone. And there's your mum.' We walk over to her painting. 'It's beautiful.'

'Thank you. But is she going to come? She wouldn't commit herself when I asked her yesterday.'

'I don't think she is,' he answers.

'So . . . how are things?' I ask quietly.

'Improving. We're, well . . . I think the expression is "building bridges".'

'That *is* the expression,' Chloë agrees. 'But she still won't speak to me.'

'Well . . . she's just got to get over it,' Roy says.

I think of the ruined wedding and of how utterly undone Mum was by Chloë's accusations – she didn't leave the house for over a week. Then, when the tent was no more than a huge yellow rectangle on the grass, I'd finally said to her all that I'd wanted to say.

'You kept my father's letters from me,' I'd said as we sat at the kitchen table. 'Dozens of them. And you lied to me about him, and about Lydia – you've lied for years.'

She'd pursed her lips. 'Sometimes it's *kinder* to lie. I was protecting you, Ella.'

'No, Mum – you were protecting yourself. Your relationship with John had ended badly, so you wanted nothing to do with him – and I understand it. But that meant depriving me of the chance to stay in touch with my own father, and to at least know that he still cared for me even if he couldn't live with me.'

'*He* was the one who did the depriving,' Mum had retorted, 'by choosing *them,* over us.' I'd then told Mum that I intended to visit John in October. She'd looked away for a moment, then murmured, 'Poor Roy'.

'Roy's *happy* for me to go. His attitude is generous, Mum, unlike yours.'

'Well . . . go, if you must. But please don't tell me about it.'

'All right.' I'd heaved a frustrated sigh. 'You know, Mum, I'd like to think that you regret the way you've handled things, but I don't think you do.'

'I regret having caused you any unhappiness, ever,' Mum said, which I knew was as much of an apology as I was ever going to get. With that, she'd got up and had gone into her studio to put her body through its daily ritual of stretching and twisting.

In the gallery Lucy offers Roy a glass of wine and he takes one, smiling his thanks. 'Everything will settle down over time,' he says to Chloë and me. 'Hopefully

359

well before your mother's sixtieth – we'll want to throw a party for her. And how's Max, Chloë?'

She smiles. 'Max is fine. I'm meeting him later.'

'You do realise that there's no cash left in the wedding kitty,' Roy says with mock seriousness.

Chloë grins. 'Well, if we did ever tie the knot, it would be in a register office with two witnesses.' She looks at me. 'Maybe you and Nate,' she suggests with a laugh.

'We'd be glad to,' I say.

'I *like* Nate,' Chloë goes on. 'But I love Max – I always have.' She nods at Nate's portrait, a few feet away. 'And it's screamingly obvious who Nate loves.'

I hug Chloë, then remember the conversation that I had with her two days after the wedding.

'Couldn't you *see* it?' she'd asked me wonderingly as we sat in her sitting room in Putney.

'No,' I'd answered. 'I really couldn't – perhaps because I was so close to it. But now I know why you reacted to the painting the way that you did.'

Chloë had nodded. 'It was a . . . shock. I felt so humiliated and upset – especially as Nate's *mother* was there. I knew that Vittoria had noticed it, and I was trying not to let her see that *I'd* noticed it too. I was in agonies. And I was just standing there, thinking that no one must *ever* see that painting. I thought I'd have to burn it, like Churchill's wife burned that portrait of him that she didn't like.'

'But . . . if you knew that Nate was in love with me, why did you go ahead with the wedding?'

Chloë had thrown up her hands. 'Because it was less than twenty-four hours away! As I left the studio I tried to convince myself that perhaps you'd painted Nate badly, and had accidentally *made* him look like he was in love with you when he wasn't. But I knew that couldn't be true because you're such a *good* painter. So then I told myself that you had some fantasy that he was in love with you, and that you'd projected that on to the portrait. I *couldn't* acknowledge the truth, because that would have meant cancelling the wedding and I simply couldn't face it.'

'Then, that night, Dad told you about Mum.'

Chloë had closed her eyes. 'It . . . knocked me for six. Then I was awake all night, trying to work everything out and I realised what Mum had really been trying to do. She hadn't been trying to protect me—'

'On one level I'm sure she was,' I'd countered. 'She's your mother – she loves you.'

'Okay,' Chloë had conceded. 'But I also think that she was reliving her own past. I even wondered whether she'd been motivated by envy of me: she'd been unable to have the love of her life, so perhaps she didn't want me to have *mine*. My thoughts were all over the place. As the sun came up, I knew that I *had* to go through with the wedding – it was too late not to. I couldn't lose face. But when I stood there on the altar, the words simply wouldn't come . . .'

The gallery is filling up now, as everyone arrives. Chloë looks at her watch, then sips the last of her drink. 'Gotta go – I'll be late for Max.' She gives me a hug. 'Bye, Ella. Bye, Dad.' She blows him a kiss.

Roy smiles. 'Goodbye, my girl.' Then he goes to chat to Polly and Lola and look at their portraits. As I make my way through the crowd, I hear my sitters swapping notes with each other.

– *She's really caught your smile.*

– *Not sure about my hair.*

361

– Hard work sitting, isn't it?

– Like therapy really.

– Feel I know a lot more about myself.

I feel a light tap on my shoulder and turn. 'Mike!' I smile. 'How nice to see you.'

'It's nice to be here – I've even remembered to wear the blue jumper.'

I point to his portrait. 'There you are.'

But Mike doesn't look at it – doesn't even notice it – because he's staring at Grace. I would never have asked Grace's parents if I could borrow her portrait, but her uncle, seeing the show listed in *Time Out,* phoned me to ask if it could be included. I said I'd be delighted.

Grace has one hand under her chin, and is smiling. 'You've caught her radiance,' Mike says. 'Her inner light.'

'If I have, it's thanks to you,' I respond quietly. 'And did you go to the memorial service?'

He nods. 'It was held at her school. They put your painting at the front of the stage. I overheard Grace's parents telling someone that they find it very comforting.'

'Well . . . I'm . . . glad. And I hope you're okay, Mike.'

'I'm . . . fine.' He heaves a sigh. 'Sarah and I have separated . . . so . . .' He shrugs. 'I keep myself busy. That's all one can do.'

'Let me get you a glass of wine.' We go over to the drinks table. 'Lucy, this is—'

'Mike Johns,' she interrupts with a laugh. 'That's the nice thing about this exhibition: no introductions needed – just match the person to their picture. Hello, Mike.' She smiles warmly at him. 'I'm Lucy. I work at the gallery.'

I leave Mike and Lucy chatting as I now see Celine arriving, in her blue linen dress, with Victor. She looks sun-tanned, and her hair is short. 'Happy birthday, Ella!' She says.

'Thanks. It's great to see you. I was sorry you weren't at home when I went to collect your portrait. So tell me – how was your trip?'

'It was wonderful. Especially Venice,' she adds, with a smile at Victor. 'But now . . . back to real life. I'm going to retrain – as a French teacher. There's a post-graduate course at Roehampton that I've applied for.'

'That sounds great.'

'So . . . where am I?' She looks around. 'Ah – *there*.'

We walk towards Celine's portrait, but before we reach it Celine is distracted by another, much smaller painting. 'And there *you* are, Ella,' She says. 'That's a lovely self-portrait.'

'Thank you. I did it last month. I hadn't done a self-portrait for over twenty-five years, so I . . . thought I'd have another go.'

'And this handsome man?' Celine is looking at Nate's portrait, which I've hung next to mine. 'He's in love, isn't he? Lock, stock and barrel.' She laughs suddenly. 'Of course – how slow of me Ella – he's in love with *you*. I hope that you're equally enamoured of him.'

'I am, actually.'

'So . . . is *this* the man you told me about?' she adds quietly. 'The one who was . . . attached?'

'Yes. But then everything changed.'

Celine smiles. '*Très* bien!'

Now I overhear Polly chatting to Iris. 'My feet have modelled for all the major shoe designers,' she's explaining. 'I do hands, too – I've been Helena Bonham Carter's hands, and Twiggy's, and Joan Collins's – which was a bit ridiculous as she's years older than me.' Then I hear her telling Iris about her new boyfriend, Ian. 'We met through Lola's school. He's a publisher. In fact, I'm going to do a book for him.'

'Is it a novel?' Iris asks.

'No – it's a cultural history of footwear from the Bronze Age to the present day. It'll be beautifully illustrated and full of fascinating facts – it's right up my street – the idea is to sell it in shoe shops as well as book shops. Oh – there's David Walliams. Ella said that he'd promised to pop in.'

Then Honeysuckle arrives with Doug, James and Kay. They look at the paintings, then come and find me.

'So we get to see Nate's portrait at last,' Doug says as he looks at it. He puts his head to one side. 'It's very striking, Ella. But is it a "great" portrait?'

'I don't know . . . I can only say that I'm happy with it. *Very* happy,' I add, as I see Nate standing in the doorway. He makes his way through the throng towards me, and suddenly I want to cry with simple joy.

'You told us that a "great" portrait reveals something about the sitter that they didn't even know themselves,' Doug is saying. 'So what was it that Nate didn't know?' He smiles. 'That he was in love with the woman who was painting him?'

And now Nate is by my side. 'I *did* know that,' he says. He slides his arm round my waist. 'I knew it from the start.'

As Nate pulls me to him, I recall the night of the wedding. We'd kept our distance, but when everyone else had drifted away, he'd come to find me. I was sitting on the bench by the horse chestnut tree.

He'd sat down next to me and had taken my hand. Then he'd just held it in both of his. 'It's nice to be able to do this,' he'd said quietly. 'I've wanted to for so long.'

'But then why . . .' I'd heaved a sigh. '*Why* did you . . .?'

'Go ahead with the wedding?' I'd nodded. 'Because . . .' He'd heaved a painful sigh. 'Because I didn't know what you felt for *me*. And because I thought that Chloë was committed to marrying me and I believed that to have pulled out would have destroyed her; plus the wheels of the wedding were turning *so* fast – the thing was like this . . . juggernaut, powering on.'

'Thanks to Mum,' I said balefully.

'Yes.'

'Well . . . she wanted fireworks,' I said. 'And she got them. But did you really feel that Chloë was in *love* with you?'

Nate inhaled. 'She seemed . . . glad to be with me. There were two or three weeks when she became a bit remote – now I know why; but then she was suddenly full on with the wedding again, really involved with all the arrangements, constantly telling me how wonderful everything was and how happy we were going to be. But now I know that she was just trying to convince herself.'

'Were you in love with her?'

'I really liked her,' he said carefully. 'I was . . . charmed by her. But we'd got engaged in such a rush – almost by accident; I panicked at first, but then told myself that I was thirty-six years old – why *not* get married? So I convinced myself that I could be happy with Chloë. But then I got to know you. And I fell in love with you, Ella. I was in agonies, not knowing what to do, and not being able to tell you how I felt because it would make me look so bad. But you must have realised how I felt.'

'I . . . did.'

'But you gave me no indication.'

'How could I? You were marrying my sister! I wasn't going to wreck her happiness – or publicly humiliate her. And I wasn't going to risk her having another breakdown like she'd had over Max. Added to which, you and I had spent so little *time* together Nate. Less than a day.'

Nate turned to me. 'Well we've got all the time we need now.' So we sat side by side, under the tree, just looking at each other. Nate smiled. 'What are you doing? Counting my eyelashes?'

'No. I already know how many you've got. One hundred and sixty-two on the upper lid . . .'

'Really?'

'And seventy-four on the lower – but don't worry, that's perfectly normal.'

'Good. You had me worried there.'

We were still gazing at each other. 'I can see myself,' I said.

'Your face in my eye . . .' he murmured.

'Thine in mine appears.'

Nate touched his lips against mine. I felt my insides dissolve. 'You kiss with your eyes open,' he said.

'That's because I don't want to stop looking at you. I love looking at you, Nate.' His lips touched mine again, his hands cradled my face.

In the gallery Nate greets his friends. 'Honey!' he exclaims softly. 'Kay. James. Good to see you all.'

I slide my arm around him. 'You're here,' I murmur happily.

'Of course I'm here.' Nate kisses me. 'Happy birthday, sweetheart.'

'We were just talking about your portrait,' Kay says. She looks at Nate, then at his painting. 'It's the very picture of you.'

Honey tilts her head as she studies it. 'It is. You've really . . . *captured* him, Ella.'

Nate kisses me again. 'She has.'

ACKNOWLEDGEMENTS

I'm indebted to the portrait painters Jonathan Yeo, June Mendoza, Nick Offer, Fanny Rush, Paul Benney and David Noakes, who kindly shared with me their insights into the art of portraiture. Any inaccuracies are entirely my own. I'd also like to thank Rodney Baldwin, of the art supplies shop, Green & Stone, and Amanda Wright for giving me the low-down on life as a hand and foot model. At HarperCollins I'm very grateful to my wonderful editor, Sarah Ritherdon, and to Lynne Drew, Hana Osman, Victoria Hughes-Williams, Liz Lambert, Laura Fletcher, Laura Mell, Charlotte Abrams-Simpson, Oliver Malcolm and Lisa Doyle. For her hawk-eyed copy-editing, huge thanks to Anne O'Brien. I'd also like to thank Rachel Hore, Louise Clairmonte and Ellie Howarth, who read the manuscript and encouraged me along the way. I'm indebted, as ever, to my brilliant agents, Clare Conville and Jake Smith-Bosanquet, and to everyone at Conville and Walsh. Jodie Terry kindly corrected my Australian, Shani Blich my Italian. Finally, I'd like to thank my family, who were endlessly supportive and tolerant during the writing process. So huge gratitude and love, as ever, to Greg, to our children Alice and Edmund, and to my stepsons, Freddie and George.

AUTHOR'S NOTE

The Very Picture of You is a work of fiction, but I wish to acknowledge that the inspiration for the story of Guy Lennox was reading about the sale at auction of a picture by the portraitist, Sir Herbert Gunn. Called 'Design for a Group Portrait', it was painted in 1929, and was of Sir Herbert's three children, from whom, following his divorce, he had been estranged. The story of Grace Clarke was in part inspired by the tragic death of Eilidh Jake Caims, who was knocked off her bike at Notting Hill Gate in February 2009. Every day I use the pedestrian crossing close to the spot where she died, and was moved by the many touching tributes to her that were placed there. I also wish to acknowledge that I have taken one or two liberties with the history of the Northern Ballet Theatre, whose production of *Giselle* was in 1978, not 1979.

The following books were a useful resource during the research and writing of the book:

Northern Ballet Theatre: 40 Years in the Making: published by Biskit Ltd.

Portraiture: Facing the Subject edited by Joanna Woodall, published by Manchester University Press,

Portraiture by Richard Brilliant, published by Reaktion Books

Painting People by Charlotte Mullins, published by Thames and Hudson.

A Face to the World by Laura Cumming, published by HarperPress

Changing Face: Contemporary Portraiture by Peter Monkman, published by Watts Gallery.

Read on for
an exclusive

Q&A with Isabel

Q. Ella makes her living by painting portraits of people. If you were to have your own portrait painted, who would you ask to paint it?

It would be very hard to choose as there are so many brilliant portrait painters around. Every year I go to the BP National Portrait Award exhibition and am awestruck at the talent of these artists who can evoke not just the physicality of a person – their skin, musculature, sinew, hair and bone, but their character and spirit too - what Picasso said is 'behind the face'. This is what a really good portrait achieves. I very much admire Jonathan Yeo, his drawings as much as his paintings – his sketch of Denis Hopper has such vitality that you half expect him to climb out of the frame. Dean Marsh, who won the BP Award in 2005 would also be on my shortlist – his portrait of the Kids Company founder, Camilla Batmanghelidjh, is one of the loveliest portraits in the National Portrait Gallery. She's reclining on a daybed, swathed in silk, in a large oval frame, in the style of Ingres - it's beautiful. Anastasia Pollard is a wonderful portraitist too – I can never quite tear my eyes away from her quiet, but enigmatic paintings – and I admire the portraits of June Mendoza and Fanny Rush. If I could travel back in time I'd choose to be painted by Sir Thomas Lawrence – his portraits are ravishing without being in any way over-glamorous or sentimental - added to which he painted several portraits of his friend Isabella Wolff, so perhaps he'd be happy to paint me too.

Q. Ella finds relief in leaving London to go to Chichester. Is there anywhere that you go to escape from life at home when you need a break?

We go sailing in Chichester in the summer months – the harbour is very lovely. For a longer break we go to Cornwall where we have a small house near St Mawes on the Roseland Peninsula. The beach is just down the lane, so we spend much of our time peering into rock pools and walking along the coastal paths. My next novel will be set in that part of Cornwall so I'm looking forward to spending more time there.

Q. The theme of fatherhood features in the book. Do you think there is an ideal type of father to be or do you think that there can be many different types of good fathers?

Any father who is there for his children is a good father, whether he lives with them or not. It's the involvement, affection and effort that matters. My own father was a lovely dad – he was very clever but kindly, and I think of him as having been an ideal father to me and my siblings.

Q. Is there any character that you particularly identify with?

I always identify with my main character – not because my life has been like hers – it hasn't - but because I need to identify with her in order to write about her in the first person in a believable way. I like the intimacy of the first person voice, and the fact that it also provides scope for irony – there's a gap between what the heroine says she feels, and what the reader believes she may truly be feeling, and this can provide a tension and edge. So there's a huge element of impersonation in my books. I'm not an artist, but I did a portrait painting course, spoke to portrait painters and read a lot of books about portraiture so that I could imagine how Ella might think. Ella was abandoned by her father when she was five, but my own father was always very present in my life. So Ella isn't me, but it's not hard to imagine how she'd feel, her curiosity about her father inevitably clashing with her anger at his rejection of her all those years before. Equally it's not hard to imagine Ella's anguish as she realises that she's falling in love with Nate. So I put myself not just in Ella's shoes, but, as far as I could into her head and heart too, so that her voice would feel authentic, and I very much hope that it does.

Q. Do you tend to follow your characters as they grow, or do you stick to a planned path for each of them?

I always plan my novels as much as I can, as I need to know where I'm going. So I have a strong idea of the emotional development that my main characters are going to undergo. I knew that Ella would reject her father's overtures to start with, but that something would then happen to her, to make her think again. I knew that she'd fall in love with her sister's fiancé, but didn't know how such a difficult attachment could end. I knew that she'd paint an elderly woman who owned a picture with a very poignant story attached to it that would affect Ella in some way. I knew that Ella's mother would be very manipulative, forever choreographing things to her own satisfaction, but I hadn't worked out how she would get her comeuppance: that came to me only once I'd started writing the book. Writing a novel is, in many respects, like being a psychologist. You decide what your characters are like then work out what's happened to them in the past to make them as they are now. Everything has to hang together in a believable way, and yes, the reader has to be able to see, by the end, that the characters were on some discernible path.

Q. Do you follow a particular pattern as you write? Where do you write?

I don't have a pattern to my writing, but *The Very Picture of You* is my ninth novel, and I think that the tone of them – I aim for a blend of humour and pathos – has been fairly consistent. I write about women who face huge dilemmas or emotional problems. I then work those problems out in as involving and entertaining a way as I can. I put in a lot of mystery, because it keeps the pages turning. And I always make sure that there's a satisfying ending – though not necessarily an easy 'happy ever after' one. But I try to conclude my books in a way that the reader will find emotionally fulfilling - they've kept faith with me by reading this far, so I want them to feel uplifted as they turn the last page. I write in the basement of our home in west London, while the children are at school.